WHAT OTHERS ARE SAYING

Now that I have retired, time is available for me to read for my pleasure. *On the Run in College Park* by Jon K. Elliott is an outstanding book. It is exciting, spell binding, and a thriller to the end. It ranks with the best of Alex Patterson, John Grisham, David Baldacci, and Nora Roberts. Mr. Elliott has combined faith, foreign intrigue and espionage in this must read book. You will enjoy!

—Don W. Stephens
Former Kentucky Legislator,
Commissioner of Alcohol and Beverage Control,
And Commissioner of Insurance

Jon K. Elliott has given us a thoughtful issue embedded in a suspenseful and exciting scenario. The settings are iconic and familiar to us residents of the "Old Line State" of Maryland. Underlying the action is the challenge of relating to Muslims in our culture not as "the other" but as worthy and needing of our witness. The fast-paced action and surprising developments remind us of our need for trustworthy and supportive friends like those enjoyed by our young protagonists as they confront unexpected dangers. This is an exciting read which engages our character and beliefs.

—Jerome Smith, Rear Admiral, US Navy (retired)
Annapolis, Maryland

In *On the Run in College Park* Jon K. Elliott utilizes the interface between Christianity and Islam as a backdrop for a first rate modern mystery. He sensitively explores political and theological issues ranging from terrorism, street crime and greed to the atonement, forgiveness and the universality of sin. This fast moving drama invites the reader to enter the narrative with questions like "Would my faith be sufficiently strong to deal with a matter like this?" This novel not only keeps the reader interested, it gets the reader thinking about one of the most significant and sensitive issues of our time.

—Dr. R. Robert Cueni, Retired Pastor and
Seminary President Lexington, Kentucky

Jon K. Elliott tells a tale of treachery, terror, and truth. This story is great for Christians and Muslims alike. Mr. Elliott takes time to help the characters, both Muslim and Christian, and the readers learn how to get along with one another and help each other through trying times. The twists in the plot leave the reader guessing from one page to the next about what the real truth is. *On the Run in College Park* will keep the reader running through the pages to find out what happens next.

—Jan Sullivan, Author of
Forever Family, Never Alone, and Stand Strong

ON THE RUN IN COLLEGE PARK

ON THE RUN IN COLLEGE PARK

JON K. ELLIOTT

TATE PUBLISHING
AND ENTERPRISES, LLC

Published by Tate Publishing & Enterprises, LLC
127 E. Trade Center Terrace | Mustang, Oklahoma 73064 USA
1.888.361.9473 | www.tatepublishing.com

Tate Publishing is committed to excellence in the publishing industry. The company reflects the philosophy established by the founders, based on Psalm 68:11,
"The Lord gave the word and great was the company of those who published it."

Book design copyright © 2014 by Tate Publishing, LLC. All rights reserved.
Cover design by Nikolai Purpura
Interior design by Mary Jean Archival

Published in the United States of America

ISBN: 978-1-63185-273-2
Fiction / Romance / Contemporary
14.11.12

To my two grandsons, Ben and Paul Elliott,
students at the Colorado School of Mines
and Colorado State University
as this book goes to press

ACKNOWLEDGMENTS

I am particularly grateful to Mrs. Deborah Rice, Dr. Robert Cueni, and Mr. Andy Elliott for their careful review of the manuscript, suggesting changes, both literary and technical, to make the book more accurate and realistic. Thanks also to Dr. Amir Youssefi for his advice in details of Islam and Middle Eastern culture, and to Mr. Harry Richart for advice on international money transactions. Credit is due to Mr. Ken Taylor, with whom I deliberated in conceiving the basic story of *On the Run in College Park*.

CHAPTER 1

"Rashid! Rashid! Let me in!" Ahmed shouted in Arabic as he pounded on the door. It opened with a jerk. He faced a scowling Egyptian, with a three-day stubble of beard, in an undershirt and undershorts. Ahmed pushed into the room and pulled the door shut. "Rashid! We've got to get out of here. They've got Masoud!" He half-whispered and half-shouted.

"Who's got him?" Rashid sounded annoyed.

"FBI? Mukhabarat? Some other agency? I don't know. I just saw two men in suits taking him away." Ahmed's eyes were wide open. "We can't wait to find out."

"Oh! Could be serious. Okay."

Ahmed paced impatiently while Rashid pulled on jeans and a sweatshirt. *Come on Rashid, please hurry,* he pleaded in his head. He opened the door to see if anyone was approaching while Rashid put on his sneakers. *No one there.* He looked back at Rashid, now behind him, and nodded. They dashed into the empty hall.

Ahmed could hear his feet slapping the hard floor as they ran through the Worcester Hall corridor toward the exit. He glanced behind him to make sure Rashid was coming, turned into the stairwell, and raced to the ground floor. There he paused. *Take a look first,* he told himself. He cracked the door and peeked out to see if anyone was outside watching. Seeing no one, he beckoned to Rashid. They ran from the door, down Chapel Lane, to the edge of Chapel Fields, a broad green field that lay between Baltimore Avenue and the University of Maryland campus. He felt Rashid's hand on his shoulder to make him stop. He looked around the field and up and down Regents Drive but saw no one who looked suspicious. The field, still wet with dew, was now vacant.

"Where are we going?" Rashid panted.

Ahmed checked his watch. Nine thirty. "I don't know."

Ahmed and Masoud had always looked to Rashid as the leader. He had the dominant personality. He was the idea man. Ahmed wondered why the FBI, or whoever had Masoud, hadn't come after Rashid. *They're probably after all of us,* he thought.

"We can't go to the house. If they know about us, they know about the house." Ahmed looked with questioning eyes at Rashid.

"But that's where all our stuff is," Rashid said, without looking at Ahmed. They kept only their minimum needs in the dormitory, a few of their clothes, toilet articles, and books for their classes. All the rest was in the house. "Nobody knows about the house but us. We've got to get in the house and get our stuff out before they make Masoud talk."

"Now?"

"Yes. And then get out of town. Out of the country."

"Yeah." *Good idea,* he thought.

They ran along the edge of the field, crossed Baltimore Avenue, and jogged down College Avenue to the corner of their street and stopped to see if anyone was watching. "You stay here. I'll go across the street to look," Rashid said and immediately walked nonchalantly to the opposite corner.

Ahmed watched Rashid walk purposely along the street, past their rented house, and then turn west and out of sight on the other side of the block. *Where's he going?* Ahmed asked himself. *I can't just stand here. It looks too suspicious.* He crossed College Avenue and walked slowly back toward the campus. At the next corner he could see Rashid coming toward him, having walked around the block. When Rashid rejoined him, he said, "It looks safe to me." They crossed the street, walked to the house, and went in. It was apparent that no one had been inside, searching the place. They gathered any incriminating documents, their passports and laptops, and hastily stuffed them into their backpacks along with a few items of clothes. They left Masoud's things, in case he would be released and would return for them.

They were ready in ten minutes. Both of their cars were parked on the street, in front of their house. Rashid instructed, "We need to get both cars away from here. Do you have a permit for a lot close to Route 1?"

"Yes, 11b."

"Park yours there, and we'll take mine to the airport."

"This is a football weekend. They'll tow it."

"Just park it over on the next block, then. It'll be okay there."

Ahmed drove around the block, parked his car, and climbed into Rashid's Pontiac.

"Where will we go?" he asked, turning to look at Rashid.

"Some vacation spot. Someplace we don't need a visa." He pulled away from the curb.

"From there you go to Morocco, and I'll go to Egypt. We can see our parents. But the police have got to think we went for a vacation somewhere, wherever we can get a flight to the fastest." Rashid turned right on Knox Road.

"Maybe we should split up here."

Rashid glanced at Ahmed. After a short pause, he said, "Good idea. Let's use different airlines. You go wherever you want to but don't tell me. When you get there, get a plane to Morocco. I'll go someplace you wouldn't think of. I'll contact you by e-mail. If I tell you I'm home, I'll be in Egypt. Just don't mention where you are or anything about Masoud. He'll contact us if the coast is clear.

"Another thing, don't send any text messages or make any cell phone calls." When they reached Baltimore Avenue, Rashid turned north.

"What about the accounts?" Ahmed rubbed his forehead.

"This has really got you spooked, doesn't it?" He looked at Ahmed. "I don't know right now. We'll just have to lie low until we find out what they know." He shrugged.

"We'll need cash, you know."

"Okay," Rashid sighed. "As soon as you get to Morocco, open a new account and transfer some money from one of your other accounts. If they're tracing all this, they're very, very good. But I doubt that they'll find us following the money. It's probably a postal fraud charge. Either way, they won't freeze your account in Morocco, so you'll be all right."

Ahmed became quiet. *This is moving too quickly,* he thought. *I need to think this out. They'd expect us to leave from the BWI airport. I need to do the unexpected.*

"Twenty-five minutes. Good." Ahmed nodded to Rashid as they arrived at Baltimore Washington International Thurgood Marshall Airport. At the first departures entrance, Ahmed got out. He felt somewhat deceptive as he took the stairs to the lower level, and then took the shuttle bus to the Amtrak terminal. *Better not to trust anyone,* he thought. "Newark International Airport," he told the ticket seller. The schedule display told him the train was scheduled to depart in two hours.

Sitting in the waiting area, he tried to make himself look calm, but inside his abdomen was a tangle of wires, all being pulled tighter and tighter. *It wasn't supposed to be like this,* he thought. *I believed it was all perfectly legal. We'd be helping children in a war-torn country. And we'd be making a little money for our time and* *expenses. I thought my parents would be proud of me. I never dreamed we'd become rich. But here we are. Rich criminals. I have probably $400,000 in my Singapore account alone, and I guess another $200,000 en route. Twenty-five percent to each of us is way too much. Well, it was okay in the beginning when we didn't bring in much. But now it's way too much.*

He rehearsed the account numbers and passwords of his personal accounts: five bank accounts and two investment accounts, a daily ritual that Rashid had inaugurated, forbidding Masoud and him to ever record account numbers, to prevent their being stolen, he'd said. *I thought he was just being careful. He knew what he was doing. Masoud probably knew all the time too.*

Ahmed looked at his watch. *Oh, it's check day,* he suddenly remembered. *It's Masoud's turn. He'll probably be glad to be in jail. He always complains.* "Why do we have to use a post office in the district?" *and* "Why print the acknowledgment letters at office supply stores? Let's buy our own printer." *The poor brute.* He laughed out loud, glancing around to see if anyone was watching. "It's all for security." *Rashid keeps telling him. Rashid had this all figured out. He thinks they could never trace us. Well maybe they just did. If not today, then someday. How do I get out of this mess?*

I guess the police have relieved Masoud from check duty today. But the envelopes will keep coming, stuffed into that post office box until we get back. If we get back. It'll be overflowing if we stay gone very long. Then it'll take us all night to sort them.

Yes, I'm rich, he thought, *thanks to American generosity.* But at the moment, being rich did not relieve his anxiety. He tried to read a newspaper but was unable to concentrate, turning to a new page now and then and staring at the ads. The thought kept recurring about his father finding out, filling him with dread as intense as the US authorities finding out. The time seemed to pass slowly to Ahmed, but eventually he saw the waiting area beginning to fill up as the departure time approached. Boarding proceeded without difficulty, and the train left on time.

Ahmed felt a little relieved, although he would not feel completely safe until he was out of the United States. *My safety depends entirely upon Masoud's ability to resist telling the authorities who his accomplices are. Once my identity is known, it will take a matter of only minutes to transmit instructions to passport control stations throughout the country. Maybe I should just stay in the States,* he pondered. *If I don't try to leave, I'll not be caught. I'll bet Rashid won't go out of the country if he thinks about it. But maybe he'll think he'll have a better chance to get out now than later. On the other hand, if they find out our names, it might be impossible to get back in. I think I'll be better off to stay here.*

Ahmed's ringing cell phone shook him from his thoughts. He took it from his pocket and saw that it was Nadira. *Should I answer? Maybe it's okay to answer.* He pressed the green button. "Nadira, hi." He spoke in English to Nadira.

"Where are you? I thought we were going to have lunch together."

"What time is it? Oh, I didn't realize it's so late. I should have called you. I can't make it for lunch today."

"Well, I've been sitting here for twenty minutes. Guess I'd better order something. What's going on?"

"Something came up with the Servants that I have to take care of. I'll be gone for a while, a few days, I imagine."

"You're going to miss some classes."

"I'm afraid so. I can deal with it."

"You're good."

"I know."

"Maybe you just think you're good."

"Ha."

"When finals get here, we'll see."

"No problem."

"Yeah. Well, I'd better go if I want to eat before class."

"Guess so."

"Bye. Call me tonight."

"Okay. Bye. No, wait. Can you call me? If I don't have a signal, you'll know it if you call. But if I can't call, you'll think I just didn't want to or something."

"Where are you going?"

"Out to rural Pennsylvania."

"Oh, okay. I'll call you."

"Good-bye."

"Bye."

Maybe rural Pennsylvania would be a good place to go, he thought. *Maybe I should get off in Philadelphia. I could get a map and just pick someplace I can get to by train.*

Nadira admired the work that Ahmed did, through the Servants of Mercy, to help children in Iraq. *He told me it was an easy thing to do except that some of the paperwork to get it started was difficult. But it seems to me that it consumes a lot of their time, and when something like this happens it ruins our time together.* Yet she was unwilling to object, afraid it would affect their relationship. She loved Ahmed but had not told him that. She loved the way he looked, his slender face with a well-trimmed mustache and short very dark, almost black, hair. She loved his eyes, a little too big for his face, that conveyed all his emotions. He was of medium height and had a slim build. She liked his size. It was not threatening to her. Her father, who was much larger, had always frightened her.

Nadira had met Ahmed two months earlier during orientation week for first-year students. Ahmed, a junior international student, was ambling among the tables advertising campus organizations and activities when she saw him. He walked up beside her as she stood at a table, talking to another student about the club they were advocating, and joined in the conversation. They chatted for a while, and then Ahmed invited Nadira to have a cup of tea, which she declined. She wanted to go with him but remembered her father's stern warning about easy relationships with college men, so she said she had to go to another meeting. However, Ahmed had read her phone number as she signed the register of interested students, and it wasn't long before he was calling her, at first to say hello and then to ask her out. Eventually she had agreed to meet him for lunch. "Yes, but Dutch," she'd said.

"What does *Dutch* mean?" he'd asked.

"In America, it means I pay for my own lunch, and you pay for yours. At least it means that in Silver Spring."

"Is that where you're from?"

"Born and raised." They'd liked each other from the beginning. With her it quickly became more than a casual friendship, and from the interest he showed in her she was certain it was more for him too. Still, her father's admonitions hovered over her. She knew he wouldn't approve if she would have real dates. In her mind, her father wouldn't think she should see anybody until the man had asked for his permission to marry her. How that could happen in America was irrelevant. *He was still living in the old country,* she thought.

The restrictions he'd placed on going out with men also applied to other religions. He had told her many times that she was not to attend the worship services or functions of any other religion other than Islam. That very day her roommate had invited her to go with her to a Christian campus ministry meeting. Lauren had told her that she wanted company because she didn't know anybody yet, but Nadira had told her that she could not, that she was prohibited from going with her. She knew it was her father's rule, not Islam's, but she left it ambiguous, and Lauren had simply replied that she understood.

Ahmed got off the train at Philadelphia's 30th Street Station at about 2:00 p.m. and learned that a train going west was scheduled for 3:45 p.m. He bought a ticket for Harrisburg, where he arrived at about 5:30 p.m. With the assistance of a taxi driver, he found a good hotel, one close to the station and restaurants, and that had WiFi service, where he made his hideout. He turned on his laptop computer and tested the Internet connection. It came right on, so he opened his e-mail program. Nothing of importance was there.

His cell phone beeped. He had a text message from Masoud. "Where is everyone?"

CHAPTER 2

Lauren Stevenson walked timidly into the large room where the Collegiate Christian Association held its group meetings. It was a private room of a restaurant near the campus. A table just inside the door held blank name tags and markers. She paused there, preferring to remain anonymous.

"Hi! Would you mind filling out a name tag?" A young woman standing nearby smiled and motioned to the table.

She smiled self-consciously and wrote "Lauren" on a blank name tag and stuck it to her sweater. She gazed around the room and found an empty chair amid the rows of folding chairs that faced a lectern at one end of the room. *This place is really crowded, but there's not a soul I know here.* Lauren was not a gregarious person, and her appearance did not attract attention. She had long dark brown hair and looked pleasant, but not pretty. *I hope they don't ask visitors to stand up and say something. I just want to sit here and watch.*

Soon a young man came to the lectern, stood for a moment as the room became quiet, and said, "Hi, everyone. Welcome to the CCA Welcome Meeting. If you're a newcomer, would you please raise a hand?" As hands appeared, he said, "We're glad you're here."

I guess they aren't going to ask us do anything, Lauren thought. She raised a hand. A student appeared at the end of her row and passed her a newcomer badge. She held it for a few minutes but eventually clipped it to her name tag.

After a prayer and a talk by one of the student leaders, he asked everyone to gather in small groups. He asked all the first-timers to gather together. *I'm glad there are a lot of us. If I were the only one, it would be hard to say no if they ask me to go to another meeting, especially if I don't like CCA.* All she'd wanted to do was watch to see if this, among the several Christian groups on campus, might be the one she would join. So she was glad she didn't have to say much, just her name, phone number, and dorm. The woman who was leading the group didn't press the newcomers to talk about their Christian experiences or to make a commitment to CCA, and that made Lauren feel comfortable. The leader told them the history of CCA and how they are organized. She said that CCA provided a way for students to continue their Christian life by helping them find churches they could attend. CCA also carries out information dissemination programs to acquaint students with Jesus. *Like Nadira,* Lauren thought.

Once the small group meetings were over, several new members were introduced. Then they announced the upcoming activities, predominately training sessions. A meditation closed the meeting.

Lauren left without speaking to anyone. *Not bad,* she thought. She had already been to meetings of two other organizations. *All of these groups are good and a lot alike. I'll have to find something unique about each to decide among them.*

"How was the meeting?" Nadira asked when Lauren came into their dorm room.

"It was okay, just introductory stuff. I didn't know anyone there. I was kind of lonesome." *I wonder if she knows who Jesus is,* Lauren thought about Nadira. *CCA is the only one that said anything about that.* "I've got a ton of stuff to do tonight," she said as she plopped down on her chair at her desk.

"I have to make a phone call. Will that bother you?" Nadira asked.

"No, that's okay. I can tune it out."

"Y'sure?"

"Yeah."

As Lauren moved her mouse to bring her laptop back to life, Nadira got up and lay down on her bed with her cell phone.

Ahmed was expecting the call. "Hi."

"Hi. Where are you?"

"A little town in Pennsylvania."

"What's its name?"

"I don't know."

"Ahmed!"

"It was almost prayer time and the train stopped, so I got off."

"Where'd you go?"

"Some hotel."

"Some hotel in a town with no name."

"A place to sleep for the night."

"When are you coming back?"

"Couple of days. I should be home Monday. Maybe even Sunday. Depends on the trains."

"That's good."

"What's up with you?"

"Nothing."

"You don't have much to say."

"I'm in my room."

"Is Lauren there?"

"Yes."

"Well, not much going on here either. I need to go out and find a restaurant for supper."

"You'd rather eat than talk to me?"

"No, I just meant that's all there is to do here."

"I need to go eat too. Before the dining room closes."

"I don't know why. You hardly eat anything."

"I want to stay slim, for you."

"I like that."

"I don't know why you don't get fat, you eat so much."

"Me neither."

"You must run it all off."

"I think that may be true. Now I'm starting to get hungry. I hope the restaurants here don't close early."

"Maybe you should go."

"Yeah, I think I should."

"Okay. Can I call you tomorrow?"

"Yeah, I want you to. If I don't answer, you'll know I don't have a signal."

"I know."

"Well, okay. Bye."

"Bye." She glanced at Lauren, who was looking at her. "I'm sorry, Lauren. I should have gone out in the hall to make that call."

Lauren said, "It wasn't that. You just sounded a little—sad. I didn't mean to be listening in."

"I didn't know it showed in my voice. I was talking to this guy I know. Well, I haven't known him long. Three or four weeks, I guess. He's an international student from Morocco. We were supposed to go to lunch today, but he didn't come. He and two other Middle Eastern students are running a nonprofit organization that raises money for an orphanage in Iraq. They call it Servants of Mercy. He had to go to Pennsylvania to meet with a donor. I just sat there waiting for him for twenty minutes, and then I finally called him and found out that he was on his way out of town."

"What's his name?"

"Ahmed. Ahmed Suliman. I guess I shouldn't object. It's a good thing they're doing. I just wish he'd called me and told me he wouldn't be there."

"Yeah. I know how you feel."

Ahmed was suspicious of the text from Masoud. *What if it was actually from the authorities to get me to use my cell phone?* He decided to use e-mail instead of texting. He answered, "On vacation. Don't have good phone strength here."

"wru," Masoud asked.

"I'll tell you about it when I return."

"Is Rashid with you?"

"N."

"Where is he?"

"On vacation."

"Where?"

"IDK."

"This is weird," answered Masoud.

"I just don't know where he is. We didn't go together."

"We have checks to sort, you know."

"You can handle it."

"Yeah. And I'll stick yours down your throat."

"Just wait till we get back to pick them up."

"I'll do that."

It doesn't sound like anyone's with him. But I'll stay here for a while anyway.

Late on Saturday morning Lauren's phone rang. She pulled it out of her backpack. "Hello."

"Hi, Lauren. I'm Martha Jenkins from CCA. I'm here in the lobby of Queen Anne's with another CCA member. Do you have a few minutes you could spend with us today or tomorrow?"

"I don't have anything to do except study and church tomorrow. How much time do— "

"Oh, just thirty to forty-five minutes. We just want to get to know you a little bit. We thought we could have some coffee or something at Starbucks."

"I guess I could do it now," Lauren said. "I haven't had breakfast yet. Right now would work best for me." She heard Martha relay her message to the other CCA member.

After a few seconds Martha said, "That would be fine for us. We'll wait here for you."

"Okay. I'll be down in about five minutes." She disconnected her phone, pulled on a sweatshirt, glanced at herself in the mirror, briefly brushed her hair, and left. Two people, a man and a woman, stood near the door in the lobby. *They look like students,* she thought.

"Lauren?" the woman asked, smiling. Her dark hair was poked through the hole in the back of a ball cap. *She looks like a jogger, not a hint of fat on her. No makeup.* Lauren was not overweight, but she knew how difficult it was to keep her weight down. She envied joggers for that reason. She knew that she could become a jogger, if necessary, but something within her rebelled at the thought.

"Yes."

"I'm Martha, and this is Tom, and we're from CCA." She handed Lauren a business card.

Lauren thought, *I kind of like Tom's looks. He has an honest face and, in a way, looks alive, like he enjoys life.*

They left Queen Anne's Hall and walked down Preinkert Drive, past South Campus Dining, through South Campus Commons, and across Knox Road to the shopping center and Starbucks. It was a brisk October morning, and police were already out setting up cones to route traffic to the stadium parking for the home game at noon. They talked about the weather and the football team along the way. At Starbucks Lauren ordered a scone and a cappuccino.

"Was yesterday's meeting your first time at CCA?" Martha asked after they sat down.

"Yes, and I've been to a couple of other organizations to see what they're like," Lauren said.

"What did you think?"

"I thought everybody was nice. Not real pushy. But there was one thing that kind of stuck with me—the girl who was speaking said you have information programs to help students get to know Jesus, or something like that."

"Right. That's a major part of what we do. That brings up an important question we want to ask you. Where do you stand with Jesus?"

"I've always been a Christian. That's why I was there. I'd rather be part of a Christian group than a sorority."

"That's great. What can we do to encourage you to join CCA?" Martha said.

"Well, my roommate is a Muslim. I hardly know how to talk to her. I don't know anything about Muslims, and she probably doesn't know much about Jesus. Could CCA teach me about her religion, and maybe advise me on some way to tell her who Jesus is without turning her off?"

Tom had been sitting silently, leaning back and listening, sipping a latte. He sat up, brushed his light brown hair out of his eyes, and said, "Lauren, I'd like to answer that. The short answer is yes. It's an issue that CCA wants to understand. It's becoming a big issue, both with CCA and my church. We don't think the church in America has done a very good job with telling non-

Christians who Jesus is, so a lot of people, including a lot of church members, really don't know who he is. So yes, CCA wants to help you understand Islam and how to explain who Jesus is."

"I'm so glad to hear that. I never know what to say. I invited her to come last night but, of course, she said no."

"Well, that could have been for any number of reasons," Tom said.

"Do you have dues or anything?" Lauren turned toward Martha.

"We accept contributions. But frankly most of our funding comes from older donors. Most college students can't give much," Martha replied.

"Well, what do I have to do next?"

"To join CCA?"

"Yeah."

"If you say you want to join, you're in," Tom said.

"I want to join." She laughed self-consciously.

"Great. Welcome."

"Yes, welcome, Lauren," Martha echoed. "We do need to get your room number so we can send you stuff." She wrote it on a card she pulled from her purse. "I already have your phone number."

"From the meeting."

"Yes. This doesn't commit you to anything, Lauren," Martha said. "It just puts you in the loop to inform you when things are happening."

"That's cool."

"Where are you from?" Tom asked.

"Frederick."

"I'm from right here in College Park," he said.

"Where are you from, Martha?"

"She's from way out west," Tom answered.

"Chicago," Martha said.

"What brought you to Maryland?"

"I got a good scholarship."

"What's your major?" Lauren asked.

"Physics," Martha replied.

"Wow!"

"What's yours?"

"I don't know yet. Accounting maybe," Lauren answered.

"That means you're probably levelheaded," said Tom.

"They say I am. What year are you both in?"

"I'm a junior. She's a senior," he said.

"What's your major, Tom?"

"Engineering and business."

"That sounds challenging. What do you want to do?"

"I want to get into industrial management. But I'll go whatever way the Lord leads me."

When they left Starbucks they walked together to the corner of Knox Road and Baltimore Avenue, where Martha left them to go to her car. Tom had parked beside the Mowatt Parking Garage, so he and Lauren walked on together. "What's your roommate's name?" he asked.

"Nadira. Nadira Shalash. Her family is from Palestine. She was born here, though. They live in Silver Spring."

"Have you talked about religion with her?"

"Not really. I don't know what to say. She knows I go to church. And I see her go off with her little prayer rug."

"Where does she go?"

"I guess she goes to some other Muslim's room. She doesn't pray in our room. At least not when I'm there."

"Does she wear a scarf?"

"Yes. It covers her hair. She has this lovely long dark silky-smooth hair and the most gorgeous eyes. She's really beautiful."

"Where are you going to church?"

"I'm still shopping around. There are four protestant churches right around here, and I've gone to three of them. We go to a nondenominational church in Frederick."

"Well, here's my car. But I think I'll leave it here and walk to the stadium. It's too hard to find a parking place over there."

They walked on to Queen Anne's Hall, Lauren's dorm, and then said good-bye.

It was almost noon, and she could hear the band and the crowd at the stadium. She didn't care about football, but she liked marching bands, so she stopped and listened. After a few minutes she went in and walked up the two flights of steps to her room.

The day she and Nadira had moved in they'd rearranged the furniture to form an L-shaped space for Nadira so that only the back of her desk could be seen from the door. The desk was high enough that it shielded her and the bed from the sight of someone entering the room. When Lauren unlocked the door and went in, she saw Nadira's head look around her desk. As Lauren started toward her side of the room, she saw Nadira's prayer rug on the floor beside her bed and realized she was in prayer.

Lauren stopped, "I'm sorry," she said. "I'll come back in a little while."

Nadira simply nodded.

Lauren backed out of the doorway and closed the door. She returned in fifteen minutes.

Nadira was at her desk. She turned to Lauren and said, "I'm sorry, I shouldn't have prayed here. I just thought you wouldn't be back until after lunch."

"That's not a problem," Lauren replied. "I pray too, just in a different format."

"I'm sure you do, but I have no right to monopolize the room. You didn't have to leave. I should have gone out for prayer. I apologize."

"No apology is needed." She hugged Nadira. "You can pray here whenever you want."

CHAPTER 3

On Saturday evening during supper Tom said to his father, Martin Parker, "I met a girl today who wants us to teach her how to talk to her roommate, who's a Muslim. She doesn't know anything about Muslims, and she'd like to learn how to tell her roommate about Jesus. Do you think the church could help?"

"What do you want the church to do?"

"I don't know. I guess, give us a strategy or something."

"I'll be meeting with the evangelism team before church tomorrow. I think they'll be open to this. Why don't you come to the meeting with me and explain what you want them to do."

"That's a good idea, Dad. I will. Thanks."

Ahmed had found Saturday in Harrisburg to be slow. In his haste he had forgotten to pack something to read. He could read in English, but for pleasure he preferred to read in Arabic. He had found a bookstore open but was reluctant to ask for books in Arabic, and because the store closed at 1:00 p.m., he didn't have much time to browse. The television was full of college football games and news stations that could talk only of the upcoming elections. He eventually found a movie on television to occupy his time.

He wanted to call Masoud and had almost decided to try to find a pay phone to call him, but suspecting that it could be easily traced and that he could be found without too much trouble in a small city, he decided against it. *Maybe they can trace the WiFi internet service the hotel has*, he thought. *I could go back to College Park but not to the house. I could stay in a motel and hang around outside the house to see if anyone is coming and going.* He discovered that there were no trains on Saturday afternoon, but that there was a bus leaving for Washington at 4:55 p.m., so he checked out of the hotel, took a taxi to the bus station, and boarded the Greyhound bus for Washington.

It was a trip of slightly under three hours. He was surprised to realize how close he was to Maryland. From Washington he went by taxi to a motel near the campus. After checking in, he walked to the house and, his heart beating hard and fast, passed on the other side of the street. He could see a light on in the front room, but the blind was shut, so he could not see who was there. Only Masoud's car was parked at the curb. *That's a good sign*, he thought. *I could walk behind the houses and look back there. But someone might see me and think I'm a burglar or something.*

He hadn't eaten, but he didn't want to go somewhere near the campus, so he walked a few blocks north on Route 1 to a fast-food restaurant for a sandwich, then he returned to the corner nearest the house, a corner unlighted by a streetlight, and watched. He stood there for twenty minutes. It was nearly ten o'clock. Ahmed's feet were beginning to get cold, and his body was starting to chill, so he decided to walk past the house again and then go on to the motel. Just at that moment the door of the house opened, and a man walked out. Ahmed heard the door shut. He watched as the man turned and walked away from him. Ahmed froze. *That doesn't look like Masoud,* Ahmed thought. *Not big or burly enough.* The man walked to the corner at the other end of the block and turned right, crossed the street, and then the houses blocked his view.

The light in the house was still on. *Masoud would have turned it off if he'd left,* he thought. The man must have been a cop. He was startled by a noise behind him and turned around. A woman was walking toward him with a dog on a leash. Shaken, he walked across the street and away from his house without hesitation. He turned toward Baltimore Avenue and made his way back to the motel.

Once in his motel room he was still shaking. *They've got Masoud, and they're looking for Rashid and me. Am I safe here? Should I go someplace else? Was the woman a cop too? I should have stayed in Harrisburg.*

On Sunday morning the evangelism team of Greenbelt Christian Church met for an hour before the morning service, as it did each week. When Tom was introduced he explained that he needed help with a strategy to acquaint a Muslim student with Christ and to teach her Christian roommate about Muslim beliefs.

"We're glad you came," the chairman said. "We've not had much experience with Muslims. But one of our church members, George Lyon, seems to know quite a bit about them. I'll talk to him if he's at church this morning and see if he would be willing to work with you on this. If he is, I propose that he, you, and your dad form a working group to see if they can find a way to help you. Is that okay with you, Martin?"

"Sure," he said.

"Okay. Thanks a lot," Tom said.

Tom and Martin were standing in the foyer waiting for the service to begin when the chairman and George Lyon walked up.

"Tom, this is George Lyon." *Around sixty*, Tom guessed. He was a stocky man wearing a bright yellow sport coat and a wide flamboyant tie. As George reached out his hand, Tom saw a large diamond ring flashing.

Martin said, "Hello, George. How are you doing?"

"Fine, fine," exclaimed George in a booming voice. "So you need some training on how to convert a Muslim. I'd be happy to help with that. When do you want to start?"

"How about this afternoon?" Tom asked, looking at Martin. "Can we meet at our house?"

"That would be all right with me. How about you, George?"

George pulled out his smart phone and looked at his schedule. "I can do it after three."

"Okay, three it is."

Early on Sunday morning Ahmed checked out of the motel, retrieved his car, and drove a few miles south on Route 1, from the campus to a coffee shop with wireless computer service. He opened his e-mail and saw a message from Rashid.

"I'm home."

Ahmed did not reply. He nursed a cup of tea while he pondered his next move. *I don't like this*, he thought. *They're going to catch us. If not this time, then sometime. And when they do they'll put us in jail, and my family will be humiliated. My father's retribution will be severe.* He heard his e-mail beep the arrival of another message. It was from Masoud.

"Home where? I thought this was home. Where are you? It's lonesome here."

Suddenly he had an idea. *Nadira! She can go to the house. She can find out if anyone else is there. But that would mean telling her about the house. That won't work. I guess I could just call Masoud and tell him to meet me somewhere.* He asked the barista, "Does this shop have a back door?"

"Yeah, why?"

"Can a car go back there?"

"Sure, the garbage trucks do."

"Well, I'm having a problem with a girl, and I want a friend of mine to meet me here, but I don't want her to know. So if I tell him to come here, can you tell him to go out the back door and meet me there?"

"I guess so. What's his name?"

"Masoud. What's yours?"

"Susan. When's he coming? I get off at noon."

"Oh, that's not a problem. He'll be here in a half hour or so. Maybe sooner."

"That'll work."

"Thanks, Susan. Masoud, remember."

"No problem."

Ahmed drove around the block until he found an alley leading to the back door of the shop. *Perfect, he thought.* He then called Masoud.

"Hello."

"Masoud. Can you meet me somewhere?"

"Ahmed, where are you?"

"Nearby."

"Why all the secrecy?

"I'll tell you later. Meet me as soon as you can at a coffee shop called Strong Grounds. It's a couple of miles south on Route 1, on the right. Speak to Susan. She works there. Tell her your name, and that you're looking for a guy. She doesn't know my name, but she'll direct you to me. When can you get here?"

"Ten or fifteen minutes."

"See you soon." Ahmed hung up. He drove to the entrance to the alley and parked across the street, where he had a view of the length of the alley and was able to see anyone who would come out the back door of the coffee shop. Ahmed looked around. It was Sunday morning and the street was very quiet. *An empty street is better than a crowded street,* he thought. *In a crowd you can't see someone who might be after you. But here, if someone is following me, I could see him coming.* He did not have to wait long. In about seven minutes he saw Masoud emerge. Seeing no one on the street, Ahmed got out of his car and began waving until he got Masoud's attention. He gestured for Masoud to come to him. Then he got back into his car and drove up the street, away from the alley. At the intersection he turned right onto the street parallel to Route 1. He drove to the next street, turned right, and went to the other end of the alley where he could see Masoud standing at the opposite end of the alley. Seeing that Masoud was alone, he circled the block. When he reached Masoud he slowed down and opened the passenger door and kept moving slowly while Masoud got in.

"What's going on?" Masoud almost shouted.

"Just being cautious. I was by the house last night, and I saw a guy leave, around ten. I suspected the police had you and were waiting for Rashid and me to come back."

"Ha, ha, ha, ha, ha. That was Hashim. He—"

"Did you tell him about the house?"

"Let me explain," he said forcefully. "I started talking to him at the sub shop. He speaks Arabic, and he likes soccer. So we went to my dorm room to watch a game. When it was over he left. After a little while I went to the house. I walked down Knox, and there was Hashim, hanging out in front of his house. He lives right around the corner. So I had to tell him. He came over, and we watched some more TV, and then he left."

Ahmed shook his head. "Man, what a mistake."

"Why? It would have been worse to make up some lie about why I was in his neighborhood. 'Just going home,' I told him. He doesn't suspect anything."

"Doesn't he wonder why we have a house and have dorm rooms?"

"'Our refuge,' I told him. That's all. A place to get away from all those kids who don't understand us, where we can speak Arabic, where we can live our lives normally."

"Rashid will go berserk."

"Where is he? He said he's 'at home' in his e-mail."

"He's in Egypt. When you got picked up, I saw you being led out of the dorm with those cops, so we split."

"Those weren't cops, you idiot. They're guys from the Syrian-American Association who took me to breakfast to ask me to speak at one of their meetings."

"In suits?"

"They were on their way to work."

"How could we know? Rashid went to Egypt, and I was supposed to go to Morocco. But I went to Pennsylvania instead. I figured they'd make you talk, and our names would be at every airport, so I stayed in the US."

"Kind of overreacted, huh?"

"What would you have done?"

"I don't know. But no police are there, and it's perfectly safe for you guys to come back."

Tom, Martin, and George met later at the Parkers' home. It was a warm Sunday afternoon, so they sat on padded wicker chairs on the front porch, watching squirrels chase each other in the trees.

George waved his right hand toward Tom. "Tom, tell me about this student you want to acquaint with Christ," he said in a loud and commanding voice.

"I've never met her. Her roommate has just joined CCA, and one of the reasons she joined is so we can help her understand the Muslim faith and to help her tell her roommate about her faith."

"Ah, it's a female." He nodded with understanding. "Well, that will make it a little more complicated. But we can handle that."

"I was thinking that we should include Lauren in our working group." Tom rubbed his chin. "Lauren's the new CCA member."

"Yes, certainly." George nodded. "What year is the Muslim girl in?"

"I guess she's a freshman." He gave a slight shrug. "She lives with Lauren, who's a first-year student."

"Is she foreign born or American?" He glanced at Martin.

"American." He looked toward his father. "They live in Silver Spring."

"That means she might already know a lot about Christianity." He nodded for emphasis. "Do you know where she went to school?"

"No."

"That'll make a difference." He raised his eyebrows. "There's an Islamic school near there. If that's where she went, she might not know much." He paused. "Well, with Muslims, there are things you need to know about what not to do, or you'll turn them away from Jesus right away. So the first thing we'll need to do is to inform her—Lauren is it?"

"Yeah."

"We need to teach Lauren what not to say." George spoke with profuse use of his hands. "Islam has a pretty healthy respect for Jesus, as a prophet, but denies emphatically that he is the Son of God. It's a religion that focuses heavily on what to do and what not to do on earth and very little about having a personal, loving relationship with God."

Tom said, "I think it might be more efficient to wait until Lauren can meet with us to introduce us to Islam, don't you think?"

"I guess so," George said, nodding in agreement. "I also have a couple of books on Islam I could lend to you. But Lauren shouldn't let her roommate see them. Well, one of them anyway. One of them is okay. It's by a Muslim and explains Islam for Christians from the Muslim viewpoint. If her roommate sees that she's learning about Islam, she'll be more inclined to learn something about Christ."

Martin said, "Tom, doesn't CCA have an understanding of Islam?"

"Not really." Tom shook his head. "Some chapters have developed local approaches to relating to Muslims, but we don't have a consistent one. Not at Maryland. We're working on it. This will help us along."

"Well, let me know when you can get Lauren together with us," George stood up to leave. "I'm available about any time."

"You don't have to run off," Martin said, waving his hand toward George's chair. "We still need to work out a general strategy."

George sat back down. "That's important. You don't have a spare cup of coffee, do you?"

"Sure do. I'll be right back." He got up and went into the house, letting the screen door slam behind him.

"Tom, how's school going?" George asked.

"Going well." He smiled with a slight nod.

"What's your major?" Both hands were in motion before him as he talked.

"Mechanical engineering with a minor in business. I want to get into industrial management." He pulled himself upright in his chair.

"Hmm. Can you do all that in four years?"

"I'm trying to. But getting the right classes isn't always possible." He wobbled his right hand, with his palm down, to indicate uncertainty. "It may take an extra semester. Maybe two. I don't know. I see you're with Glimus Motors." He could see George's Cadillac parked in front of the house with a license plate that said "GLIMUS."

"Yep. And still top salesman." George sat up straight and then slumped. "Or at least I was until GM stopped making Pontiacs. It's hard to sell Buicks to students. Glimus might pick up Chevrolets. They're doing real well."

Martin returned with three cups of coffee.

"Ah, thank you. You're a good man." George said, accepting his cup.

"You're welcome," Martin answered. Turning toward Tom, he said, "Because we can't overtly work on the campus, we need to work through students."

"Yeah, I know that."

"So we'll work with CCA. You, that is, and Lauren and any other CCA people you want to work with."

"We'll probably have to have another woman involved since Lauren's so new."

"A church woman or a CCA woman?"

"A CCA woman. Someone who can go to Laurens room or meet with her privately somewhere. We just like to keep focused on the issue." He looked at George with a half smile.

"I can understand that completely," George said.

"I'll talk to the CCA campus director about it, but I'd guess we'll need another woman."

"So I suppose we'll have to get both of them together with us to get on with training," George lamented.

"I don't know. We may not have to train the other woman. She might just be involved to keep things balanced. A guy and a young female student working together can veer off track, so to say," Tom added.

"You're saying Lauren is a good-looker?" George commented, his face lighting up.

"Not particularly," Tom said matter-of-factly. "Just average. But she's pretty levelheaded, and I like that."

"Well."

Martin said, "I guess this is enough of a start. Tom, when do you think we can get back together again?"

"I'll need a day or two to make arrangements with CCA. Maybe as soon as Tuesday. But more likely Wednesday or Thursday. We'll have to meet at night during the week, won't we?"

"Right."

"Okay. Dad or I will be in touch."

CHAPTER 4

It was midafternoon on Sunday when Nadira called Ahmed. "What are you doing?" she asked.

"Looking for you."

"Looking for—are you here?"

"Yes. I'm back."

"Why didn't you call me?"

"I just got back to the dorm. And I knew you'd be calling me."

"Oh, you did, huh?"

"You said you would."

"Did you like Pennsylvania?"

"It was pretty dull, really. The leaves were nice."

"They're nice here too."

"Can I see you?"

"Now?"

"Soon."

"In an hour."

"At your dorm?"

"In the lobby, yes."

"Okay, see you then."

She wanted time to change clothes and clean up. She also wanted to put on some makeup. She usually used little makeup other than blush and muted lipstick, but today she wanted to put on mascara too. She was waiting for Ahmed when he arrived.

He smiled when he saw her. *I think he approves,* she thought.

The day was cool but sunny and still. They walked aimlessly around the campus, talking about the weather, classes, family, and each other; about everything and nothing. They laughed often at each other and at themselves, expressions of ebullience spilling uncontrolled from within. Nadira felt a warm glow inside, happy just to be with Ahmed. He listened attentively to her and seemed interested in what she had to say. Being taken seriously by a man was a new and delightful experience for her.

As the day faded, they acknowledged that they should go back to their desks and prepare for Monday's classes. Reluctantly they said goodbye. From within the lobby of her dorm, Nadira watched as Ahmed walked away.

Later that night Ahmed sent an e-mail to Rashid telling him it was safe to come back. He didn't mention Hashim's visit to the house. Yet such things were bound to occur. It seemed to him that his position was becoming increasingly perilous; that as time passed, more and more intrusions into the lives of Rashid, Masoud, and him were inevitable, and the more likely something would alert the authorities to what they were doing. He knew he was becoming more attached to Nadira, and if the Servants' activities were discovered, it would ruin what he imagined could be a beautiful relationship. Not only that, his parents would be disgraced, and his relationship with them would be forever impaired.

Rashid's response arrived later. "Are you at home? Sounds like you're in CP. How did you get there so fast?"

Ahmed responded, "I took the bus. I'll tell you when you get here."

"I'll be back in a couple of days."

Ahmed didn't sleep well that night, as his imagination conjured up ways their unlawful activities could be detected, and the kind of punishment that might be meted out to them. He thrashed about on his bed, wadding up the sheet and blankets, and clawed at his pillow.

In the morning Ahmed said to Masoud as he was leaving for class, "I think it's time for me to get out. Sooner or later they'll catch us, and then it won't be pleasant."

Masoud stared at him for a moment, then said, "Did the last few days scare you that much? I thought you had more courage than that."

"I'm just being realistic."

"You're just being a coward!"

Ahmed balled up his fists and took a step toward Masoud, who grasped Ahmed's wrist and twisted his arm. "Don't be stupid too, Ahmed. I could wreck your face, and you know it." He threw Ahmed's arm down.

"Ahmagh!"[1] Ahmed exclaimed and walked out.

On Monday Tom talked to the CCA campus director, Pete McDermott, about the need for a woman to be included in training Lauren. The director agreed and told Tom he'd contact the women's director to assign someone.

"Lauren has already met Martha. Maybe she'd be comfortable with her," Tom said.

"Good. I'll suggest her."

---

1   idiot

"I'm trying to set up our first training session as soon as possible, so the faster you can get someone assigned the better. My dad and a guy from our church, named George, will be with us too."

"Oh?"

"They're the trainers. My church has done some study and already has some experience with this."

"Well, that's great. I'll try to get back to you today, then."

That evening Lauren's cell phone rang while she was at supper.

"Hello."

"Hi, Lauren. This is Tom Parker."

"Oh, hi. You caught me with a mouth full of broccoli."

"Sorry about that. Do you need me to call back later?"

"No, that's all right. Go ahead."

"I'm calling about your roommate. My church and CCA are joining forces to help you reach her, and we'd like to start training sometime this week."

"Wow. You don't waste time, do you?"

"Well, things just seemed to fall into place. Are you available this week? It'll have to be in the evening."

"Uh, I'll have to study, of course, but I can spare an hour or so any night."

"Okay. I have to contact the others to see when they can meet. I'll try for Wednesday night. I think Martha will be with us too."

"That's nice. I liked her."

"There will be five of us in total: the three of us and two from the church, my dad and a man named George Lyon."

"Where will we meet?"

"I think the best place will be at the church. Either Martha or I will be able to drive you over there."

"That's good."

"I guess that's about it for now. I'll call you back when I find out what night we'll be meeting."

"And the time."

"Yes."

"Okay, I'll talk to you later."

"Bye."

Ahmed didn't return to the house on Monday night or on Tuesday night. On Wednesday morning he heard a knock on his dorm room door. He was immediately alarmed and didn't answer. He heard the knock again and then heard the knob rattle. Then he heard Rashid say, "Ahmed, are you there? Open the door."

He opened the door and Rashid came in, frowning. Rashid looked at him, not saying anything. Ahmed looked away.

"You talked to Masoud," Ahmed said, looking back at Rashid. Rashid nodded.

"It's just a matter of time."

"Does Nadira know?"

"No. Yes. She knows about the Servants. Nothing wrong with that, is there?"

"Does she know you want out? Does she want you to get out?"

"All she knows is we run a charity. She likes that."

"That's all she needs to know."

"Do you think I'm stupid?"

"I think you're losing your nerve. People who become frightened do stupid things."

"Like running all the way to Egypt?"

"A precaution. Where did you go?"

"Pennsylvania. No passport control there."

"I guess not."

"Did Masoud tell you about Hashim?"

Rashid shook his head.

"He was at the house when I got back Saturday night. Watching soccer, Masoud said."

"Where did he come from?"

"Ask Masoud." Ahmed shrugged. "Sooner or later one of us is going to slip up. Maybe already has. What about your friends in that automobile club? Have you told them?"

"About the Servants? Nothing more than a passing comment."

"See?"

"They don't know anything. They're only interested in cars."

"Maybe yes, maybe no."

"So you want out." Rashid stepped away from Ahmed and looked out the window. Neither spoke for a minute. He turned around toward Ahmed. "You know that would make Masoud and me very vulnerable."

"I suppose so."

"We don't approve of your idea. We all got into this together, and we must all get out together, when we all decide to do it."

"We should all get out now."

"You're overreacting. Until we make that decision, you must be very vigilant with Nadira. She will ask questions. She must know nothing about it."

"She won't."

"Don't underestimate the curiosity of her father. If your relationship develops, he will have to approve."

"Yes."

"I advise you to not let it go on."

Ahmed looked down. "We're very fond of each other."

"If you let it go on, someday she'll have to know. Do you want her to know?"

Ahmed's head rolled from side to side. "No."

"Then cut it off now. The longer you wait the more difficult it will become."

"All the more reason for me to get out now."

"That's not possible."

Ahmed looked up at him. Rashid looked at him for a few seconds then turned and walked out.

CHAPTER 5

Lauren was quiet on the ride to Greenbelt Christian Church on Wednesday. She sat in the backseat of Tom's car. Martha, again looking like she'd just been jogging, chatted with Tom in the front seat. *I'm glad Martha agreed to go with us,* Lauren thought, knowing that without her she'd be alone with three men. She didn't distrust them, but would have felt uncomfortable. She wondered about Nadira. *Can I really say anything to her about Christianity? Will she even listen? If I try to say anything will she be required to move out or something? Her prayer time could be a conflict. Do I need to be gone so she can pray? Will she try to convert me to Islam? What am I getting myself into?*

It was a fifteen-minute ride. The three joined Martin and George in a classroom adorned with paintings of Jesus. They sat on metal chairs around a folding table. George told her the history of Muhammad and the establishment of Islam. She learned about the five pillars: reciting the profession of faith, the form and content of the five daily prayers, giving alms, fasting during Ramadan, and the pilgrimage to Mecca. He told her what the Qur'an says about Jesus and how it emphatically denies that Jesus is the Son of God.

He then turned toward Lauren and said, "Now we need to know a little bit more about your roommate. Tell us about her."

"Her name is Nadira. She's from Silver Spring. She's very pretty, especially her eyes. And she has beautiful long hair that she covers with a scarf whenever she leaves the room. And she has a boyfriend, an international student from Morocco named Ahmed." She smiled. "He and some other students from the Middle East are operating a nonprofit organization to raise money for an orphanage in Iraq."

"Really!" George stared open mouthed at Lauren. "What's the name of their organization?"

"The Servants of Mercy."

"Well, that's very admirable. Yes."

Lauren told them about interrupting Nadira's prayer. "Is that always going to be a problem for me? I mean, will I have to schedule my life around her prayer time?"

George answered, "Oh, gosh no. She wouldn't want that. She might pray in the room if she thinks you'll be gone, but she would probably be very embarrassed to inconvenience you."

"I think we both were on Saturday."

"I'm sure. It's bound to happen every now and then. Just be as sensitive as you can. She could just as easily walk in while you're praying."

"I know. But I wouldn't be in the middle of some routine, down on the floor on a rug. I'd just stop, and she wouldn't even know."

"The beauty of Christianity. Freedom."

George gave her two books to read. They agreed to meet again the following Wednesday. George said he would invite Reverend Norris to next week's meeting to highlight some of the major differences between Christianity and Islam.

When she returned from Greenbelt, Lauren inserted her key into her dorm room door, then tapped twice, paused, and tapped once before turning the key and opening the door. It was a signal that she and Nadira had devised after Lauren had interrupted Nadira's prayer last Saturday. She smiled at Nadira, who was at her desk, looking at the door.

"Hi. Looks like you're hard at work."

"At work. Not hard at it though." Nadira laughed. "Did you have a date tonight?" She looked sideways from her beautiful eyes, with a knowing smile.

"No. Actually I was at church." She put her books on her desk and took off her jacket.

"Oh." Nadira feigned disappointment. "Well, that's probably better."

"Yeah, for me it is. I hardly know any boys here. Certainly not well enough to be dating."

"Do you have a boyfriend from back home?"

"No. I've not dated much. Too nerdy, I guess."

"Did your parents permit you to date in high school?"

"Oh, yeah. After I was sixteen. Did yours?"

"No. My father was pretty, you know, strict about whom I went out with, even if it was just a bunch of other girls."

"I guess that's a good thing."

"I didn't always think so."

"What about now. I saw you with some guy. Over there by the sundial."

"Oh, that was Ahmed. I told you about him. He just needs someone to talk to. I think he's homesick. But if I wanted go out with him, my father would object. In my father's culture, I could probably only go out with him if he told my father he wanted to marry me. So it's best if I keep it very, like, impersonal."

"Shish! That is strict." She hung her jacket in the closet and sat at her desk without further comment.

Ahmed was walking across campus returning from his Friday eleven o'clock class when his cell phone rang. Rashid was calling. "Ahmed, we need to get together. Come to the house. Something's happened."

"I knew it," said Ahmed.

"It's not what you think. But it's important. Come right now. I know your last class is over."

"How do you know that?"

"Your schedule's right here, taped to the refrigerator! It says your last class on Friday is Foreign Relations, eleven o'clock."

"Oh, yeah. But I'm on my way to have lunch with Nadira."

"Look, Ahmed, this is very serious. Cancel lunch and come here."

"What's it about?"

"I'd be foolish to discuss it on the phone. You'll agree as soon as you hear. Please come immediately."

"Okay, I'll come," Ahmed said reluctantly, as he veered toward Regents Drive. He called Nadira and told her he had to cancel lunch.

"Servants of Mercy business, again?" she said wearily.

"I'm sorry. I'm really very sorry. I'll look you up a little later."

It took him ten minutes. As he approached the house, his anxiety grew. It overshadowed his anger toward Masoud and the uncertainty that Rashid had created in him. As usual, the door to the house was locked. He fished the key from his pocket, unlocked the door, and went in. "I'm here," he yelled to the empty living room.

"We're in the kitchen," Rashid answered.

He walked to the kitchen door and stopped. Rashid and Masoud were standing with their backs to the counter. Masoud saw him and then turned his eyes away. Ahmed thought, *this really must be serious. Masoud looks frightened, not his usual audacious, careless self. Hard to tell about Rashid, the great stone face.*

Rashid said, "Listen, I have something important to tell you."

Ahmed looked at him, waiting.

"When I was walking across the campus this morning, a man came up to me and said he represented an organization that was promoting Islam in the United States. He apparently knew about the Servants of Mercy, and said that they needed us to include his organization as a silent recipient. I told him that our receipts were pretty small and that what we can provide was only a fraction of what the orphanage needs. He said we have great potential, and that they are thinking in terms of a million dollars a year from us. When I laughed, he stopped me and turned me toward him and said, 'This is not a frivolous matter.'

"He said they know each of us, where we go, who we associate with. I could see then that he was warning me. No, threatening me. He said we have two choices. One is a business arrangement mutually agreed to, and the other is a distasteful intrusion into our affairs that would be, at best, onerous. He said the choice is ours, and that he will find me on Monday to obtain our answer. Then he walked away."

A white-hot pillar of terror thrust itself into Ahmed's midsection. He swore. He walked into the living room, then back into the kitchen. "What'll we do? These are terrorists, aren't they? This thing is over, isn't it?"

"Oh, come on, Ahmed," Masoud chided. "Settle down."

He shot back at Masoud, his eyes glaring at him, "You tell me what we're going to do."

Rashid answered, "Let's look at our options. One is to accept their business deal. The second is to give them the whole thing, collect our profits, and disappear. The third is to report it to the authorities. FBI, I guess. And see what happens."

Ahmed shook his head. "Even if we reported it to the FBI, they'd find a way to get to us." He shuddered.

"What if we make a business deal with them?" Rashid looked at Masoud and Ahmed.

Ahmed said, "I think we should give them the whole thing." *I'm glad that's an option on the table.*

Rashid extended both arms, with his palms up. "Look, we've probably taken in over two million dollars this year alone. We could let them in and still make a fair profit."

Masoud held up his right hand, as if it was his turn to speak. "If we report it to the FBI and they catch them, then they probably won't suspect us. And they might be grateful that we helped uncover a terrorist cell. Maybe we'd be heroes."

"We need to decide something by Monday." Rashid looked at his watch. "I have to go to class. Let's talk later." He looked into the eyes of Masoud and Ahmed and walked out.

Ahmed left immediately after Rashid did. He got into his car and drove away. *I wish I could call Nadira and talk it over with her, but I know that's impossible.* He decided to go to a mosque about fifteen minutes away. *The midday prayers will be over soon, so I can just think things over.*

He waited until after one thirty to go in. Inside he found the room almost empty. There, surrounded by the beauty of the mosque, the familiar arches, and the ornately painted walls and ceiling, he was comforted. This was a piece of home in this land of uninspired architecture and plainness. Ahmed turned off his cell phone, took off his shoes, and went to a secluded corner where he could think without interruption. He sat on the carpeted floor, his legs bent in front of him and his arms around his legs, and began to reason.

These people probably only know about the money we send to Iraq, so they're thinking that all we have is around $700,000 a year. So *there's a good chance they're a small organization. Even so, they'll probably end up demanding all of the money. They'll expect us to do all the work and give all the money to them.*

Ahmed stood and began pacing back and forth across the room, trying to imagine any other scenario. Nothing else seemed probable to him. *The best solution will be to give the entire company to them. It won't take long for the orphanage to realize they aren't getting any money, and they'll start asking questions. If we don't get out, it'll be just a matter of time before they find out we're still collecting donations here. They might be smart enough to notify the US authorities, and if they investigate, they'll paint us with the same brush they will the terrorists. Those people aren't going to accept no for an answer. They want the money, and they want us to be their slaves.*

CHAPTER 6

Tom's last class for the week was over at three. Maryland's football game would be away on Saturday, giving Tom a day to himself. Sunday night's CCA gathering would be organized by others, so he felt a certain amount of freedom, although he had plenty of homework to keep him occupied. As he walked toward his car, he checked with Pete, the CCA campus director, to update him on Lauren's training and to find out who'd been selected to be her discipler.

Pete asked, "Do you think Martha would be the right person?"

Tom said, "I would have suggested her." That settled, Tom called Lauren to confirm arrangements for next Wednesday's meeting.

She answered without looking to see who called.

"Hi. This is Tom Parker."

"Oh, hi." She sounded enthusiastic. "How are you?"

"I'm good. Just needed to touch base with you about next Wednesday's meeting."

"Why don't you tell me in person? I think I'm looking at you. Are you in front of the library?"

"I am! Where are you?"

"Over here between Tydings and Key."

"No way! Oh, there you are." He could see her waving. "I'll meet you at the corner."

It was a thirty-second walk for each of them. She was wearing a backpack, and the breeze was blowing her hair back. "It's a north wind," he said as they met. "Winter's not far away."

"I know. And I dread it." She smiled as she pulled her hair back in place.

"Which way are you heading?" Tom asked.

"The way you came from. I'm going to the Stamp."

"I'll walk along with you for a minute, if you don't mind."

"Weren't you going the other way?"

"I was going to get my car. This won't take a minute." They turned toward the Stamp Student Union Building. "Every new person who comes into CCA is assigned a discipler to be that person's mentor as they get familiarized with the organization. I just talked to the campus director, and I think they're going to assign Martha to be your discipler. Do you have any problem with that?"

"Oh, no. I like her. She and I'll get along fine."

"It won't be official until she, whoever it is, contacts you. But I wanted to give you a heads up, so you'll be ready to give her an answer when she calls you."

"I appreciate that. Will she be sort of my regular contact person to keep me up to date?"

"Yes, and she'll spend regular time with you to help you get your feet on the ground, spiritually speaking."

"I like that. I really do. I wish churches would do that."

"I guess some do. I also wanted to confirm that you'll be going to the Wednesday night session next week."

"Of course. I'll be ready."

"Well, that's all I needed to say. I'm glad you saw me back there." Tom stopped. "Face to face is always better than by phone. Most of the time, anyway."

"Yeah. Well, thanks, Tom. I'll see you next week."

"I'll see you." He smiled at her as he turned and walked away. *Nice girl*, he thought.

It was Ahmed's week to pick up the Servants of Mercy donation checks. As he drove to the post office branch in Washington, he thought, *I can see why Masoud doesn't like to come clear down here to M Street to get the mail. The traffic in this city is terrible.* It took much longer to find a parking place than the few minutes he needed to remove the envelopes from the PO box and stuff them into a large canvas tote bag. *I can't believe that Masoud didn't even pick up the mail last Friday, that lazy dog.*

To save time, he chose an office supply store where he could rent computer time. He entered the names, addresses, and amounts for each donation and then printed acknowledgment letters and envelopes. *$96,000. About average for two weeks,* he thought. By 6:00 p.m. he'd completed printing the letters and envelopes, which he took to their house in College Park to stuff and prepare for mailing. Stuffing the envelopes was a regular Friday night routine for all of them.

Rashid and Masoud were both at the house when he arrived. They were eating while they watched television. "Ah, the money man," Rashid commented. "How much did we collect this week?"

"There were two weeks' worth of checks there since we fled into the desert last weekend. Ninety-six thousand. I've got a lot of envelopes to stuff here." He scowled at Masoud. "I need to eat something, first. Is there any left for me?"

"Yeah, there's plenty," Masoud waved a beefy hand toward the kitchen.

Ahmed went into the kitchen and served himself two pieces of chicken from a pan on the stove, where it had been cooking with vegetables. He added some bread, poured himself a glass of water, returned to the living room, and sat on the couch next to Masoud. As soon as he sat down, he said, "To those terrorists, we have only one choice: give them all the money and keep on collecting checks."

"What do you mean, all the money?" Rashid set his plate on the floor beside his chair and gave his full attention to Ahmed. "Do you mean our shares too?"

"Yeah. They're going to get real close to our operation. You just wait and see. The camel's nose will be under our tent all the time."

"I hadn't thought about that."

"I think they'll want all the money and make us do all the work. We'll become their slaves."

Masoud slapped his leg. "Typical little Ahmed. You're just a little piss ant, waiting to be stepped on and squashed. We need to make them think we're a whole lot stronger than we actually are."

Rashid said, "How do we do that, Masoud?"

"We could align ourselves with an umbrella organization, like the United Way or the Red Crescent. Then we tell those terrorists, 'no deal.'"

"No deal?" exclaimed Ahmed. "They aren't going to pay any attention to the Red Crescent or any other organization."

"Now, wait a minute, Ahmed. Masoud might be on to something. We're a legitimate charity. We can threaten the terrorists just as they're threatening us. We can take their picture, maybe get a real name, and report them to the government. Maybe we should reduce our shares a little for a while, just in case."

Ahmed had stopped eating as his anxiety level rose. "I think you're both smoking hash. Those terrorists won't let us off that easily. They'll do anything to get their hands on the money we raise. And that means bodily harm. Our bodily harm."

Masoud shoved Ahmed's shoulder. "Don't be such a coward, Ahmed. We're smarter than those guys are. We can stay ahead of them, just like we've done with the American authorities."

Ahmed grew quiet, waiting for Rashid to say something. But he didn't. Finally Masoud spoke again, "We could hire someone, maybe a company, to take the checks from the post office box and send them to Iraq. We'd no longer be involved except for doing appeals. One of us would go to the post office a couple of days before the company is scheduled to pick up the checks and take out our share of the checks. As far as the terrorists will know, we'd never see the checks."

"How will we convert Servants of Mercy donations to ourselves," Rashid asked.

"Just like we always do." Masoud was standing now, walking back and forth across the room. "We split up the checks we pick up and deposit them in our own accounts just like we do now."

"No, that's not good enough, Masoud," Rashid said. Ahmed nodded his agreement. Rashid continued, "It might be possible to set up a new organization, a parent organization, with a new name. We could name our local accounts the name of the parent organization. That should hide them from the terrorists. But the authorities could trace them, I expect. I'm beginning to think we ought to just tell those people 'no.'"

Ahmed almost shouted, "That won't stop them! They won't accept 'no.'"

Masoud ignored Ahmed's outburst. "I think we should go ahead with forming a parent company and make plans to start a second charity. Tell the terrorists that our plans don't include them. Then see what transpires."

Rashid added, "Ahmed, this will be our first move. They probably won't accept it, but we'll then see how they respond. We may have to make some accommodation in the future, but for now let's just find out what they say or do. I don't think they'll do anything rash at the outset."

"I hope not." Ahmed sounded calmer.

"Then we're agreed?" Rashid asked.

"Yes," said Masoud.

"With reservations." Ahmed stood and took his plate of mostly uneaten dinner to the kitchen and threw it away. "We still have a bunch of envelopes to stuff," he shouted from the kitchen.

CHAPTER 7

B ack in her dorm room after Friday prayers, Nadira checked her cell phone for messages and found none. *Why hasn't he called me? He said he'd look me up later.* The constant interference of the Servants of Mercy with her relationship with Ahmed was irritating her. *He said it didn't take much of his time. But it's always something. Maybe it's just an excuse. Maybe he really doesn't care that much for me.* She tried to study but uncertainty gnawed at her. Unable to ignore her anxiety, she picked up her cell phone and called Ahmed but hung up before it rang.

Soon her phone dinged with a text, "I'll call u later." She realized her call must have registered. *At least I know he's alive.* She continued to study, although her preoccupation with Ahmed kept her from concentrating. Lauren came in, and they chatted briefly. Lauren wasn't a lively talker, which Nadira appreciated. It was about ten o'clock when Ahmed called.

"Hello."

"You still awake?" Ahmed asked.

"Wait a minute." She turned off the overhead light and walked out into the hall. "I couldn't talk in the room. Lauren's asleep." She sat on the floor, leaning against the corridor wall.

"Is she a light sleeper?"

"I don't know, but I didn't want to disturb her. What's going on?"

"Friday's always a busy day for us. We have to get letters out to donors."

"How many letters do you send out?"

"Oh, about one thousand a week."

"Wow. That's a lot."

"Yeah."

"Thought you said the Servants didn't take much time."

"Usually it doesn't, except on Fridays."

"All day?"

"Just afternoons and evenings. But today we had to answer an urgent request, and that's why I had to cancel lunch. Sorry about that. That was very unusual."

"It doesn't seem that unusual to me."

"What do you mean?"

"It happened all last weekend too."

"Well, you just never know when something's going to pop up."

"That's what I mean."

"Is that a problem for you?"

"It could be."

"So…"

"So maybe that should limit my expectations."

"What are your expectations?"

"Right now? Someone to talk to, to hang out with. Someone who wants to be around me."

"Well, that's me."

"Every now and then."

"Come on, Nadira. Today couldn't be helped."

"I'm sure."

"You sound like an angry American girl."

"I'm an American girl. Not angry but a little bit offended."

"I said I was sorry. And I am."

"Okay. I accept that."

"Are you available tomorrow?"

"No. My father is coming to take me home for the weekend. I'll be back Sunday night."

"I'll miss you."

"Call me tomorrow sometime, after noon."

"Okay."

After a short pause, she said, "Well, good-night."

"Good-night."

Nadira slipped back into the room and closed the door behind her. Lauren stirred but didn't open her eyes. Her desk placement shielded her lamp from shining in Lauren's eyes when she was lying in bed. Nadira watched a moment to see if she'd awakened Lauren before she sat at her desk.

Nadira valued privacy. She had wanted a single room, but her father convinced her that sharing a room with another girl would be a good experience for her. She had thought he probably didn't want to pay for a single room but hadn't said so. The furniture arrangement worked for her, giving her wall space to decorate with her personal choice of artwork and giving her a place to pray without being seen from the door.

She stared at her computer screen, looking at her wallpaper. It was a family picture taken in front of the White House last summer, and Nadira looked happy and carefree. *Things were less complicated before I met Ahmed.* She replayed their conversation. *Why did I have to sound so snippy? He apologized, didn't he? He had a reason why he hadn't called. I shouldn't have let my feelings rule my mouth. But he should have called me earlier. Maybe this is not meant to be.* Her eyes grew bleary and a single tear trickled down her cheek. She let it fall onto her desk pad and watched it grow into a quarter-sized damp spot and then begin to fade away. *That's us,* she thought.

Ahmed went to his room in Worcester Hall on Friday night and didn't return to the house until Monday morning. He spoke to Nadira again on Saturday afternoon and thought she sounded like she was over being offended. However, when he asked to see her Sunday evening after she returned to the campus, she said she wouldn't be back until late and would have quite a bit of homework to do. That unsettled him.

By Monday morning his concern about Nadira had been preempted by his preoccupation with the demands of the terrorists and his fear of their reprisals. Before his ten o'clock class he went to the house. Masoud was there.

"Where's Rashid? Has he told them yet?"

"No, he's over in the park, meditating. I think."

"What park?" Ahmed took off his backpack and dropped into a chair.

"You know. Greenbelt. He goes over there all the time to get away from you." He laughed. "No, he says he can think clearly there."

"His car's here."

"It's not a long walk. He goes over the train track behind us"—he gestured with his thumb—"and just past Kenilworth. There's an old road into the park there. It's about a kilometer and a half from here."

"When does he have to appear to the terrorists?"

"Between eleven and noon. They're supposed to find him. He said he's going to be wandering between the library and the administration building."

"We should go over there and watch, so we can get a look at the terrorist."

Masoud said. "Rashid said not to. He wants us to act like it's a legitimate business deal. If they saw us, it could cause more problems."

"So we just wait, huh?"

"Right."

After a few minutes of silence Ahmed asked, "What do you think they'll do to us?"

Masoud exhaled loudly. "Nothing. It's probably some punk who thinks he can get something for nothing."

"What if it's not?"

"I hope they tear your tongue out!"

Ahmed jumped to his feet and grabbed his backpack. "I'm out of here." The sound of Masoud's laughter followed him as he marched, seething, out onto the sidewalk. He went over to College Avenue and up to the campus.

After his ten o'clock class Ahmed stopped at a sandwich shop for lunch. Sitting at a square plastic-coated table to eat his sub, he stared out the window, hoping Rashid would walk by. A small segment of Regents Drive was visible from there, although not enough to see people very well, so he picked up his lunch and walked across the highway and the block and a half to the nearest corner of Chapel Fields. He sat on the grass where Rashid would have to pass by to go to the house. There he slowly finished his lunch. His anger against Masoud had gradually subsided. *He doesn't understand what we're up against. Or rather, what's up against us. He's playing with fire and doesn't know it. If it weren't for Nadira, I'd just drop out of school and leave. I could redirect my money to the account in Liechtenstein, and I'd be out of it. Just like that. Rashid and Masoud would never find me. They wouldn't even look.*

After he'd finished eating he felt conspicuous sitting on the grass and watching people, so he walked up to the chapel and sat on the steps for a while. *What do they do in here?* he thought. *I've seen movies with scenes inside churches. They didn't tell me much.* He stood and tried to open the front door. To his surprise it opened, so he went in. He was in a foyer, with inner doors that opened into a large room that had rows of long wooden seats facing a slightly raised platform. The room was bright, lighted by large arched windows along the walls. A lectern, a table, and a piano were on the platform. Behind that platform was a second higher platform containing only three chairs. *Not much to see here, other than the imposing half dome over the platform. Extremely plain, compared to a mosque.* The room was empty. *It's time for prayers. I guess Christians don't have them. I wonder if this will become a mosque someday.* He heard a door open, so he left. *I'm not impressed.*

It was nearing the time for his next class. Ignoring the mental call to prayer with which he had grown up, he walked back to his dorm for his book and headed to the classroom, hoping it would take his mind off the terrorists' demands. He had just walked into the classroom, removed his backpack, and sat down when his cell phone buzzed. The text read, "need u now. immediately."

CHAPTER 8

"Nadira, I just saw your Moroccan friend," Lauren said as she entered their room.

Nadira, at her desk, was resting her chin on her fist. She raised her eyes toward Lauren. "Oh, really? Where?"

"He was running down the hill toward the chapel. He looked like he was in such a hurry his backpack was flapping up and down." She sat on her bed, not taking off her coat.

"As usual."

Lauren looked at her, *I don't want to pry, but I'll just let her talk about it if she needs to,* she thought.

Nadira turned toward her. "It's probably that nonprofit he's involved in. It just takes a lot of his time."

"No time for a social life, huh?" Lauren took off her coat, thinking that leaving it on made her look impatient to leave.

"We were supposed to have lunch on Friday, but he called it off because of some donor problem or something. That's twice in a week that's happened."

"Not good."

"It's just hard to get to know people here when you're a Muslim. So I was glad to have someone to talk to and, you know, be around."

"Isn't there some kind of Muslim group or club here?"

"Yeah, but it's...just different. You all have been around boys all your life. I'd like a little freedom...to mingle." Nadira laughed embarrassingly.

"Well, what about Ahmed?"

"I'm afraid I was a little too angry with him this weekend. I didn't see him. We just talked on the phone. I was upset about lunch on Friday. I guess I let my irritation show too much."

"Did he say anything or sound mad?"

"Not that I could tell, but I really don't know him well enough to know."

"I wouldn't worry about it, Nadira. If he likes you, a little thing like that wouldn't be a problem. Just keep being your sweet self." She pulled her coat back on. "I must go. It's about time for my next class." She pulled on her backpack and started for the door.

"I hope you're right. Thanks for listening."

"No problem. See you later."

It took Ahmed no more than five minutes to reach the house. "Rashid, where's Masoud?"

"On the way."

"What did that guy say?"

"He said we had a problem. I'll tell you the whole thing when Masoud gets here."

Ahmed went into his bedroom and stuffed his laptop into his backpack and whatever extra underwear and socks it would hold. Then he returned to the living room to wait for Masoud, who arrived a few minutes later.

"Here I am. What's the news?" Masoud spoke as he walked in and dropped heavily onto the couch.

Rashid glanced out the front window as if to see if someone was outside watching. "I told him our plans didn't include them. He said that was a grave error and that if we had agreed we might have worked out a suitable accommodation. But now they have no choice but to make it impossible for us to resist full cooperation on their terms. He said he would contact me again on Friday, after we had reconsidered."

Ahmed's anxiety gave way to suffocating terror. No one spoke for a full minute.

Masoud broke the silence. "Did he make it sound like a threat?"

"No question."

"Are we in danger?"

"I don't know. Maybe one of us will get beat up," Rashid said. Masoud glanced at Ahmed.

"Does he know about the house?" Ahmed waved his hand around at the room.

"We must assume he does."

"Did he say anything else?"

"No."

"What should we do?"

"Reconsider. Look, we still don't know what these people are capable of. We don't know who they are. How much risk are we willing to take?"

Masoud said. "We already take a lot of risk."

"Listen," Rashid said. "They think we give everything we collect to the orphanage. They just want a piece of that. The worst we could expect is that they'd want all of it and that we'd now be collecting money for them and depriving the orphanage."

"Let's offer them half." Masoud held out both hands as if giving it to them.

Ahmed started toward the door, then turned around and said, "Sounds good to me. I've got to go. If I have any other ideas, I'll let you know." Then he walked out to his car, parked at the curb. He drove out Route 1, turned into a residential area, turned at another street, and into a driveway where he could see the street he just left, watching to see if he had been followed. After a few minutes he felt safe and returned to Route 1, back toward College Park to the motel north of the campus where he'd stayed a week earlier and checked in. *This'll be my home for a while,* he thought.

"Nadira, can I see you tonight?" Ahmed was speaking on his cell phone. It was Monday night.

"Tonight? Now? It's already night."

"For just a few minutes. It's been a long time." There was silence for about thirty seconds. "Nadira, are you there?"

"Sorry. I was looking at my class schedule for tomorrow. I guess I can see you for a little bit. When?"

"Right now. I'm in front of Queen Anne's."

"Can you wait ten minutes?" She sounded some-what exasperated.

"Sure."

"Okay." She sighed. "I'll be out."

Ahmed sat on the front stoop facing the library, waiting for Nadira. As he waited, he watched the passersby. A man walked by whom Ahmed was sure he had seen only moments earlier, walking in the opposite direction. Ahmed frowned. At any other time it would have been nothing more than an idle occurrence. But as things were, it troubled Ahmed, especially because it was a man with a heavy beard, about three or four days' growth, and dark hair. *It could be nothing, just a student returning to his dorm,* he told himself. Yet anxiety clawed at him. He watched with heightened vigilance but not staring at anyone.

"Ahmed?" he heard Nadira behind him.

As they talked, Ahmed tried to watch the people walking by. He saw a young woman walking toward them. He noticed that Nadira saw her too and smiled.

"Hello," the woman said. "It's too nice out here to be in studying, isn't it?"

"Hi, Lauren." Nadira turned toward Ahmed. "I'd like for you to meet my friend, Ahmed."

Lauren extended her hand. "It's very nice to meet you, Ahmed." Ahmed hesitated to take her hand.

Nadira took her hand, instead, and clasped it in both of hers. "It's a Middle Eastern thing," she said to Lauren.

Ahmed smiled, to put her at ease. He said, "I'm happy to meet you too. You are Nadira's roommate?"

"Yes. And we're good friends too."

"Yes, I'm sure," he said.

"Well, I'd better get going. I still have homework to do. I'm glad to have met you, Ahmed."

"Good-night," he said.

Just as Lauren walked away, he saw the man again, just entering his field of vision. This time the man stopped and was clearly looking at them. He then turned and walked away. *He's obviously Middle Eastern*, he thought. A wave of panic washed over him.

"Nadira, I need to go. I just wanted to see you for a few minutes. I wanted you to know that I think about you often and regret last Friday's cancellation. May I walk in with you?"

They walked into the building, and Ahmed said, "I'm going out the back door—it's closer to my dorm. Good-night, Nadira."

Nadira smiled and said "Good-night" as he turned and went out toward the back door of the dorm. He stopped at the door and cracked it open to look outside. Seeing no one, he went out, but instead of walking toward his dorm, he jogged down the lawn past Van Munching to Mowatt Lane, stopped to see if he was being followed, then headed for his motel. Ahmed was frightened.

CHAPTER 9

At the Wednesday training session at Greenbelt Christian Church, George introduced Reverend Andrew Norris to Lauren and Martha and asked him to speak about the major differences between Christianity and Islam. Andrew was a chubby man with a ready smile.

"George filled me in on the reason for this gathering," Andrew began. He wore a tie and a sport coat that he could no longer comfortably button. "I'm impressed with his knowledge of Islam and its history. I learned quite a bit from him earlier today when we spoke about this session. I am going to talk about how Christianity differs from Islam, as I understand it. Believe me, I'm no authority on Islam so, George, please correct me when I say something that's not right."

He turned toward George and smiled as he hung his jacket on the back of the chair and then sat down. "I'm going to assume that you know Christianity began with the arrival of the Holy Spirit on Pentecost. Early Christianity was propagated by preaching and miracles. Islam, so I've read, was propagated largely by force. However, the time came when Christianity was forced upon people too. The history of both religions is filled with bloodshed and intolerance. It seems to me that by the Middle Ages, Christian leaders had ignored the presence and influence of the Holy Spirit and operated under their own ideas. That's just my personal opinion. From time to time the Holy Spirit has broken in on the church and reestablished its presence and influence. Islam, on the other hand, is built entirely on Muhammad's revelations. Right, George?"

"Well, that may be an over simplification," George answered. "But if you include all the things people thought they heard Muhammad say during his lifetime, you're more correct."

Andrew discussed the Protestant Reformation and the development of the church up to the present. "The last two hundred or so years have seen enormous changes in Protestantism that have largely shifted practices away from prescribed actions to more self-discipline and personal faith. Today Protestant Christianity is mostly free of requirements. The Catholic Church has retained a lot of them, such as crossing themselves, confession, genuflecting, and movements associated with worship. But you can see that as Christians have become less burdened with these things, it seems that Muslims are requiring more disciplines, especially in regard to women's dress. Would you agree, George?"

George replied, "Well, there's a lot of variation among the different denominations and sects. Islam is fairly complex in its reach now. Islam's requirements aren't confined just to prayers but to many daily tasks, such as eating, or saying certain things at certain times, such as when taking a drink of water. It governs how to treat a guest in their houses and how a woman should dress in public, for example. Some practices have crept in and have become traditional, but most of them are based on instructions by Muhammad that have been written down in books outside the Qur'an."

Lauren interrupted. "Do I have to learn all those things?"

George chuckled. "No, that would be practically impossible. I just want you to be aware of them, so that if you see your roommate doing something that looks a little strange, or repetitive, assume it's part of her religious practice. We do a few things like that. We pray before meals. In some denominations Christians cross themselves—you know, make the sign of the cross on their chest. Those are things that aren't in the Bible but are practiced. Most of the things Muslims do aren't in the Qur'an either. There's just a whole lot more that Muslims do than we do, and that depends upon how orthodox they are. I've intentionally been brief, just to give you broad knowledge of how Islam guides many aspects of a Muslim's life, far more than Christianity requires of us. There's a lot more detail to be learned if you're interested."

Andrew turned toward Lauren, "I expect it's more important for you to learn how to approach your roommate about Christianity without turning her off. Don't you agree, George?"

"Yes, I do. You're absolutely right about the possibility of turning her off, by being blasphemous in her view. Jesus is Islam's number two top prophet, you know. So he's highly regarded. It's easy to say something about Jesus to a Muslim that he might find objectionable, even if you're a Christian."

"I think Nadira wants more freedom than the Muslim organizations permit, or at least she thinks they permit."

"What do you mean by freedom?"

"Well, a few days ago we were talking, and she said she would like a little freedom to mingle, that is, girls and boys. She seems to think the Muslim organizations on campus would be too restrictive."

Tom commented, "Even at CCA we have some separation. For instance, we always have a woman who disciples a younger woman."

"She seemed to envy Christians because we can do a lot of things together."

"Well, that's encouraging." George looked at Lauren.

"I think she was kind of needing companionship. Her boyfriend had recently broken a couple of dates because of issues with the nonprofit, and she was feeling lonely. They weren't dates, really, just getting together for lunch. If she and Ahmed want to date, he'll have to get permission from her dad."

"Where are her parents from?" George asked.

"Palestine, I think. But they've lived in America for a long time. Nadira was born here."

"Good. The most important thing for you to learn is not to try to talk Nadira into becoming a Christian. All that will do is create debate and probably some hard feelings. Christianity must be demonstrated to be accepted. And I'm not talking about religious practices. I'm talking about acts that show her the love of God, the love that Christ brought to the earth."

On the way home, Lauren asked, "What can I do to show God's love that I don't ordinarily do just being friendly?" She was sitting in the backseat. Martha and Tom were in the front. Martha looked at Tom, eyebrows raised.

Tom glanced at Martha and laughed. "I thought you could answer that."

"That's why I looked at you."

Tom said, "Well, I guess the best place to start is to ask yourself how Jesus loved his disciples."

Martha turned around and looked between the front seats at Lauren. "I think Jesus did what was simply natural for him. Just let Jesus in you do it. Opportunities will present themselves, and when they do, just respond naturally. I think his love will show through."

Tom said, "Martha, that's good. Really good."

"It…it just came to me. I hadn't really ever thought of it before."

Nadira was glad that she could be alone on Thursday afternoons. Her last class was over at noon, giving her almost three hours until Lauren would be back. *I can have a leisurely lunch, pray, and do some homework without interruption.*

After her early-afternoon prayer she read for about an hour and then began sorting her dirty laundry to do a load, when she heard a knock at the door. It wasn't Lauren's secret knock, so she looked out through the peek hole. It was a man. She called, "Who is it?"

"Maintenance. Checking smoke detectors. Won't take a minute."

Leaving the chain attached, Nadira cracked the door and saw a man, smiling and holding out an ID that dangled from a lanyard around his neck. He had a step stool in his other hand.

"Okay. Sure. Come in," she said.

He took two steps into the room, put down the step stool, and kicked the door shut. Before she could call out, he had a cloth over her mouth and nose. She remembered nothing else.

CHAPTER 10

Lauren inserted her key, tapped twice, then once, and opened the door. Her stomach dropped, and she took in a gasp of air. Nadira was lying motionless in the middle of the floor in a pool of blood. Lauren screamed and backed out of the room, screaming again and again, her hair in her fists. Almost immediately other students ran into the hall, looked into the room, and began yelling for help. Others screamed. A few entered the room to see if they could help.

"She's still alive!" a woman shouted. "Call 911!"

Another woman held Lauren, still in shock, sobbing and gasping for air. She led Lauren away from the door. After only a few steps Lauren's knees buckled, and she collapsed. "Is she dead?" she managed to say.

"I don't think so," the woman holding her said. "They've called the ambulance."

The resident assistant was quickly on the scene, and he immediately called the campus police. Within minutes the police arrived and quickly cleared everyone away from the door. The woman who had gone in to help was holding her hands over cuts on either side of Nadira's neck. The emergency medical service arrived immediately after the police and began to administer first aid. Lauren watched as they brought Nadira out, on a gurney with an IV in her arm, and began to wheel her away. Lauren scrambled to her feet. "I'm going with her. I'm her roommate."

A policeman stopped her. "Just a minute. What's her name?"

"She's Nadira Shalash. I'm Lauren Stevenson." She kept trying to keep up with the medical technicians. "I've got to go with her," she insisted.

"How can we reach you?"

"I'll be wherever they're taking her." She rattled off her phone number. She began running to catch up, with her backpack still on her back. At the ambulance, Lauren tried to climb in beside Nadira but was told she could not ride in the ambulance. She cried out frantically, "Where are you taking her?"

"Adventist Hospital in Takoma Park."

Feeling helpless, Lauren stood and watched as the EMTs closed the back door of the ambulance, shutting her out. It rushed off, with its siren blaring. *I need to get to the hospital.* She looked around at the crowd that had followed her to the ambulance. Spotting the resident assistant, she cried out to him, "How can I get to the hospital?"

He looked around. "Does anyone here have a car?" No one responded. "I can call you a taxi," he said to Lauren.

"Okay. Please do." Lauren searched for her wallet in her backpack to see if she had cash for a taxi. *Oh, not enough. I'll need to have him stop at an ATM on the way.* While she waited, she prayed continuously, *Please don't let Nadira die. Please protect her.*

In ten minutes a taxi arrived. She reached the hospital ten minutes later, having stopped briefly at a bank to withdraw some cash. She rushed into the emergency room, only to be told that she could not see Nadira then because she was being treated. She took a seat in the waiting room. Silently she continued to pray. *Please protect Nadira. Don't let her die. Hold her in your arms and give the doctors your wisdom and skill.*

Within a few minutes Lauren saw two police officers come in, one a plump man who looked about forty and the other a trim younger man. She could see them speaking to the emergency room doctor. The older one then stepped into the waiting room and called, "Is Lauren Stevenson here?"

Lauren stood. "I'm Lauren."

"We'd like to talk to you. Will you come with us?" They led her toward an empty treatment room adjacent to the emergency room.

Lauren was frantic. "Is she okay? Is she alive?" She glanced back toward the emergency room as they walked.

"We can't comment on her condition," the younger one said.

"Can I see her first? Or can I talk to a doctor?"

The officers looked at each other. Then the older one said, "Just a minute." He went back into the emergency room and returned with the doctor. "Miss Stevenson would like to speak to you."

The doctor turned toward Lauren. "Are you a relative?" He was wearing latex gloves.

"I'm her roommate." She pointed at herself. "I'm the one who found her. Is she okay?"

"I think she'll be okay. But I can't tell you any more than that, due to privacy rules."

Lauren lifted both hands at him for emphasis. "But she bled a lot! And she was unconscious!"

"I'm sorry, but—"

"Her parents need to know what has happened to her!" Tears welled up in her eyes.

"Do you know how to reach her parents?" The doctor spoke in nearly a monotone.

"No, but the school does."

"What school?"

"UMD."

"The school knows," interrupted the older policeman. "Her parents probably already know."

The doctor said, "They can tell you about her condition when they get here. Now, please excuse me." He walked back into the emergency room.

The police officers led her into the vacant room. The older officer did all the talking, while the other took notes. "Please have a seat. We know this is difficult for you. Please, just tell us about this attack." They remained standing.

She took off her backpack and sat on the edge of a metal chair. It was a short report. "I opened the door and there she was, lying on the floor in a pool of blood." She pressed her hands to her face and covered her mouth.

"Was she awake then?"

Lauren stared straight ahead, her eyes wide open. "No. I didn't see her moving. I thought she was dead."

"Did you touch her or try to help her in any way?" He leaned on a table with one hand.

"No. I'm sorry." She turned toward him. "I just screamed. I thought I was going to throw up."

"Was anyone else in the room?"

She shook her head. "Not that I saw."

He squinted. "Do you know anyone who might want to do this to her?"

"No." She paused to think. "No, nobody." She looked straight ahead again, "I only know one person who knows her. A student from Morocco, named Ahmed Suliman."

He straightened up. "Is she Middle Eastern?"

Lauren looked at him again. "I think her parents are first-generation immigrants. She was born in America."

"Is she in any clubs?"

"I don't think so." She shook her head slowly. "She never mentioned one."

The officer took a few steps in front of her. "What do you know about this Ahmed?"

"They talk." She began to wring her hands as she spoke. "They occasionally have lunch together. I think they like each other, but they aren't actually dating. He seems like a nice guy. He and a couple of other foreign students operate a nonprofit organization to raise money for an orphanage in Iraq."

The questioner glanced at the other officer. "Do you know where he lives?"

"No. On campus, I think. But I don't know what dorm. If you have her cell phone, his number should be on it." She looked up at him.

"Do you know if they are on good terms or have quarreled lately?"

"Well, I saw them talking Monday night, and they seemed to be very friendly. She introduced me to him. I'd never met him until then."

"Where was that?"

"Just outside our dorm, Queen Anne's. They were smiling and seemed happy." She managed a brief smile.

"Is there anyone else that she knows here?"

"No one that I know of." *Just me,* she thought.

"I think that's enough for now. Thanks for talking to us." They let her walk out to the waiting room ahead of them.

At the admitting desk Lauren asked, "Have Nadira's parents arrived yet?" The attendant said they had not. Lauren took a seat but sat on the outer edge of the chair, her right foot jiggled up and down rapidly. *I feel like I'm about to explode,* she thought. She closed her eyes and tried to calm herself. *Oh God, thank you for letting Nadira live. And help me to be at peace.* In a few minutes she relaxed somewhat and sat back against the chair back. She pulled out her phone and called Martha.

As Lauren began to tell her what had happened, she heard Martha gasp. "Oh. Oh. Oh, God. Sorry. Go on." As Lauren continued she could hear Martha reacting with short outbursts but obviously trying to not interrupt. When Lauren finished, Martha said, "What a terrible thing. What a nightmare. Are you all right? What can I do to help?"

"I need someplace to stay tonight. I don't want to go back to my dorm room. There'll probably be policemen there, and who knows what's going on?"

"Oh, yeah. It needs to be completely cleaned up before anyone can live there. If you don't mind sleeping on a couch, you can stay at my place. There are two other girls who live here, but they'll understand completely. Where are you now?"

"I'm at Adventist Hospital in Takoma Park. I'm at the ER. I'm going to stay here until I know Nadira is all right. I'm waiting for her parents to get here. The doctor won't tell me much, because of privacy rules. So I'll have to get it from her parents. I'm assuming the university has notified them."

"Do you have wheels?"

"No, I came by a taxi."

"No problem. One of us will be there to pick you up when you can leave."

"Thanks, Martha."

"I'll talk to you later. Bye."

Martha's pretty calm, considering, Lauren thought. *Like a physicist. Cool and analytical. That's what I need right now.* Lauren waited, listening for every sound that might tell her something of Nadira's condition. It was a busy place, with a steady stream of people coming and going. Another ambulance arrived, and a patient was wheeled in. The waiting room was almost full of people. She watched everyone entering. Soon she saw a man and a woman enter that she thought must surely be Nadira's parents. They looked like Lauren thought they would. She was a slim, elegant brunette, wearing a headscarf. He was a large, barrel-chested man with close-cropped hair, faintly gray at his temples. They strode to the admitting desk. Lauren couldn't hear what they were saying, but they were immediately taken into the emergency room.

It seemed to Lauren that Nadira's parents were in the emergency room for a long time. When they finally came out, she could see that Mrs. Shalash's eyes were red, apparently from crying. Her husband was searching the waiting room, looking for her, Lauren was certain. She stood and walked toward them.

"Lauren?" he spoke loudly as she approached.

"Yes. I'm so—"

"Who did this to our daughter?" He demanded.

Lauren immediately stiffened. "I don't know. I—"

"Oh, don't be so harsh," Mrs. Shalash was frowning at her husband. She turned to Lauren. "Please pardon my husband. You understand, I'm sure."

Wow! He's rough. "That's okay. Is—"

"I just wanted to know if you have any idea of who could have done this." Mr. Shalash said. "Surely you know who she's been seeing."

She paused briefly, giving herself time to recall. "Really, the only person I know of is a student from Morocco, named Ahmed."

"A man?"

He's interrogating me! "Yes. She hasn't mentioned any girls."

"Have they gone out together?"

"I don't think so. I just met him Monday night." She shrugged slightly. *His eyes are boring into my head!* "They were standing outside the entrance to our dorm talking. Nadira introduced me. He seemed like a nice person."

"How can I find him?"

She shook her head. "I don't know. I told the police they might find his phone number on her cell phone."

"You've spoken to the police?" He sounded surprised. "The campus police or the county police?"

"I didn't notice. They were here right after I arrived." She touched her neck. "Is Nadira okay? I mean—"

"She is seriously injured. The doctor believes she will live. He thinks her wounds are warnings! They are not fatal wounds," he said. "Who would want to warn her? Of what?"

Lauren was stunned. "I don't know, sir." She lowered her hand with her palm open. "She couldn't possibly have any enemies."

"How do you know that?" Mrs. Shalash asked.

"Because she is so quiet, so sweet, and so devout." She smiled. "She always prays at the right times."

"We are so sorry that you are involved in this." She wrapped her arms around Lauren. "But you're our only link to her life here."

"What did the doctor mean by a 'warning'?"

"He said the cuts were skillfully done, purposely avoiding major arteries or veins. They had apparently used chloroform to make her unconscious, so they could cut her without resistance." She began to weep again.

"I'm so sorry." She returned the embrace. "I'll do anything I can to help."

Mr. Shalash answered. "We will need your help. We will find the ones who did this and see to it that they are fully prosecuted."

Mrs. Shalash asked, "May we have your phone number?" Lauren released her and then recited the number. "May I have yours too?" She entered it into her phone. "May I have your home address so I can visit Nadira?" Her fingers flew over her phone as she entered the information.

"Thank you for helping Nadira. We are very grateful." Mrs. Shalash looked into Lauren's eyes. "We're going back to the ER now. Will you come with us?"

Lauren followed them into the ER. She understood from Mrs. Shalash's attitude that her contact with the family should be through her. That suited Lauren fine. She saw in Nadira's father an intense focus on finding Nadira's attacker. *He looks like a man who could tear someone to pieces, and who intends to do just that. I can see why Nadira is afraid of him,* she thought. She stopped at the curtain separating cubicles, now open. Nadira was awake and wide-eyed. She seemed confused or frightened, Lauren couldn't tell which. She stood back from the cubicle while Nadira spoke to her parents. Her mother spoke first, lovingly and soothingly, too quietly for Lauren to hear. When her father spoke, she could hear him asking, "Who did this?" Lauren couldn't hear Nadira's response. He continued to ask her questions until Nadira shook her head and began to weep.

Her mother intervened and said, "Lauren is here to see you," and turned toward Lauren.

Nadira saw her and smiled, holding her arms out toward her. Lauren stepped to her bedside and held Nadira's arms in hers. "I'm so sorry, Nadira. And I'm really glad to see you awake."

Nadira's smile evaporated. "What happened? How did I get here?"

"I opened the door, and there you were on the floor, bleeding all over the place. I screamed, and every one came running. Someone called 911. They brought you here in an ambulance. I tried to come with you in the ambulance, but they wouldn't let me. So I came by taxi."

"Thank you," Nadira dropped her arms. "You probably saved my life."

"I was afraid you'd die before you got here. I've prayed for you ever since the ambulance left."

"Thank you, Lauren." She began to act drowsy, so Lauren backed away and looked at Mrs. Shalash, who nodded. Outside the cubicle she told Lauren that they might be able to take Nadira home that night. She hugged Lauren and thanked her for her kindness toward her daughter.

"If you can, please come to see her. We don't live far from here."

"Thank you. I will. I promise." As she turned to go she looked again into the cubicle. Mr. Shalash was looking at her. He did not smile or nod. He just looked. It made a knot form in her stomach. She looked away quickly and walked out.

CHAPTER 11

Tom was at Starbucks, drinking a tall latte, talking to another student, when Martha called. He glanced at his phone and then hung up, not wanting to interrupt his conversation. Almost immediately he heard the text message buzz. He glanced at it. "Call me. Emergency."

"Uh oh. An emergency," he said. "Excuse me."

"Martha, sorry I didn't answer. I'm counseling someone right now. What's up?"

"Oh, Tom. Lauren's roommate has been attacked."

"What!"

"Someone cut her throat in her dorm room."

"Oh, God. Is she d—"

"She's not dead. I guess they found her early enough to save her."

"What about Lauren. Does she know?"

"Lauren found her! She's at the hospital with her now."

"What hospital?"

"Adventist, in Takoma Park."

"I know where that is."

"Lauren's going to stay at my place tonight. I was wondering if you can bring her here."

"Sure. Do they know who did it?"

"I don't know."

"Wow. We never know, do we?"

"No, not these days."

"I'll go to the hospital as soon as I finish here, in fifteen or twenty minutes. I don't want to cut this guy off."

"I understand. I'll see you when I see you."

"Okay. Bye."

Twenty minutes later Tom started toward the hospital. Now alone, he was free to think. *Lauren must be in shock. Who wouldn't be? She'll need to feel secure. Martha will be good for her. She's steady as a rock. Her parents will need to know, as soon as possible. They may need to take her home for a while. For the time being CCA will have to be very supportive of her emotional needs. I'd better let Pete know.* He slipped his cell phone out of his pocket and called the CCA campus director and informed him of what he knew at this point.

At the hospital Tom went to the emergency room, assuming that's where Lauren would be. He found her pacing the ER waiting area. He walked toward the center of her path. She looked at him as he approached.

She walked quickly to him and said, "Oh, Tom." She wrapped her arms around him and laid her head on his shoulder. "Oh, Tom. This is terrible." He could feel her trembling and racking with sobs and felt her warm tears on his neck. As her tears subsided, she pulled away and asked, "Do you know what happened?"

"Just that your roommate was attacked. Is she still alive?" He spoke gently.

"Yes." Lauren tried to wipe her tears with the sleeve of her blouse. "Excuse me." She went to the admitting window and was given some tissues, so she could wipe her eyes and blow her nose.

Then she came back to Tom and smiled a short smile. "According to the doctor, he wasn't trying to kill her. Apparently he, whoever it was, meant it to be a warning of some kind. He knocked her out with chloroform and then carefully cut her to miss all the important blood vessels."

"So she'll be okay?"

"I think so. Her mother thinks they'll let her go home tonight. Her parents are with her now."

"Have you seen her?"

"Yeah. She was awake but very sleepy. I can leave. Are you going to take me to Martha's?"

"I am. Do you have anything?"

"My backpack is on the chair over there." She picked it up and carried it, rather than putting it on. "I had it on when I found her, and just never thought to take it off until I got here."

As they walked out to his car he asked, "Can you talk about it? How you found her and everything?"

She stopped beside the car. He could see her face beginning to redden again. She grasped his right arm with her left hand. "I just opened the door, and there she was." She was choking on her words. "Excuse me." She paused to regain her composure. "I thought she was dead." Tears flooded her face again. She threw her arms around him and pressed herself to him. "Oh, Tom. I'm so scared. It could have been me." He embraced her and held her tightly. "If he'd come fifteen minutes later, it would have been me. Maybe he was after me all along, and that's why he didn't kill Nadira!" She began to bawl, no longer able to speak. As she clung to him, he could feel her fingernails digging into his neck. Tom didn't know what to say, so he simply caressed her hair to soothe her. They held each other for several minutes until Lauren's crying subsided, and Tom relaxed his arms. "No, Tom, hold me," she whispered. "I just need to be held right now." Tom embraced her again and began to rock gently from side to side, and she moved with him. He thought, *so trusting, this girl. So terrified and vulnerable. Be gentle with her.*

Gradually she loosened her grip and slowly pulled away from him. Her eyes were closed. Tom said, "Are you all right now?" She opened her eyes.

She spoke softly, "I think so." She was still holding his arms, one in each hand. She dropped them as she said, "I'm okay now."

Tom reached into his car and retrieved some paper napkins from fast-food restaurants he'd saved in the door pocket. He handed them to Lauren. "You might need these."

"Thanks. And thanks for being here."

"I'm glad I was." *And I mean it.* "Are you ready to go?"

"Yes. We'd better. Martha will think we got lost or something."

Tom walked around the car with Lauren and opened the door for her. She looked at him with a half smile as he did. They drove away in silence for a few minutes. Finally, Tom said, "What happened after you found her?"

"I just lost it. I screamed and screamed. Everyone ran over, and soon the EMS and police were there. I tried to get into the ambulance with her, but they wouldn't let me. The RA called a taxi for me. All I knew to do was to pray for her." She told him about the interview by the police, and the conversations with her parents. "Her mom's very nice, but her dad, whoa. He's some kind of a scary guy." She shook her head.

"In what way?"

"He's big and looks mean. He *acts* mean." She turned toward Tom. "And the way he looked at me when I left the ER, I think he suspects I'm hiding something. He's frightening. I mean, if he finds who did this, I can see him ripping him to shreds."

"She has a boyfriend, doesn't she?" He glanced at her.

"Well, I wouldn't call him that. She likes him. I met him Monday night. He doesn't look like someone who would hurt anyone. But you never know."

"Isn't he the one who runs a charity?"

"Yeah. That's another thing. But I don't think she knows anyone else."

"There are some crazy people out there. Someone could have been stalking her. You told us she's pretty."

"She's beautiful."

When they arrived at Martha's house, Lauren was out of the car before Tom walked around it. On the porch Tom reached to ring the doorbell. Lauren stopped his hand and looked at him, "Tom, thank you. You helped a lot." Then she rang the bell.

Lauren and Tom went in together. She and Martha hugged and said things Tom couldn't hear. When he left, Martha walked out with him and asked if there's anything she should know. He said, "She's pretty fragile right now. She's had a very traumatic experience. I rather doubt that she'll be able to sleep for a while. She hasn't eaten either. It didn't even occur to either one of us. That's about all. I expect the police will be in contact with her soon. Maybe tonight. I don't think she's in any frame of mind to talk to them—she did talk to them at the hospital. Call me if you need me. I'll check in with you in the morning."

Ahmed didn't recognize the number that showed up on his phone. In fact, he hadn't heard it ring, even though the call was only fifteen minutes old. He was immediately suspicious. *I'm glad I'm not in the dorm or even at the house*, he thought. *Those people won't stop at anything to get their way.* A knock on his motel room door startled him. He stepped into the bathroom, intending not to answer. After two more knocks he heard "Police. Open up." Then, "We know you're in there. Open up!"

Ahmed was frozen with fear. *Why the police? Maybe they're terrorists masquerading as police.* He went to the door to look through the peephole, when it opened. Startled, he backed up as two uniformed policemen walked in. He could see the motel desk clerk standing outside. "Ahmed Suliman?"

"Yes. I was in the bathroom. I'm very sorry."

"We have some questions to ask you. Why are you staying in a motel room when you have a dorm room?"

Ahmed stepped back into the room. "Sometimes I just need to get away for a while."

The questioner stepped toward him. "Away from what?"

"The noise of the dorm." He held his hands up beside his ears. "There are always people everywhere. There is no privacy. Here I can be at peace for a few days"—he held his right hand over his heart—"and I'm close enough to go to class. Why are you asking?"

One of them closed the door. "When did you last see Nadira Shalash?"

"Why? Is she all right?" he asked with alarm in his voice. "Did you try to call me? Something's happened, hasn't it?"

"When did you last see her?"

"I saw her Monday evening. What has happened?" He was now very agitated.

"You need to come with us."

"Where?" Ahmed demanded.

"To the police station."

CHAPTER 12

I knew this was going to happen. If not the terrorists, the government. But what's Nadira got to do with it? Ahmed's mind was racing as he sat in the back of the police cruiser. I can't even talk to those guys through the glass divider. How did they find me? What do they want to know? What can I tell them? They probably know all about the Servants. What's happened to Nadira? These questions and more flooded his mind until they arrived at the police station.

The policemen walked him into the station and, after booking him and taking his fingerprints, led him into a small room with a mirror on one side. A one-way window, Ahmed thought. It was a room with bare walls, a vinyl floor, a small table, and three chairs.

"Sit at the table," he was told.

He sat without speaking. Soon another policeman, apparently more senior, judging from his insignia, entered, and one of the other two policemen left. "Tell me what you've been doing all day," the senior policeman ordered.

Ahmed sighed a deep sigh of impatience. *Be careful*, he told himself. *I must be respectful.* He named the classes he'd attended and their times. "Why do you ask?"

"I'll ask the questions," he said gruffly. "Where were you at about 4:00 p.m.?"

Ahmed was sitting erect and spoke without any movement. "I was at the motel. Please. Has something happened to Nadira?"

"How do you know her?" he asked.

"We are good friends." He touched his chest with his right fingertips, revealing the depth of their friendship.

"Why are you staying at a motel?" He raised his right hand, palm up. "You have a dormitory room, don't you?"

Ahmed repeated what he'd told the policemen at the motel.

"Can anyone corroborate that you were there then?"

He squinted. "What do you mean by *corroborate*?"

"It means, did anyone see you there?"

"Surely the desk clerk saw me come in."

"When was the last time you saw Nadira?" the man asked flatly.

"I saw her Monday night. In front of her dorm, Queen Anne's. We stood and spoke for a short while. Then she went in, and I left. Please tell me if something has happened to her!" He pleaded with both his hands.

"Can anyone corroborate that?"

"Yes. Nadira's roommate walked by. Nadira introduced us. Her name is Lauren." He placed both palms on the table. "What has happened to Nadira?" he demanded.

The man stood and immediately a policeman entered. "I'll be back in a moment," the man said to the policeman, and he left the room. The policeman did not look at Ahmed.

Ahmed asked, "Will you tell me what has happened to Nadira?"

"Who's Nadira," the policeman said.

Ahmed dropped his hands into his lap and sighed. In a short time the man returned, and the policeman left. "Look, someone attacked Nadira this afternoon. We think you did it."

Ahmed jumped to his feet. "What do you mean attacked? Was she injured, or worse?" His arms flailed as he spoke. "Was she sexually assaulted? In the name of God, tell me."

"Sit down. You tell me."

"Tell you what?"

"What you did to her."

"I did nothing to her," he yelled. "I haven't seen her since Monday night. Why won't you tell me what happened to her?"

"She was attacked with a knife. They cut her throat."

Ahmed was suddenly filled with terror. "Did they kill her?" he whispered.

The man looked at him, staring into Ahmed's eyes, his eyes seeming to Ahmed to be boring into his soul. His eyes were beginning to fill with tears, dreading the answer. *His answer is too slow coming. How can I bear to hear this?*

The answer finally came. "No." Ahmed closed his eyes and tears rolled down his cheeks. His breaths came in short gasps as if he'd been running. As he regained his composure, he asked, "Where is she? I want to see her?"

"In a hospital. Adventist Hospital in Tacoma Park. You're free to go now but stay in the area. We may have more questions."

"Where am I?"

"This is the Hyattsville station."

"Is the campus near?"

"Two or three miles north of here. Just go up Route 1."

"Can someone take me back to the campus?" *I need to tell Rashid what has happened. I can't risk using my cell phone. I'll have to tell him in person.*

The police drove Ahmed to the campus and dropped him off at the corner of Baltimore Avenue and College Avenue. He walked down College Avenue and then turned right to the house. A light was on. He went in. No one was in the living room, and he walked into the kitchen. No one was there, either. "Hello," he yelled.

"Hello to you." It was Masoud.

Ahmed poked his head into Masoud's room. "Is Rashid here?"

"I don't think so. Why?" He didn't look up from his desk.

"Those people just attacked Nadira."

"What people?"

"Those guys that are trying to get into our business."

"You're joking." Masoud sat up and turned his head toward Ahmed. He wasn't smiling.

"No joking, Masoud. They cut her throat." He was still holding the doorknob with one hand and leaning on the doorframe with his other hand.

Masoud stood up. For a moment he didn't speak. "I'm so sorry, Ahmed. I don't know what to say."

Ahmed pushed the door open but stood in the doorway. "They didn't kill her."

"Call Rashid."

Ahmed shook his head. "They're listening in on my phone."

"Who?"

"The police. They found me through my phone. They took me to the police station and interrogated me. They released me twenty minutes ago."

Masoud searched amid the papers on his desk for his cell phone. "I'll call."

"I need to see Nadira." He turned to leave.

Masoud held up his left palm toward Ahmed. "Don't go yet. Wait till I talk to Rashid. He'll have questions." He paused with the phone at his ear. "Rashid, we know what they're capable of." There was a pause. "They attacked Ahmed's girlfriend, Nadira. Cut her throat but did not kill her." He turned to Ahmed. "Where did it happen?"

"I don't know."

Masoud continued. "He doesn't know. I guess the police didn't tell him." Ahmed nodded. "The police questioned him but let him go." Masoud listened. "He wants to talk to you." He handed the phone to Ahmed.

"Ahmed, you need to find out everything you can about who attacked her." Rashid sounded intense. "As soon as possible. Tomorrow is the deadline."

"I'm going now to the hospital. Maybe I can find out something." Ahmed left the house and walked to his motel, where his car was parked. He located Tacoma Park on his road map and drove off to find Nadira. He found Adventist Hospital without difficulty and went into the emergency room and saw the admitting window.

"May I see Nadira Shalash?"

"She's been discharged."

"Where did she go? Did she walk out?"

"All I can tell you is that she isn't here. I'm sorry. Privacy rules, you know."

"When did she leave?"

"I can't tell you."

"Is there a phone here I can use?"

"There's a phone there in the waiting room that you can call out on. Local calls only."

He turned and looked around. She pointed toward the back wall, and he saw it. "Okay," he said. He called her cell phone, but it rang until her voice mail came on. *Oh, yes, the police have it.* He walked back to the admitting window. "Can you tell me where she went?"

"No. I'm sorry. I don't know."

"She's my girlfriend. I know she's been hurt. How can I reach her?"

"You might try her home."

"Yes. Thank you."

Ahmed returned to his car. *How can I find her?* he thought. *All I know is that she lives in Silver Spring. Ah, maybe I can find her in the directory.* He returned to the emergency room borrowed the telephone directory from the admitting clerk. There was only one Shalash listed, and Ahmed wrote down the address and phone number. Afraid to use his cell phone, he went to the courtesy phone and started to dial the number but stopped before he dialed all the numbers. *She won't answer. Her parents don't know me. They would not approve. And I can't go there and simply knock on the door. Not at nine at night.* He replaced the receiver and dropped his hands in helplessness.

He sat in the nearest waiting room chair, thinking about how he could reach Nadira. He was startled when his cell phone rang. The caller ID listed Shalash, so he answered.

"Ahmed, this is Nadira."

"Oh! Nadira. Oh, I'm so glad to hear your voice. Are you okay?"

"I'm alive. I'll survive." Her voice was thin.

"The police told me you were attacked. I've been so worried. They interrogated me. What happened?"

She spoke haltingly, telling him what she recalled.

"I'm so glad you're alive. Very, very glad."

"The doctor said I was intentionally not killed. He said it was a warning. My father thinks it was someone who hates Muslims. Or maybe someone who didn't like my rooming with a Christian."

A chill ran up Ahmed's spine. He was silent for a moment.

"Are you still there?" she asked.

"Yes. I don't know what to say. This is terrible."

"But I'm safe here."

"Can I come to see you?"

"No. Please don't. My father will kill you if you come here. He thinks you did this."

After the call Ahmed used the courtesy phone again to call Rashid. "They did this to Nadira clearly as a warning. Her doctor told her father that. The attacker was very careful to cut her so she would not die. They are not playing games. I'm finished. I'm out. Give them the whole thing. I don't care." He hung up.

Ahmed barely slept. *The police think I'm a suspect. Nadira's father thinks I attacked her. How can I prove my innocence?* In the mental fuzziness of half sleep, he was unable to reason. *I know who did it. But I don't know who did it. Rashid knows. But he doesn't know.* All night he wrestled with confusing thoughts and contradictions.

Finally, around five o'clock in the morning he gave up and got up. He dressed and went out for breakfast. He sat in the parking lot of an all-night fast-food restaurant and thought. *I could go home to Morocco. But sooner or later the US authorities are going to find out about the Servants. When they do, I want to be clean. I'll allow ten percent for administration. We've already kept out money for the accountant and postage. I'll figure out how much to pay myself, and send the rest to the orphanage. Then I could leave without being a criminal.* That decision gave him a great sense of relief. He carried his backpack into the restaurant and took out his laptop. When he turned it on he discovered there was not WiFi available there. After breakfast he drove to a coffee house near the campus where he could get on line. There, in about thirty minutes, he transferred all his funds to the Liechtenstein bank except for $50,000, which he transferred to his local account. *I've probably already spent about $5,000,* he figured. He closed all his other accounts. *Wow. They'll be glad to get this money.* He'd just transferred almost $600,000 to the orphanage. He smiled. He was surprised at the feeling, as if his whole insides had been replaced with air. He bought a latte and went to his car.

Back at the motel, he was alone with his thoughts. *Should I tell the police about the Servants? If they have any chance of finding who did this to Nadira, they've got to find out about the Servants. But I still have income taxes to worry about. I need to fix that before I tell the police anything. Even if I tell them about the Servants, how did the terrorists know about Nadira?*

CHAPTER 13

"Martha, do you have time to drive me to the dorm so I can get some clean clothes? Actually, I want to get all my stuff out of there." Lauren was eating breakfast.

Martha said, "It looks like you're feeling better this morning."

"Not much. But I am hungry. I couldn't eat last night."

"I have a class at nine. But if we go right now I'd have time for you to get some clothes."

"Good. I feel very grungy after sleeping in these clothes."

Martha glanced at her watch.

Lauren stood. "Okay. I'm ready."

It was a cool gray day. Clouds diffused the sunlight so nothing cast a shadow. Even though many of the leaves were wearing their fall colors, to Lauren they appeared colorless. Nausea and fear mingled in her stomach. As they approached the campus Lauren said, "I'm not sure I can go in there." She was looking out the passenger side window.

"Just to get your clothes?"

"Ever."

They drove down Campus Drive and stopped behind the dorm. Martha looked at Lauren. "Lauren, honey, you don't have to do this. I can go up there and get some of your things."

Lauren was looking straight ahead. She paused and then said, "It would be too hard to tell my stuff from Nadira's. I need to do it."

As they approached the second floor room, they could see wide tape across the door: "CRIME SCENE. DO NOT ENTER." The door was closed. They stood for a moment staring at the door. Lauren took a deep breath. "Okay." She turned and walked away.

Back in the car, Lauren said, "I should've known. I'm going home today, so I can clean up there. But thanks for taking me."

"Have you already called your folks?"

"Yeah. Last night."

"When are they coming?"

"About one."

"Good. Will you be coming back?"

Lauren turned toward Martha. "I don't know. If they don't find who did it, I won't. I'm afraid the guy was really looking for me, and that's why he didn't kill Nadira."

"Oh, Lauren! Don't even think that."

Lauren shook her head. "It might have been a hate crime aimed at me for rooming with her."

"Think about it, Lauren. If he was after you, he wouldn't have attacked Nadira!" Lauren took a short breath, with an audible catch in it. "He'd have just left. He wouldn't have done it when he saw Nadira instead of you."

"Unless he was some crazy guy who was after me. Nadira answered the door and he just acted." They were back at Martha's house. As they got out of the car, Lauren said, "I don't really know what happened. I'm going to try to see Nadira today, and maybe I'll learn more about it."

"I have classes until noon. You probably want to see her before your parents arrive don't you?"

"Oh, yeah. Maybe Tom can take me. He's really a nice guy, isn't he?"

Martha looked at her and smiled faintly.

Nadira woke slowly on Friday morning. She had slept deeply, both from the effects of the injuries and the pain medication. She rolled over to look at her alarm clock and was surprised that it wasn't there. Then she remembered that it was in her dorm room. *My own room. This is so nice. But I have classes today. Should I go?* She touched her neck. It was tender to the touch. Thick bandages were on both sides. She sat up on the edge of her bed and then stood. *I feel all right. I'll see what my parents say. Oh my goodness, I'm wearing this old nightgown.* She fingered the embroidery around the neck. *I guess this is all they found here. Where's my watch?* She looked around the room. *Mmm. I need to find my stuff.* She found an old robe and started downstairs.

She met her mother coming up the stairs. "Oh. You startled me. I thought you were still sleeping."

"What time is it?" She stopped on the stairs.

"About nine thirty. How do you feel?"

"I feel pretty good, considering."

Her mother gently touched Nadira's bandaged neck. "When I think of what almost happened…"

Nadira saw her eyes glisten. She took her mother's hand and pulled it to her lips.

Her mother took a breath and managed a smile. "The police called and want to talk to you. And your roommate called a while ago and asked if she could come to see you."

"What did you tell them?"

"The police want to come as soon as possible. Should we call them back and tell them to come at, say, ten o'clock?"

Nadira glanced at her bare wrist. "Okay, I guess. That doesn't give me much time. I'd like to have some breakfast first. What about ten thirty?"

"Lauren wants to come this morning because she's going home this afternoon."

"Oh. To Frederick?"

"I suppose so."

"That's odd. Let me call her first. Did she give you her number? Is it all right with you if she comes this morning?"

"If you feel up to it. But let me call the police first."

After her mother's call, she found the number and called Lauren. Afterward she said to her mother, "I told her to come at eleven fifteen. She'll be with a friend of hers, a guy named Tom. He has a car."

Nadira had breakfast and located the bag from the hospital with her watch and a bracelet. After eating she looked at her mother questionably.

"Is something wrong, Nadira?" She frowned.

"Please tell me the truth." Nadira hesitated. "Was I, uh, violated?"

She raised her palm toward Nadira. "Sexually? No. You were carefully examined and there was no evidence. Your father demanded an absolute certainty about that."

Nadira closed her eyes and sighed deeply. "Yes. I'm sure he did. I'm glad to know." She turned in her chair to get up. "But why did he do it?"

Her mother, still seated, asked, "Had you ever seen him before?"

Nadira shook her head. "No. Never. I don't go out uncovered. I dress modestly. I hardly know anyone."

"What about this man, Ahmed?" she raised her eyebrows.

"He's—just a friend. An international student from Morocco. He's hardly a man. A lonely boy. We've talked a few times. It wasn't him. He couldn't hurt a flea." She stood and turned toward the door.

"Is there anyone else?" Her mother persisted.

Nadira turned back toward her mother. "Just Lauren, a girl I pray with sometimes, and my professors. Really, I know almost no one."

"Did he appear to be Middle Eastern?" Nadira could see the intensity of her questions by the widened eyes and straight mouth.

"He could have been. He had a beard, several days old. I had a good look at his face. I opened the door. He stepped in, looking at the ceiling, as the door closed. Suddenly he grabbed me and covered my face, and then I was at the hospital." In her stomach she sensed an unwelcome sensation, like a rough edged balloon being inflated.

"So his face wasn't covered?"

"No. He just looked like a proper repairman with an identification badge." It was a deeply etched image in her mind. "There was nothing to suspect when I looked at him. At first I peeked through the hole in the door, and then I only opened the door as far as the chain would permit. He looked perfectly harmless and official."

"Your father is now attempting to have your attack investigated as a hate crime under federal hate crime laws."

"So he thinks it was because I'm a Muslim?" She sat down again, sideways.

"Yes, or perhaps because you're sharing a room with a non–Muslim. It's clear that he did not intend to kill you."

Anger now seeped in. "He did a good job of barely not killing me, though. He had to know exactly what he was doing to not kill me."

"And we're grateful for that."

She sat straight up and looked directly at her mother, "I want you to know that I won't be driven out of school by some zealot. I intend to continue at Maryland."

"Right now you'd better get dressed. The police will be here soon. By the way, they asked that you not bathe until after they see you."

She was dressed and ready when the police arrived. There were two women and a man, all in civilian clothes. They handed Nadira a baggy containing her cell phone, which gave her a moment of happiness. Their questions were very detailed, and the two policewomen made very careful physical examination of her neck, face, hair, arms, and fingernails. "They did this last night at the hospital, but we're looking to see if they missed anything," one of them said. They took a few samples and meticulously placed them in containers. When they were finished, Nadira felt as if she'd been plucked clean, like a chicken about to be roasted. They left without any comment about suspects or conclusions they'd drawn from her answers.

Tom had been unexpectedly delighted when Lauren asked him to take her to see Nadira. All the past evening the sensation of her clinging to him, the warmth of her body pressed against his, remained with him. He knew she was reacting to her terror. Yet it had captured his imagination as only the feel of a woman's body in the arms of a man can do. When he saw Lauren on the porch waiting for him as he drove up to Martha's house, a quick pang of excitement sped through his midsection. She hurried to the car.

"Hi, Tom," she said, quietly.

Tom could sense that she was still troubled. "Good-morning! How are you on this fine morning?"

"Cold." She sat with her shoulders hunched. "I had to borrow this sweater from Martha. We went to my dorm to get my clothes but couldn't get in."

"Really?"

"The room was blocked with police tape. I'm glad I'm going home today, so I can get some clean clothes. I must look pretty dowdy."

"Not to me."

Lauren turned halfway toward him but said nothing.

They drove in silence for a while. Tom asked, "How did Nadira sound when you talked to her this morning?"

"Okay, I guess. Really, she sounded better than I expected her to." Tom could see her nodding almost imperceptibly.

"How are you feeling?"

"I don't know. Numb. Martha said I shouldn't think he was after me. He wouldn't have hurt Nadira just because I wasn't there. I'm not sure."

"I think she's right."

"But what if it was some crazy guy who was all set to attack me and just couldn't stop?"

"A crazy guy probably wouldn't have been so careful not to kill her. Besides, a crazy guy probably couldn't get into the dorm."

Lauren didn't respond.

They arrived at the Shalash home in ten minutes. "Should I wait here for you?" Tom asked.

"Oh, no. I want you to meet Nadira. Come in with me."

When Mrs. Shalash opened the door Tom was struck with her elegance. Even though she was wearing a head scarf, he could see that her hair was pulled back into a bun on the back of her head. She appeared to have a light suntan, and her eyes were the shape of almonds.

"Hello, Lauren. Please come in."

Lauren introduced Tom as they entered an entrance hall. Mrs. Shalash ushered them into the living room and left to call Nadira. Soon she returned with her daughter who, except for the bandages on her neck, looked very much like her mother, and except for her long shiny, smooth hair visible under her head scarf. *Wow,* Tom thought. *This is one pretty woman.* Lauren stood and hugged her and then introduced Tom. They were all seated, Lauren and Nadira on the front edge of a sofa, and Tom on an overstuffed chair. Mrs. Shalash sat on a straight-backed chair near the door.

Lauren said, "It looks like you survived your ordeal pretty well. How do you feel?"

"Surprisingly good. I'm not in much pain. My neck is just a little tender. I apparently didn't lose that much blood. I think I could have gone to class today."

"I couldn't have," Lauren shook her head.

"Really?"

"Nadira, I thought you were dead." She paused. "When I came in and saw you lying there in all that blood, I freaked out." She held her head in both hands. "And it takes a lot to do that to me."

"Oh, Lauren." She reached out and took Lauren's hand.

"I spent a very traumatic couple of hours. But I was so happy to find out you were okay. And now look at you. Put on a turtle neck and no one would know the difference."

Nadira withdrew her hand. "Whoever did this"—she touched her bandages—"really knew what he was doing."

"A surgical strike," Tom added.

"Do they know who might have done it?" Lauren folded her hands together.

"I don't think so." Nadira looked at her mother, who shook her head. "While I was in the ER, the police searched me for clues, you know, DNA samples and stuff like that. And they took some more when they were here a while ago."

"I went to our room this morning to get clothes, but couldn't get in. Looks like they're still looking for something there too."

"Lucky for me most of my winter clothes are still here. The police brought me my cell phone, so I know they've been through the room."

Nadira changed the subject. "So you're going to Frederick for the weekend?" she said brightly, looking at Lauren.

Lauren frowned. "Maybe for good. I don't think I'd feel comfortable in that room. Or maybe not that dorm."

"But I want you to stay with me. I might have bled to death if you hadn't come in when you did. You probably saved my life!"

Lauren looked down at the floor. She spoke softly. "What if the attacker had been after me but found you instead?"

"How could that be? You're a Christian. Why would someone want to warn you?"

Lauren slowly looked from the floor to Nadira. Tom could see her facial expression change from self-conscious fear to incredulity. She said, "You think he attacked you because you're a Muslim?"

"Why else?"

Silence filled the room. Lauren looked at Tom, asking with her eyes, "What should I say?"

Finally Nadira spoke. "It might have been a Christian that did it, but more likely I think it was a radical Muslim who was warning me because I'm rooming with a Christian."

Tom interjected, "Are there such types around here?" He looked at Mrs. Shalash for an answer.

She said, "I suppose there could be. There's everything else. My husband seems to believe it was a hate crime, though. And I suppose that would rule out Nadira's theory."

"Regardless of who or why," Nadira said resolutely, "I'm not going to be frightened off. I know who I am. No amount of warnings will change who I am. And I don't know anyone I'd rather be rooming with than Lauren." She again took Lauren's hand.

Lauren slid over to her and hugged her. "Thank you." She pulled away. "I have to leave now to meet my parents at Martha's house—you don't know her, but I stayed there last night. I'll call you after I talk to my parents this weekend."

She stood, and Tom stood. They said their good-byes and left.

Ahmed's cell phone rang. It was Rashid. He thought, *I told him I was out. But he's the only connection to the terrorists. I need to keep in touch.* "Hello."

"Ahmed, can you pick up the checks today?"

"It's your turn. Why are you calling me?"

"Ah—I'm not able to do it now."

"Then call Masoud. I told you I was out."

"I can't reach him."

"Is somebody listening to this?"

"No."

"Is somebody close to you?"

"Yes."

"Are they going to hurt you if I don't do it?"

"Yes. Yes."

"Will they hurt me if I do it?"

"No. Just get them and put them on the porch of the house. Then call me and tell me they're there."

"How can I believe you?"

"Ahmed, please. Just do it. I've never been dishonest with you. I very much need you to do this."

"I assume it must be done secretly, or you get hurt, right?"

"Yes."

"If I call the police, you're in danger, right?"

"Yes. Yes."

"Are they inside the house?"

"No."

Maybe they'll abduct me too. "Will they be watching?"

"I don't know."

They can't do anything to me if I drop the checks someplace else. "Okay. I'll call you."

"You'll need to prepare the acknowledgment letters too."

Ahmed was silent.

"Ahmed?" Rashid pleaded. "This has to go smoothly."

They might hurt him if I don't do it. But probably not. They need him unharmed. Maybe they'd hurt Nadira again!

"All right. I'll do the letters. That's the last you'll have of me."

"Thank you, Ahmed."

CHAPTER 14

Ahmed had never heard Rashid sound so desperate. *Rashid can pick up the checks as well as I can. Maybe the terrorists think it's too risky to go inside the post office with him, and he might escape if he goes in alone.*

Ahmed drove to Washington to the post office. Once inside he looked around to see if anyone looked suspicious. Apart from an old man teetering on a cane and a young mother bouncing a little girl on her hip, waiting for mail clerks, there was no one there. He'd been afraid to go to the house to pick up the tote bag they regularly used for pickups, so he'd picked up a plastic grocery bag from the dumpster outside the motel. The key to the PO box was still in his pocket from last week's pickup. He unlocked the box and shoved the envelopes into the bag and then walked briskly to his car. Breathing a sigh of relief, he returned to the motel to open the envelopes, enter the donor acknowledgment data into his laptop, and download the file into a flash drive.

I'm pushing my luck by coming back here to do this, Ahmed thought. He loaded all his belongings into his car and checked out of the motel. The next stop was an office supply store where he printed out the acknowledgment letters and envelopes. He loaded them into a box that a clerk gave him and then used the store's shredder to get rid of the donors' envelopes.

Now, he thought, *where am I going to leave this stuff?* Ahmed was afraid to go to the house. *Maybe I should leave it at the Chabad student center on Hopkins. That would ruffle some feathers.* He laughed out loud. *Ah. I know. I'll leave them in the chapel.* He drove onto the campus, parked beside the Chapel Fields near the Armory, walked across the field to the entrance of Memorial Chapel, and finding it open, set the box and plastic bag inside the door. Then he called Rashid.

"Hello?" Rashid answered.

"The checks, letters, and envelopes are in a cardboard box just inside the door to Memorial Chapel, to the left of the door. Good-bye." Ahmed pushed the off button.

It was late Friday afternoon. The Chapel Fields were filled with students playing football, tossing Frisbees, kicking soccer balls, and watching others. Ahmed walked back across Regents Drive to the field and mingled with the people there. Within five minutes he saw a car park on Chapel Lane. A man he did not recognize emerged from the car and went into the chapel and almost immediately came out, carrying the box. Ahmed was holding his cell phone at his ear, but as soon as the man came out Ahmed began taking his picture, frame after frame, until he reached the car and got in. Then Ahmed took several pictures of the car as it drove behind the chapel. It turned around and came back down the short lane, then turned right onto Regents Drive and drove away. As it did Ahmed could see three people in the car; a driver in front and two people in the back. One of them was Rashid.

Ahmed returned to his car and as quickly as he could he drove through the campus and continued west to a motel on New Hampshire Avenue and checked in.

"The president of the university called today," Mrs. Shalash said at dinner. "He'd like to visit us and, of course, Nadira, tomorrow."

"Really? What time?" Mr. Shalash smiled and sat up straight.

"Ten o'clock, if that's convenient." She looked at her husband and then at Nadira.

"That would be a good time for me," he said and turned to Nadira.

"Yes, ten would be fine," Nadira said.

He put both his palms on the table beside his plate. "I suppose he wishes to express his regret and to assure us that nothing like this will ever happen again, as if it were in his power to prevent it." Then he picked up his fork and began to eat.

"Nadira wants to continue at Maryland." Mrs. Shalash looked at her husband. "What do you think about that?"

He looked at Nadira, finished chewing, and said, "Are you aware of the danger you're facing?"

"Yes, of course," Nadira responded. "But I don't think it is in our best interest for me to run and hide. That could be just what my attacker was trying to accomplish."

Mr. Shalash looked at his wife but said nothing for a moment. "Before I decide anything, I need to know something about this man, Ahmed." He turned to look at Nadira. "What do you know about him?"

Nadira put her fork down. "He's from Morocco. He speaks English well." Her tone became more emphatic. "He seems to be thoughtful and a gentleman. I think he likes me, but he's never made any advances towards me. I've always been covered when he sees me. We just talk."

"What year is he in? What is he studying?"

"He's a junior—third year. I don't know what his major is. He and two other international students have started a charity to raise money for orphaned kids in Iraq. That keeps him very busy. I don't know how he finds time to study." She saw her father snap his head toward her.

His eyes bored into hers. "Do you know that Muslim charities in America are important supporters of terrorists? What's the name of his charity?"

"The Servants of Mercy."

"The Servants of Mercy," he repeated. "I'm going to look into that organization. We'll see how legitimate it is." He nodded.

"I was hoping you'd let him come here to see me," she said weakly.

"Absolutely not. You'll have nothing to do with him until my investigation is complete. Is that understood?"

She looked down at her plate. "Yes, Father."

"What is his last name?"

"Suliman."

He stood and walked into the kitchen and then returned with a pen and piece of paper in his hands. "Ahmed Suliman?"

"Yes."

"Servants of Mercy," he recited as he wrote.

"Do you know the names of the other men involved?" He raised his eyebrows.

Nadira shook her head. "No, sir." She could see by his expressions that he was searching his mind for other questions for her, but he asked nothing more.

"It won't take long for me to find out if that's a legitimate charity and if there's any sign of irregularity. I have access to all that information in my office. I can do some preliminary research tomorrow, even though it's Saturday. Now, if you'll excuse me, I'm going off to the mosque. Are you going?" he looked at his wife and then at Nadira.

"I think it would be better for us both to stay at home tonight," said his wife as he stood and walked out of the room. "We're fortunate that he works for the government, aren't we?"

"I suppose so," Nadira said, "but I hate the thought that my father is investigating a friend of mine to find out if he's a criminal. It's so—sneaky!"

"It's because he loves you, Nadira. You understand that, don't you?"

Nadira paused. It was a telling pause. Before she spoke, her mother added, "Someday you'll be grateful for him." She got up and began clearing away the dishes.

Lauren's phone sounded her familiar musical ring tone. "Hello."

"Hi, Lauren. This is Nadira."

"Nadira! It was so good to see you today."

"Same for me. I'm just sitting here at home with no one to talk to but my mother."

"Yeah. Same with me. My folks are pretty upset about your attack, as you might guess."

"I'm sure. The president is coming to see us tomorrow."

"The president?"

"The university president."

"Oh, I thought *the* president."

Nadira laughed. "He wants to talk to my parents and me."

"That's nice. Very nice. He should, really."

"Yes, I think so too. Hey, can you do something for me?"

"Sure."

"Call Ahmed and tell him that I can't talk to him. My father says I'm not to have anything to do with him until he finishes investigating the charity he runs. He still thinks Ahmed had something to do with my attack. Tell him not to call me until I call him and tell him it's okay."

"How's your father going to do that?"

"He works for the IRS, so he has access to all kinds of information."

"Wow. That's frightening."

"I'm not concerned about Ahmed. Those guys might have made some mistakes but nothing to be worried about."

"You're probably right. Sure, I'll call him. What's his number?"

Nadira recited the number. "Just tell him it'll only be a couple of days."

"Okay. How are you feeling?"

"Pretty good. Still a little sore, that's all."

"When you talk to the president tomorrow, ask him when we can get our stuff out of the room."

"Okay. Let me know if you're going to come back to school on Monday."

"You're really going to stay, huh?"

"Unless my father says no. But I think he'll let me."

"I don't know yet. But I'll call you before Sunday night to tell you something."

"Good. I'll talk to you then."

"Bye."

Lauren immediately entered Ahmed's number. No one answered. She left a message, telling him what Nadira had wanted her to say. A few minutes later her phone rang. "Hello."

"This is Ahmed. I got your message, and I'm very sorry for that. Did Nadira say how her father is going to investigate me?"

"Not you. The charity you run. He works for the Internal Revenue Service, so he has access to a lot of information."

Ahmed was silent for a moment. Lauren waited. He asked, "Do you know anyone who knows about income taxes?"

"No, I've never paid income tax. But I can ask around. I assume you're talking about someone in College Park or nearby."

"Yes, I'd like some advice for my own taxes."

"I'll see what I can find out."

"Thank you. Good-bye."

"Bye."

Lauren called Martha and asked if she knew anyone who could advise Ahmed, but Martha only knew of the commercial tax preparers. She suggested calling Tom. So she did.

"Hi, Tom. This is Lauren."

"Hey. A surprise. How are you doing?"

"All right. I'm calling because Ahmed, Nadira's friend, is in need of someone to advise him on his income taxes."

"In October?"

"Well, yeah. Why?"

"They're not due until April."

"Oh. He asked me that after I told him that Nadira's dad is investigating his charity. Her dad's with the IRS."

"Hmm. Sounds ominous. Yeah, I've been doing my own taxes for several years. His couldn't be that complicated. I could help him."

"Great. When could you see him?"

"If it's urgent, I could see him in the morning. I'll be at the football game tomorrow afternoon. If it isn't urgent, we can arrange a time in the next couple of weeks. Just tell him to call me. What does he look like?"

"He's a skinny guy with a mustache. Dark hair. He looks Middle Eastern. I've only met him once, but he'd be easy to spot around here. I'll call him now and see what he says. I'll tell him to call you."

"Fine."

"Thanks, Tom. Bye."

"See ya."

Tom's phone rang again five minutes later. "Hello."

"This is Ahmed Suliman. I just spoke to Lauren, and she asked me to call you. I am in need of someone to advise me on income tax in America."

Tom thought, *I'd put him off for a while, but this is an opportunity to use what George has been teaching Lauren and me.* "I've done taxes long enough to know something about them. And what I don't know I can tell you how to find out. Are you free tomorrow morning?"

"Yes, I am."

"Why don't we meet tomorrow at the Starbucks in the College Park Shopping Center?"

"There's a coffee shop further south on Route 1, Strong Grounds. It would be more convenient for me if we met there. Would that be all right for you?"

"Yes, that'd be fine. Is ten o'clock a good time for you?"

"That's perfect. You can recognize me by my jacket. It's black with a wide white stripe on each side."

"I'll be wearing a red sweatshirt with the word *Maryland* on the front."

"Very good. I'll be there at ten o'clock."

"I'll see you then. Good-bye."

CHAPTER 15

The Shalashes welcomed the president's Saturday morning visit. He was accompanied by an assistant, a woman not much older than Nadira, whom he introduced as Helen McGovern. He was very apologetic about the attack yet was very frank about the inability to absolutely control access to dormitories. "The man who did this to Nadira had to have been a student or had help from a student to gain access. He had to have had a key, and the only way to get a key is from another student." Nadira saw her father glance at her and nod, almost imperceptibly. "The community assistant at the desk yesterday had not been approached by someone posing as a workman nor did he see such a person coming in. So that is an important piece of knowledge."

Mr. Shalash looked directly at him. "My daughter wants to continue her studies at Maryland." He extended his hand toward Nadira. "But I have grave misgivings about subjecting her to any future assault."

"I'm encouraged that she wants to remain at UM. We have one of the most secure campuses in the country, with an extensive personal security system in place. Even so, it's not perfect, and I've asked our security people to consider additional surveillance cameras in the dorms. I agree with you that until we find her attacker your daughter should remain in a safe place. We have not released her name to the press, as you may have seen in this morning's *Post,* although it's only a matter of time until it becomes known. I think we can arrange to have her homework assignments sent here so she can keep up with her classes until he is found." He turned toward Nadira. "Would that be acceptable with you, Miss Shalash?"

"Yes, sir." She replied.

"Have the police made any progress toward finding the man?" Mr. Shalash asked.

"Not that I know of. I spoke to the chief of police last night. They have questioned one man but found nothing that would warrant arresting him."

"The police were here yesterday and questioned Nadira, and I'm grateful for that." He nodded.

"Well," said the president, "I just want you to know that I regard this incident with utmost gravity. I will personally do all I can to facilitate your daughter's education and to ensure her safety to best of our ability." He stood, and his assistant rose as well. "Please don't hesitate to contact my office if you need any assistance whatsoever. I've assigned Miss McGovern as the point of contact from all parties regarding this matter."

Ahmed arrived at the coffee shop early, ordered a cup of tea, and waited. He sat where he could watch the door, and so he could exit out the back door if necessary. *I probably wasn't followed here, but I'm not taking any chances.* He immediately identified Tom when he came in and stood so that Tom would see him. They shook hands, Tom ordered a cup of coffee, and they moved to the most remote table in the shop, so they could speak more privately.

"Where are you from, Ahmed?" Tom smiled.

"I'm from Morocco." He lifted his chin almost imperceptibly when he said *Morocco*.

Tom raised his eyebrows. "You're a long way from home. What brought you to Maryland?"

"They advertised very much in my home, near Casablanca. They welcomed me very much. They helped me make the applications."

"What year are you in?"

"Junior year." He laughed at the term. *It sounds like an inferior year.*

"What's your major?"

"Business Administration."

"I guess they haven't covered taxes yet."

Ahmed laughed again. "Yes."

"Tell me about your income tax needs."

"I made a little money last year and more this year. I have heard about income taxes in America and was told that even foreigners should pay taxes. But I don't know how to do it."

"How did you earn money? I understand that foreign students are not permitted to work here."

"After their first year they can, if it's related to their major. I and two other men started a charity last year to raise money for kids in Iraq whose parents have been killed. We received approval from the university and the government to earn money in that way. My income is from the 10 percent retained for the administration of the money collected. I don't have a good record, but I think my income is about $55,000 in total."

"Okay. Well, you'd be what's called self-employed. You must pay two taxes to the federal government and one tax to the state of Maryland." He explained each tax in broad terms.

Ahmed was immediately confused and frequently interrupted to ask questions or the meaning of some words. "Can you help me to fill out the required forms, Tom? I think it would be a terrible job for me."

"Yes, I can do that, but this year's taxes aren't due until April 15 of next year."

"Oh!" His eyes widened. "Were last year's taxes due last April?"

"Yeah. But I just remembered, you probably should pay estimated taxes for this year to prevent being penalized in April. We're supposed to pay estimated taxes throughout the year, either through our employers or by quarterly payments ourselves. It's the right time to pay third quarter's estimated taxes." Ahmed was confused. He squinted his eyes as if that might help him understand. "Sorry," Tom said. "I know I'm not making sense. Do you have the money to pay the tax? I think it will be 25 to 30 percent of your income."

"Yes, I have it. I've had to spend very little. My parents pay for housing, tuition, and meals. Books too."

"I can download the forms on my computer and print them out. I'll do that tonight. When would you like to get together again to fill out the forms?"

"Could we do it tomorrow?"

Tom checked his schedule on his phone. "No, not tomorrow. I could do it Monday, late afternoon or evening. I'd prefer afternoon."

"Monday afternoon will be fine. Thank you very much. Where shall we meet? And when?"

"Do you live in a dorm or off-campus?"

Ahmed was afraid to return to his dorm room, thinking the terrorists might be watching for him. *They have Rashid, and for all I know they have Masoud too. They probably need all of us to get access to bank accounts. What can I tell him? Just be obscure.* "I'd prefer to meet someplace away from the campus. Someplace private."

"We could meet at my house or at my church."

"You are a Christian?"

"Yes."

"Perhaps your house would be better."

"I live with my parents. They would be happy to meet you." He gave Ahmed his address. They set the time at four thirty. "Well, I'm heading off to the football game. Do you like football?"

"Yes, of course. But not American football. My game is called soccer here."

"Oh, yeah, yeah. I should have known. I'd better get going, though, so I can get into the stadium before the game starts."

They shook hands and left, separating outside to go to their own cars.

Tom left the meeting with more questions than before they'd talked. Tom parked his car on the north end of the campus and sat in it while he thought about Ahmed. *How could they have organized a charity without being informed about income tax? Surely they had an accountant. How could he not have a record of his income? Their accountant would have issued them 1099s. Maybe they don't have an accountant. Then they probably aren't reporting what the charity took in. Wow. This could be messy. I'm not sure I want to get involved any deeper than just helping him fill out forms.* He walked across the campus to the stadium and became immersed in the game, forgetting for the time being his questions about Ahmed.

That evening at dinner, Tom said, "On Monday afternoon I'm going to meet with a Moroccan foreign student here to help him with his income taxes."

"That should be interesting," Martin said.

"Really." Tom looked at his father. "Did you see in the paper where a girl was attacked in her dorm room?"

"Yeah, sure."

"Wasn't that terrible?" his mother said.

"This guy is her boyfriend." He nodded.

There was a momentary silence at the table. Martin looked at Tom, then his wife. "How did you get to know him?"

Tom said, "The girl is Lauren's roommate."

"Are you kidding me?" Martin exclaimed.

"Isn't Lauren the girl you're getting lessons on Islam for?" his wife asked.

"Yes, she is." Tom chuckled. "We never know what tangled webs we weave, do we?"

Martin put down his utensils and turned toward Tom. "Isn't he under suspicion about the attack on the Muslim girl?"

"From what Lauren told me, her roommate's father suspects him." He told them about the charity and that Mr. Shalash works for the IRS and is looking into it.

"What did this guy tell you about all this?"

"We didn't discuss it. I didn't think it would serve any purpose. I want to gain his confidence before I give him any reason for mistrusting me. I intend to be cautious about what I say to him in the process of filling out tax forms. I don't want to be on record as his tax advisor. On the other hand, I want to show him the love of God, which is what I think Jesus would want."

"Good point. Good point. Just be careful." Martin nodded slightly as he looked at Tom.

CHAPTER 16

On Sunday night Lauren called Nadira. "Hi, Nadira, how are you feeling?"

"I'm feeling really good. I'd feel better if my father would let me go to class tomorrow. But I don't think he will. The president said they could send my assignments to me by e-mail, so I can stay at home until my attacker is found."

"Would you move back into the room?"

"I'd guess it's not cleaned up yet. But I doubt that my folks will let me even if it is. But, you know, I'd like to, just to make a statement."

"That you're not being scared off?" Lauren asked.

"Yeah, and that I can room with anybody I want to."

"That's pretty heavy. I admire you for it. My mom and dad want me to go back too. But I just can't go back to that room."

"So are you coming back?"

"I'm still not sure. I need to go to college, and I've made some good friends at Maryland, especially you. My dad is going to call them tomorrow and get their opinion about security. So I'm not coming back tomorrow. Probably not."

"Well, midterms are on us, and we shouldn't miss them."

"Yeah, I know. And I need to get a lot of stuff out of the room. I can't even get to most of my books."

"Tomorrow I'll see if we can get back in the room. I'll let you know."

"Okay. But if I go back to UM, I'll want a new room. Preferably a new dorm!" Lauren was insistent.

"I'll see what it's like if I can get in tomorrow. Then I'll call you."

"Great."

After his meeting with Tom on Saturday, Ahmed spent the weekend in the motel. Breakfast was free, and for lunch he ordered in pizza, which was enough for supper as well. He spent most of the time watching the motel parking lot for the car he photographed at the chapel on Friday or for any car that looked suspicious. His vigil also provided him a great deal of time to think.

Ahmed surmised that Rashid and Masoud would want to find him to prevent his going to the police. *I suspect they will have no trouble in convincing the terrorists that I am a danger to them. Since I know how the money is collected and distributed, I can help the police follow the money trail to find them. So I'm not safe. If they find me, they could kidnap me, kill me, and hide my body. No one would know for a long time.*

His primary goal now was to find a way to prove he was not guilty of attacking Nadira and to help identify whoever did it. By Sunday evening he had formulated his plan. *The only way I can prove myself not guilty is to tell the authorities about the Servants and the intervention by the terrorists. I can show them the photos I took at the chapel. I have to take the chance that our illegal activity won't be discovered. It might endanger Rashid and Masoud if I'm compelled to tell the police about the money, but I'm more concerned about Nadira than I am about them. It's one or the other, and I choose Nadira.*

Ahmed tried to imagine how the terrorists would set up their banking arrangements, so that they could not be detected. *If they're smart, they'll require that checks adding up to the amount they want be mailed to a post office box somewhere. Then they can set up several bank accounts, so they can deposit it and move it in small enough amounts that won't raise suspicions. Once they've set it up, they'll never be seen again unless, of course, Rashid and Masoud stop sending them the checks each week. Then there'll be more mayhem. They may have already disappeared, and their car will never be found. So I need to act quickly. Tomorrow.*

On Monday morning Ahmed drove to the police station in Hyattsville, south of the campus. He did not hesitate, even though his palms were sweating, and he was raging inside as if he were being led to the guillotine. He went to the desk and said, haltingly, "I need to talk to the officers who questioned me on Thursday. I have more information about the attack on Nadira Shalash."

The desk sergeant, a fat man whose cheeks almost obscured his eyes, said, "Who?" Then in a flash of recollection, "The student who was wounded in her dorm room last week?"

"Yes." Ahmed was afraid he appeared guilty because of his nervous state.

"One moment." The sergeant called someone on his phone.

In a minute an officer, a compact man who was completely bald or shaven, Ahmed couldn't tell which, appeared. Ahmed recognized him from his interrogation. "I'm Captain Parsons. Will you come with me please?" He gestured toward the door from which he'd emerged, led Ahmed through a corridor to an office, and asked him to sit down. He stuck his head out of the door and said loudly, "Ed, will you come in here please?" Parsons sat at the desk, and Ahmed's chair faced him across the desk.

Ed came in and sat to Ahmed's side, near the door, with a notepad in his lap. Parsons turned to Ahmed. "What do you have for us this morning?"

Ahmed took a deep breath. *I hope this is the right thing. It's too late to back out now.* He tried to speak, but he was shaking so hard that he couldn't form the words. He cleared his throat. "Excuse me, sir. I'm very nervous."

"Take your time, son. We've got all day." He leaned back in his chair.

He took another deep breath. "After you questioned me on Thursday, I learned that Nadira's wounds were meant to be a warning. She was carefully cut, so she was not seriously wounded. It was apparently done by an expert—"

"Who told you it was a warning? How do you know that?" He leaned forward, frowning.

"She told me." Ahmed gestured with his right hand. "The doctor said that to her father."

Parsons glanced at Ed. "Okay, go on."

"When I learned that, I immediately thought it was someone who had intruded himself into our business. Two—"

"What business?"

Ahmed gestured with both hands. "Two of my friends and I have, since last year, operated a charity to raise money for abandoned and orphaned children in Iraq. Last week—"

"What's the name of your business?"

"The Servants of Mercy." He nodded.

Parsons gestured with his head toward Ed, who, speaking through a portable intercom, said, "Check out the Servants of Mercy."

"Continue."

Ahmed took another deep breath. He clasped his hands in his lap. "Two weeks ago a man came up to Rashid—he's one of my friends—and said his organization wants to become partners with us. He didn't give his name. He was very stern and Rashid instantly understood that this was probably a terrorist organization that wants money. He said that if we didn't cooperate they would make things difficult for us. He gave us a week to give him an answer. We decided to tell him no. He appeared to Rashid last week, and when Rashid gave him our answer, he said we'd made a grave error. When I learned that Nadira's attack was a warning, I knew it was caused by them."

"Do you know who these people are or how to reach them?" Parsons bobbed his head forward with each question.

"No." Ahmed raised his right hand and pointed up, as if to make an important point. "But on Friday, the day we always go to the post office to pick up contribution letters, Rashid called me and pleaded with me to pick up the letters, even though it was his turn to do it. I could tell by his voice and his responses to my questions that he was in the custody of the terrorists, and that if I didn't do it, he'd be hurt. He told me to leave the letters on the porch of a house we rent near the campus. I decided not to place the letters on the porch as they required but left them inside the door of the chapel. Then—"

"Is that Memorial Chapel on the campus?" Parsons asked.

"Yes."

"Please go on."

"When they arrived to pick them up, I was able, by mingling with the people on the Chapel Fields, to photograph the car." He pulled out his cell phone. "Here, you can see the photographs." He pulled them up for the officers to see. "I could see Rashid in the car, but I don't think he saw me. You may download them if you wish." He handed the phone to Parsons, who looked at the pictures carefully and then handed the phone to Ed.

125

"See if we can download these and blow them up." Ed left the room. "How much money are you talking about?"

What shall I tell him? I'll try to be vague. "Several thousand dollars each week."

"Two thousand, ten thousand? About how much?"

"Maybe ten or fifteen thousand." *That's what goes to the bank.*

"Whew. That's not chicken feed."

Ahmed did not understand but did not comment.

Ed returned without the phone. "They're going to try."

"Good," said Parsons. "What do you do with the checks?"

"First we write letters to the donors to acknowledge the gifts and to thank them. Then we deposit them in a bank."

"What bank?"

"The Bank of America, not far from here."

Parsons glanced at Ed, who made a note on his pad. "Then what becomes of the money?"

"About once a month we wire most of it to a bank in Liechtenstein, which then sends it to Iraq."

"Most of it?" Parsons squinted.

"Yes. We retain some for expenses and our time." He laughed briefly.

"Tell us what you can about the terrorists."

"Sir, I know nothing about them. I've not seen them or heard their voices. The pictures from my cell phone are all that I have. It is apparent that they want money, and will stop at nothing to obtain it. But who they are and what they are planning to do I have no idea. I've been wondering how they knew about Nadira, but I remember seeing a man watching me when I was talking to Nadira outside her dorm last Monday night. He looked Middle Eastern, but he was too far away to see his features clearly. He had a three or four day's growth of beard and dark hair. That's all I can remember."

"Someone watched you?"

"He walked by a couple of times when I was waiting for her, and then I saw him watching us when we were talking." He heard a knock on the door and then it opened, and a woman handed a piece of paper to Ed, who glanced at it, and passed it to Parsons.

Parsons read it and set it on the desk without comment. He held both his hands up to his lips, in a praying position, and stared at Ahmed. It made Ahmed very uneasy, sensing that the captain was about to pronounce his verdict. After a very long pause, he said, "Young man, you've provided us with some valuable information. Why?"

Ahmed was surprised by the question. He searched for words. "Sir, I do not want Nadira to be hurt again. I also think I may be in danger. I expect the terrorists know I have resigned and have probably come to you or, at the least, might do so. I have the knowledge of the money handling that could lead to their discovery, so they probably want me eliminated. These people are lawless and cruel and may be planning some terrible thing against America. They must be apprehended."

CHAPTER 17

It was midmorning on Monday when Ahmed returned to the motel. He recognized Masoud's number when his cell phone rang. "Hello, Masoud."

"Well, Ahmed. I guess the terrorists didn't get to you?"

"I guess you mean 'did they find me and capture me?'"

"Yes."

"No. They have Rashid, though," Ahmed said.

"They had him. They let him go Friday after you gave them the checks."

"Did they take all of them?"

"Of course, you little worm. What did you expect?"

"But Rashid sounded like he was in such trouble—"

"He was. But not $30,000 worth."

"I don't care. I'm out of it. I sent all of my money to Iraq."

"You did what?" he shouted.

"You heard right. I sent all but a small fee. I figured 10 percent is an appropriate administration fee. The rest has gone to the orphanage."

"You're some kind of idiot. What does that do to Rashid and me?"

"I don't care. You can bring in Hashim to replace me. I'm no longer a partner in the house either."

"So you're out of it completely. Are you running back to Morocco?"

"No. Where are you?"

"At the house. Where else?"

"Where's Rashid?"

"He's here too."

"Well, tell him good-bye for me. You'll not be seeing me again unless we have a class together."

"You little hen. I hope those guys find you and rip your guts out. You'll be on their hit list now, you know."

"Yeah, I know."

"Here, talk to Rashid."

"No, I'm finished. Good-bye." Ahmed hung up.

Ahmed threw his phone on the bed. Almost immediately it rang again. He picked it up, saw that it was Rashid's number, and threw it down on the bed again. He paced back and forth across the motel room, his lip curled in anger, but satisfied with all that he'd done. After a few minutes he regained his composure and picked up the phone again. It showed that he had a voice mail message. He called to listen to it.

It was Rashid. "Ahmed, you piece of snot. You've compromised both of us. If any information about our role with the Servants gets to the authorities, we'll come after you. Do you understand?" An icy chill shot through Ahmed's midsection. *This confirms my need to stay out of sight*, he thought. He saved the message and, as he stood at the window staring at his car, he thought, *it's time to change cars*. He had bought his car from Glimus on the recommendation of Rashid when he'd arrived at Maryland. *I have time to change cars before I meet with Tom. I need to check out of this motel too and find someplace a little farther away.*

Nadira called Lauren on Monday afternoon.

"Lauren, it's Nadira."

"I thought it would be you calling. What happened today?"

"Nothing. I didn't go to class. But I did get into the room. The police were all finished and the carpet's been cleaned. I got my books and clothes. My mother went with me."

"How did you feel in there?"

"It just seemed—normal to me. Like nothing happened there."

"That's weird."

"Why?"

"I guess you don't remember anything about it. To me, it's the scene of something terrible. A place I never want to see again."

"So what are you going to do?"

"Dad called a while ago and told us he'd talked to the president, and he said we'd be as safe as any college student at any university. He said the dorm security exists but is not tight, so students need to protect themselves by being cautious."

"I guess he thinks I was at fault," Nadira said.

"Dad apparently got a little uptight with him, and the president said this isn't a military compound. He said a student can get hurt playing touch football or could be attacked in a parking lot. It's like a little city. He said they have a police force, but they can't be everywhere at all times."

"Will your dad let you come back?"

"I don't know if I want to come back. Dad will be home in a little while. We're supposed to talk about it after dinner."

"I think my father will let me go to classes tomorrow. If I don't, I'll start falling behind."

"Same for me. I need to make a decision. I'll call you as soon as I've talked to my parents, and I've thought it over."

"Okay. Talk to you later."

Ahmed checked out of the motel and drove to Greenbelt where Glimus Motor Cars was located. He parked his car and walked into the used car lot. Soon he realized he didn't know enough about cars and their prices to make a decision alone and started back toward the showroom when a salesman intercepted him.

"Can I help you?"

"Uh, is George here? I bought my car from him and thought I should speak to him about a replacement."

"Sure. Come with me." He pulled out his cell phone and called. "George, there's a young man here who wants to see you."

Soon George appeared, attired in his customary flamboyant way. "Well, hello, my friend. Long time no see. Tell me your name again, I see so many students that I can't remember all your names."

"Ahmed. Ahmed Suliman."

"Ah, yes. How have you been?"

"Just fine, sir. Thank you."

"Are you in the market for a new car?"

"Not a new car. I want to replace this one," he pointed at his Saturn. "I'm afraid it will stop being supported, now that it is no longer being produced. I'm looking for a car that is about the same price."

After a brief conversation about the used cars on the lot, Ahmed asked to test drive a Chevrolet and decided to buy it. George had the Saturn appraised and stated that the Chevrolet could be Ahmed's for a measly $1,500. After a suitable period of hemming and hawing, not wishing to appear too eager, Ahmed agreed, and soon he was off in his new car.

He arrived on time for his meeting with Tom, who was waiting for him at the door, and warmly welcomed him into his home. He led Ahmed into the dining room, where he'd already piled forms for the work ahead. "I want to first explain the taxes on your income unless you already know how it works." Tom had taken the chair at the head of the table, and he gestured to Ahmed to sit on the side of the table to his left.

"No," he shook his head. "I know nothing about income taxes, except that you have them."

Tom laughed. "We have a saying 'Nothing is certain except death and taxes.'"

Ahmed smiled. He liked Tom. *A man with a sense of humor.* He liked the way Tom's eyes narrowed when he smiled. *He has a genuine sort of happiness,* he thought. "In Morocco we have taxes too, and we say the same thing." He laughed and suddenly realized he hadn't laughed for several days, probably since he'd talked to Nadira a week ago.

Tom began, "As I mentioned Saturday, in America we have two kinds of federal taxes. One is the general income tax. The other is a tax to pay for retirement and medical care in retirement. If you have an employer, he must pay half of your retirement taxes. If not, you have to pay it all."

Ahmed interrupted. "If I'm not going to retire here, do I have to pay that?" He extended both his hands, with his palms up, to emphasize his rationalism.

"Unfortunately, yes. And we thank you for contributing to our retirement." He smiled again.

Ahmed grimaced. "How much will I have to pay?"

"We're going to figure that out right now. It won't take long since it's just an estimate at this point." Tom pulled a form from the stack of papers and began to fill it out, asking Ahmed for the information he needed. In five minutes he was finished. "Now all you have to do is to write a check, and we'll mail it off."

"Is that all there is to it?" He pulled out his checkbook and wrote the check.

"We have to do the same for Maryland taxes, but it's much less." He pulled a second form from the stack and filled it in. "Now you'll need to write a check for the state."

Ahmed wrote the second check without hesitation. "Finished?"

"For now, yes. When you do your taxes in the spring, it'll take a little longer. But yours won't be complicated. Probably a half hour to complete. Does your charity have an accountant?"

"Yes, of course." He raised his eyebrows and looked at Tom.

As Tom stuffed the forms and checks into envelopes, he said, "Well, I suppose he'll be giving you a ten ninety-nine at the end of the year."

"A ten ninety-nine?"

"It's a form that tells you and the government how much money you were paid for the past year. That's the number of the form for self-employed people."

Ahmed thought, *How can I tell him why that can't be done?* "Is it essential?"

Tom cocked his head and looked at Ahmed. "It is for the company, your charity. I don't know if it's essential for you. Do you receive anything saying how much you've been paid?"

"No." Ahmed was not looking at Tom but was staring at the table. *He's getting too curious. I should leave.* "We're not very well organized."

"Are your partners paying taxes?"

"I don't know. We haven't talked about it." He glanced at his watch. "Oh, I see that it's getting late. I need to leave."

"Okay. My mom would like to meet you before you go, though." Tom stood and walked to the door to the kitchen. "Mom, are you in there?"

Ahmed heard a faint voice. Soon a plump woman with straight, graying hair appeared. She was wearing slacks and a matching top. He stood when she came into the room. As Mrs. Parker smiled, Ahmed could see from the smile lines a woman who smiled often. *Here's where Tom receives his kindness and sensed of humor,* he thought.

Tom introduced them, and she asked a few questions about his family and home country. As soon as it was not impolite to leave, he turned to Tom. "Thank you for the help, Tom. I'm sorry I must hurry away, but I must." He turned toward Tom's mother. "I'm very pleased to meet you. Good-bye." Smiling, he walked out to his car and drove away, relieved that he didn't have to answer any more questions.

Nadira was eager to hear what her father had found out about Ahmed. However, to not appear too interested, she would say nothing but wait until he brought the subject up, or at least made an opening for her to ask. The subject came up soon enough during dinner.

He faced his wife. "I spoke to the federal attorney today, asking him to open an investigation of a hate crime against Nadira. When I gave him the details he agreed to conduct a preliminary inquiry. It wasn't the response I wanted, but it was a positive one." He then turned toward Nadira. "I told him all the details that I thought were important, but I'm sure someone will want to talk to you soon. I want you to cooperate one hundred percent with him."

"Yes, Father." She frowned slightly. "I want to get this solved and behind us more than you do."

He looked into her eyes. "I mean that you should do nothing to protect that friend of yours from Morocco."

"I know that. But why should I?"

He sighed. "Nadira, you aren't hiding anything from me. Your feelings for him are more than simply a casual friend."

Nadira's face reddened. *Am I that transparent?* She asked herself. "I only know two people at UM, Ahmed and Lauren. They're friends that I care about, it's true. But please don't assume there is any more between us than friendship."

His voice became slightly more forceful. "I believe you, Nadira. But I also understand your personal feelings better than you think

I can. Have I not been your father for eighteen years? Have I not seen how you react to others, how you show your feelings, even in ways you think are invisible?" He faced her mother, who smiled and nodded.

Nadira was speechless. Her eyes became blurred as tears formed. Her mother rose and stood behind her, wrapping Nadira's shoulders in her arms. "Don't be surprised, dear. We women are made that way. It enhances your beauty, you know. We know you've done nothing intentional to lead him but your feelings toward him radiate just as surely as your voice does. He knows it, and we can see it. So please don't try to act as though he is no more than a friendly face."

Nadira leaned her head on her mother's arm. After a pause, she said, "I just want you to know that he couldn't do this to me." She touched her bandaged neck.

"I doubt that he did," her father said. "His charity seems to be in order, at least as far as its tax responsibilities are concerned. He has no income tax record but that doesn't mean anything. I thought you'd be encouraged by that information."

"Thank you. But I'm not surprised."

Her mother released her from her embrace. "Neither am I. I'm certain that you'd not be involved with anyone who is less than honorable."

"Mother! I'm not *involved*—with him!" She'd started to react vociferously but thought better of it.

"What would you call it?"

"Acquainted." She paused briefly. "Well maybe 'friendly.'"

"We'll leave it at that," her mother said and sat down.

"May I go to school tomorrow?" She looked at her father, then at her mother.

Her father answered, "I'm reluctant for you to be out and about until the man who attacked you is found."

Her mother asked, "How many classes do you have tomorrow?"

"Three. One in the morning and two in the afternoon."

"I was thinking that if I could park near to where you'd be having your classes, I could take you and bring you home. That way no one could follow you, and I'd be able to see you when you'd be outside the building."

"Do you think that would work?" her father asked. "Don't forget that the president said your assignments could be sent here."

Either way I'd be constantly under their eyes. I'd never be able to see Ahmed. "I guess I could try it at home, at least until midterm exams."

"When are they?" he asked.

"I'm not sure. Soon, I think. I'll find out tomorrow."

"And call Miss McGovern in the president's office about your homework."

"Okay."

"Ahmed seems like a nice young man, doesn't he?" Tom's mother commented.

"Yeah, but a little spacey. He and his partners better get some good advice before they get in trouble with the IRS."

"Oh, have they done anything wrong?"

"I have no idea. Ahmed just knows nothing about taxes. Who knows what other regulations they don't know about?" He gathered up his papers and went upstairs to his room to study awhile before dinner. *Mom's right. Ahmed seems like a good guy. I'm almost certain he's a Muslim and probably knows less about Jesus than he knows about taxes. As messy as their business might be, I need to find a way to keep a conversation going with him.* He checked his phone to make sure he had Ahmed's number.

He lay on his bed on his back with his hands behind his head, his thinking position. *It's strange that Ahmed didn't say anything about Nadira's attack. I wonder why her father is investigating Ahmed's charity. Maybe that's the only thing he could do since he works for the IRS. Lauren told me Ahmed asked about taxes as soon as she told him about Nadira's father. Would he have been interested in paying his taxes if he hadn't known that? The government would never know about him if he isn't receiving a 1099. This doesn't sound good. It may be just an honest mistake. But on the other hand, hmmm.*

"Tom, dinner," his mother called, interrupting his thoughts. *Maybe I can help keep them out of trouble,* he thought, *and that could give me a way to keep in touch with Ahmed.*

"Dad, I think the president is right. No college is absolutely safe. I don't think that's the issue."

"Go on."

"I'm trying to figure out why Nadira was attacked. Everybody I've talked to thinks I'm crazy to think the attacker was after me. Even so, if I go back I don't want to live in that room or even that dorm. But why was she attacked? She hardly knows anyone."

"What does she think?" Her father asked. He, Lauren, and her mother were sitting in the living room in their Fredericksburg home. Lauren was curled up in a large wing chair. Her parents were on the couch.

"She thinks it's because she's rooming with a Christian." She put her hand to her throat. "It was a warning attack, you know."

"That makes sense. But someone must've known she was there. What about that foreign student?" He made a suspicious squint.

Lauren shook her head. "Who knows? Nadira is certain he didn't do it. She saw her attacker, after all. That doesn't mean Ahmed didn't have anything to do with it, though. Nadira really likes him, and, like they say, love is blind. But I don't think he is as crazy about her as she is for him."

"Why do you say that?"

"For starters, he's stood her up a couple of times when they were supposed to meet for lunch."

Her mother interjected, "Well, that ought to tell her something!" She laughed.

Her father pointed at Lauren, "So you think he could have had something to do with it."

"Well, other than me, he's the only person that knows she exists. That's not exactly true. People in the dorm see her coming and going. She goes to class, and people see her. They know she's a Muslim because of her head scarf. I don't know how many people know we room together, though."

"It doesn't do much good to speculate," her father said.

"I'm just trying to be realistic. But you're right. Speculating won't help me decide to go back to school. Nadira wants to go back, and she wants to keep rooming with me. That's as much to make a statement as it is to say she likes me."

"What kind of statement?" her mother asked.

"That she won't be frightened off but will go on living with a Christian."

"That kind of defiance could get you both hurt—or worse." He stood. "I think we need to pray together about this, don't you?" Lauren and her mother stood, and the three of them joined hands while he prayed.

When he finished Lauren squeezed his hand. "Dad, there's something else to consider. I've begun some personal lessons in relating to Muslims, so I'll know how to talk to Nadira and so I can tell her about my faith. While we were praying, I had this strong impulse that I shouldn't stop that. The only way I can do that is to go back and room with her, in spite of the danger I may face."

"Is that through CCA?" he asked.

She released his hand and her mother's. "Yes. They've arranged weekly lessons at the church of one of the leaders. I think it's important to keep that going, more important than ever since her attack."

She waited while her mother looked at her father. Neither said anything. *I know they're communicating. I've seen them do this ever since I was a kid.* So she simply stood and waited. *I think they're going to leave it up to me.*

Her mother spoke first. "Honey, do you want to go back?"

I want to and I don't want to. But I think God wants me to, for Nadira's sake. "I think I should," she said softly.

Her father put his arm around her shoulders. "That's a very mature decision, Lauren. I support it. I'll call the president's office in the morning to ask for a new room, a double room. Okay?"

"That's good, because I don't want to fall any further behind than I already am. I need to call Nadira and tell her."

"Hi, Roomy."

"Does that mean what I think it does?" Nadira answered.

"Yep. Dad's going to call the president tomorrow to find me a new room—a double room. And hopefully a new dorm."

"I'm going to be staying home for a while. The president told us he'd send my assignments home. So that's what I'm going to do. Probably until they find the guy who attacked me."

"That may take a while. I'll be lonesome."

"I'm sorry."

"Have you heard anything yet about your attacker?"

"No. Nothing yet."

"What about Ahmed?"

"I'm not allowed to talk to him, remember?"

"I mean, did your father find out anything?"

"Oh. Yes. I mean no. They didn't find anything wrong. As I expected."

"That's good news." *Now it's a bigger mystery,* Lauren thought. *Maybe I shouldn't say anything about his asking about taxes.* "Well, I hope you can come back to our dorm room, wherever it is. I'll call you when I find out where it's going to be."

"Okay, Lauren. Good-night."

CHAPTER 18

"Mr. Suliman?"

"Yes."

"This is Captain Parsons, Prince George's County Police. Would it be possible for you to come back down to the station this morning? We're trying to get to the bottom of the attack on Miss Shalash, and we'd like to ask you some additional questions."

"Yes, I'd be happy to. I do have a class this morning at ten. I've missed many classes over the past few days that I'd—"

"Understand completely. Could you make it earlier, say nine? We need your help. At the moment you're our only cooperative link to the perpetrators."

Ahmed looked at his watch. Eight thirty. "Yes, I can do that."

"Good. I'll be looking for you then."

What more could they be asking? Ahmed thought. *Perhaps they don't believe what I've already told them. Maybe they will arrest me after all.* He shaved and dressed and drove to the police station.

It was exactly 9:00 a.m. when Ahmed entered the station. "I am here to see Captain Parsons," he told the fat desk clerk. He was much less apprehensive than he had been yesterday; still, he was shivering like he was cold. He looked around the station. *These places are the ugliest buildings I've ever seen. They must intentionally strive to make them so stark and colorless.*

Captain Parsons interrupted his thoughts. "Ahmed." He extended his hand. "Thank you for coming on short notice. Come into my office." He showed Ahmed to an open door. "Please have a seat."

Ahmed glanced around and was pleased to see artwork on the walls, a carpet on the floor, and a photograph, obviously of the captain's family, on the desk. *This isn't the same room I was in yesterday.* Notwithstanding his intimidation by men in positions of authority, he relaxed somewhat in those more comfortable surroundings.

Captain Parsons rubbed his forehead. "It seems that the attack on your friend has generated a great deal of urgency to find the attacker. We need to find a way to identify the person or persons who did it. At the moment, all we have is your theory that some unknown terrorist group did it. Can you provide us with a way to find these people?"

Ahmed asked, "Did the security cameras around the dorm pick up anything?"

"Not a thing."

"Did the photographs from my cell phone help any?"

"Not a lot. We did trace the license plates to a local dealer. They were dealer plates. It seems the men who picked up the checks were using a car they'd told the dealer that they were trying out. Unfortunately, the photos don't show enough of the people in the car to identify them. Has, uh," he looked down at his notes, "Rashid tried to communicate with you? Is your other friend in the custody of the terrorists?"

"Masoud was not abducted. Rashid has been released, so he might know something more. At least he should know what they look like."

Parsons face brightened. "Well, what has he told you? Could he lead us to them?"

Ahmed hesitated. *Should I tell them I've resigned? Would that make them suspicious? Maybe not.* "I haven't talked to Rashid. I've resigned from the Servants of Mercy." He sat rigidly, waiting for the reaction.

Parsons frowned. "You've resigned? Why?"

Ahmed licked his lips. "Someone I care about has been assaulted because of my association with the Servants. I don't want to subject her to any more danger, and to remain in that company makes a statement that I prefer them to her."

Parsons leaned his head on his fist. "That sounds a little precipitous. You've placed a lot of stock in your theory about who attacked Nadira. If it turns out to be someone else, won't you have acted too soon?"

"I have no doubt about who did it, sir."

"It sounds like I need to have a conversation with Rashid. I'll need the address of the house you rent." He passed a notepad to Ahmed, who wrote down the address and handed it back. "I suppose I can expect that you'll be there too?"

"I'd very much not like to be there, sir. I…uh… have severed my relations with Rashid and Masoud."

"What?" Parsons partially raised himself from his chair. "It sounds like something more is going on than you're telling me, young man."

"Captain, if you please." He held out his right hand, palm down, to calm him. "I believe they have agreed to some form of cooperation with the terrorists, which means they'll be raising money for them. I refuse to be part of that. They're now very angry with me." Parsons sank back into his chair. "And for that reason they'll be unwilling to talk to you unless they are compelled to."

"Ah. Uh, that does put a different light on it. It means they'll be involved in criminal activity, won't it? All right, I'll leave you out of it."

"Thank you, sir."

Parsons handed the note pad to him again. "Here. Write down the full names of your ex-friends, if you don't mind." Ahmed wrote their names and handed the pad back. "I think that will be all for the time being. Please stay in town so I can reach you if I need to."

Ahmed stood and turned to leave but stopped and turned back toward the captain. "I should say, I don't think Rashid and Masoud have done anything for the terrorists willingly. They are being coerced by threats to their well-being. The only reason they aren't doing the same thing to me is that they can't find me. Yesterday I exchanged my old car for a different one, and I'm staying at various motels. I will go to class, but I'll be very careful not to be caught. Rashid and Masoud have my class schedule, but unless one of them gives it to the terrorists, they shouldn't know how to find me. I must continue to attend class, so I won't jeopardize my status and, therefore, the terms of my visa."

Parsons was standing now. "Very clever. How did you finance your new car? That is an avenue by which you can be found, you know."

"Oh, it was a trade. I went back to Glimus Motors where I bought my old car and made an exchange for only a little difference, which I could pay."

"I see. You're very careful. Feel free to call us if you're being threatened with imminent danger."

"Thank you, sir. I will." With that he turned and left the office.

Tom had just finished his eleven o'clock class and was having lunch at the Stamp. *Good time to call Ahmed.* He found the number on his phone and called. There was no answer. He left a message, "Ahmed, this is Tom Parker. I'm calling to see if you could find a time when we could talk. Please give me a call." He laid the phone on the table beside his tray and finished his lunch. He'd been thinking about Lauren and wanted to call her but hadn't found a reason to call. *Maybe I should tell her about my meetings with Ahmed,* he thought. He entered her number.

"Hello, Tom," she answered.

"Hello, Miss Lauren. I thought I ought to bring you up to date with my meetings with Ahmed and see what's up with you."

"Yeah, I've been wondering. You met with him, huh?"

"Twice. We met at a coffee shop on Saturday morning and then again at my house yesterday afternoon."

"Oh, wow. Did you help him?"

"I think so. He knows next to nothing about taxes. About all I could do at this point is to fill out his estimated tax form and send in his check. It worries me that his partners in the charity probably don't know any more than he does. And it sounds like their accountant isn't helping them much. Maybe you could take over their account."

"Ha. Very funny. Maybe in four or five years."

"Do you mean you haven't learned how to do income taxes yet?" He was smiling.

"If I don't get back to school soon, I may never learn."

"Does that mean you're coming back?" *I hope,* he thought.

"Yeah, I guess so. I think it's the Christian thing to do. Nadira wants to stay in school and wants me to be her roommate. So maybe there's hope for her yet."

"That's good news. When will you be back?"

"Dad called this morning and got a new room assigned for us. It's in Carroll Hall. So I can come back any time."

"Does Nadira know yet?"

"No. She's going to get her assignments at home for a while. Until her attacker is found, if it's up to her dad. And I guess it is."

"Why do you say that?"

"He yields a pretty heavy hand with Nadira. I don't know if that's customary for Arabs or that's just the way he is."

"It's something we should ask George. That reminds me. I should call him and cancel our meeting for this week, don't you think?"

"I guess so. Dad can't bring me during the week. Mom could, but she's got some doctor's appointments today and tomorrow, so the earliest I can get there is sometime Thursday afternoon. Then I'll have to find the room, and start moving my stuff over from Queen Anne's."

"Would it help if I drove up there to get you?" *Am I appearing too eager?*

"Do you have classes this afternoon?"

"I have one, at one o'clock."

"So you could be up here by about three?"

"Yes."

"Are you sure you want to do that?"

"I don't have anything better to do." *Besides, I want to.*

"Let me talk to my mom, I'll call you back in a few minutes."

Lauren was back on the phone in five minutes. "Mom is all right with you picking me up today. It would take a big load off her."

Great. "I'm glad to be of service."

She gave Tom her address, and he went, smiling, off to his class. *I guess I'm violating one of our rules, but I think asking Martha to go along would be asking too much. Besides, she's probably in class now.*

As he walked, he called George Lyon. He answered immediately. "Hey, George. This is Tom Parker. How are you?"

"Hello, Tom. I'm doing just fine. Just fine. What's up with you?" Tom pulled the phone away from his ear. *Wow. That's way too loud.*

"I'm calling to give you a heads up. We might have to cancel this week's meeting with Lauren."

"That's no problem. No problem at all."

"I suppose you heard about the girl who was attacked in her dorm room. That was Lauren's roommate."

"Oh, my stars! How did that happen?"

"I really don't know. Lauren walked in and found her lying in a pool of blood. Someone called 911, and they got her to a hospital in time to save her life."

"Have they found the man who did it? I assume it was a man."

"Not that I know of. Lauren went home on Friday and will be coming back today, but I'm not sure she'll have time to go to a meeting. They're moving her into a new dorm, and she'll have a lot to do to get settled there."

"Of course. Of course. Oh my. What's this world coming to?"

"Well, I just wanted to give you a heads up. I'll let you know for sure, probably tomorrow."

"Okay, Tom. Thank you for calling."

"You're welcome. Bye."

CHAPTER 19

"Hi Lauren. How's it going?"

"Good, Nadira. I'm going back to school today."

"Oh, I'm so glad. Did you get a new dorm room?"

"Yeah. And a new building—Carroll Hall."

"That's real close to Queen Anne's, isn't it?"

"Yes. It's just like Queen Anne's."

"Great. So you're going back today and get all moved in?"

"Yep. I've missed too many classes already."

"So have I. I'm supposed to get my assignments today. They'll send them by e-mail, I think."

"I just wanted you to know. Do you have any idea when you'll be able to move back on campus?"

"Afraid not. But I'll keep in touch with you."

"That's good. Well, next time you hear from me might be at your front door."

"That would be wonderful."

"Okay. Bye."

Time for me to get my stuff together. Winter clothes. Tom's such a good guy. I wouldn't be disappointed if he's doing this for more than just being a good Samaritan. I'm glad Mom'll be able to meet him. To see that he's a solid citizen.

She spent the next hour selecting the clothes she wanted for colder weather. She glanced at her watch. *Lunchtime.* "Mom," she yelled down the stairs. At Mom's response she said, "Will you fix me a sandwich and maybe an apple or something?"

"Sure, honey," she responded.

She came downstairs and said, "Do we have any big plastic bags I can put my stuff in? My luggage is in my old room at school. I hope."

"Sure. In their usual place, in the pantry." She waved her arm in that direction.

As she was pulling out some bags, she said, "I'd like you to meet Tom today. He's one of the leaders of CCA."

Her mother placed a small plate with a sandwich on the table and sat down. "I'm glad you found them. I've always heard good things about CCA. What would you like to drink?"

"Juice. Grapefruit if there's any left." She sat down in front of the sandwich. "Tom and Martha, you know, the girl who put me up last Thursday night, have been really helpful." She picked up her sandwich and held it at the ready. "In our youth group at church they always told us to be prepared to share our faith with those who don't know Christ, but I didn't know how to do that with a Muslim. So CCA, Tom and Martha, that is, arranged for me to get personal lessons on how to witness to Muslims. And now Tom is driving all the way up here to take me back to school. Pretty nice, huh?" She bit into her sandwich.

"I've never known you to be shy about sharing your faith." Her mom got up and opened the refrigerator to look for the juice.

"It's always come naturally to me. But this time it's different." She spoke between bites. "Nadira is so cute. She's sweet on Ahmed, and now Tom is talking to him. We need to make them both aware of who Jesus is. It could get interesting."

"Also dangerous," her mother sat down again. "You have no idea who attacked Nadira or why." Her face took on a serious countenance.

"Yeah." She paused. "That does present a sinister element. I wonder how my instructor, George, will handle that."

"Who's he?"

Lauren uttered a little laugh. "Professionally he's a car salesman. But for some reason he knows a lot about Islam. He's a member of Tom's church in Greenbelt. That's where we have the lessons."

"Are you trying to convert Nadira?"

Her sandwich eaten, she turned toward her mother. "Yes and no. I believe that conversion is her decision. My job is to inform her who Jesus is, and that will have to be demonstrated by some strong illustrations. She probably already knows him as a prophet. But for her to accept him as the Messiah, she'll have to overcome a lifetime of teaching otherwise."

"How will you do that?"

"I don't know, Mom. That's why I joined CCA, and why I'm taking the lessons. But right now I just don't know." She shrugged.

He mother got up and picked up Lauren's plate. She looked at the kitchen clock. "You'd better get your things together. Your driver will be here in fifteen minutes."

"Oh, gosh. I'd better hurry. I got lost in our conversation." She jumped up, grabbed the plastic bags, and ran upstairs.

Soon the doorbell rang, and Lauren opened the door. "Welcome to Frederick, Mr. Tom. Please come in. I want you to meet my mom before we go. Let me find her. Have a seat for a minute." She walked toward the kitchen and almost ran into her mother. They both laughed. "Mom, this is Tom Parker. Tom, my mom, Gloria Stevenson."

Tom extended his hand. "Nice to meet you, Mrs. Stevenson."

"Thank you, Tom. It's nice to meet you too. Would you like a cup of coffee or a soft drink before you go?"

He looked at Lauren. "Are you all ready?"

"Not quite." A black plastic bag was sitting by the door. She gestured toward it. "That bag's ready. I've got one more that's not quite full yet. It'll only take me a minute."

"In that case, I'll take you up on the coffee," he said to Mrs. Stevenson.

"Good. Come with me into the kitchen. We'll leave Lauren to get herself ready." She turned, and Tom followed her into the kitchen.

Lauren ran up the steps to her bedroom to finish packing her second plastic bag. In less than five minutes she lugged the second bag down the steps and went into the kitchen. She heard her mother say, "I just can't imagine why anyone would do such a thing."

Tom replied, "Me neither. It's a crazy world we live in. Yet at CCA we try to help fulfill Jesus's words that he came to give us life more abundantly. So we keep looking at the sunny side of life and try to help each other out when we need help and to help other people too."

Lauren interjected, "And I appreciate it. I've got my other bag ready, so as soon as you finish your coffee we can go." *I guess I fall under the category of helping others. Oh, well. He's still a good guy, though.*

Tom swallowed the rest of his coffee, got up, and said, "Okay. Let's go."

At the door Tom and Lauren said goodbye to her mother. He and Lauren toted the bags to the trunk of his car, and they were on their way.

Ahmed had just finished his two o'clock class. As he emerged from the building, his phone text notification went off. "U cannot hide from us. Ur a dead man." Ahmed froze. *The police have already*

talked to them, he thought. He looked around, but didn't see them. Instinctively, he turned around and went back inside and ran to a fire exit at the back of the building. *If they find me, they'll do more than kill me.* He peeked out the door. *Good. No one's there.* He dashed out of the door and across the driveway and entered the rear door of another building. *Great. A lot of people.* He pushed into the middle of a group of students leaving the building. *I need to camouflage myself. I can put my hood on and take off this backpack. Now if I stay in the middle of this gang, maybe they won't recognize me.* He walked in the midst of the group down toward Baltimore Avenue. The group soon thinned out, but Ahmed continued north of the campus until he was certain he wasn't being followed. He entered a fast-food restaurant, sat down at an empty table, took out his laptop, and watched out the window.

He could feel his teeth chattering. His stomach was heaving in rapid spasms. *I knew they'd be after me as soon as the police talked to them. Masoud will smash me like a bug. And Rashid will cheer him on. They will have no mercy. They're certain I've told the police about the money. But surely they realize that I haven't. Otherwise they'd have been arrested already. I'll tell them. Maybe that will keep them from hurting me.*

He texted Rashid, "I have not told them about the money. U are safe." Then he waited.

Soon his text notification sounded. "U are lying. U are not safe."

The only way I can escape is to leave UM, but I'm afraid that would violate my visa. I need to find out what I can do. They won't stop hunting for me, so I need to do something.

He saw that he had a voice mail message, so he listened to it. It was Tom Parker asking to talk to him. *A flicker of hope! He might know someone who can help me.* He called Tom's number.

"This is Tom."

"Hello, Tom. This is Ahmed Suliman returning your call."

"Oh. Thanks for returning my call. I wanted to see if we could get together sometime."

"Yes, of course. I would like to talk to you as well."

"When would work for you?"

"I would like to talk to you as soon as possible. I need your advice very urgently."

"Well, I'm on my way back to College Park right now. I should be back at about four, but I need to help someone move into a new dorm room, and that'll probably take the rest of the evening. I'll be free in the morning."

"Could I see you then? It is very urgent."

"I could meet you at eight at the coffee house where we met Saturday."

"Would it be possible to meet at your home? I am in danger, and I am afraid the men who seek to harm me could find me in a public place."

"That does sound urgent! Yes, of course, we can meet at my house."

"Thank you. Thank you very much. I will see you in the morning at eight."

"Okay. I'll see you then. Good-bye."

A possible avenue of help gave Ahmed a disproportionate amount of relief from his anxiety. *I will stop attending classes until I am safe. Now I need to get back to my car without being seen.* He walked counterclockwise around the circumference of the campus until he was near his car and then walked into the campus directly to his car, and he was safely away.

Tom drove directly to Carroll Hall. *I can park in front, I think, to unload Lauren's bags.* Just inside Lauren looked up the RA to find out what room was hers, and they deposited the bags there. "Do you think we can get into your old room?" Tom asked.

"I'm pretty sure we can. Nadira was able to get her things out yesterday. I hope so, anyway. If we can't, I won't have any sheets for the bed here."

It was a short drive to the back of Queen Anne's. As she approached her old room, Tom saw her hesitate, glance back at him, and then hold her key, suspended in space for a long moment before she slid it into the keyhole and opened the door. *This must be hard for her. The last time she opened the door there was Nadira lying in her blood.* Lauren was standing before the partially opened door, obviously reluctant to step in.

Tom said softly, "Lauren, would you like for me to go in first?" She nodded. He pushed the door wide open and then stepped into the room. *I'll look around to make sure there's no evidence of the attack.* Having done so, he said, "It's okay, Lauren."

She took one step into the room and stopped. Tom reached out and took her hand. *Wow. Her hand feels like ice.* He covered her hand with his other hand and watched her. She took a deep breath, pulled her hand away, and stepped past Tom. "First I need to get those blankets and sheets off of the bed," she said matter-of-factly. "Let's use the bedspread as a bundle for the sheets and pillow."

Tom pulled the spread off the bed and started to lay it on the floor. Lauren almost shouted, "No! Don't put it on the floor. Put it on the chair."

Oh. The blood was there. "I'm sorry. I understand." *This is going to be more difficult than I imagined.* However, once the bedding was removed and they could use the bed for her luggage, Lauren seemed to have no more problems. Tom carried down the things on hangers and laid them on the backseat of his car. While Lauren removed her possessions from the drawers and closet and put them in the suitcases, Tom carried her CD player and speakers, books, backpack, the two pictures on the wall, and bedside lamp and stuffed them into the car, using both the front and backseats.

They finished in less than an hour. Lauren walked to Carroll because there wasn't room for her in the car. Together they carried everything to her new room. Tom helped her put clean sheets on the bed, and then Lauren said, "I'll save all the rest of this until later."

It was almost six o'clock. *I wonder if she'll go out to eat with me. Should I ask? Would she say no? Well, she won't say yes unless I ask.* "Are you getting hungry?"

"Yes, a little, I guess."

Here goes. "May I treat you to supper?"

"Oh, you don't have to do that. You've done so much already."

"But I want to, Lauren." *Whoops, I hadn't intended to say that.*

She looked down at herself and laughed.

I get it. Clothes. "I was thinking of a very informal place just down the road. You can go just as you are. C'mon. Let's go."

"Well, okay. Just let me comb my hair." She went down the hall to the bathroom and soon returned with lipstick on and her hair combed. "I'm ready."

Nice, Tom thought.

During dinner at the Shalash home, Nadira said, "Lauren went back to school today. They assigned us to a new dorm: Carroll Hall."

"It's not as elegant sounding as Queen Anne's," her mother said.

"It's just like it, though."

Her father paused, holding his fork in his left hand. "Are men housed there?"

"Yes, I'm sure. Almost all the dorms are coed." *What now?* she thought.

He was looking at her. "So they have dorms for women only?"

"I think they have a couple. I know of one for sure."

He pointed his fork at her. "Then that's where I want you to be."

She glanced at him and then at her mother; a pleading glance that said, "Help me out, Mother." She whined, "Lauren has already moved in and everything. She has a lot of stuff to move."

"She should have conferred with you before accepting that dormitory." He looked down at his plate and resumed eating.

"She probably didn't—"

His head snapped up and without a word he motioned with his right hand that the conversation was over.

Nadira looked at her mother, but she didn't return the look. *They think I'm still six years old. They don't care. At least he doesn't.*

Nothing more was said, and when they were all finished eating, she asked to be excused and left the table. She went upstairs to her room and called Lauren, but only reached her voice mail. "Lauren, bad news. My father wants me to move to an all-female dorm. Have you moved into Carroll yet? Please call."

CHAPTER 20

"Oh, no!" Lauren exclaimed. She was listening to her voice mail. "What?" Tom and Lauren were in his car returning to Carroll Hall.

She turned toward Tom. "Nadira's dad wants her to move to an all-women's dorm. I wish I'd known that a few hours ago."

"There's only one women's dorm. It's unlikely that there's any room available."

"Is that Cecil Hall?"

"Yes."

"It'll be easy to find out in the morning. I'm too tired to unpack anything else tonight anyway."

Tom drove to Preinkert Drive and stopped in front of Carroll Hall. "Here you are, ma'am. Let me know what happens about your room. I'll help you move if you have to."

"Thanks. You've been a really big help already. I hope I don't have to move again. Thanks for feeding me tonight. It was very nice of you."

"I enjoyed having some company for dinner."

"Good-night." Lauren hurried to the door, unlocked the door, turned and waved to Tom, and then went in. A few feet inside she stopped and turned back toward the door and watched Tom drive off. She thought, *he's either a saint, or he likes me. We've spent the last five hours together, and he hasn't said or done anything flirty, but he did take me to dinner. So he must have some feelings toward me. Maybe it's just wishful thinking. Maybe he's just being helpful to a fellow Christian who is an emotional wreck and needs a strong shoulder to lean on. Whatever. But I like it.* She turned and went to her new room.

As he drove away, Tom thought, *I don't know what draws me to her, but I find her very comfortable to be around. She just seems much more mature than most freshman girls. Pretty down to earth. And she doesn't seem to try to be something she isn't. She's been through a lot the last few days, but she seems to have survived it with her emotions intact.*

Ahmed's call pushed itself into his consciousness. *There's obviously more going on there than he's told me. He needs help, but what? I don't want to endanger my parents. Maybe we should meet someplace else. Maybe I could just drive around while he tells me his problem. That's probably the safest thing. But probably he's more involved with Nadira's attack than he let on to me. And in that case, this is serious business.*

Tom was in front of his house when Ahmed arrived on Wednesday morning. "Morning, Ahmed."

"Good-morning." Ahmed looked somewhat confused as to where to go.

"I think the safest thing for us is to talk while I drive around. If you're in as much danger as you said you are, I don't want to involve my parents."

"I understand completely," Ahmed said.

"Is parking your car here inviting trouble?" Tom gestured toward Ahmed's car.

"It shouldn't be. But just to be on the safe side, perhaps I should park someplace else. Would down the street or around the block be okay?"

"Let's put it around the block."

Tom followed him, and when Ahmed parked his car he got into Tom's car. As he drove toward Greenbelt Road, he let Ahmed talk.

"Tom, I must ask that you keep absolutely confidential what I'm going to tell you. Will you do that?"

Uh oh, thought Tom. *It's just what I was afraid of.* "Ahmed, I don't have the legal right to do that. If I were an attorney or a clergyman, I could."

"I am mainly afraid that something I tell you will be told to someone else, and then it will be retold to those who want to hurt me."

"If it's not illegal, then I'll keep it confidential."

"Good. This is about the attack on Nadira. First, let me say that I had nothing to do with it. I like her very much and would do nothing to harm her."

"I'm glad to hear that." *I hope he's telling the truth.* He turned east onto Greenbelt Road.

"You know that I've been in business with two other guys, raising money for orphaned kids in Iraq."

"Yes."

Ahmed told him about the frightening demands for a share of the contributions leading up to the attack on Nadira.

"Man! You should be telling the police this."

"I already have. That created a problem, though."

"How?"

"The day after the attack, Rashid was abducted and forced to turn over the money received the past week to them."

"This is really sounding serious, Ahmed."

"I explained all this to the police on Monday and spoke to them again yesterday. Apparently, they went to my ex-partners to try to identify the terrorists. Yesterday afternoon—"

"What do you mean, ex-partners?"

"After the attack I resigned from the Servants of Mercy. I will have nothing to do with raising money for terrorists."

"That was probably a good thing."

"Yesterday afternoon Rashid left a message on my cell phone threatening to kill me. It probably wasn't from Rashid but from his abductors. At least I want to think that."

"But you don't know that, do you?"

"No. I'm sure my other partner, Masoud, could carry out a terrible crime against me. He is a thoughtless brute. So I am a hunted man. If it weren't for my feelings for Nadira and my desire to help find the man who attacked her, I would have already returned to Morocco."

"Wait a minute, Ahmed. Something doesn't make sense here. You say the police went to them to question them about the identity of the terrorists, and because of that they want to harm you?"

"I can only think that they are under the control of the terrorists."

Tom paused, trying to apply logic to what he'd just been told. *Why would they want to hurt or kill him?* "Ahmed, do you know who the terrorists are?"

"No, I've never seen them. I'm sure they want to be absolutely invisible. But now that I've gone to the police, they know that will be impossible. And so I'm to be punished."

This is a mystery. "Why are you telling me all this?"

"I need your help to find an attorney or some person who can advise me on what to do. I am here on a visa, and I need to be certain I don't violate it if I stop attending classes. But if I continue going to classes, they will always know how to find me. They have my class schedule. Yesterday as I left the building after class, they immediately threatened me by a text message."

This guy really has a problem, Tom thought. *About all I could do is ask around. Dad might know a good lawyer for him. But surely the school has someone to advise him.*

"Ahmed, I'll see if I can find someone. I don't do any work with attorneys, so I don't personally know anyone." When he reached Glenn Dale he turned around and headed back toward College Park. "Doesn't the university have an office to advise you on things like this? They could tell you immediately what will affect your visa status."

Ahmed didn't respond. They rode on in silence for a few minutes. Finally he said, "I want to be very careful about the people I trust with this information. Although I haven't known you for very long, I think you are a man I can trust. I don't know about the people in the university office. They could even be connected to the terrorists."

"That doesn't sound very likely. At least they could answer general questions about how missing classes would affect your visa. The answers are probably contained in documents you already have."

Again Ahmed grew silent. He turned his head away from Tom and looked out the window. Eventually he said, "That's good advice. And I might find visa answers on the Internet."

Tom said, "I think you should go to the police about the threat on your life. They apparently know where to find your ex-partners, don't they?"

"Yes. They were there yesterday. But what can they do about threats?"

"For one thing, the police could warn them that if anything should happen to you, they would come directly to them."

"Of course. But if the terrorists find me, Rashid and Masoud can deny any charges."

"So you still need to remain out of their reach."

"I think so."

"Is there someone in your mosque you could go to for advice? I assume you're Muslim."

"I am, yes. But I have no relationship here with anyone in authority in Islam. Could I go to your religious leader for advice?"

That's an interesting question. "Sure. Would anything in your religion prevent that?"

"I don't think so. Would anything in yours prevent it?"

"No."

"It—just seems like there is great prejudice against Islam in America."

"I'd say more like distrust."

"Why?"

"September 11, for one thing. There's obviously a violent element in Islam that is against us—against America."

"But that's not all Muslims. Why do the Christians reject Islam?"

Tom paused before answering. "I guess accepting Islam would be kind of going backwards. We believe Jesus was God's son, revealing God to the world and teaching God's ways."

Ahmed said, "Our holy book says God has no children. But it tells us to respect Jesus as a great prophet."

Tom said, "He was more than that. The Bible says, 'God so loved the world that he gave his one and only Son, that whoever believes in him shall not perish but have eternal life.' Jesus is God's son who brings eternal life."

They were approaching College Park. Ahmed said, "That raises many questions in my mind. If I survive this current danger, I'd like to continue this discussion. But I would be interested in talking to someone in authority in your religion or an attorney about my situation."

"I'll see what I can do. I'll get back in touch with you as soon as I can arrange something."

When they arrived at Ahmed's car, he thanked Tom for his thoughts and time and left. Tom drove around the block and parked in the driveway of his house. He sat in the car and thought about the conversation he'd just had. *It doesn't sound like Ahmed knows much about Islam. He's probably like a lot of people our age, not committed to anything but interested in everything. I should talk to Pete about him. Maybe Lauren and I should meet with George tonight too. I'll call her after my ten o'clock class.*

Ahmed sat in his car too, gathering his thoughts. *I suppose I should call Captain Parsons. He asked me to do that if I'm threatened. I should have his number.* He checked his phone, found the number, and then called. When he got Parsons on the line he said, "Captain, this is Ahmed Suliman. You asked me to inform you if I'm threatened. Such a thing happened yesterday about three. I was coming out of class and received a text message saying, 'You cannot hide from us. You're a dead man.' Apparently, they were watching for me to come out—they have my class schedule—so I ran back into the building and out the back door and escaped. But I can't go to class anymore because they'll be waiting for me."

"Who sent you that message?" Parsons asked.

"It wasn't signed, and I didn't take time to look. I assume it was from Rashid or Masoud. But maybe from the terrorists."

"So you believe that you are in danger?"

"Yes, without a doubt."

"Okay. I'll deliver a warning to them. But my advice for you is to remain out of sight until this episode is resolved."

"Thank you, Captain."

"In the meantime, if you find any additional information, please notify me immediately."

"Yes, I will. Good-bye."

CHAPTER 21

Lauren awoke amidst piles of clothing, large plastic bags, and luggage. *Ugh. What a mess. I need to find something to wear somewhere in here.* She found most of what she needed in the plastic bags, and the rest, underwear mostly, was in one of the suitcases. Soon she was washed, dressed, and brushed and on her way to breakfast. After she ate she checked her watch to make sure it wasn't too early to call Resident Life and made the call. She explained who she is and why she was calling. The receptionist passed the call to someone with more authority, and Lauren repeated herself. That person referred the call to another person, and again Lauren explained the reason for the call. That person took her phone number and promised to call back.

Maybe I should just call the president's office. Or better yet, I should have Dad call. Yeah.

"Hello, Lauren."

"Hi, Dad. Well, I've moved into Carroll Hall. But I need a favor of you."

"What's that?"

"Nadira's dad wants her to move into an all-female dorm. I think there's only one here, Cecil Hall. I tried to find out this morning if there are any vacant rooms there but just got the runaround. Could you call the president's office and see if they can tell us?"

"Well, that's a surprise. Too bad we didn't know that yesterday."

"Yeah, all my stuff is still in bags and suitcases, and I don't want to unpack until I know if we're going to stay there."

"Okay, honey, I'll see what I can do. I'll call you back when I've found something out."

"Thanks, Dad. I'll talk to you later."

A while later Lauren received a call from Tom. "Oh, hi, Tom. I thought it was my dad calling me back."

"Nope, just old Tom. I'm calling to see if you'd like to meet with George Lyon tonight after all."

"Is Martha going?" *Why did I ask him that?*

"I'm sure she is. I've never told her that we were thinking of canceling."

"If I don't have to move again tonight, I'll go. That's what I'm expecting my dad to tell me. I tried to find out from the housing office, but they didn't know. So I asked Dad to call the president's office."

"Well, even if they find a room for you in Cecil you won't have to move today, will you?"

"No. You're right. Okay, I'll go."

"Good, because I want to ask him some questions about Ahmed. We had a long talk this morning."

"You two guys are becoming good pals, aren't you?"

"I wouldn't exactly put it that way. He wanted advice, and it turned into a discussion of theology. So I need to know some things about Islam. But I've got to call George to make sure he hasn't made other plans. I'll call you back when I find out."

"Okay. I'll talk to you later then."

Tom called George at Glimus Motors. "George, this is Tom Parker."

"Hello, Tom," he boomed. "How's it with you my friend?"

"Good. How about you?"

"Fine. Fine. What's on your mind today?"

"I wonder if we could meet tonight."

"That would be no problem. I've kept the date open since you told me it was tentative."

"That's great. Lauren is back in College Park, and I've got some things to ask too. I've started to meet with a Muslim student, and so I need to learn a few things myself."

"All right. Well, I see I have a customer waiting, so I'd better get off the phone. I will see you all later."

"Okay. See you tonight."

Tom called Lauren back and also called Martha to remind her of the meeting.

Ahmed, still worrying about losing his status as a foreign student, decided to take Tom's advice and talk to the university authorities about the impact of missing classes. He asked, "If I need to miss classes for a couple of weeks, how will that affect my status as a foreign student?"

He was told, "If you miss classes and as a result fail a class, you'll need to take the class over. If you miss so many that you fail all your classes, you will be dismissed from the university. So my advice is, go to your professors in advance and find out what the assignments will be and when exams will be held and make arrangements to take the exams in whatever media the professors permit."

"Will missing classes, for example, an entire week of classes, violate my visa?"

"Oh, no. Your visa is pretty flexible."

"If I am dismissed, how will that affect my visa?"

"It will depend on whether you can transfer to another school or be reinstated here. If you stop attending college altogether, sooner or later, the State Department will find out and terminate your visa."

Ahmed was encouraged by that conversation. *With five phone calls I can make the necessary arrangements with my professors. I can honestly tell them that I must be away from the campus for a while due to business matters. They should be able to e-mail my assignments, and I can study on my own.*

During the afternoon he called his professors and, as he anticipated, was able to arrange to have his assignments e-mailed to him. And in two of his five classes he can have the midterm exams e-mailed to him as well. For the other three classes he would need to go to the classrooms to take the tests. *Tom gave me useful advice. I'm glad I've discovered him.*

Ahmed returned to the motel and lay down for a short nap. *There's nothing else I can do. I'd like to call Nadira, but she probably wouldn't talk to me. But even so, she'll know I'm thinking about her. Maybe if I text her it won't ring and alert her mother.* He texted simply, "Thinking of u. Wish we could talk."

Almost immediately his phone rang. A pang of happy anticipation raced through him. "This is Ahmed," he answered.

It was Nadira, speaking quietly. "Hi, Ahmed."

"Hi."

"You know I'm not supposed to be in contact with you."

"I know. You called me."

"Yes. I'm talking softly so my mother won't hear me."

"What would happen if she did?" Ahmed's question was more a challenge to Nadira's affection for him than one of her mother's intent.

"She would probably tell my father."

"So, what then?"

"I guess he'd beat me. Just kidding."

"What does that mean, *kidding?*"

"Joking," she explained.

"Oh. But does he beat you?"

"No, never. But his disapproval is very stern and very threatening. But he has never beaten me."

"Well, how are you doing?"

"Very well. My wounds are healing, and I have no pain. But I am not permitted to go to school, or anywhere else, until my attacker is found."

"Your father's rule?"

"Yes. A prisoner in my own home."

"He's just being protective, I'm sure."

"Yes, that's true. But overprotective, I think."

"So, will you leave UM?"

"Oh, no. My assignments are being sent to me, so I can keep up. Oh, I hear mother coming up the stairs," she said hurriedly. "I must go. Bye." The line went dead.

Ahmed was happy for the first time in six days.

George Lyon met Lauren, Martha, and Tom at the church entrance and together they walked into the customary room for their meeting. The four of them gathered around a folding table. Uncharacteristically, George was subdued. He looked around the table, and finally said, "A lot's happened over the past week, hasn't it? Lauren, I understand you've had a very traumatic experience."

"Yes, I have." Lauren reached up and touched her neck. "One I'll never forget." She sighed deeply.

George said, "I thought that tonight we should discuss what you think happened and how it applies to your understanding of Islam."

No one spoke. Tom nodded gently. George said, "So solemn." He smiled. "I hope we can inject a little joy into your lives tonight. Martha, what's your involvement in the attack on Nadira?"

167

Martha answered, "I'm mostly an interested bystander. A very distraught Lauren Stevenson spent the night at my house the night of the attack."

George turned his head toward Lauren. "And Tom tells me you found her. That must have been quite a shock."

Lauren said, "That's putting it mildly."

"If I may," George asked, "can you tell us what you thought when you found her?"

"I didn't think." Pressure suddenly filled her chest as she recalled the scene. She looked at her hands on the table. "I knew she was dead, and I simply reacted to the whole thing. I was just overcome with shock and grief."

"Would it have made a difference to you if she were a Christian girl?"

"No." She glanced at George. "That didn't have anything to do with how I reacted. It may have a lot to do with why she was attacked."

"Why do you say that?" George asked.

How do I answer him? Lauren thought. *How much should I say to him without violating Nadira's privacy?* She paused to make sure of what she would say. "No one knows why Nadira was attacked. I guess the police are looking for clues, but as far as I know there's not even a reasonable motive. But it seems likely that it had something to do with her religion. But it could be simply that she's a beautiful girl."

"Has this changed your view of Islam?"

She looked at George. "Not really. It makes me sad that a human being can be so cruel. But it was probably someone without a religion."

"That's a very intelligent answer," George said. He looked at Tom.

"What do you make of all this, Tom?"

"I've seen what it did to Lauren. That's bad enough. I can't imagine what Nadira has gone through."

"Yes, it must have been horrifying."

Not really, Lauren thought. *The restrictions of her father have been worse.*

"Tell me," George said to Tom. "You say you've been meeting with a Muslim student. What questions do you have?"

"He asked me, 'Why do Christians reject Islam?' I didn't know what to tell him."

"What prompted that question?"

"He had asked me if he could get advice from a Christian leader. I said yes, and he said that it seemed like there's a lot of prejudice against Islam in America and asked, 'why?'"

"What did you tell him?"

"I told him 9/11 and things like that. He said that it's not all Muslims, and then he asked why Christians reject Islam. I said something like we believe Jesus is God's son and revealed God to the world, or words to that effect. And that accepting Islam would be going backwards. He said their holy book says God has no children but that Jesus is a great prophet. I quoted John 3:16 to him. We didn't get into it any more than that. I'm afraid my answers were pretty squishy."

"Squishy?"

"Well, you know, not very definitive. He did say he'd look into Jesus more if he survived his current danger."

George frowned. Lauren interpreted it as an expression of confusion. She asked, "That was Ahmed, right?"

"Yes."

"What kind of danger is he in?" she asked.

"Well, obviously he's a suspect in Nadira's attack."

Lauren watched George's expression change to one of understanding. "Oh, he's the boyfriend, the one operating the charity. I get it. Yes, I imagine he's a prime suspect. But," he shifted his gaze toward Tom, "how did you happen to be talking to him?"

"He came to me to get help with his income taxes," Tom said.

George said, "In relation to the charity?"

"Yes. He probably won't owe any, but he's just being cautious."

"Nadira's father works for the IRS," Lauren said.

George smiled. "That explains a lot. A lot. Well, I'm afraid I can't be very much help with tax questions for foreign students."

"No need to," Tom said. "But should I have said more to him about perishing?"

George held both his hands with palms up in front of him. "On one hand"—he moved his right hand up and down—"Islam speaks a great deal about eternal life. He undoubtedly has heard much about it all his life and likely has a great deal of confidence that Islam is the correct path to eternal life. On the other hand"— he moved his left hand—"to hear a whole new concept of the path to eternal life, and from the mouth of a prophet revered by Islam, could cause a high degree of emotional confusion, or at the very least, intellectual confusion, depending on how devout or active he may be."

"Sounds like I was probably premature in quoting him that scripture."

"I think you're right. You may have set the stage for debate for a long time. If he'd first learned more of what Jesus did, of his compassion, of his enormous wisdom, and of his sacrifice, Ahmed would be more apt to accept that statement as an ongoing expression of who Jesus really is. But saying he's interested in learning more about Jesus after this current danger is over is a significant statement in itself, one you shouldn't ignore."

George then went on to advise the students of the necessity of not only telling them who Jesus is but also of modeling Jesus before them. They'd been there for over an hour and a half when George declared the session over.

As Tom was driving Lauren and Martha back to College Park, Ahmed was studying in his motel room, the first studying he'd done since the attack on Nadira. *I'm behind but not so far behind that I can't become current,* he thought. So he forced himself to read and reread and look up words in his English-Arabic dictionary that he did not recognize. He became so deeply engaged with the material that he lost awareness of the world outside his motel window until one of the exterior lights was momentarily blocked out. He jerked his head toward the window, in time to see a shadow on the pavement moving toward the parking lot. He rose to his feet, turned off the light, and went to the window. His heart was pounding. *Have they found me? How?*

CHAPTER 22

At the window of his darkened room Ahmed watched. The parking lot was illuminated by widely-spaced lamp poles, leaving many areas in the dark. *I can barely see my car. It's almost hidden between two SUVs. Is somebody out there?* He watched for a few minutes but saw nothing. *Voices. Low, soft voices. Men's voices. Not speaking English. Arabic? I can't tell.* He reached for his cell phone. *Be ready to call 911.* His hands were shaking so badly that he doubted he could do it. *The voices have stopped. There. Someone is in the parking lot, messing with the cars. Thieves? Car thieves?* He heard a car start. One of the cars near his, but not adjacent to it, backed out and drove away. *I must report this.*

He called the office. "I think a car was just stolen from the motel parking lot."

"What kind of car was it?"

"I don't know," Ahmed answered. It was too dark to tell.

"How do you know it was stolen?"

"I heard men talking and then saw them sneaking around the cars, when suddenly an SUV started and quietly drove away."

"Okay, I'll report it. Thanks for calling."

Ahmed watched for another twenty minutes but saw or heard nothing more. Police never appeared. *Tomorrow I must find a new motel further away.* He lay on his bed fully dressed, awake and listening. Eventually he drifted into sleep.

Thursday. It was the one-week anniversary of her attack. Her knife wounds were healing well. But other wounds, emotional ones, were developing. Neither she nor her family had heard any positive reports from the police. Life seemed to be returning to normal for her friends, but hers was a cloistered existence. She stood at the window looking at the yard below.

But I'm alive. We all know that if I continue to live with a Christian roommate I may be attacked again and possibly killed. I refuse to be intimidated into a life with only Muslims. This is America, after all. I thought that after high school I'd be released from that kind of sheltered life. My parents encouraged me, but now they're having second thoughts. So I remain here until they find the guy who cut me. That may take a long time.

Her phone rang. *It's Lauren.* "Lauren! I'm so glad to hear your voice."

"Gee. Thanks." She sang, "I have some news on housing,"

"I hope it's good news."

"Yeah, it is. There's a vacant room in Cecil Hall. One girl left school and the other moved in with a friend in another dorm. So we can move in next Monday."

"That's wonderful news. Now I just hope I can be released from my captivity here."

"Is it that bad?"

"I haven't been out of the house for a week, except once with my mother to get my clothes."

"But it's for your own good, isn't it?"

"I don't know. I guess it is—we just don't know why he did it, so I could be in real danger if I come back before he's caught."

"Exactly."

"So will you move in Monday?"

"I will if you're going to join me sometime."

"I will sometime. Maybe a long sometime, though. Being cooped up here is driving me crazy."

"I'm sure. No news from the police?"

"Nope."

"They've got to keep working on it. The papers won't let the incident die. And the college has sent out caution memos to all women about admitting people to their rooms and all kinds of other safety precautions. It's all the stuff that's always been part of their advice to students. Nothing new."

"Reminders, I guess."

"Yeah."

"Can you talk to Ahmed yet?"

"I'm not supposed to. But I snuck in a short conversation with him yesterday. He sounded good."

"Well, I just wanted to tell you about the room and to find out the latest news."

"I'm so glad you called. I can't wait till I can return to campus."

"Neither can I. But I'll keep up with you by phone."

"Good. Thanks for calling. It brightens up my day. Come over and see me if you get a chance."

"Maybe I can do that Saturday. But we'll talk before that."

"Okay. Bye, Lauren."

In late morning Ahmed checked out of the motel and began to carry his possessions to the mostly vacant parking lot. As he approached his car, he noticed scuff marks on the asphalt along the driver's side. He paused to look at them, placing his books and backpack on top of the car. *They look like yellow mud.* No similar marks were visible on the adjacent spaces. He walked to the empty parking space where he thought he'd seen the SUV stolen last night. *They're here! Same color. Not as many, though.* Ahmed rubbed one with his finger. *It's mud all right.* Alarm filled him. He looked at other nearby spaces but saw no similar markings. Returning to his car, he knelt down to look underneath. *I don't know what I'm looking at.* He began to identify things he'd expect to see. *Muffler, another muffler-like thing, engine, a small box—wait, it's not dirty like the rest. It has wires to it. I don't know what it is. I'm not going to start this car until I find out.*

He called Captain Parsons at the police station. "Sir, this is Ahmed Suliman. I'm at a motel on New Hampshire Avenue. There's something attached under my car that I can't identify. It's not dirty like the bottom of the car is and it has wires to it. I don't know much about cars, so it may be nothing. But I thought I should call you to get your advice before using the car."

"Ahmed, don't touch the car! That sounds like an explosive device. Just stay there but away from the car. I'm sending a bomb squad, and they'll be there quickly, along with a lot of other people. When they get there, just tell them which car and then get out of the way. What's the name of the motel?"

Ahmed told him and then said, "How could they have found me?"

Parsons said, "Didn't you tell me you bought a new car?"

"Yes."

"Did you keep your old license plates?"

"Yes."

"There's your answer. Okay, I've got a lot of people to notify. Help will be there soon."

The line went dead. Within minutes he heard sirens, and very quickly police cars began arriving. He stood in the parking lot, and with the arrival of the first police car he pointed to his car. The street was blocked, and the few remaining motel residents were evacuated. A crowd began to gather across the street. More sirens filled the air as fire engines arrived. A policeman, followed by a large German Shepherd, emerged from a police vehicle. Ahmed was escorted to a police van that apparently acted as a mobile command center. He was told to remain there, that he would need to be interviewed. A policeman remained in the van with him. From the van he could not see what was happening at his car. He listened to the bewildering conversations of the various units on the police radio, which he could not comprehend. However, he did think he heard that what he had seen was actually an explosive device. "Did I hear correctly?" he asked of the officer in the van. "Was it an explosive device?"

"Yeah," the officer said curtly. He was obviously concentrating on the ongoing operation and did not wish to be engaged in a conversation.

A television truck arrived but was prevented from getting close to the scene. Ahmed could see a reporter and a mobile cameraman walking around, attempting to gather information. *I do not want to be seen on television.* "I do not wish to be interviewed by the press or television," he said to the policeman.

"Okay," the policeman said.

Soon a man in civilian clothes entered the van. He told the policeman, "The device has been removed and neutralized. We'll turn it over to the FBI for analysis."

When he heard "FBI," Ahmed was struck with a pang of terror. To him, FBI meant a secret police of incredible capabilities, feared the world over.

The man in civilian clothes said to the policeman, "I want to talk to the motel staff. Is this the car owner?" He pointed to Ahmed.

"Yes, sir," the policeman answered.

"As soon as things begin to thin out, we need to deal with the press. Is Stokely here?

"I haven't seen him, sir."

"Get the station on the line and have them get Stokely here ASAP."

"Yes, sir."

Ahmed watched the policeman use a mobile phone to call for Stokely. The man in civilian clothes stepped into the back of the van and showed Ahmed his badge. "I'm Lieutenant Borkowski. I'll need you to come with us to the station. We'll want to find out everything you know about this incident. Everything. In the meantime, the media will want to interview you."

"What is media?" Ahmed asked.

"The press. You know, newspapers, television."

"Sir," Ahmed began, "I do not wish to speak to newspapers or television."

"You have that choice," Borkowski said. "But they'll hound you until they can get something out of you."

"Sir, I don't understand *hound*."

"Where are you from?" Borkowski demanded.

"Morocco, sir. I am a student at UM."

"Hound means they will pester you and sit on your doorstep until you speak to them. They will follow you wherever you go, like a hound dog chasing a raccoon. Do you understand?"

"I cannot speak to them. Television pictures will reach my parents in Morocco, and they will be disgraced and frightened. The university will also be troubled, and they will have to respond, even though I do not think it is related to the university."

"Do you know who placed the bomb under your car?"

"I have suspicions only."

"Who do you suspect?"

"It's a very long story, but I do not know the names of the ones I suspect."

"You'll need to tell your story to the investigator."

"I've already told it all to Captain Parsons."

"Captain Parsons?"

"He is at the Hyattsville station."

"Oh, yes. Of course. Well, I think you'll have to explain it to some others. While you're here, I'll try to keep the press from you, but they have a right to ask questions just as you have a right to not answer them."

"When will I be permitted to use my car?" *I don't want to leave it here overnight. They may put another bomb under it.*

"Our experts will need to make sure there are no other devices hidden somewhere in the car. They will do a preliminary investigation here, and then they will move it by truck to where it can be thoroughly tested to make sure it is safe to drive."

Ahmed reached into his pocket. "Here is the key. I left some of my belongings on the top of the car. Can I retrieve them?"

Borkowski said, "We'll put them inside the car." He took the key and left the van. While he was gone, Captain Parsons entered the van. "Is Mr. Suliman here?" He glanced to the back of the van and saw Ahmed. "Oh, there he is." He stepped to the back of the van. "So, it was indeed a bomb. Who do you think did this, Ahmed?"

"The terrorists, I assume. I doubt that Masoud or Rashid would do this unless forced to."

"I will go with you to the interview with the investigator. I brought along your file, and I'll copy it for the investigator, so you won't have to repeat everything. You may feel like you are the one being accused, but that's the way they must be to get to the bottom of this intended attack."

Ahmed was taken to the Hyattsville police station. It was a long and difficult interview. Yet he successfully avoided saying anything about keeping the money and the money laundering.

The investigator said to Ahmed, "I find it difficult to understand why those people, whoever they are, would try to eliminate you, except that you have revealed to us that they are active here and are planning something. They can't change that by blowing you up. In fact, it would make finding them even more imperative. The attempt on your life has the same affect. We will go after them aggressively."

I need to explain this again, Ahmed thought. "Sir, they have been told that I know every aspect of the collection of money, sending acknowledgements, banking, accounting—everything. The longer I am left alive the more the opportunity for me to lead you to them. I am a danger to them." *And I'm a danger to Rashid and Masoud.*

"Well," the investigator said, "Until we find them, I advise you to take every precaution to avoid their finding you."

Captain Parsons added, "As a starter, you should get new license plates and, ideally, a different car."

"But how could they find my car by knowing the license plate number?" Ahmed asked. *It would be like finding a single grain of sand in the desert.*

"When you registered at the motel, you probably had to list your license number and the make and color of your car. Is that true?"

"Yes, I think so."

"Then, by imitating the police, they could call the various motels around here and ask. Did you use your real name when you registered there?"

"No, sir."

"That was smart. But by listing your license plate number you could be found without too much trouble."

"What other precautions should I take?" *These people should know better than anyone.*

"I'd get as far away from here as you can and get a new cell phone with a new number, registered under an assumed name. Just give the new number to me, so we can reach you when necessary."

"Thank you, sir. Am I free to go now?"

Parsons turned toward the investigator and raised his eyebrows. The investigator nodded. "Yes, you may go. But you'll be contacted soon by the FBI, who'll need to go over all this again."

Ahmed felt the blood drain from his face. Ice water filled his veins. He stood to leave but almost fainted, his fear of the FBI was so great. Without another word he walked unsteadily out of the station, only to recall that his car was not there. He went back in and asked for Captain Parsons. When he appeared, Ahmed said, "Where is my car?"

"Let me check. Wait here."

Most of my things are still in the motel room, even though I've checked out. The cleaning people may have already taken them. He glanced at his watch. *Almost noon. This is terrible.*

When Captain Parsons returned he said, "The forensic people are still working on it. It will be midafternoon before they're finished. Do you need to go somewhere?"

"Most of my possessions are at the motel including my computer and clothes."

"I can arrange a ride to the motel."

"The problem is," Ahmed's voice sounded anxious, "I checked out of the room and was taking my things to the car when I discovered the marks on the pavement. So I left almost everything in the room, which is probably now being cleaned."

"What was your room number?"

"Seventeen."

Parsons turned to the desk clerk and instructed him to call the motel and to tell them to protect the belongings in room 17 until last night's occupant gets there. He turned to Ahmed and said, "Your car will be returned to the motel, so you'll need to stay around there until it gets back. Sorry about that."

A police car took Ahmed to the motel, and he went first to the room but found it locked. He went to the office and asked about his possessions.

The manager, who appeared Indian to Ahmed, came out of his office behind the desk and shouted, "You are the one who caused all this trouble. Now most of our guests have gone, and we will have many vacancies for a long time! You are not welcome here!"

"What about my possessions?" Ahmed demanded.

"They are there in the room, where you left them. Here is a key. Take your things and get out!" He handed him a key card.

"But my car won't be returned to me until later this afternoon. How can I carry everything, and how can I go anywhere?"

"I don't care. It's your problem. Now go."

Ahmed glared at him, and he glared back. Ahmed looked away first, turned and walked to his room, his stomach churning like a washing machine. He went in and found that his clothing was there. That gave him partial relief. *Wait. Where is my computer? Did I put it in my backpack?* He sat down and tried to recall. *Surely I did. I always keep it there. I hope it's there. But how will I handle all these clothes?* He had less than he imagined. Gathering everything together so he could handle it all in two hands, he carried it to the parking lot and sat on the curb, facing the building, and waited. The concrete was cold, and he was soon standing.

Before long the manager appeared. "Give me the room key. And get off of the property. You are trespassing now. If you don't go, I will call the police and have you forcibly removed."

Ahmed handed him the key card. "But the police have my car and will bring it back here this afternoon!"

"That's no concern of mine. You are trespassing. You must leave."

The heat of anger boiled inside of Ahmed. With narrowed eyes he faced the manager, fighting the urge to strike at him. The urge passed, and without another word, Ahmed picked up his clothes and walked to the sidewalk, looked up, down, and across New Hampshire Avenue for a place to stay. Seeing nothing promising, he began walking along the street to find a nearby spot to wait. He finally settled on the entrance to an apartment building across the street, where he could see the motel parking lot. There he waited until almost three o'clock, when his car was finally returned, along with his books, backpack, and computer.

Ahmed was exhausted, so he drove west and took a room in a motel in the Bethesda area, using a false name, false make and model of his car, and false license number. *I hope I'll be safe for one night. Tomorrow I'll take care of the car and license plates.* Nearby was a restaurant where he had his first meal of the day, and then he returned to the room, lay down, and instantly fell asleep.

His ringing cell phone woke him several hours later. It was dark, and awaking from deep sleep in unfamiliar surroundings created a moment of confusion as he struggled toward full consciousness. His voice mail clicked on before he could answer the phone. Once fully awake, he waited for the recording to register, and then he listened to find out who called.

"This is Tom Parker. Just getting back to you about a lawyer. Call when you can."

Ahmed returned the call. "Tom, this is Ahmed. You have news about a lawyer?"

"Yes. Our organization, CCA, has a lawyer they use for legal matters. I spoke to the director about him, and he felt certain that he could advise you. He might charge you, but he charges us much less than lawyers usually charge people."

"I took your advice and called the university office. They were very helpful about my visa status. It's much less restrictive than I thought."

"I'm glad to hear that. That's free legal advice. It's not often I'm right. But I'm glad they could help."

"I don't think I need a lawyer at this time. But if things get any worse, I could."

"Has anything new happened?"

"Someone attached a bomb to my car last night."

"Oh, no! Did it go off? You're not hurt are you?"

"No. I discovered it before I got into my car, and I notified the police. So I spent the whole morning with the police. There were police and emergency vehicles all over the place."

"How did you find it?"

"It's a long story, but the short version is that I noticed mud marks on the pavement and, as a precaution, I looked under the car, and there it was."

"Wow! You are so lucky."

"Yes, I guess so. Or maybe I was spared for a reason."

"What do you think that would be?"

"Tom, I'd rather not talk about this on the phone. Nothing is secure. We should meet and talk where we can discuss this privately."

"Saturday?"

"Will you be going to a football game on Saturday?"

"Not this Saturday. Maryland is playing away this week."

"Good. Saturday would be good. But not in a public place and not near the campus."

"Have you ever been to Annapolis?"

"No. It's the capital city of Maryland, isn't it?"

"We could drive over there and take a look around."

"That would be very helpful. What time?"

"How about ten in the morning?"

"Okay. I will park a few blocks from your house and walk to your street, where I'll meet you at ten."

"Fine. I'll see you then."

CHAPTER 23

Ahmed was awakened on Friday by his cell phone. Captain Parsons asked him to appear at ten o'clock at the station to speak to the FBI. Ahmed said he would be there. *What will they do to me? What will they want me to confess to? Will they take me somewhere and hold me until I confess? Will they torture me? Will they turn me over to the CIA? Then I will surely die.*

He could not eat as the time for his meeting slowly approached. He could not think of anything other than what he could imagine about an encounter with the FBI. The dreaded FBI. The feared FBI. All his life in Morocco he had heard about the FBI and of stories of atrocities it had committed; of how people had been required to acquire entirely new identities and move away from family and everyone they knew; of how people had disappeared at the hands of the FBI; of people tortured until they confessed to crimes they had not committed. He had not questioned the authenticity of the stories. They were passed among schoolmates as if they were absolutely true.

At the appointed time he walked into the Hyattsville Station. He told the desk clerk, "I'm here to see Captain Parsons. I'm Ahmed Suliman."

The fat desk clerk looked at him and said, "Are you all right?"

"Yes sir."

"You don't look all right. Are you on something?"

"Do you mean medications or drugs? No, nothing."

"Well, sit over there. I'll tell Parsons you're here."

He sat where the clerk pointed, but almost immediately Captain Parsons appeared and beckoned for Ahmed to come with him. Ahmed rose unsteadily and followed. He was expecting two sinister looking men in dark suits but was surprised to see a young man in a sport shirt, smiling as he entered the door. The smile did not put Ahmed at ease. Parsons introduced them and invited Ahmed to sit at a steel table, across from the FBI agent. His name was Paul something. Ahmed did not understand his last name.

"I've briefed Paul on what you've already told us. So I don't think we'll need to go over much of that," Parsons sat at the end of the rectangular table. "You can take it from there, Paul."

"We're trying to identify who put that explosive device under your car," Paul began. "We need to determine why someone would want to do that to you. Do you have any idea?"

"Yes." Ahmed could not sit still. Every few seconds his body jerked. "The terrorists who have taken over the Servants of Mercy," he stammered.

"But why?"

His throat was so dry he could barely speak. "They know I went to the police after Nadira was assaulted."

"But what would killing you accomplish?"

"I think it is to punish me. Why else?" His right foot jiggled up and down uncontrollably.

"That's what we're trying to determine. You look very nervous, Mr. Suliman. I'd like you to relax a little. Would you like some water?"

"Yes, thank you," Ahmed said. Parsons got up and left the room. The agent resumed, "Tell me about the Servants of Mercy."

Ahmed told him of how they started it in the fall of last year. They were all computer knowledgeable, and they used the Internet to advertise it. He explained where the contribution checks went and how they picked them up and immediately sent acknowledgment letters. Captain Parsons returned with a cup of water.

"Do you have copies of the letters?"

"No. But our accountant has the names and amounts."

"Who is the accountant?"

Ahmed gave him the name and phone number. Then he told the agent how they moved the money from the local bank to Lichtenstein, and from there to Iraq. "But now that terrorists have forced their way in, I don't know if any goes to Iraq anymore."

"Are the terrorists taking it all?"

Ahmed shook his head. "I don't know. I resigned last Friday, the day after Nadira was cut."

"Why was she attacked?" the agent asked.

"I believe it was a warning to us to accept the demands of the terrorists."

"But why her? Why not one of you?"

"I think because they are cowards. She was not on her guard for any reason, so she was an easy target. Or maybe to demonstrate their mastery of the unexpected."

"Do you know their names or the name of the organization?"

"No, neither." Ahmed slowly began to relax.

"Now that you have resigned, what is your relationship to Rashid and Masoud?"

"I believe they are angry with me. They must take the full impact of the terrorists while I am free."

"Have you talked to them after resigning?"

"No."

"Did you receive income from your enterprise?"

"Yes, 3.3 percent."

"Do you pay income tax on that?"

"Yes, but only estimated tax so far. In April I will pay the full amount."

The agent leaned back in his chair and looked at Captain Parsons. "As soon as we get the forensic report, I'll probably want to speak to Mr. Suliman again."

Ahmed interjected, "Have you spoken to Rashid and Masoud?"

"We'll speak to them today. Why?"

"I simply think they would know more about the terrorists than I do. Especially Rashid. It was Rashid that they approached and spoke to. He should know what they look like. You should be able to catch the terrorists when they pick up the money, however they have arranged to do that."

"How do you think they'll do it?" the agent asked.

"The safest way for them is to set up an account in an Iraqi bank. Then they will require Rashid to instruct the Liechtenstein bank to transfer a percentage, or all, of the money to the new account. The new account in Iraq could even be given the name of a false orphanage or agency to avoid suspicion. From there they could move the money anywhere."

The agent looked at Captain Parsons, his eyebrows raised. "Very clever. But I still don't see what killing you would accomplish. We should be able to get the same information from your ex-partners that we got from you. The terrorists would be no safer with you gone. There must be another motive for the bomb." He turned and looked at Ahmed, his eyebrows still raised in an expression of a question.

Ahmed shrugged. "Perhaps there is something I don't know. Maybe you'll learn more from Rashid and Masoud."

"Yes, perhaps. In the meantime, stay available. We'll need to speak to you again. Okay?"

"Yes, sir. Am I free to go?"

"Yes, and thank you for your cooperation."

Ahmed got up, and Captain Parsons went out with him, escorting him to the front door. He left the police station feeling not much better than when he'd entered it. His stomach was still churning, and he was still shaking. *Sooner or later they're going to ask me to tell them something I don't want them to know. But I don't want to lie to the police or to anyone else. That FBI agent is getting too close. But for now, I need to get a different car.* So, for the second time in a week he headed off to Glimus Motors.

This time he walked into the showroom and saw George Lyon standing at a desk in a small cubicle. George looked up and recognized Ahmed and smiled. "Well, hello," he boomed. "What brings you back to see me?"

"Hello, Mr. Lyon."

"Please, call me George. How are you doing, son?"

"Just fine, sir…er, George. But I'm not satisfied with the car I bought on Monday. I'd like to look around for another one."

"Well, sure. Sure. Let's just walk out there and see what we can find. What didn't you like about the Chevy you bought?"

"I think it attracted too much attention."

"Ha, ha, ha, ha. You must be kidding. That car?"

I'd like to tell him about the bomb, but maybe I'd better not. He'd probably tell everyone he sees. Ahmed laughed, too. "It was a joke. I just don't like the way it feels."

"We have some Pontiacs that might be in your price range. We also have a couple of Toyotas and a Nissan."

Ahmed spent over an hour looking at various cars and driving a few of them. He finally settled on a Toyota that George said he could have for a measly $1,000. Ahmed agreed and bought it. "I'd also like to get a new license plate," he said as they sat at George's desk.

"Why would you want to do that?" George asked.

"The one I have has a crazy picture of a turtle on it. I just want a plain one."

"No problem. I'll just have to give you a temporary plate until the new one arrives. Do you want it mailed to you, or do you want to pick it up here?"

"I'll pick it up here."

By midafternoon Ahmed was off, feeling less vulnerable in his new Toyota. *Now I must contact our accountant so he can issue proper documents.* While at a gas station to fill up his new car, he called the accountant. His secretary said he was not in, so he left a message with her that the Servants of Mercy had transferred approximately $600,000 to the agency in Iraq, money that had been withheld until now for business reasons. He said he would provide the appropriate bank statements when he received them. He also told her that he had been paid $55,000 this year by the Servants of Mercy, and that will be all he'll receive because he has resigned from the organization. He gave her his dormitory address to send the tax documents.

"Hi Lauren." Nadira saw Lauren's name on her phone screen.

"Hi to you. What are you doing this afternoon?"

"The same as most days. Studying in my cell."

"I thought you might want a visitor, if you are allowed to."

"It depends on who it is. You're on the approved list. When do you want to come?"

"Oh, around two. My last class ends at noon. Then I'm done for the weekend."

"How are you going to get here?"

"I was about to ask if there's a bus that comes near your house."

"No, not near."

"How far is it from here?"

"Not far. It only takes ten minutes by car, depending on what time it is. I think it's about five or six miles. Too far to walk."

"I need a bike. That would be an easy bike ride."

"Hey. That's a good idea. I have a bike you could use. I'll ask my mother to pick you up, and then you could ride my bike back." *A brilliant idea, if I may say so.*

And so at two o'clock Lauren was waiting in front of Carroll Hall when Mrs. Shalash and Nadira, both with their heads covered with scarves, arrived to pick her up. Nadira's scarf was solid maroon, and her mother's was medium blue with complex designs in assorted shades of blue. *Mrs. Shalash is so beautiful,* Lauren observed. *Her gorgeous scarf makes her look even more elegant.* They drove slowly past Cecil Hall, their new dorm-to-be, but decided not to go inside.

Cecil Hall is very near Memorial Chapel, Lauren mused. *This would be convenient to the chapel if I wanted to go to church there, but their services are at odd hours. Evenings, I think. I need to find out.* She said, "I hope our room looks out over Chapel Fields and all the frat houses across Route 1."

"It looks like all those trees would block our view. Maybe we'll be on the fourth floor and can see over the trees." Nadira said.

"Ugh. I hope we're not way up there. I don't think the fourth floor has dorm rooms anyway. Look at those dormer windows. The roof is right there."

"Maybe so."

"I'll find out Monday when I start hauling all my stuff over here. I think Tom's going to help me."

"Will they let him in?"

"Surely they will, to carry heavy things in."

"Yeah. Okay. Let's go, Mother. We've gawked at Cecil Hall long enough."

It was a short ride. When they arrived at the Shalash home, Nadira asked Lauren to go into the kitchen with her to have a cup of tea. While the water was heating, Nadira took out cups and saucers from the cabinet, a tin of loose tea, a strainer, and a teapot, chattering as she did. As Nadira scurried around, Lauren glanced at the morning's *Washington Post*, lying on the table. On the front page she noticed an article about a bomb discovered under a car at a motel on New Hampshire Avenue. "Did you see this?" she asked.

"What?" Nadira leaned over Lauren's shoulder to see the article.

Lauren pointed at the print and said, "It says the car belonged to a foreign college student from Morocco! Does Ahmed have a car?"

"I'm not sure. I think so." She poured the hot water into the pot.

"It says he refused to give his name."

"Is there a picture?" Nadira asked.

"No. But it couldn't be him. He lives on campus, you know."

"Yeah. There are a lot of Moroccans around here. We even have a Moroccan restaurant now."

"Can you talk to him yet?"

Nadira put her finger to her lips and nodded yes while she said, "Not permissible yet. I expect the tea is ready. Sugar or cream?"

"Sugar, please."

She poured the tea, and gave the sugar bowl to Lauren. "Let's take this upstairs to my room." In Nadira's room Lauren sat in a small rocking chair, which was too narrow for an adult, pushing aside a stuffed elephant, and Nadira sat on her bed, their cups and saucers in their hands in front of them. Behind her closed door, Nadira, looking into her teacup, said, "Today was the first time I've been outside for a week except for picking up my books and clothes on Monday. But it's not that so much. My father is the only person in this family that can have an opinion. My mother will not contradict him for a second. I don't think she's afraid of him but was probably brought up that way. I don't know. It seems like that's how it's always been. But they're Americans now. It's different from Palestine. Or it should be. I expect freedom is why they came here. I've never asked, but why else?"

Silence pervaded the room. Lauren thought, *I want to say something but maybe I shouldn't. No, I should.* She said, "Freedom is at the heart of Christianity. That's why it goes so hand in hand with America."

"Ah, the land of the free and the home of the brave." She put her right hand over her heart. "Sometimes it takes bravery to be free."

"I'm sure. There are brave people everywhere, though. But freedom is mandated by our constitution." She began rocking the chair more forcefully as if to emphasize what she was saying.

"What does that have to do with Christianity?" Nadira looked directly at her.

Lauren raised her eyebrows and said, "Only that the federal government can't dictate what religion you must have, or what you can or can't practice."

"So people are free to practice whatever religion they wish to, right?" She set her empty cup on the bedside table.

"Exactly. There are forms of Christianity where people are required to do this or that or to refrain from doing some things. But in my opinion, true Christianity is where people have the freedom to be as much like Jesus as their abilities permit."

"I guess I could say the same about Islam."

"I don't know much about it. Does Islam give you freedom?"

"Well, the freedom to submit to God or not."

"What does it teach about obeying your father?"

"Good question. I don't know!" They both laughed, and Nadira flopped on her back on the bed.

Lauren stopped rocking and asked, "If they don't catch the guy, when do you think your father will let you come back to the campus?"

Nadira twisted around so her head was on a pillow. "I wish I knew. I've tried to convince him that I'll be safe there, but he won't hear of it."

"Is he still investigating Ahmed?" She looked around for a place to put her cup and then set it on the floor.

"I don't think so. But who knows. I think he's concentrating on the hate crime angle. But I'm sure he still thinks Ahmed was somehow involved, since he's the only person I know except you and my professors. Well, I also know this girl on the second floor I sometimes pray with. We've never done anything together and haven't even talked much."

"Have you talked to the police any more since last Friday?"

"Oh, yes." She paused. "Monday it was, I think. Yeah, Monday. They came back and asked me some more questions."

"Do they have any suspects?" She got up and picked up her teacup and put it on the bedside table and then sat back down.

"They haven't told us of any, at least as far as I know. My father talks to them all the time, but he hasn't told me much."

They both sat quietly for a minute. Lauren then said, "Can I see your scars?"

"Oh sure." Nadira sat up and Lauren stepped to the side of the bed. Nadira pulled her hair aside.

"You don't even have bandages on them!" Lauren exclaimed as she examined the wounds. *Those white things must be instead of stitches, so they won't leave scars,* she thought. "Not bad. Looking good, says Dr. Stevenson."

Nadira laughed and dropped her hair.

Lauren looked around the room, which contained a computer desk below a window that looked out over a treed yard. "So, is this where you study and everything?"

Nadira got off the bed. "This is it." She waved her hand in grand gesture that encompassed the computer stand. "I have all my books and notebooks, and I get my assignments on the net. But I can't hear class lectures, and I can't ask questions or join a class discussion. I need to convince my father that what I'm missing is vital."

"I hope you can. I need a roommate! But now I need to take a look at that bike and make sure its tires aren't flat. I want to get back to campus before it gets dark. And I'll have to think about a lock."

"I have a lock!"

"Cool."

They went downstairs and into the garage. "Oh, it's a Schwinn! Let me sit on it." *Mmm, the back tire looks a little low.* "I'll have to stop at a gas station and get some air in the tires."

"Here. You'll need this." Nadira held out a helmet. "See if it fits."

Lauren put it on. "Perfect," she said. *Close enough,* she thought.

Nadira began rummaging in a box. "I need to find the lock." She soon found it and handed it to Lauren. "I always used to lock it to the luggage rack when I was riding."

"I have this little purse." Lauren held it up. "Maybe I could strap it to the luggage rack too."

"I wouldn't," Nadira said. "Can you just put it over your shoulder?"

"Let me try that. Oh, that will work. Well, thank you. With this I can visit you whenever I want to. How do I get there from here?"

Nadira gave her directions, and Lauren went on her way, feeling good about riding a bike again.

CHAPTER 24

Ahmed had just driven away from the gas station when his cell phone rang. *The accountant again*, he thought. Without looking at the screen he answered, "This is Ahmed."

"This is Captain Parsons." Ahmed jumped in his seat and looked for a place to pull over.

"Yes, sir."

"Something has come up. I need you to come by the station if you're available right now."

Oh, no. The FBI agent has found something. Surely he found out about the money. "Yes. I'm in my car now and can be there in ten or fifteen minutes."

"That would be very good. Thank you. I'll see you soon."

After Parsons hung up Ahmed sat and thought. His hands were shaking as he put the phone on the seat beside him. *Will they arrest me even if I've turned over all my money to the orphanage? I probably should take a lawyer with me. But I think in America a person doesn't have to admit to anything. He must be accused by someone else. I know I'm not guilty of anything, at least not anything permanent. And I'm trying to correct those mistakes. If they ask anything about the money, I will refuse to answer.*

The drive to the station took only ten minutes. When he walked in the fat desk clerk wiped his mouth with his sleeve and asked, "Captain Parsons?" An open bag of chips lay on the desk.

Ahmed nodded. Within a minute Parsons appeared. "Thanks for coming so quickly, Ahmed. There's someone here who wants to talk to you." He led Ahmed into the same room they'd used in the morning. Seated at the table was a young man, obviously Middle Eastern, in a tee shirt and jeans. He looked like he was young enough to be a student but a little older than Ahmed.

Captain Parsons introduced them. "Ahmed, this is Hashim."

Ahmed was startled. *So this is Hashim. But why is he here?*

Hashim spoke to him in Arabic. "I am here because I recently met Masoud and, just this week, Rashid. I'm a student here at UMD and live near your house. I was born in Jordan but moved to America when I was nine. My family continues to speak Arabic at home, but I speak English well. Captain Parsons will tell you why I am here."

Ahmed looked at Parsons, still puzzled.

"Have a seat, Ahmed," Parsons said. "Hashim is here because of his acquaintance with your former business partners. He has agreed to help us identify the terrorists who have hijacked your charity. Now that your relationship with them has soured, we hope he might be able to learn something through direct contact. But he needs you to school him about Masoud and Rashid to help him put together the pieces of the puzzle."

"I don't understand *soured*. Does it mean become bitter?" Ahmed asked.

"Exactly. We want Hashim to begin to associate with Masoud and Rashid and to try to find a way to contact the terrorists. We want you to help him understand all about the Servants of Mercy and the habits of Masoud and Rashid."

Ahmed looked at Hashim, then at Parsons, then back to Hashim. *He must be some kind of policeman. Or maybe FBI.* "Are you a policeman?" he asked of Hashim.

"When they need me. A part-time policeman of sorts, just for special cases."

Parsons said, "Look. The president of the university is very insistent that we find who attacked Nadira. The newspapers are continuing to publicize the security issue at the university. The FBI is very interested in finding who placed a bomb under your car. You know there are terrorists active around here, and the people that hurt Nadira are probably the same ones who tried to kill you. So Hashim is one man who might be able to find out some answers. Okay?"

Ahmed shrank from Parsons' forceful invective. "Yes, sir." *I'm just glad they aren't trying to find out about the money.*

Parsons took hold of Ahmed's arm and looked him in the eye. "Ahmed, we need you to help with this case. I know you want to find the perpetrators as much as anyone. But I must have your word that you will not tell anyone, not a living soul, about Hashim. If asked about him, you may say you've met him but know little about him. And that's true. If asked where you met him, just say somewhere near the campus. I must have your promise that you will not reveal to anyone that Hashim is a policeman of any sort. I've spoken with you enough that I think I can trust you. Will you promise me you'll keep silent about Hashim?"

Ahmed looked at the table. His hands were folded in his lap, and he rubbed his fingers as he thought. "Could there be a time when, perhaps in court, I must acknowledge him?"

"There may be. But if that becomes necessary, I will tell you if it's all right. He is only valuable to us as long as he is not known."

Ahmed nodded. "Yes. You have my pledge."

"Good. Now I want you to spend time with Hashim this weekend, today if possible, so he can began to unravel this case. All right?"

"Yes, sir." Ahmed continued to act intimidated, even though he was privately relieved. He looked at Hashim. "I'm free to talk to you now or whenever you want to, except for a couple of hours tomorrow morning. I have something planned for then."

Hashim replied, "Let's just talk for a while here, and then we can decide where to go from there. What do you say?"

"That's all right with me." Ahmed turned toward Captain Parsons.

Parsons nodded at both of them, and said, "Good. I'll leave you two boys alone. You can stay here as long as you like." He stood and walked out of the room.

"Let's talk in Arabic," said Ahmed.

"Fine. First, tell me about Masoud and Rashid." He leaned his head on his fist.

Ahmed looked directly at Hashim. "Rashid is the leader. He is from Egypt and older than Masoud or me. He is a thoughtful, intelligent guy who does not make decisions quickly, but once he makes a decision, he will not change. I know nothing of his family. He does not practice religion. None of us does here. He is serious most of the time. He is not patient with foolishness. Masoud is very different. He is profane and disrespectful. He is strong physically and often threatens me with his brutality when he wants to intimidate me. But he's never attacked me. He is very smart. But he's also brash. He's not a good thinker like Rashid."

They talked together for about half an hour about the lifestyle and habits of Rashid and Masoud, and then Hashim said, "It's about prayer time. When can we resume this discussion?"

"I'll be available any time after about three tomorrow."

"Okay. Give me your cell phone number, and I'll call you once I've looked at my schedule."

Ahmed gave Hashim his number and then they shook hands. Hashim said, "You go ahead, and I'll go out a little later. We don't want to be seen together."

When Nadira's parents returned home from Friday prayers at the mosque, she came into the kitchen while her mother made tea. "May I have some too?" Nadira asked.

"Yes, of course."

Nadira rubbed her father's back. She asked, "Have you heard anything from the police yet?"

"Only that they are aggressively looking for your attacker. Earlier this week I was speaking to the campus police, but yesterday they told me they've turned their investigation over to the Prince George's County police force."

"I suppose that's good," her mother said.

"Probably. They said the local police have a wider jurisdiction and greater resources."

"Have you talked to them?" her mother asked.

"I did, and I told them of my suspicions about the Moroccan. The captain I spoke to said he'd follow up on that lead. That was today."

Nadira stopped rubbing his back but continued to stand behind him. "Surely they would have investigated him immediately," she said.

"The campus police told me that he had stopped attending classes and was receiving his assignments by e-mail. Doesn't that sound suspicious to you?"

"Well, I'm doing the same thing."

"Has anyone tried to kill *him*?"

"Maybe. Today I saw an article in the paper about a foreign student from Morocco who found a bomb under his car yesterday."

He turned and looked at her, with his eyes squinting. "Did it give his name?"

"No. It said he wouldn't give it."

"Where was it?"

"At some motel on New Hampshire Avenue. Let me get the paper for you." She went into the pantry where they collected newspapers for recycling. It was lying on top of the pile. She picked it up, laid it before him, and pointed to the article.

He read quickly and then looked first at Nadira, then at his wife. "Obviously the police know all about this since they removed the bomb. But if that was Ahmed, why would he have been staying at a motel?"

"You said he's getting his assignments by e-mail." Nadira said.

"There are a lot of Arab people around here. A lot of North Africans. It would be an enormous coincidence. But it's something that should be investigated."

"But if it was Ahmed, wouldn't that prove that he is also a target of someone and not guilty of hurting me?"

He turned and fully faced Nadira. "Not in the least. In fact, it would place him in the middle of some kind of terroristic activity, making it even more likely that he was behind the attack." His voice became very forceful. "Now I want you to stop protecting him. He had to be involved in your attack in some way. You'll see." He stood, picked up the paper and his tea, and walked into the living room.

Tom heard the phone ring only once. "Hello," Lauren answered.

"This is Tom Parker."

"Oh, hi," she said, enthusiastically.

Encouraged by the tone of her voice, he asked, "How're you doing?"

"Okay. Still camping out here in Carroll Hall. That makes it a little hard to find my clothes. Other than that I'm just peachy."

"I was wondering if you'd like some company tonight."

There was a slight pause. "I'd love it. I'd like to get out of this mess for a while."

Great! he almost said. "I thought you might."

"Do you have something in mind?"

"Are you hungry?"

"Not really," she said. "I just had supper a half hour ago. Dessert, maybe." She laughed.

"That sounds good to me too. When can you be ready?"

"Twenty minutes?"

"How about seven o'clock?"

"That'd be good."

"I'll pick you up in front of the dorm."

A few minutes before seven he was parked in front of Carroll Hall. *I like this girl,* he thought. *A rare mixture of pragmatism and femininity.* Just then he saw her emerge from the dorm, wearing jeans and a sweater. *I like the way she carries herself too.* She waved when she saw his car. He got out and walked around the car and opened the door for her.

"Such formality," she commented.

"Something my mother taught me." He grinned. He hustled around the car and got in. "There's a place about a mile from here that makes their own cupcakes. Amazing cupcakes. Like a meal in themselves. And they have ice cream by the ounce. Serve-yourself ice cream."

"Umm. Sounds like my kind of place," she said.

"All right!" he said, and off they went.

Sitting before huge cupcakes and cafe lattes on a tiny table, they talked and laughed about food they liked and disliked, foods their parents made them eat, foods they grew to accept, and foods they refused to try. The conversation turned to movies, music, celebrities, and social websites. It all seemed to Tom as meaningless chatter, yet he was getting to know Lauren in the process. More than her preferences, he was unconsciously evaluating her personality. It had begun at their first meeting at Starbucks several weeks earlier, and it had accelerated eight days ago at the hospital in Tacoma Park and had continued ever since. He had seen her in many circumstances in a short period of time. Even though he was unaware of what was happening in his subconscious mind, he knew that his attraction to her continued to increase.

They left the sweet shop after about an hour and drove back to the campus. Tom asked, "What do you hear from Nadira?"

"I saw her today! She's feeling like she's in jail. Her father won't let her go out until they find the guy who attacked her."

"I really don't blame him. I mean, if I had a daughter who'd been attacked like she was, I'd probably do the same thing."

"This could go on for a long time. Apparently, they don't have a suspect."

"Wow. No motive, no suspect, not even a guess."

"Her dad still thinks Ahmed had something to do with it."

"I'm going to see him in the morning."

"More taxes?"

"No, he just wants to talk. Someone planted a bomb under his car Wednesday night."

Lauren sat up straight and jerked her head toward Tom. "I saw that in the paper! I was at Nadira's. We both saw it. But we didn't think it could have been Ahmed. This is serious business!"

"He was very, very lucky that he found it before it went off."

"How?"

"He saw mud marks on the pavement beside his car and looked under it as a precaution and saw it."

"Does he know who did it?"

"I don't know. He didn't want to talk about it on the phone. That's why we're getting together tomorrow."

"Why you? Shouldn't he be going to the police?" Lauren frowned.

"He's already done that. Did the paper say anything about police being there?"

"I guess it did. I'm not sure."

"Well, he told me the police were there in force."

They stopped in front of Carroll Hall. Lauren said, "Tom, this is very scary. First Nadira, now Ahmed. Who's next? And why?"

CHAPTER 25

It was cold on Saturday morning. Tom waited inside, watching through the window beside the front door for Ahmed to arrive. He held a small paper bag containing two warm cinnamon rolls. When he saw Ahmed walking briskly toward his house, he went out. They met at Tom's car.

"Howdy, Ahmed," Tom said.

"Good-morning. You sound like a cowboy." Ahmed laughed.

"Yep. And here's our wagon." He pointed at his car. "Climb aboard."

Inside, Tom said, "My mom sent you some cinnamon rolls she made this morning. We can stop for coffee to wash them down with."

"Wash them down?" Ahmed laughed. "I understand."

Before they drove off Tom asked, "Do you have an ID card with your picture on it?"

"I have a driver's license."

"Maryland?"

"Yes."

"Good. I checked online this morning. Navy does not have a home football game today, so we can get around Annapolis. On game days it's impossible. With your license we can get into the Naval Academy."

"I don't understand. What is *navy*?"

"It's what we call the US Naval Academy. It's a college to prepare people to be naval officers."

"Oh, I understand. That would be interesting."

After a brief stop to buy coffee to go, they took the beltway toward Route 50. Tom said, "Ahmed, do you want to talk about the bomb incident or something else?"

"I want to tell you that I think God spared my life Thursday morning. I believe he drew my attention to the markings on the pavement and prompted me to look under my car. I would normally have ignored something as obscure as mud on a parking lot pavement. But I will tell you what happened, so you can help me know if God has some reason for saving my life." He related having seen people in the parking lot late Wednesday night, thinking they were car thieves. He told Tom of the warning he had received from Rashid. He had thought he was safe by staying in motels, but the police told him how they probably found him. "I am very surprised that Rashid and Masoud could have devised a bomb. They must have cooperated with the terrorists. Even so, they failed. I am still alive. Is it possible that God has a reason to spare me?"

Tom said, "Sure, it's possible. I have no inside information about you, specifically. But, yeah. Sure." Ahmed sat silently for a minute. Tom thought, *what can I say that won't confuse him?* Tom asked, "Did something, or someone, lead you to talk to me about this?"

"No. I simply think of you as someone who has knowledge of godly things."

"All Christians, when they are baptized, are given the Holy Spirit. Those who accept the Holy Spirit can begin to learn of godly things, over time."

"Why would anyone not accept the Holy Spirit?"

"I don't know. It seems unbelievable to me. It was the main thing in the establishment of the church—the giving of the Holy Spirit."

"I think the Christians grew cold."

"Some did, but today there are many very warm Christians filled with the Holy Spirit."

"You are one of these warm Christians?"

"Yes."

"I can see that."

"Thank you."

"That's why I thought you might know about why I was spared on Thursday."

"I'll pray about it. Maybe God will give me some knowledge. That will be up to him."

"Yes, I'm sure."

The traffic was light on Route 50, and soon they exited onto Rowe Boulevard. As they passed the vacant Navy-Marine Corps Memorial Stadium, Tom said, "Here's where the Naval Academy plays their football games. We'll take a walk around the academy grounds if we can get in. But first we'll take a drive around town." They drove around Church Circle, where they admired the old Episcopal Church, and State Circle to see the state house. Then they went to the waterfront where they parked and walked around the piers to see the boats and the shops nearby. It was an overcast day, and the wind from the Chesapeake Bay was biting as it blew up the Severn River. Not many boats were out, so the piers were crowded with shiny pleasure craft, both sailboats and powerboats. Tom watched Ahmed as they walked alongside the piers. Ahmed appeared only slightly interested in the boats, so after a brief walk they returned to Tom's car and drove to Maryland Avenue where they found a vacant parking space and walked to the Naval Academy's Gate 3.

They were permitted to enter, and they began a walking tour of the "Yard" as they quickly learned it was called. After the congestion of the city, the spaciousness of the Yard was a welcome relief to Tom. *I hope this will distract Ahmed from whatever is occupying his mind,* he thought. They walked around the perimeter of a large open space filled with brick walks and monuments, ringed by buildings on all sides. Midshipmen in uniform walked briskly and visitors sauntered about the Yard.

Ahmed seemed disinterested in the buildings. None of them, except the chapel, were open to visitors. When they entered the chapel, he said as they walked in, "This is quite beautiful, although very stark, almost harsh. Perhaps it is appropriate for a military post."

"Yes, all that stone does give it a cool feeling," Tom observed as they walked down the center aisle.

When they reached the end of the nave, Ahmed stopped, gazing at the windows. "Oh, my, such beautiful windows. Now this is superior. These windows make this building into a place of worship."

Shortly after leaving the chapel Ahmed shivered in his light jacket and said, "It seems to be getting colder."

"I agree. We've seen enough, I think. We should probably be heading back."

As they were walking to the car, Ahmed's cell phone rang. "Oh, hello," he answered. Ahmed looked at his watch. He turned to Tom and asked, "Will we be back in College Park by three?"

Tom glanced at his watch and then nodded.

"Yes, I'll be available then," Ahmed spoke into his phone. He appeared to listen for a few seconds and then said, "Okay, I'll be there."

Ahmed slipped his phone back into his pocket. "This whole attack on Nadira and the attempts on my life are wearing me down. I should probably go a long way from here. Maybe back home."

"What's keeping you here?" Tom asked.

"Mainly, Nadira. I want to continue to help the police apprehend who did it. I think I'm the only one with reliable information."

"What about your business partners?" They arrived at the car.

In the car Ahmed continued, "I suspect my ex-partners have joined with the terrorists. They are obviously afraid I will reveal some of their questionable business practices to the authorities, and then the source of money for the terrorists will be gone. I really think that's why they had a bomb put under my car, although I doubt that they know how to do it. They probably asked the terrorists to do it for them."

"Questionable business practices, huh? Like what?" He turned his head toward Ahmed, then back toward the street.

"Tom, I don't want to in any way involve you in this matter. It might endanger your safety or bring police questioning to you. The less you know, the better it is for you."

I don't know how to respond to that, Tom thought. He said nothing.

Ahmed continued, "I look to you for guidance on spiritual issues. I want to be on the same side as God. In you I see someone who is on God's side. You are a trustworthy man."

Tom looked straight ahead. "Thank you, Ahmed. I hope I won't disappoint you."

"Don't worry. I know you are a man, just like me. No one is without faults. I don't think you can know everything. But I know you'll be honest with me."

Tom thought, *Does he see Jesus in me? Somehow I need to make him understand that.* He said, "Does it bother you that I'm of another faith?"

"It might to some Muslims. But I know you follow a great prophet. You would not have told me about the Holy Spirit if it weren't true."

This is astonishing! And challenging. "I'll pray about your question, and if I learn anything, I'll let you know."

"Is that how you learn, in prayer?" In his peripheral vision Tom could see Ahmed looking at him.

Tom glanced at Ahmed and then returned his eyes to the road. "To learn if God has a special purpose or a particular message or meaning for someone, yes. But we learn from pastors and teachers about Jesus and our religion."

"Our prayers are more structured. We learn from our teachers too. But I don't think I'm worthy to hear directly from God. To be honest, I haven't spent much time in prayer lately, since I've been in America really."

"Why is that?" Tom asked.

Ahmed raised the palms of his hands. "It's just that it seems so, you know, futile. I mean, why does God need us to repeat these things over and over and over? Perhaps I am being disrespectful in even saying this. Does Christianity have required prayers?"

"I think some forms of Christianity do, but my church doesn't. There is just one prayer that Jesus taught his disciples, but we understand it to be more of a prayer outline than a required prayer. We recite it often, though," he shrugged.

Ahmed became quiet as they turned onto Route 50. They drove in silence for a while. Suddenly Ahmed said, "Tell me about Christian forgiveness."

Lord, give me wisdom, Tom prayed silently. "Forgiveness has been a central part of Jesus's ministry from the time he began to preach in public. According to the Bible, he often told people their sins were forgiven before healing them. It has been a major part of Christianity ever since. We believe that if someone stops doing the wrong he is doing and asks God, in Jesus's name, to forgive him, God will forgive him."

Ahmed asked, "Do your laws recognize God's forgiveness?"

"No. This country's government is separated from religion."

"Then of what value is forgiveness?"

"It's of value when we die."

"So, if I steal from you and later give it back, I could still be arrested for stealing?"

"If you stole money from me and then gave it back, I would forgive you because of Jesus. If the authorities asked me to charge you with theft, I would not. So the authorities would not prosecute you. But if you stole money from a non–Christian or committed a crime against the government and later repaid it, that person or the government might not forgive you and might turn you over to the prosecutors. It depends a lot on the crime and the nature of the government officials."

"I don't understand the value of forgiveness. If I am punished by the authorities for a crime, wouldn't God honor that? Would God punish me again when I die? I don't think so. God is merciful. Why would I need to be forgiven?"

Tom thought, *Lord, help me.* After a few minutes of silence, Tom said, "I agree with you that if you were punished for a crime, God wouldn't punish you again. The value in forgiveness is that when we die we know our sins, wrongs for which we weren't punished while alive, won't be held against us if we repented and asked forgiveness when we were alive."

"What does that word mean, that word you said, if we... something?"

"Repented?"

"Yes."

"Basically, it is a decision to not sin any more. When you decided to give back the money you stole from me, that was repentance. It also means turning to a new direction, such as, turning away from godlessness toward Jesus."

Ahmed didn't respond. Tom glanced at him, but he was turned toward the side window. After awhile Ahmed said, "That causes many questions for me. More than I can ask right now." He was quiet for the remainder of the ride back to College Park.

When they were close to Tom's house, he said, "Can I drop you off at your car?"

Ahmed answered, "Please, just let me out at the corner of the street and then watch to make sure I am safely in my car and away."

"Can do," said Tom.

"Can you give me the name of the lawyer you told me about and his phone number?"

Tom looked at his address book on his phone. "I don't have it with me. I have it at home. I'll call you in a few minutes and give it to you."

Tom watched as Ahmed walked to his car and drove away. *What's going on in that guy's brain?* he thought. He shook his head. As soon as he went into his house, he found the lawyer's name and number and called Ahmed.

Ahmed had just enough time to buy a sandwich and get to the police station for his meeting with Hashim. On the way he attempted to call the lawyer but only received a message saying the office was closed until Monday. *I definitely need some legal advice on what to expect if I confess to the police about the money. If I could do that, it might explain to the police why Rashid and Masoud and the terrorists are trying to eliminate me. But, doing that will incriminate them, and they'll be arrested. I'm no better than they are. I was part of the illegal operation for almost a year. What a hypocrite I'd be. And I could be endangering my safety for the rest of my life.*

Ahmed finished his sandwich in the police station parking lot. He was guessing that Hashim would try to infiltrate the Servants and through them make contact with the terrorists. Even so, he knew it would be hard to identify who attacked Nadira. Inside the station he told his name to the desk clerk, who asked him to wait. In about five minutes he saw Hashim come in. Hashim was not much taller than Ahmed but was broad shouldered and considerably more muscular than Ahmed. He walked with an easy stride like someone who exercised often. Hashim saw Ahmed but ignored him, walking past him down the corridor. In a minute the desk clerk told Ahmed to go to room 3. In the room Hashim greeted Ahmed with a smile and shook his hand. "Sorry I had to ignore you out there but you know the procedure." Hashim said.

They sat in metal chairs facing each other. Hashim began, "I need you to tell me all about the charity you guys run. Just start talking, and I'll stop you when I need to and ask questions."

Ahmed told him everything about the Servants of Mercy except for their keeping three-quarters of the money for themselves. He gave him all the details of where the donations arrived, how they acknowledged them, what bank the money went to, and how they forwarded it on to Iraq.

Near the end of the conversation Hashim asked, "Who does your accounting?"

Ahmed hesitated, instantly realizing that if Hashim dug very deeply into the money, he would find out about his recent transaction and request for an IRS form 1099. He covered his hesitation by looking into his cell phone address book, and then he told him the name of the accountant and his phone number. A wave of dread washed over him, and then his whole abdomen grew cold. He hoped that Hashim hadn't perceived his discomfort with his question, yet he knew that what was to happen may have slipped out of his control. Their meeting was over five minutes later, and Ahmed was grateful.

When her phone signaled that she had a text message, Lauren saw that it was from Martha. "Will u b at the mtg tomorrow?"

She texted back, "I guess so. Where is it?"

"I'll call you."

Soon her phone rang. "Hi, Martha. Happy Saturday."

Martha laughed. "Hi, Lauren. How's it going? Still camping out?"

"Yeah, and it's a mess."

"When are you moving?"

"Monday, if my help shows up. Tom said he'd be here. He's such a good guy."

There was a noticeable pause. "Yes, he is, isn't he?" Lauren perceived a sight change in her voice.

"Well, where's the meeting tomorrow? The regular place?"

"That's why I wanted to call. Tomorrow we're meeting at the chapel."

"Oh. That's cool. I can almost roll down there from here."

"Yeah, but you might arrive looking kind of grungy."

"I suppose so. I guess I'll walk. Anything special we'll be doing?"

"Communion."

"That's good. Okay, I'll be there. Thanks for letting me know."

"Good. I'll see you tomorrow. Bye."

"Bye."

Lauren's head dropped onto her arm on her desk. *I hope it's just my imagination. But there's something there. Is he going out with her too?* A heavy cloud had formed around her heart. After a few minutes she lifted her head and said, "Lauren, listen to me. You have no claim on Tom. A lot of girls probably like him. But he asked you out last night. That's all you need right now."

CHAPTER 26

First on Ahmed's agenda on Monday morning was to contact the attorney. He started calling at eight o'clock, and called every fifteen minutes until he received an answer at nine. "Mr. Henry, my name is Ahmed Suliman. Tom Parker gave me your name. I need some legal advice. Can I see you today?"

"Not today, I'm afraid. I have appointments all day long."

"Please, sir. This is very urgent."

"I'm very sorry, Mr. Suliman, but as I said—"

"I think I'm about to be arrested. But I'm sure it can be avoided with the help of an attorney."

"I don't believe I'm the person who can help you. I have a partner who deals more in criminal matters. Let me see if he can help you today. Just hold on for a minute or two."

Ahmed paced around his motel room, his nerves on edge after a weekend of anxiety about Hashim's impending conversation with the accountant. In about five minutes he heard a new voice on his cell phone.

"This is John Kelly. How can I help you?"

"My name is Ahmed Suliman. I'm afraid I will be arrested soon, maybe today. But with legal representation I may be able to avoid it."

"What is your situation?"

"I'd prefer to discuss it in person if you can give me some time today. The sooner the better."

"Yes. Of course. But please give me some basic information. What are you to be arrested for?"

"Financial things, like hiding money in other countries and not paying taxes, but things I have—I think the word is repented of."

"I see. Well, can you meet with me at eleven?"

"Yes. Certainly."

Kelly gave him the address and asked for Ahmed's phone number.

After the call Ahmed dropped onto a chair and exhaled a chest full of air, as if he'd been holding his breath since Saturday afternoon. He closed his eyes and rocked back and forth as his body began to relax somewhat.

In the meantime, on the campus Lauren busied herself with moving from Carroll Hall into her new room in nearby Cecil Hall. Lauren had already carried over a plastic bag full of linens and towels when Tom called.

"Hi, Tom."

"Good-morning. Are you ready to move your stuff to Cecil?"

"Ha. I've already carried one load over, and I'm on my way back for more."

"Well. No flies on you."

"The sooner I can get my things organized the better. I'm weary of living in a heap."

"I'm glad to know that."

"Why?"

"I just am. I'll be up there in about ten minutes."

"Wonderful."

"Okay. See you soon."

Back in her room at Carroll Hall she used the few minutes before Tom arrived to put things in bags that she'd left hanging on chairs and on the closet door. *I don't want him to see that I contribute to this mess.* She looked at herself in the mirror, straightened her hair, and put on lipstick. As she busied herself, a warm and jittery sensation was inside of her, and she knew it was there because Tom was on his way. *My heart is smiling,* she thought.

Soon she heard two raps on the open door frame and turned as Tom came in. Inside her it was like a bell rang, although a silent bell. She stood with her feet together and her arms extended toward him. "Tom! My savior!"

"Not quite," he said, laughing. "Just your helper."

"Well, I'm glad you're here." She dropped her hands to her sides.

He glanced around. "This doesn't look like much of a heap to me. Maybe a neat heap. Any particular order for this stuff to go?"

"Nope. Everything goes except the furniture."

In no more than an hour they moved all of Lauren's belongings to Cecil Hall. As they brought in the last of it, she sat on the edge of the bed and looked around the room. "Now I've got a heap here." Having worked alongside Tom for an hour, the warm glow inside her had become an intense fire. She stood and walked over to where he was standing. She rubbed his left arm and said, "I really appreciate all the help you've given me."

"It was my pleasure," he said and took her left hand in his right hand. She involuntarily moved slightly toward him. She looked into his eyes and smiled as his eyes met hers. They gazed at each other for a long moment. Her heart almost leaped out of her chest as he drew her to him and kissed her, a long and soft kiss. As their lips separated, she pulled her face up against his.

"Oh, Tom. Is this really happening, or is it a dream?" Fireworks were bursting inside her, her joy glorious.

"I hope it's not a dream," He whispered. His breath was warm on her cheek.

Tom gently took her face in his hands and pulled her lips back to his, and she could feel his hands caressing her hair as they kissed. *I love this man,* she thought. *Should I tell him? Maybe not.*

Tom stepped back and glanced at his watch. "I don't want to leave, but I have a class I can't miss in about four minutes. Midterm."

"I understand."

"I don't want this to end. Can I see you later? For lunch maybe?"

"Anywhere you want. I want to be with you."

"Okay." He bent toward her and kissed her lightly. "I'll call you when class is over." He turned and jogged down the hall to the stair and disappeared.

Lauren closed the door and leaned on it. She held her eyes closed for a moment and then let out a guttural noise, a deep, throaty moan. She threw herself on the bed. "Oh, Tom. Tom. I love you, Tom." She stood on the bed and jumped up and down. "I'm in love. I'm in love. I love you, Tom," she yelled, bouncing as if she were on a trampoline. She stepped off the bed and danced around the room as if she were being held, all the time smiling broadly.

"I need to tell someone! Martha? No, no, no. She would be crushed. Nadira." She found her phone and punched in Nadira's number.

Ahmed was parked at the lawyer's office at 10:45 a.m. He waited for five minutes before he went in. John Kelly was a large man. He looked huge to Ahmed. *This is good,* Ahmed thought. *He could intimidate most people to get his way.* The two of them sat at a large polished wood conference table, Kelly at the head and Ahmed at Kelly's left side.

Kelly said, "Tell me in detail what your situation is and what you want me to do for you." His voice was deep and forceful. He placed a pad of legal paper before him and prepared to take notes as Ahmed spoke.

"Will this be completely in confidence?"

"Yes, of course."

Ahmed told him the entire story, beginning with forming the Servants of Mercy. "From the start, Rashid seemed like he knew how to set this up. He knew how to deal with the tax system in America. He said we needed tax-exempt status, so we got it. Support for orphaned kids in the Middle East, the application stated. He said we'd get an accountant and send him a list of the checks that go to the orphanage, but not our shares. He assured us that is how it should be done. If they ever audited us, the books would be there, all very proper. Why would the authorities look any further? They'd never see the money we were putting into our own accounts, which we gradually transfer overseas in small amounts, so it won't attract attention. I was amazed at how much money came in and how much we accumulated." Ahmed explained how they had hidden it, each of them setting up his own network of accounts.

He told him of the demand of the terrorists and the attack on Nadira. He explained that he had resigned from the Servants of Mercy and had transferred most of his money to the orphanage, all except what he thought was a reasonable administrative fee, and paid the estimated income tax.

"I did not wish to implicate my former partners, and I told them that I had not done so. I didn't want to be seen as—what is the English word?"

"A snitch?"

"No, a funny word, something about a bird."

"Oh, yeah," Kelly laughed. "A stool pigeon."

"Yes, that's it. However, knowing that I had been questioned by the police, they did not believe me. They warned me that they would kill me, so I went into hiding, staying at motels, and receiving my school assignments by e-mail. Then last Wednesday night someone attempted to blow up my car, but I discovered the bomb. I'm sure they were behind it."

"They who?"

Ahmed looked at Kelly and said impatiently, "Rashid and Masoud. Then I learned last Saturday that the police are going to talk to our accountant. He will certainly reveal that a large sum was transferred to Iraq recently, and that I registered a salary of $55,000 and asked that the proper documents be submitted to the tax authorities. The police will easily see that something irregular has been happening and may quickly deduce that Rashid and Masoud are guilty of the same kind of activities I was engaged in." He glanced at Kelly.

"Go on." He waved his hand at Ahmed.

"Mr. Kelly, I am afraid that all three of us will be jointly implicated and all charged with the same crimes. I'm asking that you go to the police in my behalf and secure some form of immunity for me if I confess what I've done and have repented, before they speak to the accountant and reach their own conclusions." He looked directly at Kelly, with his eyebrows raised and his face long, imploring him to help.

Kelly said nothing for a minute or two while he glanced over his notes, then he returned Ahmed's look of entreaty. "Ahmed, the police you've been dealing with have no jurisdiction over money laundering crimes. In addition, the IRS will probably find reason to charge you with tax fraud. Your having paid to the orphanage the money you had collected will not protect you from having participated in the money laundering and tax fraud crimes still ongoing by your associates. If you confess these things to the local police, they will have no alternative than to turn you over to the federal authorities. I believe it would be better for you to go to the federal authorities."

"What will happen if I do?"

"They will expect you to cooperate fully, revealing everything about your financial dealings, and I mean the three of you. You will have to be a stool pigeon. And if you do, you can expect a measure of leniency, but you'll probably not escape prosecution altogether. But tell me more about the attack on the girl. Is this the same attack at UM that's been the newspapers recently?"

"Yes." Ahmed nodded.

"Do you think your confession and cooperation would help find the perpetrator of that crime?"

Ahmed thought for a moment. "That would probably require the cooperation of Rashid and Masoud. They don't know who the terrorists are, but they may be able to give the police enough evidence to find them. I was able to take some pictures of them. I—"

"How did you do that?"

Ahmed told them about leaving the checks in the chapel and taking pictures of the terrorists when they picked them up. "I gave the pictures to the police, but they said they couldn't tell much from them."

"Do you still have them?"

"Yes, they're in my cell phone."

"Good. Well, Mr. Suliman, I will take your case. As you say, we'll have to act quickly. You will have to be completely honest with me. So let's get to work."

CHAPTER 27

As he walked away from his eleven o'clock class, Tom was smiling. *Wow!* he thought. *Wow! Zing! That was so good. I think she likes me.* He pulled his phone from his pocket and called Lauren.

"Hi, Tom," she purred.

"Hi. Ready for lunch?"

"It'll have to be fast. I have a one o'clock class. Where are you?"

"I just left Martin Hall. Since you're pressed for time, why don't we just have a sub? I can be there in five minutes."

"That's good. I'll see you there."

They arrived simultaneously. The line was long. They chatted as they waited their turn. Lauren, standing backward in the line said, "I talked to Nadira this morning. I told her you helped me move. She likes you. She said you're handsome."

"Hmmm." He smiled a smirky smile. "Maybe I should get to know her better."

She frowned, then brightened and said, "That would be hard right now since she can't leave home until they find her attacker."

He shrugged, "Does she think they're making any progress?"

"The police?" She looked over her shoulder at the line and moved a step.

"Yeah."

"No. I didn't ask her today, but on Friday she said they haven't. Her father thinks Ahmed is involved. What do you think?" Her eyes narrowed. "You spent some time with him on Saturday, didn't you?"

Tom frowned. "He's a complex guy, and something seems to be bothering him." He shook his head as he said, "But I don't think he'd hurt Nadira. I believe he loves her. If he didn't, he'd have gone back to Morocco."

"Sounds like Romeo and Juliet." She grinned. "But if he can't see her, what good does it do him to stay here?"

With a look of skepticism he said, "He says he's trying to help the police find her attacker."

"Oh. But I'll bet he'll try to see her." She turned around as they reached the counter.

They ordered their sandwiches. Lauren said, "I'll pay. It's the least I can do for all the help you've given me."

Tom smiled. "Thanks."

They ate quickly so Lauren could get to her class on time. They went out, held hands for a moment, and then parted on the sidewalk, she to her class and Tom to his car, parked beyond the engineering buildings.

Tom thought he should let Pete know of their growing relationship. He was in his car but still in the parking lot. Pete answered promptly, as he usually did, eager to keep in touch with the ministry participants.

"Hi, Pete. Thought I should give you a heads up. Lauren Stevenson and I have been seeing a lot of each other lately, and it seems that a relationship is growing here. It grew out of the aftermath of the attack on her roommate."

"Well, well, well," Pete answered. "So Tom Parker has been smitten. I'm glad you told me."

"I wanted to let you know before you hear about if from someone else. I know it can be a little awkward."

"Not if you aren't hanging all over each other in public. When you're ready for it to be known, Sharon and I will let the word get around to avoid rumors. But don't wait very long if it looks like this will be permanent."

"Up till now we've just been to eat together, but it's inevitable that someone'll see us and put two and two together. I'll talk to Lauren about that and let you know."

"She's new to CCA and hasn't had time for the class on dating and morals. Who is her discipler?"

"Martha."

"Oh, yeah. I knew that. I'll have Sharon talk to her about that class."

"That's good. Well, I just wanted you to know. We're having midterms now, so I must be off to study."

"Okay, Tom. Thanks for letting me know."

Tom drove home but before he could get out of his car his phone rang again. He saw that it was Pete. "Hey, Pete."

"Hey to you. Uh, Tom, I just talked to Sharon. It seems that we might have a touchy situation here."

"Oh?" Tom frowned.

"Yeah. It seems that Martha has had eyes for you for a long time."

"Martha?"

"Yeah."

"Martha. Hmm. I never knew. I don't suppose it would have made any difference to me. No, that's not true. I would have been uncomfortable around her. She's been like a sister to me. But no sparks. Well, what now, coach?"

"Sharon and I both thought you should know, and that Lauren should know. Sharon will speak to Martha as soon as she can and gauge her reaction. In all probability she'll need some time to grieve, so for the time being you should try to stay away from her, if you can."

"She's been going with us on Wednesdays for the Islam class."

"Oh, yes. Well, I'll have Sharon talk to her right away and get back to you about that."

"That's good. I'm sorry to have sprung this on you. You have enough on your plate as it is."

"No, it's just part of life. It happens more than you might think. It's perfectly natural. So don't worry about it. We just want to avoid division or other complications. I'll let you know about Wednesday."

"Okay, Pete. Thanks."

Ahmed met with John Kelly again after lunch. Kelly began, "We need a stronger link to the attack on the girl than you've given me. At this moment all we have to go on is your hunch that the attackers were the same people who want part of the take of your nonprofit. I don't think the police can establish a connection, do you?"

"But who else could it be?"

"Look. Attacks on women happen all the time and for all kinds of reasons. They probably already have some DNA material belonging to her attacker. But unless they can find someone with matching DNA it doesn't do them much good. Right?"

Ahmed sighed deeply. "I suppose you're right."

"Besides, how on earth would the terrorists even know the girl—what's her name?"

"Nadira."

"Nadira even existed?"

"Well, I think I was being watched while I was with Nadira Monday night two weeks ago." He gave Kelly the specifics of that incident as he remembered them.

"So this guy saw you talking to two girls, you're telling me, and for about ten minutes. How do you suppose he found out her name and her room number?"

"I don't know. How did they find out about the Servants?"

"That's on the Internet, for heaven's sake. Her attacker had to know she was alone! How did he know that?"

Ahmed shook his head. "I don't know," he whispered.

"Ahmed, this isn't enough to make your confession worth anything. You've got to have a lot more concrete evidence about who attacked Nadira. Period. Now, who knew anything about her besides you?"

"She has a roommate and other students who live around her know of her, of course. Rashid and Masoud know about her. Rashid had warned me to stop seeing her, thinking I would sooner or later reveal our operation to her."

"Oh. Now that's something. Tell be about that."

Ahmed told him of their conversation shortly before Nadira's attack.

Kelly made some notes. "How long have you known Rashid?"

"About two years."

"Have you considered the possibility that he is connected to the terrorists?"

"I suppose it's possible that Rashid was involved with them since the beginning." A sudden realization struck him. "Maybe all along he's been raising money for the terrorists and now they want more, and he attacked Nadira as a warning to Masoud and me." Ahmed stood and began pacing around the room. "How could I have been so stupid?" He stopped and asked himself, "But why would he have advised us to refuse the terrorists?" Immediately he answered his own question. "To appear to us that he was against them. Mr. Kelly, I think that is a very likely idea."

"But it's only a theory at this time. We need more evidence to make it a probable scenario. Even a plausible scenario would help us. Sit down, Ahmed. Let's think this through."

They spent the next half hour talking about Rashid and all the interactions Ahmed could remember that would point to him as the perpetrator of Nadira's attack. Finally Kelly said, "Ahmed, we're no closer to positively implicating Rashid than when we started. Let's talk about Masoud."

They spent another fifteen minutes exploring Masoud's relationship with Ahmed. But other than showing him to be a bully, nothing pointed to him as Nadira's attacker. At about three o'clock Kelly said, "I think our best approach to the police is to tell them that, one way or another, Rashid is connected voluntarily to Nadira's attack. But it's all related to the money. Although we can't prove it, Rashid is probably an agent for the terrorists. You may not be aware of it, but I'd guess that the FBI is already investigating him and will soon have some of his DNA to compare with that found on Nadira. The information you've given me will undoubtedly strengthen their case against him even if the DNA comparison is inconclusive. Rashid may not have carried out the attack himself, but he's the only one beside you who could have known enough details of Nadira's life to make it happen. Do you agree?"

Ahmed was elated. "Yes, it sounds very possible to me."

"The only problem is that money laundering is a federal crime, and the attack on Nadira is a state crime. I think we can avoid any problems with tax evasion because you've paid estimated taxes for this year. It would help even more if you paid taxes for last year, and do it as soon as possible. You'll have a penalty for late filing, but it won't be much. But money laundering... I don't know. I think if you confess to money laundering and fraud to the local police, they'll have no alternative than to notify the federal attorney. And he'll probably treat the three of you the same. But if you confess to the federal attorney, he might agree to some kind of plea bargain."

Ahmed frowned at Kelly. "So what are you telling me to do?"

"I think we go to the local police with the theory that Rashid is connected materially to the terrorists and is responsible for the attack on Nadira. Then we should go to the federal attorney and confess about money laundering on the basis of remorse and—"

"What is *remorse?*"

"Remorse is recognizing that you've done something wrong and are sorry about it."

"I understand. Go on."

"Confess out of remorse and hope that he will be lenient with you."

"But you expect some punishment?"

"Yes."

"Imprisonment?"

"Probably."

Ahmed stood again and walked around the conference room without speaking for a few minutes. Kelly waited for his response. Ahmed placed both his hands on the back of a chair and looked at Kelly. "Mr. Kelly, I trust Captain Parsons. I wish to confess everything to him. If he thinks it should be reported to the federal attorney, let him make that decision. I do not trust a federal attorney I do not know."

"So be it," Kelly said. "You should know that you'll be Rashid's accuser, and Rashid will be entitled to know that."

Ahmed's stomach tightened when he heard that, but he quickly realized that they'd already attempted to kill him so matters couldn't be worse.

Kelly concluded their meeting with explaining to Ahmed what to expect over the next few hours. "The next thing to happen is I will have a conversation with the police. That's the Prince George's County Police, right?"

"Yes. I've been talking to Captain Parsons since the beginning."

"Good. I'll talk to him, telling him that we have information to present to him. But first I want to write down what I think you've told me, and I want you to review it to make sure it's accurate. I'll call you when it's done, probably in an hour or so."

"May I wait here?"

"Sure. Just hang out around here, and I'll come and find you."

An hour later, Ahmed reviewed the summary John Kelly had written, made a few corrections, and approved it. Kelly called the Hyattsville police station and spoke to Captain Parsons and then said to Ahmed, "He'll see us at eight tomorrow morning. Can you go then?"

"Yes. That'll work well. I have a midterm exam at one, and I have to go to class to take it. I'm doing all my classes by e-mail, but I have to be there in person to take the tests."

"All right, I'll meet you there."

CHAPTER 28

On the way to the police station on Tuesday morning, Ahmed reflected, *I thought I'd be frightened to be doing this, but more than that I'm eager to get it over with. I will trust Allah to make Captain Parsons merciful or, at least, so grateful for the information I'm bringing him that he'll be lenient with me. I wonder if Allah knows me. Surely he does, but he may be punishing me now for what I have done. Perhaps Jesus would forgive me and spare me this. Is he still alive as the Christians think he is? How does a man find the answers to these questions? Growing up among Muslims I knew no other way. But the Christians, who grew up among other Christians, knew no other way. Who is correct?*

It was a short drive to the police station, and soon Ahmed and John Kelly were being led into a room familiar to Ahmed. Captain Parsons and another officer were there waiting. Kelly introduced himself to Parsons and said, "I believe you know Mr. Suliman."

"Oh, yes. How are you, Ahmed?" Parsons appeared more serious than his greeting suggested.

"Nervous, sir," Ahmed answered as he shook Parson's hand.

"Mr. Kelly tells me you have new information for us, is that correct?" He looked at Kelly.

"Yes, and I'd like for Ahmed to tell you in his own words. First, it is information about the probable attacker of Nadira Shalash and, secondly, reasons why Ahmed's former business partners wish to harm him. These two items are interconnected and may be considered a confession of sorts on Ahmed's part, and I'll have more to say on that matter after Ahmed speaks."

Parsons said, "Ahmed, you are under no requirement to say anything to incriminate yourself, and if you choose to speak, anything you say may be used against you in a court of law. You are entitled to an attorney, which you have with you, and I assume that you are acting in accordance with his advice. Do you understand?"

Ahmed responded quickly, "Yes, sir."

"Please have a seat," Parsons said to Ahmed and Kelly. "This interview will be recorded." He looked at Ahmed and Kelly, neither of whom objected. "Go ahead, Ahmed."

Ahmed sat upright. He rubbed his hands together, looked at them, and then wiped them on his pants. He swallowed hard and then began, telling them in detail how he, Rashid, and Masoud had set up the Servants of Mercy. "Among the many topics was our administrative fee and payment to ourselves for the work we do. Of course, we did not know how much money we would raise. Rashid said 25 percent to each of us. I didn't question that, having had no experience in those matters, so that became our standard.

"In about eight months all was in order, and we began soliciting money. Money arrived slowly, but we began sending small amounts of money to Iraq via a bank in Liechtenstein. The response from the orphanage was deep gratitude, and I was extremely happy to be doing something good for others. Each of us deposited our payments in our own personal bank accounts. At first our personal payments were small, so 25 percent seemed appropriate. But the contributions increased steadily, and our personal payments increased as well. Rashid told us that soon we would have too much money in checking accounts, and that we should begin investing it. He explained to Masoud and me that we should move our money to other countries and into multiple accounts where it would not be questioned by authorities. That seemed reasonable to me. At that time I knew nothing of American laws about taxation and hiding money. So I set up a system for myself that involved sending money from my local checking account to a bank in Switzerland and from there on to a bank in another country and then to investment accounts in Hong Kong. I would deposit proceeds of stock sales in a bank in Singapore."

Parsons interrupted, "What was the other country that money from Switzerland went to?"

"Turkey," Ahmed replied. "Ankara. At some point earlier this year I learned about what is called *money laundering*, and that it is illegal. That's when I realized I was a criminal, although I hadn't intended to be. It just happened. I was afraid of being caught and lived with that fear up until the time that Nadira was attacked. You know about that. Until my conversation with Mr. Kelly, I had assumed that Rashid and Masoud only learned about the laws we were breaking as I had. But when I spoke of the matter to them, they already knew. Mr. Kelly made me realize—well, helped me realize—that the only person that could have injured Nadira was Rashid. He says his name is Rashidi in Egypt, but everyone here calls him Rashid. It is probable that Rashid wanted to…what is the word…*establish* the Servants of Mercy to raise money for the terrorists. And when he knew how much was going to Masoud and me, had to invent a way for the terrorists to get it. So—"

"How much was that?" Parsons asked.

"I had received approximately $600,000."

"Had you spent it, or any of it?"

"Very little of it. And immediately after Nadira was attacked, I sent it all to the orphanage. Well, all except for $50,000. I calculated that a reasonable administration fee should be 10 percent. Some of that went to the accountant and for postage and similar expenses, and so $55,000 is my legitimate share. I figured I'd spent about $5,000." He looked at Parsons to see if he had other questions. Parsons waved at him to continue. "So I now believe that Rashid invented the threat from the terrorists, pretended to disapprove of our agreeing to let them into our organization, and even attacked, or arranged the attack on Nadira, to hide his own relationship to the terrorists."

"When did you first learn that money laundering was illegal?" Parsons asked.

"Last summer."

"Three or four months ago."

"Yes."

"But you kept sending money to your offshore accounts."

"Yes."

"Why?"

"I was reluctant to break faith with my friends. I thought that to do anything else would jeopardize them. That's why I spent very little of it. I was terribly afraid that we would be caught, even though Rashid and Masoud assured me that we would not. But after Nadira was attacked, things looked different to me. I decided that I did not want to be a criminal and should send the money on to the orphanage. I then resigned from the Servants, so I would not participate in collecting money for terrorists."

Parsons rubbed his forehead, then his whole face. "Let me get this straight. You think Rashid set up this whole operation to raise money for a terrorist group. More than likely a quarter of what you received, that is, Rashid's share, was ultimately going to the terrorists. But when the receipts became significant he, or his terrorist friends, wanted more of it, so he invented a threat and either committed the attack on Nadira or had it done to punctuate the threat, And now the terrorists are in charge. You, in the meantime, learned you were breaking the law, and after a three to four month period and an attack on your girlfriend, you decided it was time to come clean and sent all your money to the orphanage except for $55,000. Mr. Kelly, is this a valid summary?"

Kelly said, "Ahmed, tell him why you think Rashid is the only one who could have committed the attack."

Ahmed said, "Oh, I should have told you this. No one knew that Nadira existed except for her roommate, a few residents of the dorm, and me. Rashid learned about her from me. Some time before the attack on her, he warned me to stop seeing her. He thought I would tell her more than I should, or that our relationship would become deeper, and she would sooner or later learn enough to endanger our operation. That was at the same time I told him I wanted to get out, but he warned me that I should not unless the three of us agree to disband.

"Masoud knew about her too, but I don't think he knew about the terrorists until they threatened us, but maybe he did. No one else knew enough about her and me to do what was done to her. I should add that when I resigned and sent my share of the money to the orphanage, they assumed I would tell you what I just did, especially about the money. They warned me that they will kill me. I told them I hadn't told you about the money, but they didn't believe me and said that I'm a dead man."

"So the bomb under your car was almost certainly initiated by them."

Ahmed nodded.

Parsons said to Ahmed, "Go out to the desk and have a seat there. I want to talk to your attorney for a few minutes. He'll tell you what you'll need to know."

Ahmed stood and walked out to the seating area across the room from the fat desk clerk. He waited for almost an hour, and then he was called back into the room.

"Sit down, Ahmed. I listened to your story and read the summary that Mr. Kelly prepared. Certainly your friends are guilty of money laundering and tax evasion. You've paid estimated taxes for this year covering your total income of $55,000."

"Yes, sir."

"But there's not enough evidence to prove that Rashid, or he and Masoud both, intended to set up the Servants of Mercy as a funding mechanism, or that Rashid perpetrated the attack on Nadira Shalash. I intend to report what you've told me to the US attorney. I will recommend that you not be charged, on the basis of your statement, and especially since you came here on your own volition. However, if new evidence is uncovered that proves that you are more culpable than you have revealed, you'll be subject to being charged too. In the meantime, the investigation into Nadira's attack will continue, and I want you to tell me any additional information you may obtain or that you've forgotten to tell me. Do you understand?"

"Yes, sir. Thank you."

"You're free to go now." Parsons stood. He nodded to Kelly, who gestured to Ahmed to stand and leave.

Ahmed shook Parsons' hand. "Thank you very much, sir. It feels very good to tell you all this. And soon I hope we will find Nadira's attacker."

"So do I. So do I," Parsons said.

Ahmed left the police station and, after a few words of instruction from Kelly, he returned to his motel room. He spent some time reviewing for the midterm exam, but as the time to leave drew closer, his anxiety grew more intense. He was aware that both Masoud and Rashid had classes from time to time in Van Munching, the building where the exam was to be held. At about noon, unable to focus on the material any longer, he left for the campus, leaving time to have lunch on the way. He parked near the University College, in an open lot where he could quickly get to his car and get away. Leaving his backpack and cell phone in the car, as his professor had required, he walked to Van Munching.

It was an easy exam, and Ahmed finished before the allotted time was over. He watched as some others finished and left the room. *I could leave now,* he thought, *but I'd be easier to see, out there alone.* He glanced at his watch. *There's only eight minutes left. I'll wait for the whole class to leave. I'll be safer that way.* When the proctor called time, he turned in his paper and walked out, shielded from view by the crowd. Most of the students walked toward the library, so he followed the crowd. *I should check my mail,* he thought, so he headed toward Worchester Hall. He stopped to look around, before he left the crowd. There, not twenty yards away, staring at him with his phone at his ear was Masoud.

Sudden fright invoked pinpricks over his body. Masoud stood between him and his car, so he ran in the opposite direction. He ran between Carroll Hall and the Preinkert Field House. At the street he stopped and looked back. Masoud was running toward him. *I can outrun Masoud, but I don't know about Rashid.* He ran past Worchester Hall and across McKeldin Mall. Students were stopping to look at him and his pursuer. On he ran, past Patterson Hall and across Campus Drive. Behind the Microbiology Building he swung left, beginning his wide turn toward the west and his car.

Glancing over his shoulder, he saw Masoud dropping far behind him. *I think I'm losing him,* Ahmed thought, panting hard now. He ran past the Stamp and up Fieldhouse Drive, feeling confident now. Suddenly he saw Rashid, directly ahead and coming toward him rapidly. Ahmed swerved to his right. Byrd Stadium was now blocking his way. He was breathing very hard and was tiring quickly. He could see the fence around the stadium extended all the way to the baseball field. *That's where Masoud is! I can't get around that fence! Oh! There's an open gate.* He dashed through the gate, which opened to a wide concrete walk, leading to at least four sets of stairs, each separated from the next set by a flat concrete walk. Each set of stair steps included three bright red handrails, which Ahmed found he could slide down to the next level. Very quickly he reached the bottom level. The football field stretched out before him, surrounded with high seating. He glanced back and saw that Rashid and Masoud were already entering the gate. Now exhausted, he thought, *I need a place to hide.* As he ran across the east end zone, he saw a door to the Team House and tried it. It opened and he sped inside.

A surprised student stared at him. Ahmed, panting as he spoke, pointed at the door and exclaimed, "Lock the door! Two guys are after me to kill me!"

The student stared at him, as if stunned.

Ahmed, terrified, repeated, "Lock the door! Please. And call the police. Call 911."

This time the student complied and locked the door. Through the door's window Ahmed saw Rashid and Masoud run across the field and then stop and look around.

"Are any other doors open?" Ahmed asked.

"Yeah, on the side." The student gestured toward the north side, pointing with his cell phone.

"Lock it too, please. Don't let those guys in here." He pointed out the window. As the student went to lock the other door, Ahmed watched Rashid turn toward the door Ahmed had entered and run toward it. Ahmed ducked inside a room nearby. He heard the door rattle briefly.

Seconds later he heard the student yell, "Hey, buddy, where are you?"

Ahmed answered, "I'm in here." He stuck his arm out. "Are they gone?"

The student looked out the window. "I don't see them anywhere. Who are they? What's going on?"

Ahmed, still breathing hard, said, "They're criminals, and I'm the only one who knows what they've done. Is there a way out on that side?" He pointed north.

"Yeah. The gate's open. They probably think you ran out there."

"It's too bad they're not trapped in the stadium." He heard a siren approaching.

Two police cars arrived. Ahmed explained what had happened and asked them to call Captain Parsons at the Hyattsville station to confirm his story. After they were assured of the validity of Ahmed's story, they drove him to his car. His heart was still pounding as he drove safely away.

CHAPTER 29

"Mother, I need to go to class tomorrow to take my midterm exam. Will that be all right?" Nadira was at the kitchen door as her mother prepared dinner.

"Oh. How many midterm exams do you have?"

"One tomorrow and one the next day, Thursday."

"I wonder if they'd let me sit in the classroom during the exam," her mother said.

"I think it would be very distracting for the other students. Out in the hall, maybe."

"Could you find out? I'd want to talk to your father about it."

"Yes. Of course." Nadira waved both hands in the air. "We must talk to my father about it."

Her mother's head snapped toward her. "That's uncalled for, Nadira."

Nadira glared at her, her lower lip puffed out. After a moment she dropped her eyes. "I'll find out," she said contritely as she turned and went back upstairs. She sent e-mails to both the professors and then called Lauren.

"Nadira, hi."

"Are you still on cloud nine? Can you talk like a normal human being yet?"

"I'm floating on a moonbeam," she sang.

"Oh, good grief. Come back to earth for a minute, so I can complain."

"Must I?"

"You must, if you want to have a normal conversation."

"All right, all right. Here I am. But my heart is still floating somewhere above this room that maybe, someday, you'll be able to join me in."

"Okay, heartless one. It doesn't look like I'll be joining you there any time soon. My mother wants to come with me for my midterms and even sit in the classroom, guarding her little chick while she takes her tests. Can you believe it?"

"Hmm. They probably wouldn't allow it. Maybe she could sit in the hall. She'd have to bring her own chair, though."

"A lawn chair, maybe. Or how about a chaise lounge."

Lauren laughed. "Can't she just drop you off and come back again and pick you up?"

"She knows my father wouldn't agree to that. We're going to talk about it tonight."

"Are they worried that some assassin is going to be waiting for you in a classroom full of people?"

"I guess. This is getting a little old, y'know."

"Yeah."

"So do you have another date with Tom?"

"We had lunch together yesterday. At the sub shop. Very romantic."

"I'm sure."

"We're going to church together on Wednesday night."

"That should keep you out of trouble."

"We won't even be alone in the car. Martha always goes with us. I think she likes Tom too. That might become an uncomfortable situation."

"Do you mean if she finds out about you and Tom? That's bound to happen. Soon."

"Yeah, I worry about that. She's a really nice person. On the night you were attacked she put me up, you know."

"You told me. She's a senior, isn't she?"

"Yeah. In physics."

"She must be terribly smart."

"I guess so. But I can't say anything to Tom about it. I don't know if they've dated, or what."

"Well."

"So tomorrow I'll probably just sit in the back of the car and let her sit in front and talk to Tom about CCA stuff all night. I'll just pretend nothing's going on."

"That doesn't sound right."

"What would you do?"

"I don't know. Maybe take someone else with you for her to talk to."

"Tom's dad went the first time I went. But he hasn't gone since. That's a good idea, though. I'll try to find a way to suggest it to Tom. Have you heard about any progress in finding your attacker?"

"Nothing. I'd probably be the last to know, though."

"I doubt that. Your staying home is probably as much of a burden to your mom as it is to you."

"Why? She's here all the time anyway. Most of the time. She can go out any time she wants to. And she does. She doesn't have to stay here and watch me."

"Oh. She's not a prison guard, then. That's good. For her."

"Yeah. They think I'll not break the rules. I might be here until I die if they don't find the guy who cut me."

"I hope not. I miss you being here."

"Thanks. That's nice to know. I just hope they find him soon."

"Me too. Well I'd better hit the books. I've got a midterm tomorrow, and I'm not ready for it. Thanks for the advice. Bye."

Tom's cell phone rang, breaking his concentration. He saw that it was Pete. "Good evening, Peter."

"Hi, Tom. Are you busy?"

"I'm studying for tomorrow's midterm. But I always have time to talk to you."

"You're too kind. I've got an update from the senior staff woman."

"Good. If Sharon can make some good come out of this, then she should get a medal."

"Aw, it's not such a big deal. As I told you today, this happens a lot. Sharon talked to Martha and, as we expected, it hit her pretty hard. But it's not like you and she are dating or anything, and she realized that she didn't have any claim on you. Martha cried, and they prayed together. She'll need some time to recover, and she will."

"Well, will you replace her as Lauren's discipler?"

"I don't know yet. I'll need more information from Sharon as she interacts with Martha over the next few days or weeks. I do think you should go to the training session on Wednesday without her this week. I think I'll ask Sharon to speak to Lauren in the next day or so, to ask her to be sensitive to Martha for the foreseeable future."

"That's great, Pete. Thank you. Martha's a great gal, and she's a good Christian. I'm sure she'll be all right. But, it could have turned ugly if you and Sharon hadn't stepped in."

"You're welcome, Tom. I'll see you Sunday, if not before."

"Bye."

Tom mused, *I'm so grateful to Pete for this. He's a great guy and a great leader. I can't imagine how this would turn out without him and Sharon.* He folded his hands on his desk and prayed. *Lord, thank you for CCA and how it holds us together through people like Pete and Sharon. Thanks for their willingness to minister to our emotional needs. And thank you for Lauren. I'm very fond of her, Lord, and I pray that you will protect her. Make me protect her too, and to never take advantage of her but to always respect her as one of your children. In Jesus's name, amen.*

Tom stood, stretched, and went downstairs to the empty kitchen to see if any coffee remained in the coffee pot. He had lived in the house all his life. His parents had remodeled the kitchen in the 1990s, not long after he was born. It showed its age. *It's about time they redo this place,* he thought. He'd mentioned it to his parents more than once. His father liked it the way it was, but his mother said it was time to update it. His parents were comfortable there, so changes weren't a high priority for either of them.

Tom was their only child. He didn't know if that was the way they planned it, or if it just turned out that way. He'd always had friends, at school and at church, so didn't miss having siblings. Church was like a large family to him, and he felt comfortable living among people with many generations around them. Living at home while attending college gave him a place without the interruptions many of his classmates faced. At times like the night before two exams, he was consciously grateful for that.

He found the coffee pot empty, so he opted for a Coke instead. Back in his room he looked at his cell phone. No calls. He texted to Lauren, "r u studying?"

A reply was almost instantaneous, "trying. thinking of u."

Ah, he thought. *I like that.* He texted, "that's nice. must concentrate. 2 tests tomorrow."

She replied, "too bad. I like thinking of u."

"me 2. duty calls. so sorry," he wrote,

"ok. see u tomorrow?"

"Yes. Muslim lesson. pick you up at six thirty?" he asked.

"okay, bye," she answered.

Tom smiled and then returned to his book and class notes.

While Tom studied, Ahmed was sitting in front of the single window in his motel room, staring out into the night. He hadn't moved since returning from the campus that afternoon. When he arrived at the motel he was still very frightened, and his thoughts had been too jumbled to have any rational ideas about what had just happened. Gradually his pulse and mind slowed, and now after dark, his eyes were fixed on his car, parked just outside his room. One question began taking shape: why hadn't Rashid been arrested? *Maybe they just hadn't had time to do it. Or maybe they didn't agree with my theory. Maybe Hashim needs them to be free for a while to identify the terrorists. Maybe I should go back to Morocco. If it weren't for exams, I could still do my homework by e-mail. But what about Nadira? Besides, Captain Parsons wants me to stay available. He told me to get a new cell phone. I should do that.* Late into the night, despite hunger and fatigue, he peered into the darkness, trying to develop some direction for himself. Finally, without deciding anything, he collapsed on the bed and fell asleep. A few hours later he woke, removed his shoes and went back to sleep.

Ahmed was wakened by his cell phone.

"Ahmed Suliman?" The terror of the day before immediately returned.

"Yes."

"This is Sergeant Beeman. You are wanted here at the Hyattsville Police Station."

"Again? I thought we'd been through everything."

"Apparently not. You must come directly here. Immediately."

What has happened? Why this impolite treatment? They know everything. What more can they ask? Anger welled up inside him. He washed, brushed his teeth, and left. After a ten-minute drive, he arrived at the station, where two officers ushered him into the room in which he had been questioned the day of Nadira's attack, the room with the two-way mirror on one side. He was told to sit at the small table, and immediately Captain Parsons and another man in civilian clothes came in. The two officers that brought him in left.

Ahmed stood. "Captain, what's going on? Why am I here?"

"Sit down, Ahmed. We have some questions to ask you. This is Mr. Landry."

Ahmed turned toward him. Landry nodded but did not rise or offer his hand.

Parsons said, "Mr. Landry will ask you a few questions. Go ahead." He gestured to Landry.

Landry cleared his throat. "Mr. Suliman, tell us about your family."

Ahmed shot a questioning glance at Parsons and then turned toward Landry. "My father is an engineer, my mother works at home, that is, she doesn't have a paid job. I have two sisters, one older and one younger. My older sister has recently finished college in France and is looking for work in Morocco. My younger sister is still in high school."

Landry watched him very closely when Ahmed answered his questions. "How do you get along with your sisters?"

"I admire my older sister. She is beautiful and smart. But because she is older she always regarded me as an irritant—I think that's the word—and tried to ignore me. She had her friends, and I had mine. My younger sister thinks I'm wonderful. We are nearer in age and we are closer friends than my older sister and I are. I like my younger sister, but she is sometimes a pest. Uh, what else do you want to know?"

"How do you get along with your mother?"

"We get along well. She seems closer to my sisters, and my father closer to me, although he is the authority in the family, and for that reason there is separation between us. I think my mother is proud of me, especially for going to college in America."

Landry pushed on. "Do you feel resentment because your mother is closer to your sisters than she is to you?"

"Resentment? No. Why? She needs to teach them things that only she can do. And she has to help them more." Ahmed turned to Parsons. "Captain, why these odd questions? What is going on?"

Parsons answered, "Just answer his questions, Ahmed."

Ahmed turned back toward Landry.

"Have you ever struck one of your sisters or your mother?"

"No, of course not. That would be cowardly. Absolutely forbidden."

"But have you ever wanted to strike one of them?"

"Oh, there have been a few times I would have picked up my younger sister and carried her into another room, to remove her from annoying me. But I like her too much to hurt her in any way."

"How do you feel about Nadira?"

"If you pardon me for being selfish, I am very fond of her. Her attack was a terrible thing, and I am dedicated to do all I can to help find the man who did it. I am trying to be of help to Captain Parsons to do that."

Landry smiled faintly. "How would you feel if you discovered she was seeing another man?"

Ahmed drooped noticeably and his hands fell into his lap. He sighed deeply and said, "I think it would break my heart. I would feel very sad."

"Would you be angry with her?"

Without hesitation Ahmed said, "It would be very difficult to be angry with Nadira. She is very gentle. She is a person without deceit."

"Do you trust her?"

"In what way?"

245

"To be faithful to you?"

"Sir, I have no legitimate claim on her. I would hope that she would reserve her affection for me. But I would not be surprised at all if other guys found her as attractive as I do."

"Do you watch her?"

"What do you mean?" He frowned.

"Do you watch her from a distance? Do you wait outside her dorm to see her?"

"Do you mean, spy on her? No, I never have. I usually call her first and arrange for us to meet. We really haven't dated or things like that—just walked around campus and talked."

Landry looked at his notes. "Tell us why you stay in motels. You have a dorm room and a house. Why stay in a motel?"

"I am staying in a motel to avoid being accosted by my former business partners who are trying to kill me."

"Do you know that as a fact, or are you assuming that?"

"They have told me so! And yesterday they chased me across the campus to capture me. The police came and saved my life."

Landry looked at Parsons, who nodded. Landry asked, "But weren't you staying in a motel when Nadira was attacked?"

"Yes." He looked at Parsons. "Does he know about the terrorists?"

Parsons said, "Yes, he knows the full story."

Ahmed said, "I was hiding from the terrorists. They knew everything about us including where we lived and where we went and everything we did, it seemed. They had threatened us. So I took a room in a motel to avoid being found."

Landry looked at his notes again and then said to Parsons, "I think I have enough here."

Parsons said, "Ahmed, it seems someone thinks you hurt Nadira and that you have stalked her and waited for an opportunity to injure her. This person thinks you have a love-hate relationship with her and are disposed to hurt people you love. Mr. Landry is a psychologist who is helping to verify that charge."

Ahmed looked directly at Parsons. "Captain, please ask Nadira about that. She would have recognized me. Ask her."

"Good idea, Ahmed."

"I can probably guess who told you that. Apparently you found Rashid or Masoud after yesterday's chase. They will tell you anything to turn suspicion away from them."

"Well, that will do for today. Sorry for the disruption."

With that dismissal, Ahmed drove back to his motel. *Now they know for sure that I've told the police about the money. They'll be looking for a way to find me. I can't trust anyone, not even the police.* As soon as he arrived, he decided to move to another motel. He found a telephone directory in the room and located a store where he thought he could buy a new cell phone. Then he packed up his belongings and checked out.

While he drove around looking for a new motel, his thoughts drifted. *I need to get into my dorm room and get some clean clothes and check my mail. Without being seen. Rashid and Masoud might be using their dorm rooms during exams. Very risky now. Maybe on the weekend. Early Sunday morning.* His wandering took him to the Bladensburg area, and there he found his new motel. After he checked in he went out to a store that sold cell phones. There he outfitted himself with the newest technology in portable devices.

CHAPTER 30

Tom finished his first exam and returned to his car to go home for lunch when his phone, which he had left in the car during the exam, beeped. He saw that it was a message from Martha. *Uh oh*, he thought. The message read, "will u pick me up at the regular time tonight?" He checked the time she sent it. Eleven o'clock. *I guess I should check with Pete.* He called but was sent to Pete's voice mail. "Pete, Martha just texted me and asked if I'd pick her up tonight. Has Sharon said anything to her about not going?"

Somewhat troubled, he drove on home, putting aside calling Martha until he heard from Pete. But by the time he parked his car for his second midterm exam at two o'clock, Pete had not called. Tom returned to his car at three forty-five and immediately checked his phone. There was a second message from Martha, "Tom, r u avoiding me?" and a message from Lauren, "pls call."

Again he called Pete, but still there was no answer. *I'd call Sharon, but I don't know her number. This could be very awkward.* He called Lauren.

"Hi, Tom."

"Hi, Lauren. How did your test go?"

"It was hard! I almost didn't get finished but just barely made it. How were yours?"

"Ahh, pretty easy."

"Hey, I was wondering if maybe your dad could go with us tonight."

"Dad? Why?"

"I was thinking about Martha. I guess you could put me in the backseat as usual and let Martha sit in the front seat, so you and she can talk. Or if you let me sit by you and put her in the back, she'd probably feel demoted or something. I just thought if your dad came along Martha and he could talk in the back, and it wouldn't be too awkward."

Tom was silent for a moment while he collected his thoughts. Finally he said, "That's a pretty good idea. I'll call him and see. He hasn't come since the first time because he's been too busy. But I'll ask him. I can call him right now. I'll call you back, okay?"

"Okay, bye."

Tom reached his dad right away and asked if he could go with them tonight.

"I'm sorry, Tom, but I've got a meeting at church tonight. Why?"

"Oh, I was just trying to find a way to smooth out an uncomfortable situation between a couple of people. I thought if you weren't busy you could help out. It's no big deal. But it might be to Martha."

"Is she having a problem?"

"I don't know. It's an emotional issue. I'll tell you about it sometime. Sometime, soon."

Martin laughed. "Okay. It doesn't sound life threatening. Sorry I can't help."

"No problem. I'll see you at supper."

He called Lauren again, "Well, he can't come with us. I appreciate your sensitivity, though. I'll just pick you up first, and she'll have to take a seat that's left."

"Yeah, I guess that will be all right. Okay. Thanks for trying. I'll see you in a few hours."

"Okay. Bye."

Next he pulled over to the curb and texted Martha, "So sorry. 2 exams today. couldn't take phone, u know. will be 10 min later than usual tonight."

He pulled back into the street and continued home. Before he got out of the car he checked his phone. Martha had replied, "I understand."

I guess she does.

Later, when Martin came home from work, Tom heard him come upstairs. The door to his room was open, so Martin stopped and said, "How'd your tests go today?"

Tom turned his swivel chair toward Martin and crossed his legs. "Pretty easy, I thought. I hope that doesn't mean I didn't understand strength of materials." He laughed.

"You'll find out soon. What's happening with Martha?" He stepped into the room.

"Well," Tom paused, "I guess Lauren and I have developed a relationship." He emphasized 'relationship.' "It's nothing serious but could become."

"Hmmm. Is Martha…?"

"I told Pete just so he'd know. He needs to know that kind of stuff. And since Martha is Lauren's discipler, he told Sharon—"

"Sharon?"

"She's the senior staff woman."

"Okay. Got it."

"Sharon told him that Martha has liked me for a long time."

Martin sat on Tom's bed. "Uh oh."

"Yeah. I never knew that." He shrugged. "Pete told Sharon to tell Martha, and she did."

"Hmm. This is beginning to make sense. So what are you going to do about tonight's meeting?"

"We're just going, like nothing's changed. Lauren doesn't know about Martha. Even so, she was very sensitive toward Martha's position, as an older woman and as her discipler. Martha's always sat in the front seat and talked to me on our way over to Greenbelt, but Lauren didn't want to just sit in the back and pretend that nothing's going on between us. So I'll just pick Lauren up first and she can sit up front, and Martha will have to sit in the back, which she probably will be glad to do, since she already knows about us."

Martin said, "Hell hath no fury like a woman scorned."

"So I've heard."

"Just be ready for anything."

Tom sniffed and grimaced while he did. "Like a knife in the back?"

"Do you have any bad habits that she knows about?"

"She knows me pretty well. We've spent a lot of time together on CCA work. Who knows?"

"And you never knew she liked you? Mercy." He stood. "I don't envy you. By the way, take it slow with Lauren." He walked out.

Lauren waited outside for Tom. He was on time, and she hopped into the front seat and smiled at him. "Hi," she said. *Will he kiss me?* she thought.

He looked at her and smiled. "You look nice tonight."

"Thanks." *I tried to. No kiss. Probably not the right place.* Lauren was wearing jeans, a yellow polo, and a jacket. She was made up with only blush and lipstick. She'd taken particular care of her hair tonight, so it was brushed smoothly.

"Are you doing all right?" he said as he pulled away from the curb.

"I'm doing great, Tom. Are you?" She sat with one leg tucked under her, turned toward Tom.

"Couldn't be better." He smiled broadly and reached over and squeezed her hand.

She smiled. After a brief pause she said, "I talked to Nadira this afternoon. I wanted to find out how her parents handled her exam. They don't want her to be out of the house without one of them, you know."

"Yeah."

"Her mother wanted to go into the exam room with her. But her professors didn't allow that. They did allow her to stay in the hall outside the room. So that's what she did."

"That's not so bad."

"Nadira feels like an inmate."

"I would too. But they should be about ready to arrest someone."

"If they are, Nadira doesn't know it."

"When I talked to Ahmed on Saturday it sounded like the police were working actively on it."

"I hope so."

"It's only been two weeks. The press won't let it rest, so they've got to do something."

"For Nadira's sake, I hope they find him soon."

Soon they arrived at Martha's house. Tom honked the horn and she came out. Lauren straightened on her seat and turned toward the window, saw her coming and looked ahead, and then did a double take. It was Martha, but not Martha as she had ever seen her. *Oh my goodness,* Lauren thought. *I didn't know she could be so pretty!* Martha's hair was no longer in a ponytail, but curled beautifully to her chin. As Martha approached the car, Lauren could see that she was very attractively made-up, with eyeliner, mascara and eye shadow, blush and lipstick. *I thought she didn't own any makeup.* She glanced at Tom. He was staring with his mouth open. Martha had on a knee length skirt and matching top, and a sweater.

Without any hint of moving toward the front seat, she got in the back. "Hello, everybody."

Tom answered first. "Is that you, Martha?" He was looking over his seat at her.

Martha laughed. "Who else?"

Lauren didn't know what to say. *I didn't expect this kind of reaction from her,* she thought.

Tom said, "I thought some strange woman had gotten in my car." He turned around in his seat and steered the car out into the street.

"I was getting pretty grungy after midterms and decided to take a shower, if that's what you mean."

"Well, showering seems to suit you," Tom said.

Lauren had to say something. "Hi, Martha. You look very nice tonight."

"Thank you," Martha said with a sweetness to her voice that Lauren had never heard before. "How is your roommate?"

"She's healing up well, but she's getting cabin fever from being confined to her parents' house."

"Still no arrest?"

"No. Nadira doesn't even know if the police are making any progress."

"That's too bad. Will Nadira be coming back to school?"

"Not if they don't find the guy."

"Then our classes might be all for nothing."

Tom said, "She's not the only Muslim around us. I'm trying to learn how to witness to Ahmed."

"Oh, yes. I forgot about him."

"And there are a lot more at UMD."

It was a short trip to Greenbelt, and by seven o'clock they were assembled in the customary room with George Lyon.

George began, "Tom, will you introduce the new lady to me?"

Tom laughed. "George, this is Martha. Martha, meet George."

George, for once, was momentarily speechless. He simply stared at Martha. Then he smiled broadly. "Well, so it is. So it is. Martha, I apologize for not recognizing you. But it's a new you, isn't it?"

"Not really," she said. "Just cleaned up for a change."

George turned toward Lauren. "And I must say, you look very nice tonight too. Are all of you going someplace special after our meeting?"

"No," Lauren said. "At least I'm not." She looked at Tom and Martha, who both shook their heads.

"Well, then, let's get started. Tonight we're going to talk about who Jesus is and how to reveal him to others."

Lauren glanced at Tom, who was looking at Martha. A feeling of tightness had formed inside Lauren's chest as soon as she had seen Martha. Now it was becoming like a large lump of clay. Martha looked so happy. Lauren slumped and hunched her shoulders. *She's a woman, and I'm just a little girl. I could never look as good as she does.* She pretended to be listening to George but couldn't hear him.

At the end of the session Lauren and Martha walked out together, but as they approached the car Martha strode ahead, reached the car first, and climbed into the front seat. Lauren, without pausing, sat in the back. Tom looked back at her from the front seat with a look that Lauren interpreted as, "It doesn't matter to me." She said, "Please take me home first." Tom nodded.

When they arrived at Cecil Hall, Lauren jumped out and simply said "Good-night" and ran to the front door, entered, and didn't look back. She climbed the stairs rapidly and briskly walked down the hall to her room. As soon as the door closed behind her, she let the tears she had been holding back for nearly two hours burst from her eyes. She fell onto the bed, face down, and sobbed until her pillow was soaked. The lump inside her chest was strangling her heart. She lay there, not caring about the wet pillow or anything else, for an hour. She thought of nothing, except the pain inside her, expecting it to end her life at any moment, and not objecting if it did.

Eventually the pain began to subside, and she thought, *I guess I won't die, but I would have been happier if I had.* She sat up on the side of the bed. *If Tom cared about me, he would've called a long time ago. He's probably still with Martha.* She felt tears fill her eyes again. She shook her head to try to make the tears stop. She lay down again on her back, trying to think of nothing, and gradually drifted off to sleep.

In the meantime, as Tom drove Martha to her house, he was quiet, not knowing what to say. Beside him was a Martha he'd never known: a very attractive woman who liked him. After Lauren left she turned in her seat toward him, the hem of her skirt lying across her thighs. Passion edged itself into him, having been kept in check for the past two hours. He didn't know what to expect from Martha who, until then, had been modest and pleasant.

"Lauren acted like she doesn't feel well," she said. "She didn't say a word at the meeting, and was awfully quiet in the car."

Tom thought, *I know exactly what her problem was, and so do you. Should I make an issue of it?* He decided not to, responding more to the rising excitement he was feeling than to good judgment. "She's always quiet," he said.

It was a short ride to Martha's house. When he stopped at the curb Martha said, "Can we talk awhile?"

"Sure," he said and turned off the engine. He leaned against the door and turned toward her.

She unlatched her seat belt and dropped her hands nervously into her lap. "I don't know how to say this, so I'll be blunt. Tom, I've liked you for a long time. I don't think you knew it, but when I heard about you and Lauren I thought, 'he doesn't know the real me.' You've only known the informal, business side of me. By business I mean the organizational, Christian activists side of me, not the recreational me. Not the off-duty me. Well, now you get a little peek at a more relaxed, casual me."

"You look pretty dressed up to me."

"Yes. But that's just an expression of the me you don't know." She pointed at herself. "The Martha you've known up till now is the dowdy, drab physicist. But outside of classes and meetings, I'm a more social, congenial person."

"Well, it's nice to meet you, off-duty Martha." He reached out his right hand to shake hers. "Now I need to find out which one is the real Martha." He held onto her hand while he spoke, and then let it go.

"They both are!" she said with eyebrows raised.

"I can see the differences in how you look, but you sound like the same Martha I've always known."

"I want you to get to know the casual side of me." She smiled. "Would you like a Coke or something?"

"Sure."

He started the car and she fastened her seatbelt. It was a one-minute drive to a fast-food restaurant two blocks away, and then they waited their turn in the drive-thru lane.

"Tell me about yourself, Martha Two." Tom said.

"Hmm. I'm five foot five, a hundred and fifteen pounds. I won't go into any more physical measurements."

"Aww." *She looks really good, whatever they are,* he thought.

"I like classical music. I once studied violin, but found out I'd never be a concert violinist, so I gave it up."

"Really?"

"I love math and physics, and I already have a job waiting for me when I graduate."

"Where?"

"The Lawrence-Livermore National Laboratory."

"Is that in California?"

"Yes, Livermore, California."

"Do you know what you'll be doing there?"

"No. They started out developing nuclear weapons. But now they do all kinds of things. I'll probably make coffee and sweep the floors for a while." They both laughed.

"Coke?" he asked as he opened his window.

"Diet." she said.

As they pulled away from the window, with drinks in hand, Martha said, "I don't eat much meat. I could be a vegetarian if I wanted to. I eat meat occasionally for the protein, but I like veggies better. I jog almost every day."

"It shows. You look like someone who's in good condition."

"Thanks. I'm serious about my studies and about my involvement in CCA too. I enjoy being with other people, but I don't like partying and that sort of thing. Some people call me highbrow, but I think that's because of my choice of music. Umm, what else can I tell you?"

"Tell me about your family."

"I have a younger sister. She's starting college at Illinois this fall. My parents have been married for about twenty-five years. They're Christians too."

"And you don't wear makeup very much."

"That's true. Most days I can't be bothered when it's just school or CCA. But to go out I do."

"Well, I'm glad to know you, Martha the second," Tom said as they arrived back at her house.

She got out but looked back in and said, "I'd be glad to hear more about you, Tom. Sometime soon."

"You probably know all about me. But yeah, maybe."

"Goodnight."

"Night."

Tom waited until she was inside and then drove away. *Well, now what? She really looked nice. Stunning. But I don't think it made her any different than she's always been. She's a nice girl, though. But she sure had a negative impact on Lauren.* He glanced at his watch. Almost ten. *I'd better text her.* He pulled over and sent a short message, "r u ok?"

He waited a few minutes for a reply but when nothing came he continued home.

CHAPTER 31

On Thursday morning Tom was finishing up his usual morning meditation time when his cell phone rang.

"Good-morning, Tom. This is Ahmed. I hope I didn't wake you."

"Nope. Been up for an hour and a half. How are you doing?"

"I've had a very hard two days. That's why I'm calling. I have a new cell phone, and I want to give you my new number."

"Won't it show up on my phone?"

"It shouldn't."

"Okay, give it to me." Tom wrote it down on a note pad.

"I also would like to ask if you would serve as a point of contact for me if something should happen to me."

"What's going on?"

Ahmed told him about the chase across campus on Tuesday and the interrogation on Wednesday. "I've moved to a new location and gotten this new phone to try to keep as far out of sight as possible."

"I see."

"I think the police questioned Rashid and Masoud on Tuesday. They didn't tell me that, but something they said made me suspect it. Apparently they accused me, so I was called back in for questioning yesterday. But they let me go. Even though the police know everything that has happened to me, they can't protect me."

"Why not leave, go back to Morocco?" Tom asked.

"Until Nadira's attacker is found, I need to stay around here. I will try to remain hidden to the best of my ability, but the threat against me is very real. If they find me and kidnap me or worse, I need someone to know that something's wrong."

"Why me, Ahmed."

"You're the only one I trust. My location and phone number must be absolutely secret. My well-being too. I know I can rely on you."

"Well, what do you mean by 'point of contact?' What can I do?"

"I simply need you to know if I'm all right or not. I'd like to call you or text you every other day simply to say I'm all right. And if I don't call, you'll know I'm not all right and should contact the police. They can tell the school and the school can contact my parents. I assume you could inform Nadira through her roommate."

"Is there anything else that I might be involved in?"

"Not that I can think of."

"If you don't call, should I call you?"

"No. If someone is holding me, they can force me to say things, or they can imitate my voice or respond to a text. No, I must initiate the calls myself."

"Tell me about the police. If I call them can they help you?"

"Maybe. They might be able to find me through my cell phone. I'll give Captain Parsons my phone number too. If he calls me, I believe they can confirm my voice or detect an imitator, through their special equipment."

"Wow. That's interesting."

"Anyway, I wouldn't ask you to do this if it would endanger you or your family. I just want to have the confidence that if I'm not able to contact you, you'll call the police. If you're willing to be my contact point, I'll tell Captain Parsons about you."

"I guess I can do it. I don't see any reason why I shouldn't."

"Thank you very much, Tom. That's a big comfort to me." Ahmed gave Tom the phone number of Captain Parsons. "Wait until noon to call him if you don't hear from me. I'll call you during the morning."

"Okay, Ahmed. I hope all this is unnecessary."

"Of course, I do too. But those guys mean to find me and do me harm. There's no question about that."

"Apparently so."

"All right. Thanks, Tom."

"You're welcome. I'll be looking for your call on Saturday."

"Yes. Fine. Good-bye."

Poor guy, Tom thought. *I wonder if the police found some DNA from the attacker. It would be easy to tell if it was Ahmed or one of his old partners that attacked Nadira. Lauren might know.* He checked his phone for messages. *Ah. She's alive.*

A text message had arrived from Lauren while he was talking to Ahmed, "I guess so."

How do I answer? I know her problem was Martha. She's a problem for me too. She really looked good last night. And she was pretty straightforward about how she feels. I like that. But, now what? What can I say to Lauren? How should I act around Martha? Hmm. Maybe Pete could help.

Pete answered. "Pete, Pete, fount of all wisdom. I'm so glad you're there."

"Maybe I shouldn't be." Pete laughed. "Sounds ominous."

Tom chuckled. "Well, I do need your advice. It's about women."

"Yeah. I'm so sorry I couldn't answer you yesterday. I was completely tied up all day. So what transpired last night?"

"That's why I called. Martha wanted to go last night. I'm assuming Sharon advised her not to. But she went. When we, Lauren and I, picked her up she looked gorgeous! I'd never seen her with makeup on or her hair down. But she was made up very nicely and dressed in a skirt. I've always seen her in jeans, no makeup, hair in a ponytail. But, boy, what a transformation!"

"Oh, my. How did Lauren react?"

"Lauren was just knocked out, like a prizefighter hit in the gut. She didn't say two words all evening. I texted her last night to see if she was all right. She didn't answer until this morning. She just said 'I guess so'."

"But, tell me. Didn't you take Martha home first? Lauren didn't say anything in the car with you?"

"No, Lauren asked me to take her home first. So Martha was in the car until Lauren got home."

"Oh. Now you're alone in the car with the beautiful Martha. The plot thickens."

"Y'know, she did a real classy thing. First she told me she liked me. And then she introduced me to the *other* Martha, who was quite a nice lady. We went out and got a Coke while she talked about herself, her family, and what she likes. Things like that. But other than how she looked, it was the same Martha."

"She's not giving up without a fight, is she? Well, how do you feel about her?"

"I don't know, Pete. It's just too early to tell. But my real question is how do I respond to Lauren?"

"Again, how do you feel about Martha? And Lauren?"

Tom paused and then said, "I like Lauren. I'm intrigued by Martha."

"All right. The first principle here is to be forthright. Don't try to be obscure. Be completely honest, and that may mean saying you don't know."

"Okay."

"In your conversation with Lauren, bring Martha into it very early. Clearly she's the cause of Lauren's discomfort. So get that on the table. She'll probably want to know how you feel about Martha. Just tell her what you told me. Don't say you don't know if you can put your finger on a reason. It could be that you've never seen that side of Martha, or that a few minutes together don't create any cohesive feelings. It's too easy to say you don't know, although sometimes that's the only thing you can say."

"That's helpful. Just tell it like it is. Right?"

"In a nutshell, yes. But don't be brutally frank. You can speak the truth without slashing and burning. Tell the truth gently."

"That's a challenge," Tom said.

"I knew a guy who had known for months he wanted to break up with a girl, but because he'd not been honest all along with her about what he was feeling, when the time came to break up he realized that he'd talked himself into a deep relationship that existed only in her imagination. She'd say something like, 'I love you,' and he'd say 'I love you too' or 'me too,' even though he didn't mean it. When he wanted to break up with her, he knew that he'd be seen as a class A hypocrite. When he finally did break up with her, he drank three or four beers to bolster his courage and then just told her they were finished, and he turned around and left. Of course, she was devastated and mystified because it came right out of the blue. 'How could he love me one day and break up with me the next?' Lying to her did them both more harm than good because she talked to other girls, and the word got around."

"Ugh," Tom said. "I think I get the message."

"I hope that helps. I must run. Stay in touch."

"Okay. Thanks. I'll see you." Tom hung up. He sat for a few minutes letting Pete's advice sink in. *I need to know what I think and feel before I talk to Lauren. But I should talk to her soon. By telephone, though, not in person. That'll give her more space.*

Tom pondered his thoughts and feelings for about fifteen minutes, said a prayer, and then called Lauren.

"Hello," she answered, even though Tom knew she could see who was calling.

"Good-morning. This is Tom."

"Good-morning." She sounded a little sheepish.

"Are you feeling all right?"

She didn't say anything for a minute. "No, not really."

"I'm sorry. Let me ask you something. Are you reacting to Martha?"

"I...I guess so. I mean, how should I react if a beautiful model got in the car with us?"

"I don't know. Say hello or something. But 'beautiful model' is a little over the top, isn't it?"

"Well, how would you describe her? You seemed pretty interested?"

"I think I was astonished, mostly. I'd always seen her in jeans and a tee or sweat shirt, and a ball cap, and pony tail. It was quite a transformation."

"Yes. I knew right away what she was doing."

"Uh, yeah, I think I did too."

"Did it work?"

Tom, surprised by that question, wasn't prepared to answer. "That's a question I don't know how to answer. I've known Martha for a long time. She's always been like a sister to me. To see her dressed up and made-up is intriguing to me, but it's still Martha."

"But she got your attention."

"Yes, and she got yours too, I'd say."

"Well, yeah, but that's different."

"Listen. There are plenty of attractive women at UM, including you. But that's just the wrapping. What counts is what's inside. I'm no more interested in what's inside Martha than I ever was, if that's what you're asking."

Another moment of silence ensued. Tom wondered, *I hope I haven't just shot myself in the foot.* She said, "You know, if you're trying to make me feel better, you're doing a good job."

"Thank you. But now I've got to get myself to class. I'm glad I was able to talk to you."

"Me too. Thanks, Tom. Bye."

I think I was honest with her. Not completely open but honest. The new Martha's wrapping is interesting to me, but I didn't have to tell Lauren that. I like Lauren a lot. Just sort of fascinated with Martha's new look, and that she likes me. Just play it cool, Tom, and see what happens. You'll see Martha all the time, and it'll be interesting to see what turn that takes.

As he began to drive to the campus, Tom had another call. It was George Lyon. "Good morning, George."

"Good-morning, my friend. Good morning. I'm trying to get in contact with Ahmed Suliman. Do you have his phone number?"

"I can't help you with that, George. What's up?"

"We've received a recall notice on the car I sold him, but I can't reach him. We sent a notice to his campus address but haven't received a reply. I realized he's been staying in a motel, so I tried to call him this morning, but the number I have for him isn't in service. I thought you might be in touch with him."

"Not unless he calls me, which he does now and then. Just out of curiosity, how did you know he's staying in a motel?"

"Oh, you know how it is. I do a lot of business with college kids. I think all the Arabic exchange students come to me to buy their cars. I try to treat them right. They're in here all the time, sometimes just to chat. They know what's going on. Word gets around."

"Yeah. It's pretty amazing. Well, if he does call, I'll tell him to get in touch."

"He doesn't have to call, just have him bring the car in and ask for me. I'm here Monday through Saturday noon. It'll only take about half an hour. We just have to replace a switch. It's a safety issue, so it should be done as soon as possible."

"Okay, George. If he calls, I'll convey the message."

"Thanks, Tommy. Give my regards to your dad."

"Will do. See you Sunday."

After talking to Tom, Ahmed called Captain Parsons and left his phone number with him. He asked, "please don't give my number to anyone. I'm afraid that someone who wants to hurt me can find me if they have the number. I will give it to Hashim myself. I've also given it to a friend that I trust, Tom Parker. He's a student at Maryland. I'll call him every two days to let him know I'm all right. If I don't call him, he will call you so you can do what you can to find me and alert the college if anything serious happens to me, so they can call my parents to let them know."

Parsons said, "Okay, Ahmed. I'm glad you're still around. We need your help to find Nadira's attacker."

"Thanks, Captain. Good-bye."

Ahmed then called Hashim. "I want you to have my new cell phone number. But I must ask you to keep it absolutely secret. I know that someone's location can be determined using cell phones."

"Yes, that's true. Certainly I'll keep it confidential. I was about to call you. I would like your help tomorrow afternoon."

"Of course, I'll help if I can," Ahmed said.

"I want to go to the post office to see how the money is picked up and follow them through the processing of the contributions."

"Oh. Well. That shouldn't be hard. Do you want me to go with you?"

"Yes. I don't know where they receive the checks and where they go from there. Do you receive contributions on the Internet?"

"No, not yet. Or at least we couldn't when I left. We had plans to do it but hadn't had time to set it up."

"It's fairly easy to set up, isn't it?" Hashim asked.

"Not for us, it wasn't. We didn't want the Internet contributions to automatically go to our checking account or to any checking account. I'll explain in more detail tomorrow."

"What time should we start out tomorrow?"

"To be sure we don't miss the pickup, we should be in place by one o'clock."

"Okay. Where is the pickup place?"

"It's a post office in Washington. We'll need to give ourselves a half an hour to get there."

"All right. I propose that I pick you up at the Hyattsville police station at twelve thirty. Will that work for you?"

"Yes, I can be there at twelve thirty."

"Fine. I'll see you then."

Ahmed hung up. He clapped his hands and smiled for the first time in many days. *Finally! Finally I'm able to do something to help find Nadira's attacker! It will be dangerous, though. The terrorists might be following him too. If it's Rashid, he might see us, but if it's Masoud, he's so careless he wouldn't be looking. I should be disguised, though. They know Hashim too. I hope he'll be disguised.*

He rummaged through his backpack for something that he could use to disguise himself but could find only a pair of sunglasses and a scarf. He decided to go out and try to find a store that might furnish him with something better. But before he left he realized that he had no idea of where such a store might be. *I'll call Tom to see if he knows,* he thought.

When Tom answered, Ahmed said, "Hello, again, Tom. I hope I'm not disturbing you. I just wanted to find out if you know where I can buy something to disguise myself with."

He heard Tom laugh. "What are you planning to do?"

"I'm, uh, going to be someplace where Rashid or Masoud might see me, and I don't want them to recognize me."

"I could've guessed that."

"I just want to be careful."

"I can't blame you. I'd think that a five and ten might have something, like a wig or fake eyebrows. Stuff like that."

"What is a five and ten?"

Tom named a few stores that might help him. Then he said, "I'm glad you called. I just had a call from George Lyon, who's trying to reach you. He says you know him."

"Yes, I do, but how do you know him?"

"He goes to my church."

"But—"

"I was talking to him a few days ago and mentioned that I'd helped you with your taxes. He told me that he'd sold you a car. Is that right?"

"Yes."

"Well, he'd tried to inform you that they've received a recall notice on your car but that he'd been unable to contact you by mail or by phone. I knew about the phone, of course. He wanted to know if I had a good number for you, but I told him that I couldn't help him. He said to tell you, if I see you, that you need to bring the car in to his dealership to replace a switch."

"Did he give you a day and time to bring it in?"

"Any time. He said bring it in any time, and they could install the new switch in about a half an hour."

Ahmed asked, "Do you know if they're open on Saturday?"

"Yeah. He said they're open until noon on Saturday."

"So I could just go in on Saturday morning without an appointment?"

"Yeah."

"Do you think it's important to do that?"

Tom said, "He seemed to think so. That's why he was personally trying to reach his customers."

"Well, I guess I should do that. Thanks for telling me and for not giving away my phone number."

"You're welcome."

"Good-bye."

"Bye."

CHAPTER 32

On Friday afternoon Ahmed drove to the Hyattsville police station. When he saw Hashim arrive, he walked over to his car, holding his disguise aids in his hand. The driver's side window was open, so he went there to greet Hashim. In order to shake hands he transferred his disguises to his left hand.

Hashim said in Arabic, "What do you have there?" pointing to Ahmed's disguises.

Slightly embarrassed, Ahmed answered, "Uh, just some things I brought to change my appearance."

Hashim grinned and then laughed. Ahmed's face grew warm, and he laughed nervously.

"Come on, get in. You're probably smart to bring that stuff. It just struck me as funny to think of you with heavy eyebrows and a wig on."

Ahmed got in and dropped his disguises on the floor. "I just thought I'd be easy to recognize if either Rashid or Masoud sees us."

"Yes, of course. I usually wear sunglasses and a ball cap. Sometimes I have a beard. We must do it. I'm glad you came prepared."

They left immediately, with Ahmed giving directions. They drove south on Route 1, which became Rhode Island Avenue in the District. When they reached M Street NW, Ahmed told Hashim to turn right, and then in slightly more than two blocks they were at the post office. They circled the block several times before a parking place became available on 20th Street near the intersection with M. There they waited.

It was a long wait. Eventually Ahmed recognized Masoud's car as it slowed down on M Street. "There he is," he told Hashim.

"That blue car?"

"Yeah."

"Put on your disguise," Hashim said as he wrote down the license number.

Ahmed donned a black wig, a short black beard, and fake glasses.

"Hey, that's very good," Hashim said. "Very authentic."

Soon Masoud's car passed them as he circled the block, looking for a parking place to open up. Eventually Ahmed saw Masoud walking from M Street into the post office. A few minutes later he emerged, carrying a bulging cloth bag. "There he comes," Ahmed said.

"Okay," Hashim said. "As soon as he turns his back to us, we can ease out so we can see him get in his car."

Traffic was brisk, but they had no trouble following Masoud, who returned to Rhode Island Avenue as soon as he could and headed back north on Route 1. Shortly after Masoud passed into Maryland he turned off of Route 1. Ahmad said, "I know where he's going. There's an office supply store near here that we use sometimes. He does it differently than I do. I usually enter the information using my laptop at the house and then go to a store to print out the letters. He does it all using a rented computer."

"Tell me when we get close," Hashim said.

"We're close now. You can see the sign up there on the left."

They slowed as the watched Masoud pull into the parking lot beside the store.

Hashim asked, "What's he going to do there?"

"He has a memory stick with him that contains the Word set-up he'll use to enter the names and addresses of each donor and the amount of the check. Then he'll print letters and envelopes to each of them. He also prints a report of the donors and amounts."

"Gotcha. How long will he be there?"

"I could do it in about a half an hour. I don't know about Masoud. I've always felt he didn't know as much about computers as I do. It also depends on how busy they are. Usually on Friday afternoon there are computers available."

Forty minutes later they saw Masoud come out and get in his car and leave.

"Get down," Hashim directed when he saw Masoud's car turn towards them. Ahmed ducked below the window until Hashim told him he could sit up. "Where's he going now?"

"Probably back to the house. The next step is to put the letters in the envelopes and get the checks ready to deposit."

"Then what?"

Ahmed turned toward him. "The acknowledgment letters go to the post office. And probably the terrorists will demand that some of the checks be mailed to them at that time. I doubt that they will want their share of the checks deposited in a bank by Rashid and Masoud. But I don't know how they've arranged to get the money to the terrorists. I'm only guessing about that."

"Then the next step is the crucial one," Hashim said. "When will they go to the post office?"

"Sometimes we'd go on Friday afternoon and sometimes on Saturday morning."

"Always the same post office?"

"Yes."

"Where?"

"Very near to the house. Just a few blocks."

"Oh, yes. I go there often. Let's go there."

Soon they were at the Calvert Road post office. Hashim parked beside the building. "Wait here. If you see Masoud or Rashid, hide but keep your disguise on." Hashim went in the post office.

He returned in less than ten minutes. He said, "Now take me to the bank you use."

"It's just up the street, on the corner of Route 1 and Knox Road."

"Good." He drove to the bank and went in, and returned in fifteen minutes. Before leaving he looked at Ahmed and asked, "Ahmed, do you suppose they'll use another bank to deposit checks for the terrorists rather than mailing them?"

Ahmed shook his head. "I doubt it. The banks are so thoroughly regulated that everything done there is easily detected."

"But they'll have to deposit the checks somewhere." He gestured with his right hand.

"Yes, but they can do it in several accounts and in several banks, to avoid large transactions that will draw attention. That's what I think they'll do, anyway."

"Hmm. That makes sense. Okay, I'm going to take you back to your car now, and you can go home or wherever you're staying."

"What did you do in there, and at the post office?" Ahmed asked.

"Investigating, my friend. That's what you and I have been doing."

Ahmed grinned. "Pretty boring. Is it always like this?"

"Usually. The fun begins when we make arrests."

"Do you think you'll catch them?"

"It's hard to say. We don't know enough about them yet. We think they're part of a Washington-based Islamist group, unrelated to any known international movement. But they haven't tipped their hand yet by any attempted attacks that would identify them more fully. There's apparently a lot more to their intelligence network than we know about. For example, how did they know about the Servants of Mercy? And more elusive is how they knew about Nadira. All about Nadira."

"Yeah. I've asked myself the same questions."

Hashim said, "We may never answer those questions, but there's a pretty good chance we can catch the guys that are taking the money from your partners. But finding who attacked Nadira—I don't know."

If not, I'll never be able to prove my innocence to Mr. Shalash.

At the Shalash house, Nadira was happily anticipating the absence of her parents for the next two days. They would be leaving for the weekend soon after her father arrived home from work. Without specific intentions, yet realizing the possibilities, she was excited that her guards would be absent for forty-eight hours.

Her parents left at five thirty, and soon she was on the phone to Lauren. "Guess what."

"What?"

"My parents have gone away for the weekend and have left my cell unguarded."

"Uh oh. Now what?"

"I'd really like to get out of this house tonight or tomorrow."

"And do what?"

"Anything. Well, not anything. But something other than staying cooped up here. I tried to call Ahmed a minute ago, but his phone is no longer in service. I'm wondering what's happened to him."

"Why were you calling him?"

"Lauren! You know why."

"Wouldn't your father object?"

"If he knew."

"This doesn't sound like the sweet, obedient Nadira I know."

"It isn't. I was just thinking that, since he has a car, we could just take a ride somewhere and talk. Or maybe you and Tom could meet up with us and go get something to eat. Do you think Tom knows what's happened to Ahmed?"

"I guess I could call him to find out."

"I wish you would. I'm a little bit worried about him. I haven't talked to him or anything for two weeks."

"I think Tom's seen him. He's probably just fine."

"It would be fun to see him again. And if you and Tom go with us and if my father finds out, at least he'll know I wasn't out with Ahmed alone. Y'know?"

"Well, if Ahmed can't do it, I'll ride your bike over tomorrow afternoon. I might do it anyway, and if Ahmed can take you out, we can get together near your house."

"I'd love for you to come over, but I wouldn't want Ahmed to come here and pick me up. Mother would hear about it from the neighbors the minute she gets back."

"Oh. The cell guards are gone, but the guard towers are still manned. How are you planning your jailbreak?"

"It'd be hard during the day. But after dark I can just walk away and nobody would see me."

"It's almost dark by six thirty. That would be a good time to plan our rendezvous."

"Yeah. Seven would be safer. You'd have to leave earlier on the bike, but maybe Tom could pick you up near here if he can put the bike in his car."

"I don't know about that. Does it fold up somehow?"

"No. It's just a regular bike."

"It's no problem to ride back to the dorm if Tom will pick me up there. There'll be a lot of traffic near College Park because of the game, but by six thirty it should be thinned out."

"Well, no matter what else, please come over. Come for lunch. I'll make something good. Something Middle Eastern."

"Great. I'll call you back after I talk to Tom."

"Okay. Bye."

Tom was at work on the talk he was scheduled to give at the Sunday night CCA gathering when his cell phone rang. "Hello."

"Hi Tom. This is Martha."

"Oh. Surprise. Hi."

"I was just wondering. Are you going to the game tomorrow?"

"Of course. Especially this game. Virginia Tech is going to be tough."

"Will you sit with me?"

Tom hesitated. Then he said, "Is there an empty seat beside you?"

"We can make one. It will be a little cozy."

"Where's your seat?"

"Eleven. Row L. There's always a lot of movement. There'll be room for you."

"I'm in section twelve. I might come over and visit with you for a spell if the guys I sit with will let me."

"Huh?"

"Hey, it's football. We get pretty emotional."

She paused and then said softly, "So do I."

"I'll bet you do. Okay, I'll look for you."

"And I'll look for you."

"Bye."

"Bye, Tom."

Whew. She means business. He tried to resume preparing his talk, but his mind wouldn't focus on the subject. *This could turn into a mess. Lauren and Martha are supposed to be friends. I can't let this go on. I probably ought to break it off with both of them right now. Or at least one or the other of them. Which one?* He stood and walked to the window, gazing onto the street, illuminated by a street light. *Everything's at peace out there. The trees, the squirrels, the birds. All nestled down for the night. Hey out there, lend me some of your peace, will you?*

His cell phone ring interrupted his reverie. He walked back to his desk and picked up his phone. He could see that it was Lauren. *Oh, no,* he thought. "Hi, Lauren."

"Hi, Tom. Sorry to disturb you, but I need to ask you something."

"Sure, no problem."

"I was just talking to Nadira, and she told me her folks are gone for the weekend, so she wants to get out of her house for a while—sneak out, really."

"Can hardly blame her for that."

"Yeah, I know. She'd like to get together with Ahmed. She tried to call him but his phone is no longer in service. She wondered if you knew how to reach him or if he's still around or what."

"He's still around. But he has a new phone number, but he's not giving it out. He'll be calling me from time to time, and I expect him to call tomorrow. I can tell him to call her."

"Oh, good. She'll be so happy. What she told me is that she'd like for the four of us, Ahmed and her and you and me, to go out to eat tomorrow night. Is that possible for you?"

"It depends on what time. There's a football game tomorrow, you know. So the earliest I could do something would probably be around four o'clock."

"She doesn't want to leave the house until after dark."

"That'll be around seven. Sunset is at about six thirty, isn't it? So yeah, I can do it."

"I'm going to ride her bike over to her house earlier, about noon. Will a bike fit in your car?"

"I know what you're thinking. I don't think so, Lauren. My trunk is pretty small."

"I don't want to leave it at Nadira's because it may cause her parents to become suspicious."

"I'd be willing to try, but what would you do if I can't get it in?"

275

"Maybe I'd better just ride back to the dorm. Could you pick me up there?"

"Yes, sure. The football traffic should be cleared out by then."

"This all depends on whether or not Ahmed calls you. If he does and if he calls Nadira and wants to go out with her, then I'll call you back or text you tomorrow after I get over to Nadira's."

"That's fine. I'll just not make any other plans for tomorrow night."

"Good. Okay, I'll talk to you tomorrow."

"Okay. Bye."

Hmm, she sounds better than the last time we talked. She and Martha are as different as night and day. Lauren is so natural, so unpretentious. And Martha has suddenly become something of a vamp. But she's so good-looking, it's hard to ignore her! And now both of them have just asked me for a date! Some guys would think this is a good problem to have. But I don't have enough time for two women.

CHAPTER 33

While waiting for his car to be repaired on Saturday morning, Ahmed called Tom. "Hello, Tom. I'm calling to tell you that I'm all right."

"I was hoping that would be the case."

"I plan to spend the weekend catching up on my studies."

"Well, listen. Nadira wants you to call her. She tried to call you but, as you know, she couldn't get through."

"Oh. Yes. I should have informed her. I'm so happy that she tried to call. How did you know?"

"Nadira's roommate, Lauren, called me to ask if I'd heard from you and, of course, I had. Nadira wants us to all go out together tonight. Maybe I shouldn't have told you. If you call her, don't tell her I spilled the beans."

"Spilled the beans?"

"Yeah. It means told something I shouldn't have."

"Like a lie?"

"No, like something private or something someone said about you."

Ahmed laughed. "Spilled the beans!" He laughed again. "Where do you Americans get these sayings?"

Tom laughed too. "I don't know. We just learn them as children."

"Oh, here comes George. That didn't take long at all. Okay, I'll call Nadira. Thanks for telling me."

"You're very welcome. I hope to see you later today."

"Yeah. Me too. Good-bye."

He turned to George. "Is it ready?"

"Yes, indeed. Yes, indeed. And I trust that you will be safer now."

"Is there a charge?"

"Oh, no. When car companies recall cars, it's because they've made a mistake, which they must pay for."

"Well, thank you. I'll be on my way."

The car was waiting just outside the showroom door. Before Ahmed left, he called Nadira.

"Hello." she answered her cell phone.

"Nadira, this is Ahmed."

"Oh, Ahmed." He could hear the smile in her voice. "I'm so glad you called. It's been so long!"

"Yes. Are you no longer a captive?"

"Not really. It's just that my prison guards are out of town."

"Your parents?"

"Yes." She laughed. "So I hoped we might be able to see each other."

He lowered his voice. "Your parents would not approve."

"Maybe not. But they won't know. I thought you and I and Lauren and Tom could go someplace to eat. At least if my parents found out they'd know we weren't alone."

"Oh. I thought you wanted me to come to your house."

"No, that wouldn't work. That could cause major problems."

"Well, I'd like very much to see you. But I don't want to be the cause of your disobedience."

278

"Ahmed, I'm going out tonight. Somewhere. Whether you go with me or not. So you're not causing my disobedience."

"In that case, I'd better go with you to make sure nothing bad happens to you."

"I thought Tom and Lauren could pick you up and then come and get me."

"That might be difficult."

"Aren't you in your dorm?"

"No, I'm in a motel, a few miles from the campus."

"Why are you staying there?"

"For my own convenience."

"But—"

"I'll tell you more about it sometime."

"Ahmed! It was you!"

"What?"

"The bomb, under the car." She spoke in a loud whisper.

There was silence. After twenty seconds or so Nadira said, "Was it you, Ahmed?"

"Uh, yes."

"But why? Why you?"

"I can't talk about it over the phone."

"But why, Ahmed? There's nobody else on the line."

"We don't know that. Phones are very insecure."

"You have a car, then. Can we just meet you someplace?"

"That would probably be best."

"Lauren and I are getting together this afternoon. After we figure it out, I'll call you back and tell you where to meet us. Where is your motel?"

"It's a few miles south of CP."

"Oh, clear down there. Do you know of any restaurants around there?"

"No."

"How about someplace near the campus?"

"I'd prefer not near the campus," Ahmed said. "Maybe something nearer to Silver Spring."

"That would work."

"Good. But don't call me. I'll call you back later. Would four o'clock be okay?"

"Yeah. Lots of mysterious stuff going on. I hope you can tell me more tonight."

"I will. I promise."

"Okay. I'll talk to you later."

"Bye."

Ahmed drove away from Glimus Motors, thinking about what he would be willing to tell Nadira. *I just can't tell her I was involved in criminal activity. I should have left the Servants the moment I learned about it. I can't change that, though. I'm sure her father would never let me go out with her if he knew about that. Now if I can help identify her attacker, maybe he'd see some good in me. But that is the problem, identifying her attacker.*

Still, I need to tell her why I'm hiding. If I tell her that Rashid and Masoud are after me, I'll have to tell her why. But they didn't attack Nadira, even though Kelly made me think so for a while. I still think it was the terrorists. I can tell Nadira that terrorists attacked her to force the Servants to give them access to the money we were collecting, and that I'm working with the police to find them. The terrorists know I'm cooperating with the police and want to silence me. So I'm hiding from them.

I hope the FBI will find them before they do something terrible, something even more terrible than attacking Nadira or killing me. But what are they planning?

Nadira had lunch waiting when Lauren arrived around twelve thirty. "You're really bundled up. Is it that cold?"

"It is on a bike! Riding a bike creates its own windchill factor."

"Your face is all red."

"Yeah, it was pretty cold."

As Lauren took off her coat, scarf, hat, and gloves, Nadira said, "You're just in time for lunch. Hope you worked up an appetite."

"It depends on how exotic it is."

"Not too. You'll see in a minute." They walked into the kitchen. The table was set for two.

Lauren sat down. "What are we having?"

"Just pita stuffed with an eggplant mixture and saffron rice."

"Hmm. Sounds exotic."

Nadira spooned the rice and eggplant dish into the pita halves and set them on the table. As they ate, she said, "Mother called last night. She said she wanted to make sure I'm all right. But you know why she really called. I'll bet they'll call again tonight. We probably shouldn't stay out too late."

Lauren asked, "What time did she call?"

"Around eight thirty."

"Did she call your cell?"

"No, the house phone."

"Do you have call forwarding?"

"Ah, I know what you're thinking. I don't know. But I can find out. I'll just call the phone company."

"I really like this," Lauren said of lunch.

"I thought you'd like it. My mother has made this ever since I was a little girl."

After lunch Nadira called and found that she did have call forwarding. "I'll just forward their call to me." She smiled a self-satisfied smile.

In the meantime, Tom was in the stadium. He'd arrived at eleven thirty and made his way to his seat. The people sitting near him were familiar to him by this late in the season, and he enjoyed the banter among them about as much as he did the games. After the game began he was distracted by the awareness that Martha was in the adjacent section and was probably looking for him. *It's getting cold in here. It might be warmer close to Martha. She'll be looking terrific, no doubt. She'll probably want me to go out with her after the game. What'll I say? If she asks me if I have a date, I'll have to tell her. And I'll have to tell her it's with Lauren if she asks. And maybe that would be the best thing.*

As the game went on, Tom was evaluating his feelings, trying to decide whether he felt more attraction to Martha or Lauren. *They are so different from each other. Martha is more intentional, actively trying to win me over. She's hands down the better looking. Lauren is more passive but somehow that appeals to me. Martha is older, of course, and three years is a lot at this age. Maybe that makes her more decisive. Or maybe she's that way because of her scientific mindset. Lauren is pretty down-to-earth too. Although she seemed pretty emotional Wednesday night.* By the end of the first half, he was no closer to knowing his own mind and emotions than when the game had begun.

During halftime he went to find Martha. He didn't have to look very long. She was in her seat, waving at him with red-mittened hands, as he came up the aisle toward her row. "Is there room for me in there," he yelled over the band blaring on the field.

"Of course. Come on over." She beckoned.

He made his way to her seat, and Martha scooted over to make room for him. As he sat down, she grasped his left arm with both hands.

"I'm freezing. I need you to keep me warm."

She does look great. He observed. "I hoped you'd have already warmed it up here."

She laughed.

Pretty teeth. White and straight. "Do you think we can pull this game out?"

"No," she said. "Not unless we make an adjustment to let the outside linebackers blitz. The inside receivers are drawing the linebackers away from the line, so no one is there to stop their off-tackle plays. That's where they've been picking up their first downs."

Tom was astonished. He hadn't noticed the linebacker versus tight end play, and he'd been playing football ever since he was eight. He turned and looked at her. "But won't that open up the tight ends for short passes?"

"They'd have to make those passes very quickly. But they won't be anticipating the blitzes, and this late in the game it will be harder for Tech to make the adjustment."

"That's very astute. I had no idea you knew so much about football."

"I just watch. That's how I learn. I think most people just watch the ball carrier. But you can learn a lot more by watching the others."

"What else have you seen?"

"Well," she paused. "Well, notice how effective the pulling guard is on those off-tackle plays. He's out there to block either a linebacker or safety, if they come up. But he leaves the door open for the inside linebacker to blitz. That could be very disruptive."

"Wow. I'm impressed. Have you considered applying for a job as a defensive coach somewhere? I can't wait for the third quarter to start, so I can see what you're talking about."

"There's probably something going on that I don't realize that would preclude my ideas from happening. I don't know that much about football."

Soon the game resumed, and it wasn't long before, on third down, Tech ran the off-tackle play, and Tom could see exactly what Martha was talking about. Tech's tight end ran downfield, and the linebacker went with him. With a pulling guard running interference, the ball carrier made a good gain and a first down. "There it is. It's exactly what you said, Martha."

"It's too bad. Too bad for Maryland." She looked at Tom and smiled.

"Yeah. We could have three blitzing linebackers and their backs would be running for their lives."

"Oh, well. It's only a game," Martha said. "What are you doing after the game?"

"I hope to get together with Ahmed, the guy I've talked about at our Wednesday meetings."

"You hope to?"

"I'm just waiting for a call to let me know. But I'm pretty sure it'll happen. Why?"

"I thought we could do something. You know, hang out."

"I'll just have to wait and see."

"Can you just tell him 'some other time'?" She rubbed his arm.

I was afraid of this, he thought. *I need to be honest with her but also careful.* "Ahmed is in a lot of trouble. No, not trouble, jeopardy. So he remains hidden most of the time. Hidden alone. He needs contact. Especially with a Christian. I don't know if there's any chance he'll accept Jesus, but I need to do all I can to acquaint him with Jesus. So I think it's important to take advantage of any opportunity to spend time with him."

She pulled her hand back. "I understand, Tom. That's what I like about you."

"Well, thanks." He looked at her and nodded. *I hope she doesn't ask any more questions.*

She didn't ask any more questions and appeared to become more attentive to the game. She didn't yell or jump up, but he guessed she was analyzing. *Her mind is frightening. She's probably going over everything I've said and figuring out what I'll be doing this evening without my telling her.*

As the game went on, and Maryland fell further and further behind and people began to leave, in ever increasing numbers. "It's really getting cold up here without a lot of other people around," he said.

"Yeah, there's no chance Maryland can pull this one out. I think I'll take off."

"Me too." Tom said.

"How about going someplace to get something hot to drink." She looked inquisitively at him.

"I can do that. I need it."

They walked out of the stadium to Tom's car, inched their way out of the parking lot, down to Route 1, and headed south. At the coffee shop where he'd met with Ahmed not long ago, they went in and found an empty table, a small brown round table with two brown café chairs with wrought iron backs. The aroma of freshly ground coffee was accentuated by the coffee colored shades of the lamps.

"I guess Ahmed hasn't called yet, or did I miss it?" Martha took her coat off and draped it over a chair.

"Nope, no call yet." *She's fixed up the way she was Wednesday. She sure does sparkle.*

She leaned her elbows on the table, rested her chin in her hands, and looked at Tom. "What kind of jeopardy is he in, if I may ask?"

He hesitated and looked around to see if anyone near them could hear him speak. "I really can't say much without compounding his problem. It's somehow related to the attack on Nadira. He is trying to help the authorities find the perpetrators, and the perpetrators know that. So they are out for him. They tried to blow his car up a week ago, and they chased him across the campus on Tuesday, but he got away. His life is in danger. That's about all I can say. It's about all I know."

"That's terrifying. Why does he stay here?" She frowned.

"It's because of Nadira. I think he'll go back to Morocco if they find Nadira's attacker."

She almost smiled. "Oh, they're a couple?"

"Not really. A budding couple, maybe." He shrugged. "Let's order something to drink."

She wanted a hot chocolate, and he ordered one for himself. While he was at the counter, his phone rang. "Hello," he said and stepped toward the door, out of earshot of Martha.

"Hi, Tom. It's Lauren. Are you still at the game?"

"No. We were losing and it was freezing in the stadium, so I left."

"Here's the plan. You're supposed to pick me up at about ten till seven. Then we'll pick up Nadira near her house. She doesn't want us to drive up to the house, but she'll meet us at the corner. Then we're going to meet Ahmed at Josie's Restaurant not too far from Nadira's. Is that okay with you?"

"That's great."

"We haven't talked to Ahmed yet, but when he calls and if we have to change anything, I'll call you back. Okay?"

"That'll be just fine."

"I'm still at Nadira's and have to ride her bike back to the campus. If I don't freeze on the way, I'll be ready in the lobby at ten till seven."

"Good." He saw that the hot chocolates were ready. "Gotta go. I'll see you in little bit."

He picked up the drinks and took them to the table. As he sat down, he said, "That was the call. So the meeting with Ahmed is on. But I've got a little time till I need to meet him." He glanced at his watch. It was shortly after four.

"Are you going to talk to him about Jesus?" She was sitting back in her chair with her legs crossed.

He raised his eyebrows. "Probably. He has some issues that bother him. To me, Jesus is his answer, but he tends to take our conversations in directions I can't anticipate. It hasn't been easy, you know."

"Is that because he's Muslim?" She lifted her cup to test the temperature and set it down again.

"Partly, I guess. But he's also very bright, and his mind is always running ahead of the conversation."

She uncrossed her legs and leaned forward. "What do you think would happen if you let him lead the conversation?"

He looked past her to form his answer. "In the past, he's asked me questions. Then he lets my answer generate new questions. And that's not bad, but it just keeps me on my toes. I can't think ahead because I don't know what he's going to ask me."

"A challenge." She smiled.

"Yeah."

She cocked her head. "But you like that."

"To some extent." He nodded.

She looked directly at him. "Do I challenge you?"

"To some extent," he said, without hesitation.

She threw her head back and laughed.

He continued, "Martha, you have an exceptional mind. You're probably the most intelligent person I know. That can be challenging."

She continued to smile. "Well, challenging I can accept. I just don't want to be intimidating. You're no mental slouch yourself, you know."

"I get by," he said flatly.

She continued, "I think of you as a very focused man. A very dedicated man."

"I'll take that as a compliment."

"I meant it that way." She was still smiling.

"Thank you."

"I think we have a lot in common." She was looking at her cup.

Tom gazed at her without commenting.

She gave her head a slight sideways tilt and smiled. "You don't agree?"

"I'm thinking about it." He lifted his cup and sipped. "It's cool enough to drink."

She also took a drink.

He said, "I'd have to know you better to agree with you."

She looked directly at his eyes. "The opportunity is yours."

Tom smiled broadly. *She's not at all subtle about it,* he thought. "I sensed that."

She smiled again and looked down.

There was a brief silence.

Tom said, "You've presented a conflict, you know."

"Yes." She glanced at him and looked down again.

"I hope you don't expect an answer today." He looked at her with raised eyebrows.

"I could hope."

He looked at his watch. "It's about time for me to get going." He picked up his cup. "We should talk again soon."

"I hope we do," she said with a note of anxiety in her voice. She picked up her cup too.

He finished his hot chocolate and waited for her to finish. *She is just gorgeous,* he observed. *And very intelligent.*

They left without further discussion. He drove Martha to her car and went home to get ready for the night with Lauren, Nadira, and Ahmed.

CHAPTER 34

It was a cold ride back to Cecil Hall. Lauren locked the bike to the bike rack behind Kent Hall next door and hurried inside Cecil, grateful for a warm building. Once in her room she looked at herself in the mirror. *Wow. My face is so red!* She went to the restroom and ran warm water and splashed it on her face. *I'm going to look awful tonight unless I do something.*

She didn't own many cosmetics, but she did have eye makeup and blush as well as lipstick. As she went to work on her face she thought, *If Martha can transform herself the way she did, surely I can make some improvement. But I don't have as much natural beauty to work with. The two things I'm going to work on are my skin color and my eyes.* As she applied eyeliner, eye shadow, and mascara she looked at herself for a long minute and then thought, *That's just too overdone. That's not who I am.* She removed as much as she could and started over. She skipped the eye shadow and made the eyeliner as thin as she possible could. *That's better. It helps a little, but it doesn't look like I'm trying to be a model or trying to compete with Martha. I don't want Tom to like me because of how I can make myself look but for who I am.*

She waited until just before Tom was to arrive to apply blush and lipstick. By that time the redness had left her face, and she was happy about that. *I'm me, and I'm glad.* She put on a jacket over her sweater and went down to the lobby to wait for Tom. She saw him coming and met him at the curb.

"Hello, Mr. Parker," she said as she got in.

"And hello to you, Miss Stevenson." He gazed, studiously, at her for a minute. "You look very nice tonight." He refastened his seatbelt.

"Thank you." She smiled a satisfied sort of smile.

As he steered the car away, he said, "So, are we going to Silver Spring?"

"Yes. She should be at the corner waiting for us."

"This is unusually cold weather for late October, isn't it?" He glanced at her.

"Yeah. I about froze coming back to the dorm." She rubbed her hands together.

"Oh, that's right. You rode your bike, didn't you?"

"Nadira's bike."

"I knew that."

"Have you ever been to Josie's?" She asked.

"No. I've never heard of it."

"Nadira says it's very good."

"What kind of food is it?"

"I don't know. She didn't say."

They chatted on until they reached the designated corner. Nadira was standing there. When Tom stopped the car she peered in, smiled broadly, and got in the backseat.

"Right on time," she said. "Hello, Tom. It's nice to see you again."

"Nice to see you again too, Nadira. I hope I won't be accused of abetting your disobedience."

Nadira laughed. "I'll tell you what I told Ahmed. I'm going out tonight, whether you go with me or not. So you shouldn't feel guilty."

"Thanks. I feel better already. So which way to the restaurant?"

She gave him directions, turn by turn. As they approached the restaurant, her phone rang. Tom heard her say, "Are you there yet? Oh. Where are you? You're just a few blocks behind us Okay. We'll wait for you in the parking lot. See you soon."

Tom asked, "Was that Ahmed?"

"Yes. He's not far behind us. There's the restaurant up ahead on the right."

"I see it." He swung into the lot and found a space where there were two empty spaces side by side. He stopped and said, "I'll go up to the entrance and make sure he sees us." He got out and walked to the curb beside the entrance. *I don't know what his car looks like. But he'll see me.*

Soon a car approached and slowed. Tom saw Ahmed who'd opened his window to wave. Ahmed stopped and said hello. Tom said, "We're parked in the first row. There's an empty space beside my car."

"Okay." Tom started back to his car, but stopped to let another car pass as it entered the parking lot behind Ahmed. As he watched Ahmed park, the other car stopped immediately behind Ahmed's car. As soon as Ahmed got out of his car, Tom saw two men emerge from the other car, grab Ahmed, put a white cloth over his face, and push him into the backseat of their car. The car sped to the back of the parking lot, turned back toward the street in the next parking lane, and swung past Tom onto the street. Tom pulled his cell phone from his pocket, took a picture of the back of the car as it left, and then ran back to his car, where Nadira was screaming, and Lauren had gotten out. Tom shouted, "Get back in. We've got to follow them."

They jumped into the car, and Tom quickly pulled out and onto the street. Nadira took in a sharp breath and stopped screaming. Traffic was not heavy but in the darkness he could not see the car ahead. He gave his cell phone to Lauren and said, "I took a picture of the car. See if you can bring it up."

He sped in the direction they saw the other car go. Nadira was moaning in the backseat. Lauren said, "I have it. It's a black car. I can't tell the make. And I can't see the license plate."

"Not much to go on. Oh, hey, I think that's it up ahead at that red light. Call 911 and give me the phone."

She punched in the numbers and handed him the phone. When the operator answered he said, "This is Tom Parker. I just witnessed an abduction of a friend of mine. He was taken in the parking lot at Josie's Restaurant, and they're now driving north from there. I'm behind their car, which is a black car. That's all I can tell right now. I'll keep following until you can stop them. My car is a silver Ford Focus." He gave them his license plate number.

"Are you calling from a mobile phone?" the operator asked.

"Yes." He gave them his number.

"Okay. Hang up. Another agent will call you in a minute."

Tom disconnected. "They'll call me back. Just keep watching the other car so we don't lose sight of it." He eased a little closer to get a better view of it. He handed his phone to Lauren. "Here, Lauren, take some more pictures of it as we get closer. It looks like a Chevy Malibu. Yeah. Hey, there's no license plate on that car!"

"Are you okay?" Lauren looked over her shoulder at Nadira.

"Yes. No. This is awful," she blubbered through tears. "What are they going to do to him? It's all my fault." She began to moan again.

"The police will catch them. We just have to keep them in sight," Tom said.

His phone rang. Lauren handed it back to Tom. It was a police officer. "Where are you now?"

"We've made a couple of turns. We're coming up on Colesville. Yes, and they're turning toward the beltway."

"Okay, just keep them in your sight. Who is the abductee?"

"An international exchange student named Ahmed Suliman."

"Are you driving?"

"Yes."

"Is there someone else who can use the phone?"

"Yes. Her name is Lauren." He handed her the phone.

"We're about to the beltway," Tom heard her say. "Yes, they're on the ramp now, going east."

"Man, a lot of traffic," Tom said. "Don't take your eyes off of them."

After a brief pause Lauren said, "They're turning off. What is that, Tom?"

"University Boulevard," he shouted. She repeated it to the officer. "They're stopping at the light at Franklin. They must not know we're behind them. There's just one car between us. Okay, they're moving again, down University Boulevard toward Tacoma Park." Again Lauren repeated him.

Lauren told Tom, "They're going to try to stop them at University Boulevard and New Hampshire."

"Uh oh. They're turning on, what is that? Piney Branch. Going east." Tom slowed down. "Not much traffic here. I need to stay back. There's New Hampshire ahead. They've got a green light. Oh, no. It's changing! What'll we do?"

"He heard you. Run it if you can," Lauren repeated.

"It's clear to the left, but cars are coming on the right." Tom was shouting so the officer could hear.

"Go across and merge with the traffic. Be aggressive."

"Here goes. I'm across—merging. I made it. But I'm pretty far behind. I think they're going back to the beltway." Horns were honking at them. Nadira was still moaning and reacting to every turn.

After a thirty second pause, Tom shouted, "Yes, they're turning onto the beltway, going east."

293

"Don't lose them." Lauren repeated the instructions.

"I'm trying. A lot of traffic. Is that them on the outside lane?"

"I think so. Get closer," Lauren said. "They're moving back, they crossed two lanes. Yeah, that's them. No license plate. Now they're in the right hand lane. I think they're going to exit again. Yeah, they're exiting on Route 1, going south."

"Okay. We've still got them," Tom shouted.

A minute later he said, "They're moving into the left turn lane at Greenbelt Road. We'll be right behind them. I can see three heads in the car. How did they know Ahmed would be at Josie's? They're turning now. We're right behind them. I'll drop back. They're moving pretty fast."

Lauren said, "They're trying to set up a roadblock ahead."

"They'd better hurry. They'll be at the interstate in a minute. Oh, look. They're turning into the park! This doesn't look good. They'll be hard to find in there." He heard Lauren relay his words to the police.

She said, "The police said they'll block both entrances. But we are not to go after them. Wait at the entrance. They said they don't have jurisdiction there. They can go in, but the park police have to make the arrest."

Tom muttered, "This'll be messy. It'll take forever, and they'll never find them." He parked just inside the park entrance.

Laura added, "They're contacting the park police now."

"They're right over there." Tom pointed toward the Park Police headquarters building. "I know this park really well. I've camped in here many times with the scouts. But this time of the year there's probably only a few campers here." He drove into the park and waited at the entrance to the park police headquarters. In a few minutes two Prince George's police cars passed them. Tom followed them. A park police car then appeared behind Tom with its lights flashing. Tom pulled over, and the park police car stopped behind him. Tom got out, but the police officer shouted, "Stay in your car!"

Lauren told the county police office they'd been stopped.

Tom rolled down his window and waited. After a long pause, the park police car's flashing lights went out, and it pulled out and zoomed around him. Tom said, "I knew it," and he followed the park police car.

"Ask them if the south exit is closed."

Lauren asked and then said, "They don't know for sure. It's supposed to be." She shrugged.

The park police car turned off toward the picnic area, but Tom continued south toward the camping areas. "The police won't find them. They've either hidden in the forest, which is easy to do here, or escaped at the south end."

Just as Tom approached the camping area he saw a county police car coming toward him. It turned on its flashing lights when Tom came into view. Tom pulled over to the side of the road. The police car, going north, stopped opposite him, and an officer got out and walked across the road to Tom's car. Tom rolled down his window and said, "I'm Tom Parker."

"I thought I told you to stay out of here," the officer said.

Tom said, "Look. I know this park like the back of my hand. I live near here and camped in here many times. Have you seen anything of the terrorist's car?"

"No. Are you sure they came in here?"

"Absolutely, but they may have gotten out at the south end before your people got there."

"The park police said the gate at the south end is closed, and there's no way they could get around it. Well, look." He pointed at a gate just beyond them. "They'd have to get by that gate too."

"It's usually not locked. But they could have gotten out by the fire road, if they knew about it. Are there campers in there?"

"Yeah. A few. Mostly RVs and some scouts."

"Maybe they just drove up into the woods, out of sight. I know of some places they might be. I'd like to take a look. They could be doing something terrible to Ahmed, and the campers nearby wouldn't even know." He heard Nadira gasp and whimper in the backseat. "By the way, Captain Parsons is very familiar with Ahmed and knows his circumstances."

The officer said, "We'll go back over this area too. Don't do anything foolish. And stay in touch."

"Yes, sir." Tom rolled his window up.

The police car backed and turned into the camping area. Tom followed. The police car proceeded slowly, shining its spotlights into the forest. After passing the Ranger Station it turned right into the scout camping area.

Tom said, "The terrorists wouldn't go in there with a bunch of scouts all over the place." Instead, he turned left into the B Loop. They saw several RVs parked there but no campers and no lights. Tom drove around the loop until they came to an opening among the trees, with a paved walk leading downhill into the woods. He knew the walk led to a campfire circle. Tom turned off his headlights and turned into the entrance and stopped and turned off the motor. "This goes to a campfire area," he said. "I'm going to take a look. Roll down your windows so you can hear me if I yell."

He quietly opened his door and intentionally left it open. He walked noiselessly on the walk, which rounded a bend to his right, leaving the car out of sight. He thought, *A car could easily get down in here.* A half-moon shone enough light that he could see the path. It opened onto an open area that he remembered contained a fire pit on his left and a semicircular seating area of log benches facing a large white display board, approximately eight feet square, held up by two heavy posts. As Tom came into the opening, he heard what sounded like a moan. He stopped. It was too dark to see anything among the trees. *I should have brought a flashlight,* he thought. He crept on, listening as he went. He was near the benches now. There it was again, *definitely a human sound, straight ahead.* Dread filled his chest and goose pimples formed on his arms and legs as he moved slowly toward the sound, looking at the ground before him as he heard another moan in front of him. He looked up at the white board and in the dim light of the moon he could see the form of a man, with his arms outstretched to either side, like Jesus on the cross. Although Tom was already filled with adrenalin, the sight before him created a sudden burst of additional adrenalin that felt like a knife had been thrust into his stomach.

"Ahmed?" he cried.

Another moan.

Tom could see Ahmed's feet, about four feet above the ground. By feel he could tell that one foot was standing on a large spike driven into the wall but not through his feet or legs. Ahmed's foot was covered with a sticky fluid. *Is that blood? Must be,* Tom thought. *Lord, what have they done to him?* He couldn't reach Ahmed's hands, about ten feet from the ground.

He said, "Ahmed, I'll get you down. Hold on."

Ahmed moaned again.

"I'll be right back," he yelled. Tom ran back to the car.

"I found Ahmed!" he shouted. "Lauren, tell the police we've found Ahmed and that we need an ambulance. Let me back the car out of the way." He started the car and backed it out to the drive. *I'm getting blood all over the steering wheel,* he thought. "Tell them we're in the B Loop. They'll see my car here. Stay here 'till they get here. You can show them where he is. Tell them to please hurry. He's really hurt bad."

Nadira was already out of the car and running down the path. Tom pulled his flashlight out of the glove compartment and ran after Nadira. Soon he caught up with her. He could hear a siren not far off. With the help of his flashlight he led Nadira to the aisle between the log seats, toward the white board. Then he turned his flashlight on Ahmed.

Nadira gasped, and then screamed. She ran to him, "Oh, God. They've crucified him!"

CHAPTER 35

The county police arrived in less than a minute. Lauren pointed the way and followed on foot down the asphalt path behind their car. They followed the path easily to the campfire ring and then shone their spotlights at Tom and Nadira, who had begun to yell for help. Now, brightly illuminated by spotlights and headlights, Lauren could clearly see Ahmed. She cringed as he came into view. *His hands are nailed to that board!* she realized. She could see blood covering his hands and running down his arms and onto his chest. A lump formed in her throat. From where she stood it looked to her like one of his feet was nailed to the board by a large spike and that his other foot was on top of it. She moved closer to get a better look *I don't think his foot is actually nailed to the board*, she thought. *The sharp end of the spike is facing out. He has to stand on that spike!* He'd been stripped down to his underwear and his shoes and socks had been removed. She was beginning to be nauseated. *Standing on that spike must be terribly painful. He must be freezing too.*

In spite of her nausea and aversion to the suffering Ahmed, Lauren held up Tom's cell phone and began taking pictures. She continued taking pictures as the police officers worked to free Ahmed's hands. She could see that his hands were actually nailed to a narrow board, no more than six inches wide and five or six feet long. That board was nailed in turn to the display board. As the officers tried, unsuccessfully, to loosen the nails, Tom and Nadira held up Ahmed so that his weight would not have to be borne by his hands and arms alone. Lauren could hear Ahmed moan as they worked. *He seems to be only semiconscious,* she thought.

A second police car had driven up the path. In its trunk was a crowbar, with which they were able to loosen the six-inch board, and they lowered Ahmed and laid him on the ground. The police officer decided to wait for the ambulance to arrive before attempting to remove the nails holding Ahmed's hands to the six-inch board.

Lauren turned to an officer who was not busy with Ahmed and said, "Do you have a blanket in your car."

The officer said, "I'll look," and he walked away. Soon he returned with a blanket and spread it over Ahmed.

The ambulance arrived within minutes. While Lauren continued to take pictures, Tom watched as the EMTs cut off the heads of the nails with a bolt cutter and then carefully slid Ahmed's hands off of the nails, amid much blood. Ahmed was lifted onto a stretcher and loaded into the ambulance. Nadira attempted to get into the ambulance with him but was told she could not ride with them.

Lauren asked, "Where are you taking him?"

"Do you have a preference?" the driver asked.

"Ask Nadira," Lauren said.

Nadira said, "Adventist, in Takoma Park."

The park police were on the scene and began collecting evidence and information. A county policeman approached Tom. "How did you know to look here for him?"

"I know this park really well," Tom said. "I've been to several scout campfires here, and I saw that the entrance was wide enough for a car, so I just thought it could be a place they'd take him."

A park ranger walked up to join in the conversation. "Do you think they're still here someplace?" the policeman asked.

Tom replied, "The terrorists? I doubt it. If they knew about this place, they probably know about the fire roads."

The ranger added, "Yeah, there's a fire road just below us, but the easiest place to get to it is at the D Loop. From there it leads directly to Good Luck Road."

Tom said, "If you go over there, you might see if there are any fresh tire tracks."

"Good idea. Come with me," the policeman said.

Tom beckoned to Lauren and to Nadira, who'd been picking up Ahmed's clothes, and they walked up the short trail to his car."

"Are we going to the hospital?" Nadira was visibly agitated.

"First we're going to help the cops find out if the terrorists escaped by the fire road."

"What can you do?" Lauren asked.

"Sometimes I can tell if a car has recently been there. It's grassy at the entrance and that might be a help." Tom drove to the D Loop to where the fire road intersects the paved road. A police car followed him.

Tom got out and said to the officer, "Shine your spotlight over here. My flashlight's not bright enough." The entrance was immediately illuminated by the police car's spotlight. Tom carefully examined the grass, looking at it from various angles. He looked at the officer and said, "I think these are the tracks."

He pointed. "I'm going to move my car so the headlights will shine down the road."

He went back to his car and repositioned it. "There," Tom said. "Now you can see how the tire tracks are shinier than the grass around them. The grass is bent away from us. See that? They've gotten away, and you may never find them."

The officer returned to his car and spoke to someone on his radio. Soon a second park police car arrived, and they started down the fire road. As they passed Tom, the officer said, "Please go back to the B Loop. A police detective wants to talk to you."

Tom did as the policeman directed. Back at the campfire circle they found the detective and spent twenty minutes answering questions. He had Tom forward all the photographs Lauren had taken to a police address. After he wrote down Tom's and Lauren's phone numbers he let them leave.

They reached the hospital nearly an hour after the ambulance had delivered Ahmed to the emergency room. Ahmed had arrived without identification and with little explanation of what had happened to him, except that his hands had been nailed to a board. The ER desk attendant seemed glad to have someone there who knew who he was and what had happened to him. "Are any of you relatives?" the attendant asked.

Tom answered, "No, we're just friends, but we were with him and know what happened to him."

"Good." She said. "Before you go in, tell me what his name is and how we can contact his family."

Tom said, "His name is Ahmed Suliman. He's from Morocco and is a student at UMD. He has no family in the United States that I know of. We have his clothes, so his insurance card is probably in his pocket." He glanced at Nadira, who quickly found his wallet in his pants pocket, pulled out his insurance card and gave it to the attendant.

"Okay, you can all go in and see him."

Ahmed appeared to be asleep, but when he heard their voices he opened his eyes. "So happy to see you. What happened to me?" He said groggily.

"Do you remember anything?" Nadira asked.

"At the restaurant, I parked the car." He spoke haltingly. "When I got out they grabbed me and threw me into their car. The next I knew they were doing something to me. It hurt but not a lot. It seemed like I was in a dream."

"How do you feel now?"

"My hands and arms and shoulders hurt now. What did they do to me?"

"They nailed your hands to a board like you were being crucified. We found you hanging there."

"I'd be dead if you didn't find me." He smiled. The nurse also smiled, first at Ahmed and then at Nadira.

Two policemen came into the cubicle. One said to the nurse, "Is it all right if I ask him some questions?"

"I think so," she said.

"Ahmed, do you know who did this to you?" he asked.

"No. Terrorists. Captain Parsons knows they were after me."

The policeman glanced at the other officer, who took out a pad and began taking notes. He turned back to Ahmed. "They had to have known where you were going to have followed you, wouldn't they?"

"Only Nadira," Ahmed turned his head toward her, "and Tom and Lauren knew where we were going. One of them must have told someone."

Nadira said, "I only told Lauren. No one else."

Ahmed said, "No one knew what my car looked like. It was new. Rashid couldn't find me. They didn't know where I live. Tom didn't know either. No one knew. How could they follow me?"

Nadira said, "They came into the parking lot right behind him. They must have followed him."

"I assume the car is still there," the policeman said. "What kind is it?"

"Toyota. Silver. Corolla."

"What's the license number?"

"It has a temporary license. I just bought it."

"Do you have the key?"

Ahmed hesitated. He looked at Nadira. "Where are my clothes?"

"Right here." She had laid them on a chair beside the bed. She pulled the key from the pants pocket and gave it to the officer.

He got directions to the restaurant, and then he said to Tom, "I need to speak to you privately for a minute."

Tom and the two policemen walked out into the waiting room, to a corner of the room away from others.

The lead policeman said, "Do you know who abducted this man and tried to kill him?"

"No, sir. But I suspect it's the same guys that tried to blow his car up last week."

"Where did that happen?"

"I don't know. I haven't known Ahmed very long. Just a couple of weeks. I helped him with his income tax. He's told me a few things, but the gist of it is that his former business partners are doing something illegal. He's blown the whistle on them, and they're after him."

"What's your relationship with him? Obviously, you were going out together. That's more than tax advice."

"Nadira and Lauren" —he gestured toward the ER— "are roommates. Nadira arranged this dinner tonight because she and Ahmed are something of a couple, and I've been seeing Lauren."

"I get it. A double date. A double date gone bad. And you didn't even get to have dinner." He laughed.

"Right."

"Did you tell anyone about going out with him tonight?"

"Well, I told another girl that I'd be seeing him tonight, a girl I'd sat with at the football game. But I don't think I told her where we'd be going, and I certainly didn't tell her I'd be with Lauren and Nadira too." *This could cause a problem,* he thought.

"Who is she?"

"Martha Jenkins. She's a senior at Maryland."

"Where does she live?"

"She lives off campus, but I forget the house number."

The policeman looked at his watch. "Do you have her phone number?"

Tom gave it to him, and added, "Hey, look. Don't tell her anything about Lauren and Nadira, okay?" The officer asked for Tom's number, and he gave it to him too. Then he told Tom he could go back into the ER. Tom asked, "Are you going to move Ahmed's car, or should I go retrieve it?"

"We'll move it to the police station where we can examine it. We'll let Ahmed know when he can have it back." He followed Tom into the ER.

Soon after Tom returned to Ahmed's cubicle, the doctor returned and said to Ahmed, "We'd like to keep you in the hospital overnight for observation. You've had traumatic shock and maybe hypovolemic shock as well as exposure to the cold. You were given chloroform too, and all that could cause some adverse reaction, so we want to keep you here and keep an eye on you for a while. We'll move you into the intensive care ward where you'll spend the night." He turned to the others. "His wounds aren't life threatening. Fortunately, you found him soon after he'd been abused and that prevented him from serious injury. There's no need for you to remain here. He'll need to sleep, and we'll give him something to help him rest comfortably."

Nadira asked, "Can I stay here with him?"

"You may, but he'll be sleeping all night."

"Well, then, I can just sleep too."

"All right. Just wait here until we move him, and you can follow him to the IC unit."

The policeman said to Nadira, "While you're waiting, I'd like to ask you a few questions if you don't mind."

"I don't mind. I'll do anything I can to help find the people who did this to Ahmed."

Lauren hugged Nadira. "We missed dinner. Do you want us to bring you something?"

"I'll just get something here in the cafeteria."

"Call me in the morning and tell me how he is."

"Yeah, I'll have to call to get a ride home, if that's okay with you, Tom." She looked at him with a combined smile and grimace.

"That's just fine." Tom grasped her arm lightly.

Tom and Lauren left the hospital and found a nearby fast-food restaurant where they had sandwiches and soft drinks. Tom looked at Lauren. Her face was pale and drawn. "This has been hard, hasn't it?"

"Awful."

"What's on your mind?"

"First it was Nadira. Now Ahmed. Will you be next? I don't think I could go through this again."

Tom took her hand. It was cold, and she seemed to be shaking a little. "Will you be all right in the dorm?"

"Before Nadira said she'd stay with Ahmed, I was hoping I could spend the night with her."

"Do you want to go to Martha's?"

She gave him a sick look.

He nodded and squeezed her hand.

"I'll be okay. Just—don't take me back to the dorm for a while." Her eyes pleaded.

They were silent for a minute.

She said, "How could anyone be so cruel?"

"I don't think you can blame it on religion."

"But—"

"I know how it appeared, but I don't think we can jump to conclusions. They are probably motivated by hatred and revenge."

"Then why did they crucify him?"

"I can only guess. But remember that the attack on Nadira was a warning. This may have been something like that."

"Do you mean that they weren't trying to kill him?"

"Yes. Otherwise they'd have actually killed him and dumped his body. That was a pretty public place. It wasn't that late at night, and there were people staying nearby in their RVs. I think they wanted him to be found."

Lauren was silent for a moment. "So cruel."

"Yes."

Lauren and Tom stayed for about a half an hour, and then he took her to her dorm. He walked with her to the door, and there she hugged him tightly. He held her until she relaxed.

She said, "You were a superstar tonight, you know."

"I didn't know. I just did what my instincts led me to do."

"You have noble instincts, Tom Parker. Good-night." She kissed him on the cheek, turned, and went inside.

Tom wasn't even off the campus when his phone rang. He pulled over and saw that it was Martha calling.

"Tom Parker, you have some explaining to do!"

"I thought I might be hearing from you." He chuckled.

"This is no laughing matter. What was that call from the police all about?"

"Are you at home?"

"Yes."

"I think it would be better to talk about this in person. May I come over?"

"Please do."

"I'll be there in about five minutes. Watch for me, and come out to the car. I don't think we should discuss this in earshot of others."

"Okay."

Soon he stopped in front of Martha's house, and she immediately came out to the car and got in.

Tom didn't drive away. "Martha, what I'm going to tell you has to be kept strictly between us. Okay?"

"Yes, sir," she said and saluted.

"You'll understand why in minute. You remember Nadira."

"Sure."

"Ever since she was attacked she has been forbidden by her parents to leave the house, unless one of them is with her. However, they went out of town this weekend. So Nadira decided that she wanted to go out with Ahmed." Tom explained how Nadira had arranged the dinner and told her how Ahmed had been abducted.

"Oh, no!" Martha was staring at Tom, her hands holding her head on either side of her face, apparently shocked.

"I got back in my car, with Lauren and Nadira, and we followed them. While I drove, Lauren called the police and kept them informed of every turn. She also took a lot of pictures of the car. Eventually they turned into Greenbelt Park, and we lost sight of them. So did the police. The park police and the county police were there by then. We all began searching. I know that park very well, and on a hunch we went to one of the campfire circles, and there we found Ahmed. They had crucified him on a large screen—you know, for showing movies."

"Good Lord!" Martha cried. "Was he dead?"

"No. We called the police and the emergency squad, and they got him down and the nails out. They'd actually only nailed his hands."

"Wouldn't that be extremely painful?"

"Well they'd driven a large spike through the wood from the back for him to stand on. But he was so drugged up that he had a hard time keeping a foot on it. His feet were pretty bloody."

Martha had her hand on Tom's arm. "This is just too painful to listen to!"

"Well, the reason the police called you was to try to find out how the abductors knew he'd be going to that restaurant. They asked me if I'd told anyone about getting together with Ahmed, and I told them I'd told you. So I guess they were trying to find out if you'd told anyone about it."

"Yeah. Well, I'd gathered that. And I told them I hadn't told a soul."

"No one has been able to find out how the abductors knew where he was going."

"Who else knew other than you and me?"

"Lauren and Nadira, of course. The police talked to both of them. Surely Nadira didn't tell anyone, since it was a clandestine operation to her. Lauren told me she hadn't told anyone."

"In that case, he either had to be followed or tracked."

"Tracked? Do you mean with a GPS locator or something like that?"

"A GPS tracker." She was looking straight ahead. "But, Tom"—she turned toward him— "why was he crucified? Could they be sending some sort of message?"

"I don't know. Maybe so."

"Do you know if the abductors are Muslim?"

"I think so, but I'm not positive."

"Just look, Tom. He'd been talking to you about Christianity. Maybe they wanted to make a statement. Maybe they wanted to punish him but in such a way that would also warn Muslims about considering Christianity."

"But how would they know that he'd been talking to a Christian? He doesn't even know who they are," Tom said.

"Who have you told about him?"

"Uh," Tom paused to think, "Pete."

Martha said, "And George."

They stared into each other's wide-open eyes.

"Could it be?" He whispered.

"George has a big mouth."

"And he does talk to a lot of students. He could have told a lot of people."

"Yeah."

"Well, that's the story. I just didn't want to tell you all this over the phone. But it's late, and I have church early. So I'd better head on home."

"Okay. Thanks for filling me in. Whew. Pretty heavy." She spoke as she got out. "Good-night, Tom."

"See you tomorrow night." She closed the car door, and he drove off toward home.

CHAPTER 36

Tom barely slept, more questions without answers filling his head. By morning he had decided that he needed to tell his father what had happened. He was up and dressed before Martin got up. The Sunday *Washington Post* arrived with a heavy *thud* on the wooden porch floor, and Tom brought it in. There on the front page was a picture of Nadira holding Ahmed's head, with the caption "Exchange student after botched crucifixion in apparent hate crime." *Wait until Nadira's dad sees this,* Tom thought. *And the university will go berserk. Oh, God,* he silently prayed, *what have I gotten myself into?* Eventually he heard footsteps upstairs, then the shower running. Tom started a pot of coffee while he waited. It was ready when Martin came downstairs.

"Well, good-morning." He sounded surprised. "And coffee ready! What a treat."

"Have a seat, Dad. I'll pour you some." He handed Martin a cup of black coffee. "I need to talk to you about something."

Martin looked up at him inquisitively. Tom handed him the paper and pointed at the picture, watching for his father's reaction. Martin slowly raised his head and eyes toward Tom. "Pretty serious stuff," he commented.

"I was there."

Martin shot upright. "You were there? Did you see this? I want to hear all about it."

Tom told him the whole story, beginning with the call from Lauren about the dinner plan.

"Is Ahmed going to be all right?"

"The doctor thought he would. They said he might be released today."

"If you hadn't found him, would he have died?"

"Surely someone else would've found him. It was a fairly public place. But, I don't know. It was pretty cold, so there weren't many scouts out running around in the woods. The only campers nearby were in RVs. I guess he'd have died if someone hadn't found him before morning."

"They didn't mention your name in the paper."

"I suppose they thought I was one of the EMS squad."

"I told you to be careful."

"I thought it was just a harmless double date. How was I to know?"

Martin paused for a moment. Tom said, "After church I'm going back to the hospital. If they let him out, he'll need a ride to someplace. I don't know if he'll be able to drive or even walk."

Ahmed woke looking into Nadira's eyes. "What a wonderful way to wake up," he mumbled. "Maybe I've died and gone to heaven."

"How are you feeling?"

"Not well. That's how I know I'm not in heaven. My hands and feet hurt. Especially my feet. And I ache throughout my body."

"I'm so sorry."

"I'm sorry I spoiled your dinner party."

"Speaking of food, are you hungry?"

"Not really."

"They brought breakfast a while ago. The eggs are cold by now but all the rest was cold anyway. Would you like some?"

"Some juice would be good."

He drank some orange juice, and a nurse appeared and took his vital signs. "A doctor will be by soon to check on you, and he'll probably release you if he thinks you're well enough. Do you think you're well enough?"

"That depends on if I can walk. May I try?"

"Sure."

He rolled to the edge of the bed and dropped his feet to the floor. He began to stand but sat back down on the bed with a loud grunt. "Oh, oh, oh. That really hurt." He grimaced.

"You may have to rent a wheelchair for a few days," the nurse said. "Let me have a look." She pulled the sheet off his legs and removed the bandage on one foot. "I can see why it hurts. There are a lot of cuts but none very deep."

As she replaced the bandage, two police officers came in. "Oh!" she said. "Just a second, and I'll be out of here." Soon she left.

"Miss, may we speak to Ahmed alone, please?"

"I was there. I probably know more than he does," Nadira said.

"Just give us a few minutes, okay?"

"Sure." She left the room.

The officers introduced themselves. Then one of them asked, "Do you know why they did this to you?"

"Yes, and Captain Parsons knows too. They want to eliminate me because I might reveal their crimes."

"Do you know who they are?"

"I'm not certain. I saw only one face, and I didn't know him. There were others in the car. Maybe two more. But they knocked me out so soon I was not able to see them."

"Who do you suspect may have been in the car?"

"The others may be my ex-business partners, Rashid al-Jaber and Masoud al-Shahrani."

"Why would you suspect them?"

"It is obvious that my ex-partners discussed me with the terrorists, to warn them that I am a threat to them. Certainly that is why they attempted to bomb my car a week and a half ago. I guess you didn't catch the men who did this to me."

"No, we didn't."

"That means they will continue to look for me so they can kill me. I cannot remain here."

"Captain Parsons would like for you to come to the police station tomorrow."

"I'll try. I can't walk, though, and I am in great pain. Is my presence here a secret, or can anyone call and find that I'm here?"

"You'll need to talk to the hospital people about that."

"Please let Nadira come back in. But tell Captain Parsons that if I can't come to him, I will call him."

The officers left and Nadira came back in, followed by a doctor in a long white coat and a stethoscope around his neck and the nurse. He listened to Ahmed's heart, asked a few questions, and then told him that he'd be discharged before noon. He left without further conversation. The nurse said, "We'll take you in a wheelchair to the office to check out and then to the hospital main entrance. We'll arrange a rental wheelchair for you if you want. Do you have someone who can pick you up?"

"Please arrange a wheelchair. I'll have to make a phone call to see about being picked up. Are my clothes and cell phone here?"

Nadira said, "Your clothes are right here." She gestured to a plastic bag on a metal stand. She handed the bag to Ahmed. "See if the phone is there."

The nurse said, "I'll be back in a few minutes." She left the room.

He felt around in the bag, then pulled his pants out and searched the pockets. "It's not here. They either stole it, or I left it on the seat in my car. I need to call Tom to see if he can pick us up, but I don't know his number."

Nadira called Lauren and got the number. Ahmed listened to her end of a long conversation about his well-being, after which she called Tom's number and handed the phone to Ahmed. It rang four times, and then his voice mail answered. He left a message.

Five minutes later Tom called back. He'd been in church and felt his phone vibrate. Could he pick up Ahmed and Nadira? "Of course. I'll be there in an hour. But what's your situation? Can you walk or drive?"

"I can't walk. It's too painful. The hospital is arranging a wheelchair for me. I don't know about driving. My hands are bandaged, but I can use my fingers. Whether I could use my feet or not, I won't know until I try it. Oh, the nurse is back. Please hold on." He turned toward the nurse. "I will be picked up. What time should I tell him to come?"

"We'll have you at the front door at eleven thirty," she said.

Tom said, "I heard that. I'll be there."

"Okay. Thank you. I'll see you soon." He handed the phone back to Nadira.

Tom was waiting at the hospital entrance when Ahmed appeared in a wheelchair. The nurse pushed him to Tom's car and helped him into the front seat. Nadira got in the back. Tom lifted the wheelchair into the trunk.

When the doors were closed Tom said, "Ahmed, I'm going to take you to my house. My parents and I don't think you'll be able to take care of yourself in the dorm or in a motel."

Ahmed said, "That's very kind of you. But it should remain secret, so the terrorists will not come there looking for me and endangering you and your family."

"We talked about that. In spite of the risk, we want to help you get back on your feet. Nadira, we'll go to your house first so you can be there when your parents come home."

"My mother called last night after Ahmed was moved to intensive care."

"What did you tell her?"

"She thought I was at home because I had forwarded calls to my cell phone. I simply told her that I was fine. I told her that I'd spent much of the day with Lauren, and she approved. She thinks highly of Lauren and so do I. You have found a very fine woman, Mr. Parker."

"Yes, I think you're right."

"Have you looked at the pictures she took of the car last night?" Nadira asked.

"Oh, yeah. She got some really good shots."

"She did that while she kept in constant contact with the police. She kept a very cool head while I was blubbering in the backseat."

"You know, I hadn't thought about that. Yes she did, didn't she?"

"You two make a very good pair."

Tom laughed. "Thanks. I guess you're right."

When they were close to the Shalash home, Nadira instructed Tom to drop her off at the corner where he picked her up the night before. She said to Ahmed, "I hope your phone is in your car, so we can talk."

"So do I." he paused. "Nadira, thank you for taking care of me all night. You are a true angel."

"I'm glad I could be some help. After all, I'm partly to blame. Tom, thanks for the ride home. Bye, Ahmed." She got out and hurried up the street.

As they pulled away, Ahmed said, "Captain Parsons wants me to come to the police station tomorrow. Is that something you can help me with?"

"I have a couple of classes tomorrow morning, one at nine and the other at eleven. I want to show him the pictures Lauren took of the car, so they'll have something to look for. Do you know what time he'll be there?"

"No, but maybe you could call the station and find out. I would call but I left my cell phone in my car. Are you thinking about going early?"

"Yeah."

"You have his number, don't you? I gave it to you last week."

"It's in my phone. I'll call when we get home. I hope you don't mind sleeping on the couch."

"I could sleep anywhere now. The nurse told me to take Tylenol. They gave me some this morning, but it's beginning to wear off. Do you have any?"

"We probably do. If not, I can go get some."

When they arrived at the Parkers' Tom took the wheelchair to the porch, then went back to the car, and helped Ahmed up the steps and to the porch. In the house Tom's parents welcomed Ahmed and helped him to the couch. They offered lunch, which Ahmed declined. Soon he was asleep.

The newspaper was still on the porch when Nadira went into the house. *They're not home yet,* she thought, gratefully. *I'm glad to be home. I'm starved, and I need a nap.* She made herself a sandwich and then changed clothes. *Uh oh. There's blood all over these things. I'd better look at my coat.* She had thrown her coat on a chair in the living room. She found that it had blood on it, too. *Gosh, how will I get it off?* She soaked all her blood-stained clothes in cold water and then, except for her coat, treated them with all-color bleach, and ran them through the washer. Soaking didn't work for her coat. She called Lauren.

"I've got blood all over my jacket, and it wouldn't come off in cold water. What can I do? I can't let my mother see that."

Lauren said, "I have an idea. I'll ride over there and trade you coats. I'll take your jacket to the dorm and work on it. I might take it to the cleaners. That way you'll have an honest answer if your mom wonders where your jacket went. I'll wear something that's too light for this weather."

"Lauren, you're a lifesaver. I would never have thought to do that."

"Okay. I'll be over in about a half hour. Do you have blood on your other clothes?"

"Yeah, but it came out. Mostly. I might have to run them through again."

"By the way, do you get the *Washington Post*?"

"Yeah."

"Tom just called and said your picture is on the front page."

"What? Oh, no." A sharp pang of anxiety shot through her chest. She ran down the stairs and into the living room where she'd thrown the paper.

"You may want to get rid of it somehow before your parents get home. When do you expect them?"

Nadira unfolded the paper. "Good grief. This is awful." In her midsection a storm erupted.

"Are you looking at it?"

"Yes, and there I am with Ahmed's head on my lap. If my father sees this, I'm as good as dead. He'll crucify me!" She continued to stare at the picture.

"Well, don't throw it away until I get there, so I can see it."

"But what am I going to do? He'll want to see the paper."

"When are they coming home?"

"Probably not until tonight, unless he's already seen the paper someplace."

"Hide it until I get there. I'll leave in about five minutes."

"Good. Lauren, this is a disaster. I know he'll see it sometime. Come as soon as you can."

"On my way. Bye."

She removed the front section and ran back upstairs to her room and hid it under her mattress. *What'll I say to him? I know he'll want to see the paper. At least they didn't print my name. Does it really look like me?* She pulled the paper out and looked at it again. *Enough that they'll think it's me. Maybe I can give it to Lauren. I can tell him there's a story about a student she knows. I won't lie to him. I can't lie to him.*

Ahmed awoke after a three-hour nap. Although alone in the living room, he could hear voices in another part of the house. Needing to go to the bathroom, he put one foot on the floor, and then quickly lifted it, because of the pain, and uttered a small cry. Mrs. Parker appeared at the doorway and said, "Do you need to get up?"

"Yes, if you don't mind."

She turned and called, "Tom, can you help Ahmed get up?"

"They gave him a bedpan, Mom." Tom said as he walked into the room. He picked up the bedpan from the floor and handed it to Ahmed. "I'll come back and get this in a few minutes." He grinned and left the room.

A little later, after Tom had taken care of the bedpan, Ahmed said, "I really need to call someone. But his phone number is in my cell phone, and I don't know where it is. If the terrorists stole it, that person will be in serious trouble. You have the number of the police station. Can you call them and ask about my car and my cell phone?"

"Sure." Tom placed the call and handed the phone to Ahmed.

Ahmed's conversation with the officer who answered was inconclusive. The officer said, "I don't know anything about your car. I'll have to find out and call you back."

Ahmed gave him the number and told him who would answer. He handed the phone back to Tom. "Have you called Captain Parsons yet?"

"Thanks for reminding me. I'll call him now."

Ahmed listened to Tom's end of the conversation. After identifying himself he asked, "Is this Captain Parsons?" Pause. "Is he in today?" Pause. "Do you know what time he'll be in tomorrow?" Pause. "Okay. Thanks. Good-bye."

Tom said to Ahmed, "He doesn't come in until eight tomorrow. But if we're there waiting for him, I should be able to get to class on time. The station isn't far from here. We should be able to get there in five or six minutes."

"Good," Ahmed said. "Is there any possibility today or tomorrow you could take me to the motel where I've been staying so I can check out and get my clothes and books and things?"

Tom glanced at his watch. "I have a meeting to go to tonight at six. If we go right now, we can do it today."

"I will need some clean clothes soon," Ahmed said. "And I'll need my computer, so I can keep up with my classes."

"Okay, let's hit the road." He helped Ahmed into his wheelchair, told his parents where they were going, and left.

They were still on the way to the motel when Tom's phone rang. Tom pulled over and answered. "Yes." Pause. "Repeat that address, please." Pause. "Can we get in today?" Pause. He held his hand over the phone and said to Ahmed, "Do you have your driver's license with you?"

Ahmed touched his back pocket. "Yes."

"Yes, he has it." Pause. "We can be there before five. Thanks a lot." He disconnected the phone. "We can look in your car for your phone if we get there before five. I have the address. It's pretty close to the police station."

"That's good." *I really want to call Hashim,* he thought.

At the motel Ahmed, with Tom's help, retrieved all his belongings and then checked out. From there they drove to the warehouse where his car was being examined. He and Tom were admitted by showing their licenses, and Tom pushed him, accompanied by a police officer, to the car. Inside, lying on the front seat, was his cell phone. *Wonderful, wonderful, wonderful.* "May I take this?" he asked the officer.

"Sure. But you can't have your car back yet. The guys that will go over it won't be in until tomorrow."

He held up his bandaged hands. "Well, as you can see, I probably couldn't drive it anyway."

"What happened to you?"

Ahmed glanced at Tom. "The story is too long to tell. The short story is that I fell into the wrong hands. My friend here saved me. But he must go to a meeting now. We should leave so he won't be late."

Back in the car, as they started out for the Parker home, Ahmed said, "Will you get to your meeting on time?"

Tom looked at his watch. "I should make it with time to spare."

"What kind of meeting is it?"

"It's the weekly meeting of the Collegiate Christian Association, CCA."

"What do you do there?" He was twisted in his seat, looking at Tom.

"We sing praises to God, have prayer, and then one or two people talk about their experiences in becoming Christians or in becoming part of CCA. After that we have some snacks and have some games or just talk."

"Men and women together?"

Tom laughed. "Yes. Why?"

"I wondered. Would it be permissible for me to go with you?"

"Sure. I'd like to have your company."

"I wouldn't need to change my clothes, would I? These," he pointed to his shirt and pants, "were clean yesterday afternoon when I left for the restaurant. They washed me well at the hospital."

Tom laughed again. "You look fine. Everyone there will want to know about your bandages and the wheelchair, though. Are you ready for that?"

"If you give me the opportunity, I would like to say something about what happened to me."

"Fine. I think everyone will be very interested. I can arrange for you to say a few words, if you wish."

"Thank you."

Back at the Parkers', while Tom prepared for the meeting, Ahmed called Hashim. "This is Ahmed. Do you know what happened last night?"

"No. Should I?"

"It was on the front page of the *Washington Post*."

"Do I need to buy the paper to find out, or will you tell me?"

Ahmed laughed. "I'll tell you." He told the whole story. "So here I am all bandaged, hands and feet."

"What a terrible thing. Did you get a look at any of them?" Hashim asked.

"Just one. I think there were three in the car. But I'm not sure. We're to see Captain Parsons tomorrow morning. Tom Parker will take me."

"I'll see what I can find out about it from Rashid and Masoud. If they have any connections with your attackers, they should make some mention of it unless they're being very careful. I'll also talk to Parsons and set up a meeting with you and him, so we can share information. But not with Tom Parker there."

"I understand."

"All right. I'll be in touch."

In the meantime, Lauren pedaled to Silver Spring on Nadira's bicycle. She rang the doorbell at the Shalash home. Nadira opened the door immediately.

"Oh, Lauren. I'm so glad you're here. Let me show you the paper." She thrust it into Lauren's hands before she had a chance to take off her light jacket.

Lauren looked at it for a long time, studying the picture of Nadira carefully. "I can't really tell this is you." She laid it down. "Let me take my jacket off. I got cold coming over here. Do you have something warmer I can borrow so I won't freeze going home?" She handed her jacket to Nadira and sat down and examined the picture again. "It could be anyone," she said.

"But look at the coat! My mother will recognize that."

"Maybe. Can I have this picture? I'd like to have the whole section so I can sit on it. The bike has been outside for days and the seat was so cold, I could hardly stand it."

Nadira smiled broadly. "Of course. You can have the whole paper if you want it."

"No, it's too big. One section will be fine. But I particularly would like the front section because I'm told it has a story about someone I might know."

Nadira began to giggle. Then she hugged Lauren. "You are a genius."

"I know." Lauren laughed and pushed Nadira away. "May I see your bloody clothes?"

"I can show you the coat. My other things are in the washer. They should be about done, though. Come on upstairs."

In her room Nadira had hung her coat over the back of a chair. Without moving it Lauren carefully examined it. "Did you try to wash it?"

"No. It's supposed to be dry-cleaned. I did soak it in cold water."

"Yeah. The blood is pretty obvious. Do you mind if I take it to a cleaner?"

"Not at all. They should be able to get it out, shouldn't they?"

"I think so. We'll find out. I hope it's not ruined."

"Me too."

Lauren looked directly at Nadira. "You know, sooner or later, your folks are going to find out all about this."

"I know. But maybe by then the police will have found my attacker and Ahmed's attacker, and we can all look back on it and have a big sigh of relief. My father might be a little mad at me for disobeying my confinement, but by then it won't be so serious. Hopefully."

"Yeah. Hopefully. Well, I've got to get back to the campus. I have a meeting at six tonight. May I wear your coat? The jacket I wore over here wasn't warm enough."

That evening, at the CCA meeting, Tom watched Ahmed during the praise singing, trying to gauge his reaction to the joyful songs and enthusiasm of the students. *He looks like he's interested, but he doesn't seem to be caught up in it. That's okay. He's just familiarizing himself with Christianity.* During the prayer, Tom saw that Ahmed didn't bow his head or close his eyes. *He probably thinks the prayer should be more organized, that we should all be doing some prescribed actions.*

Following the prayer, the leader asked Tom to introduce his guest. Tom pushed Ahmed's wheelchair to the front, and then took the microphone in his hand, and said, "I'd like to introduce Ahmed Suliman. Ahmed is an exchange student from Morocco and is a Muslim. He wanted to come here tonight to say something about the bandages and the wheelchair. So, here's Ahmed." He handed the microphone to Ahmed and asked if he could hold it. He tried it and then nodded that he could.

Ahmed began without hesitation. "Last night Tom Parker saved my life."

Tom jerked his head toward Ahmed.

"He saw me being kidnapped by several men, and he followed the car until it reached Greenbelt Park. He called the police who also came to the park. They all looked for me, but it was Tom who found me. They had nailed my hands to a wall, and they made me stand on a large nail. It was to imitate what was done to Jesus. I think they did it because I had been speaking to Tom about the Christian religion. They wanted to discourage me and other Muslims from even speaking to you. They do not represent Islam, but they are bad people who misunderstand the Holy Qur'an and misunderstand the teachings of the Prophet Muhammad. Tom found me before I died. But if he hadn't found me, I would have probably died by this morning. I am grateful that Tom, a Christian man, saved me, a Muslim man. May God bless him, and may God bless all of you for learning about caring for others. Thank you." He handed the microphone back to Tom.

The applause was long and enthusiastic. Tom was embarrassed. *It was a good speech, though,* Tom thought. When the applause stopped he started to make a comment but then thought, *What could I say?* He handed the microphone to the leader and then wheeled Ahmed back to where they had been sitting.

Lauren suddenly appeared and hugged Tom and hugged Ahmed. Tom heard Martha's voice before he saw her. She had the microphone in her hand. "I want to second Ahmed's thanks to Tom. And I'd also like to say that Lauren Stevenson was also there and was very much instrumental in the whole episode. Lauren has just recently joined CCA and has shown herself to be a true follower of Jesus."

A second round of applause filled the room. Lauren's face became very red, and she crouched behind Tom's chair. Eventually, when the applause stopped, she returned to her seat. Martha handed the microphone to the leader and went back and hugged Lauren. *I don't know how to interpret that,* Tom thought. *But I'm sure it will become clear to me at some point.*

At about the same time as the CCA meeting, Nadira's parents arrived at home. Nadira met them at the door and hugged them and said she was glad they were safely home, although inside she was filled with the turbulence of great anxiety. *I would love to go and hide, but I can't do that. I'll just have to hang around and go with whatever happens.*

CHAPTER 37

On Monday morning Mr. Shalash was already gone when Nadira awoke. She lay still. *I'm still alive. He didn't say a word about the paper. Thank you,* she breathed a prayer. After she dressed she called Lauren.

"So, what happened?" Lauren asked.

"Nothing. Nothing yet, anyway. They were very tired and they went to bed early. They didn't say anything about anything."

"I'm so happy for you. But thanks for letting me wear your coat home. It was cold, cold, cold. It's not supposed to be this cold in October in Maryland."

"You're welcome. Mother will ask me questions. But I don't worry about her."

"It's just the opposite with me. I can handle my dad. But Mom can see right through me."

"Well, I just wanted you to know. I should be getting downstairs."

"Okay. Bye."

When Tom told Martin that he and Ahmed were going to the police station, Martin insisted on going with him. Tom said, "What are you going to do? You don't know anything about what happened. I don't see why you should be involved."

Martin looked straight at Tom's eyes. "Tom, you're twenty years old. There are things you aren't familiar with when it comes to crime and police. I want to be there to make sure you don't incriminate yourself or get talked into some form of entrapment. No, I'm going with you."

They drove to Hyattsville to the county police station. Inside Martin told the clerk, "We're here to report a crime."

"What kind of crime?" the clerk asked.

"Attempted murder."

"All right. Give me the specifics."

"Tom, tell him what you saw Saturday night."

Tom said, "The police already know all about this. I was present at Greenbelt Park where Ahmed Suliman was crucified."

"Oh. There's someone here you need to talk to. Wait just a minute, please." The clerk called someone on his intercom.

"I'll be right there," Tom heard the reply.

Almost immediately a uniformed officer appeared. "I'm Captain Parsons." Looking at Martin and at Tom and back, he said. "One of you must be Tom Parker."

"That's me. This is my dad, Martin Parker."

"Tom, Martin, nice to meet you. Good morning Ahmed. Come with me."

They followed Parsons along a corridor to a room with a desk and comfortable chairs. Parsons said, "Have a seat. Tom, Ahmed told me about you just Thursday. He must have known something was about to happen." Another officer came in and sat behind them.

"I don't know about that, Captain. I guess you know all about what happened at Greenbelt Park Saturday night."

"I only know what they've told me. Are you the boy that tailed the car that Ahmed was abducted in?"

"Yes, sir."

"That was some very fine detective work. You're to be commended."

Tom glanced at his father, who was looking at him. "Thank you, sir."

Parsons turned toward Ahmed. "Ahmed, you look awful. Do you feel as bad as you look?"

"I have a great deal of pain, Captain."

"I'm very sorry, Ahmed. Tell me what happened."

"All I remember is being dragged into the car and then waking up hanging by my hands. Tom and Nadira and his friend Lauren were there and the police and medical people were there. It was all very confusing because they had drugged me. The doctor said it was chloroform."

"Did you see any of the men who abducted you?"

"Just one. It was no one I know. But I don't think I will ever forget his face."

"Tell me, why were the four of you together?"

"It was to be a dinner together at a restaurant. Josie's. Tom brought Nadira and Lauren in his car, and I drove my car there to join them. Tom was there when I arrived and stood at the entrance to the parking lot to direct me to a parking place."

"Tom, tell me what you saw."

Tom glanced at Martin, who nodded, and then he told Parsons the entire story, including Lauren's role in communicating with the police and taking pictures.

When he finished, Parsons said, "May we see your pictures?"

"Yes." Tom pulled his phone from his pocket, touched the appropriate app, and handed it to Parsons.

He looked at each photograph carefully. After almost five minutes he said, "Some of these are very good. This could be most helpful. Unfortunately, the car didn't have a license plate, so it will be hard to track. May we copy these?"

"Sure," Tom said, again glancing at Martin, who nodded again.

Parsons handed the phone to the other officer. He looked at Ahmed. "Do you know how the abductors knew how to find you?"

"No, sir. Only the four of us knew where we were going. It is a great mystery to me."

Parsons looked at Tom. "Are you aware if anyone else knew where you were to meet or even knew the meeting was to happen?" The other officer returned and sat down.

Tom said, "A friend of mine, Martha Jenkins, knew I'd be getting together with Ahmed, but she didn't know where. The police spoke to her on Saturday night. She had not told anyone."

"Hmm." Parsons looked at Ahmed. "Do you think they could have followed you? Are you still staying in a motel?"

"Yes, sir. But I had moved to a new motel and until yesterday no one knew where that was. Tom took me there yesterday to get my clothes and things and to check out. So I don't know how they could have followed me."

"Well, they could have just waited until you arrived at the restaurant and just followed you into the parking lot."

"But they would have had to know I was going there. Are they able to tap into my cell phone?"

Parsons waved his hand. "Anything is possible. I understand tapping into cell phones is very difficult. The authorities can do it. We'll investigate that possibility. Do you know of any other possible ways to find out who did this to you?"

"Of course. You should suspect Rashid and Masoud."

"Yes, of course. They will be interrogated."

Ahmed held his bandaged hands together below his chin, like a child clutching a doll. "I would expect to find that the ones who did this are the same ones who attacked Nadira. Because I was crucified in a public place they surely anticipated that I would be found before dying. Although they must have known that if I would not be found, I would soon die. From the cold if nothing else. They had taken my clothes off, all except my undershorts. But, as in Nadira's case, I think they were sending a message. I don't know what the message would be, although it must have had something to do with Christianity. I have found friends among the Christians, you know. Why else would they choose crucifixion? For that reason I worry that by staying at the Parkers' house I am endangering their safety. So I intend to leave there as soon as possible."

Parsons said, "I think you're right in that. Well, that's all we need to talk about today. I'll call you if we need to talk again. I wish you a fast recovery." He turned toward Tom and Martin. "Thank you both for coming. We may have to talk to you again, Tom." He spoke to Martin. "And you're welcome to come along with him. I'm glad to have met the father of a courageous young man." He shook Martins hand and then Tom's hand and smiled. "Oh, and here's your cell phone."

Tom drove Ahmed and Martin back to the house and then rushed off to his first class of the day.

As soon as he returned to the Parker living room, Ahmed lay down on the couch, happy to be off his painful feet and to rest his aching shoulders and back. Within minutes he fell asleep. He awoke to the sound of his cell phone ringing. Sleepily he groped for it in his pants pockets, finally finding it in his jacket. He saw that it was Hashim calling.

"Good morning, Ahmed. How are you feeling?"

"Not much better. I need some Tylenol."

"I spoke to Captain Parsons. We set up a meeting for tomorrow morning. Eight o'clock."

"I'll try to arrange a ride. If I can't, I'll call you."

"No, call Parsons. I can't be seen with you. He can send out an unmarked car for you."

"Okay. I'll see you in the morning."

Ahmed disconnected and, looking up, saw Mrs. Parker in the doorway watching him. She smiled and asked if he needed anything.

"Some Tylenol, if you have it, please."

She brought him a bottle of pills and a glass of water. "Are you hungry? I couldn't tell if you had any breakfast. It's lunchtime now. You must be starving."

"Yes, madam, I could eat a little, thank you."

In ten minutes she brought him a sandwich and a bowl of cut up fruit on a tray. After he ate he tried to do some homework on his computer but soon fell asleep. When he awoke, Tom was sitting in the chair next to the couch, reading.

Ahmed leaned on one elbow and pulled the blanket and sheets back. Tom looked up at him. "There's still some life left in him."

"I've done nothing but sleep and eat all day." He looked at his watch. "Three o'clock. My body must need the sleep to heal. Your mother gave me some Tylenol and lunch." He yawned.

"How are you feeling?"

Ahmed sat up, put his feet on the floor, and rocked forward to put some weight on them. "Ouch," he said. "Not much better. But I think if I had some padding under them it might not hurt so much." He rolled over on his side.

"I'll see if I can find something." He stood, but Ahmed had more to say.

"I have another meeting at the police station tomorrow morning."

"What time?"

"Eight."

"Hmm" Tom thought a few seconds. "I could drop you off, but I couldn't stay. I have a class at eight."

"If it's no inconvenience"—Ahmed looked up at him, his eyes wide—"that would be all right. I think the police can bring me back. I guess my car will be available tomorrow. If I'm able to walk tomorrow, I would like to go without my wheelchair, so I can drive my car. But if that is not possible, I may need your help to move the car if they require me to do so."

"We can see about that in the morning. If they need you to move the car, my dad and I can do that if you can't drive."

"Thank you, Tom. I'm sorry to be a burden to you. Unfortunately, I am very helpless at the moment."

"No problem. That's what we're here for. Let me see if I can find anything to pad your feet with." He left. Ahmed listened as Tom climbed the uncarpeted, wooden stairs and then heard his footsteps as he walked above him.

After a few minutes, he returned empty handed. "We couldn't find anything that would work. Mom suggested we try a medical equipment store." He bent and looked at the label on the wheelchair. "This place, where the wheelchair came from, probably has something. I'll give them a call." A quick discussion with the store confirmed that they carried a number of things that might help.

Later, Ahmed had his first dinner in an American home. Although accustomed to American food, his experience was mostly from eating at a university dining room, presented cafeteria style, where he could choose foods he thought he'd like. At the Parkers' there were no choices. At home in Morocco, although there was a distinct French influence, the diet was typically North African.

During dinner Martin said, "I'm planning to go over to Annapolis on Friday for a parade to honor the Navy Seals. Tom, would you be interested in going along? How about you, Ahmed?"

Tom said, "I have a one o'clock statistics class I might have to skip. What time would we have to be there?"

"It starts at four. But we'll need to be there about an hour before, and even then it will be hard to find a place to park. I'd like to leave at two, to give us enough time to get parked, and then get to the parade ground."

"I could do that," Tom said. "Would you like to go with us, Ahmed?"

"I might be able to walk by then. Is it possible in a wheelchair?"

Martin said, "Of course. I think you'd really like it."

"Are you going, Mom?" Tom asked.

"I don't know. I've been to several. It depends on the weather."

"What's it like?" Ahmed asked. *It must be unlike the parades I've seen. The French have some wonderful parades.*

"It's a military parade. All the midshipmen are lined up, company by company. They go through the manual of arms and then march past the reviewing stand. There are a couple of bands and a bagpipe band, so there's a lot of marching music. It takes about an hour. It's just a beautiful and thrilling spectacle, with all the students in their full dress uniforms and all."

I've never been to a military parade. He pictured banners flying, goose-stepping soldiers, and weapons on trucks "Will we need to stand?"

"No, they have bleachers."

"What are bleachers?"

Tom said, "Like at a ball field. You know, like wooden boards." He used his hands to show how the seats are stacked.

"Oh, I know. Yes, I think that would be very interesting. I will be happy to go."

"Good." Martin raised both hands. "That's good. How are your feet doing?" He looked at Ahmed.

"They are still quite painful. Tom has found a place that sells or rents padded shoes and that would probably help very much."

Tom said, "We'll go out and try to get some tomorrow. He has to go back to the police station in the morning, and I have an eight o'clock. But after that we could go. Dad, they might need for Ahmed to move his car tomorrow. Is there any way you could help with that? I don't think Ahmed will be able to drive by then."

Martin thought a minute. "I suppose I could come back at lunchtime, and we could do it. After work would be better. That would be about five thirty. So, are you thinking of driving his car over here?"

"Yeah. But not park it here. We'd park on the next block or a couple of blocks away."

"That would be smart. They obviously know what his car looks like."

When dinner was over, Tom went upstairs to study, and Ahmed returned to the living room, also to study.

CHAPTER 38

Ahmed rode with Tom to the Hyattsville police station, to the underground parking lot, where he could use the elevator. As he had anticipated, Ahmed had some difficulty propelling himself due to the wounds in his hands. However, he was determined to be no more of a burden on Tom than was absolutely necessary, and even though it was painful for him, he eventually reached the clerk's desk. "I'm here to see Captain Parsons," he said.

"One moment." The clerk called someone, and in a few seconds an officer arrived.

"Mr. Suliman?" Ahmed raised his hand. "Come with me please. Do you need help?"

"I'm sorry, but with these bandages," he held up both hands, "I have trouble with this wheelchair."

To Ahmed's relief, the officer pushed him to Captain Parsons' office. As he entered, he saw Hashim seated near the corner of Parsons' desk. Parsons was seated behind the desk. The officer rolled Ahmed to the center of the desk as Parsons and Hashim both stood to greet him. The officer left.

Parsons began, "I'm glad you could make it this morning, Ahmed. Are you feeling any better?"

"No, not much," Ahmed said.

"So sorry. Well, I wanted you here to listen to Hashim's report. I think you'll find it encouraging. Hashim, why don't you go ahead?"

Hashim, wearing a short-sleeved tee shirt and jeans despite the cool weather, smiled. "We have a video of the people who picked up the checks."

"Oh, that's amazing. How?" Ahmed asked.

"Thanks to you, we were able to intercept the package that Masoud mailed. It was addressed to a PO box at the M Street post office, the same place where we saw Masoud pick up the letters last Friday. We were able to set up cameras that recorded anyone in the room and any who opened that particular PO box, and we were successful Sunday night."

"Did you recognize him?"

"No. There were two of them. We followed them to their home. We'll find out their names soon."

"May I see the video?" He looked at Parsons.

Parsons gestured toward Hashim.

Hashim said, "Sure." He turned on a projector that was sitting on Parson's desk and turned off the light. The room was instantly dark. As the video began to play on the wall facing Parson's desk, he said, "This occurred at about nine thirty Sunday night. No one else was in the room. As I mentioned, there were two cameras recording. The one you're looking at now was aimed at the PO box."

"I only see one guy," Ahmed said.

"The other man was near the entrance, apparently watching, or maybe just waiting. You'll see him in a minute. Do you recognize this one?"

After a brief pause, Ahmed said, "No. He's new to me." He continued to watch as the man removed the package from the box and closed it. Then the scene changed to the entrance, where he could see a man standing, apparently watching the other man. "Stop!" Ahmed said loudly. "That's the guy who grabbed me. Yes, I'm sure of it. His face has been imprinted on my mind. That's him. There's no doubt." His heart beat fast as he looked at him. He looked at Hashim, then at Parsons. "Who is he?"

"We don't know his name yet. But we'll identify him soon."

"You should show these videos to Nadira."

"We'll be taking some still shots of these to her home today."

"Good. So, will you arrest them?"

Parsons replied. "Not quite yet. We need to build a very strong case against them."

Hashim said, "Don't worry, though. They're being watched, so they won't escape. There's more to this story than attacks on you and Nadira. They're planning something, probably something much larger."

"How do you know?"

"Mostly it's an educated guess. We're watching their house now to learn who is coming and going and what is being brought in and taken out. We're seeing a lot of activity. This effort isn't foolproof though. An explosive device can easily be hidden under someone's clothes or in a grocery bag. There are obviously some other people involved."

Ahmed frowned. "Like Rashid and Masoud?"

"Maybe. What do you know about Masoud?"

Ahmed took a deep breath. "He's a brute, a brute without dignity. I can imagine him being a criminal."

"What makes you say that?" Parsons asked.

"He has no fear or respect of authorities or other people."

Parsons looked at Hashim.

Hashim said, "I've spent some time with those guys recently. Rashid doesn't say much. But Masoud is a talker. He has no reluctance to speak badly of you." He pointed at Ahmed.

"Do you think Masoud is in contact with the terrorists?"

"I don't know. Something has compelled Rashid and Masoud to increase their advertising. Masoud has muttered about that. Reading the tea leaves, as we say, I have a theory that the terrorists have demanded more money, and that Rashid has agreed, hence the increase in advertising, but on the provision that they, the terrorists, do away with you. Rashid and Masoud see you as a threat, since you've gone to the police. You've violated the code. But they don't want to do away with you themselves, at least Rashid doesn't. I imagine that Rashid was able to convince the terrorists that you are a threat to them too."

"Well, Rashid and Masoud chased me all over the campus!" Ahmed waved his two bandaged fists.

"I know. But I think Rashid just wanted to beat you up, not kill you. He would have too much to lose to commit murder. Masoud, I'm not so sure."

"Yeah. I think he would." He nodded to add emphasis.

Parsons said, "Did you say there were three men in the car? Could either of the others have been Masoud?"

Ahmed shook his head. "I didn't get a good enough look at them. But Rashid is very familiar with Greenbelt Park. He goes there often to be alone."

Parsons said, "We'd like to find a stronger tie between the terrorists and Rashid and Masoud. Hashim thinks there probably is, but he hasn't seen it yet. And there has to be someone else." He held out his fist and then opened it, with his palm up. In his hand was a small metal object. "This was found in your car. It was attached to your car."

Ahmed bent toward it to see it better. "What is it?"

"It's a GPS tracking device. It's how your abductors were able to follow you Saturday night."

Ahmed looked at Parsons. "How could they have found my car to attach it? I've only had the car for a week. I've been to a gas station, stores, restaurants, this police station, the dealer, a couple of motels—it could have been anywhere. But they would have been looking for me. Oh," he paused. He said, more slowly, "I parked it at school for my midterm exam last Tuesday. Rashid and Masoud know my class schedule. They must have done it while I was taking my exam and then waited for me to come out of the building. That's when they chased me across the campus."

"That sounds very probable." Parsons nodded.

They all sat silently for a minute or two. Eventually Parsons said, "Will that do it for now?" He looked at Hashim and Ahmed.

"I think so," Hashim said.

Ahmed nodded.

Parsons continued, "We're making progress. Keep your eyes and ears open for any hint of an attack. If Hashim and the Bureau's boys are right, we might be the only ones that can head it off. We'll reconvene if anything turns up."

The meeting adjourned.

Ahmed said to Parsons, "I don't have a way home. Can you have someone take me?"

"Oh. How did you get here?"

"Tom Parker brought me and then went to class. Is my car available to pick up?"

"Yeah. sure."

"Can Tom and his father pick it up?"

"Yes, but you'll need to be with them."

"We plan to do that at noon."

"No problem. I'll have someone take you home. Just wait by the elevator."

When the doorbell rang at the Shalash home, Nadira heard Mrs. Shalash open the door almost immediately. *She must have been waiting at the door,* she thought. Nadira left her room and started down the stairs. A policewoman was in the hall with a manila envelope in her hand. She watched her mother show the officer into the living room and then start to call her, but stopped when she saw her. "I'm on my way, Mother." Nadira came into the living room and the officer stood and showed her badge and said, "I'm Lieutenant Price, Prince George's County PD."

"I'm Nadira. I'm so excited about this. They said you'd be bringing pictures."

"Yes," she said as she opened the envelope and pulled out the photographs.

"Here, sit beside me on the couch so we can look at them together." Nadira sat down and gestured for the officer to join her. "Where did these pictures come from?"

"I don't know," she said, "I asked the same question but didn't get an answer." She laughed. She handed the stack of pictures to Nadira.

Nadira looked at each picture carefully. After the first three she said, "These are all the same man. I've never seen him before." She turned to the next picture and drew in a sharp breath. "It's him!" She sat motionless as she stared at the image in her lap. She whispered, "It's him. It's the man I saw through the peephole. I watched him come in. I know it's him." She looked at the next two shots. "These are all him." She looked at the rest. "Just these three." She held them up, clutching them in her left hand like a just-completed manuscript. She looked at her mother. "This is the one. Here, look at him."

Her mother stood and took the pictures from her fist. She stared at them, hatred quickly growing on her face. She looked at each one, carefully memorizing his image. Then she handed them to the officer. "When will he be arrested?" She demanded, her voice husky and throaty, threatening.

"Soon, I think. We must be sure he can be convicted. Victim recognition can be fairly easily discredited by a good defense lawyer. We'll need other evidence. Knowing he's your attacker, we'll keep a close watch on him while we develop the case against him. We already have some additional charges. It shouldn't be long."

"My husband will be very happy at this progress. And I'm sure Nadira is too."

Nadira nodded. "Thank you."

Late in the morning Martin called Tom. "It looks like I can get away at lunchtime. I'll be there at about noon to pick you up."

At noon he came in the front door. "Are you guys ready to go?"

"Just about." Tom said. He moved the wheelchair to the couch, helped Ahmed up and into it, and then pushed him out the front door. He loaded Ahmed and the wheelchair in Martin's car and headed for the police garage. At the garage Ahmed identified himself, and they were given permission to take the car.

"That was easy," Martin said. "I'll head back. See you at supper."

"Thanks, Dad."

"Yes, thanks, Dad," Ahmed repeated.

Martin laughed.

Tom said to Ahmed, "Let's go over to the medical equipment store and see about padded boots."

"Yes, please."

On the way Ahmed told Tom about the GPS tracking device the police had found in his car and how they think it was placed there.

Tom said, "That explains a lot. Those guys aren't about to let you get away, are they?"

"Unfortunately, no. I don't know why the police haven't already arrested them. I'll have to continue to hide out until they do."

They found the store, near the hospital in Tacoma Park. There they found silicone pads and post-surgery shoes. Tom said, "Let's try them on here before we go out to the car."

Ahmed put them on and then gingerly stood up. Tom looked at him quizzically, but Ahmed said nothing. He took a step, then a second step.

Tom said, "Well?"

"It still hurts but not nearly as badly as without them. Let's go to the car and see if I can drive." He sat back in the wheelchair and wheeled himself out to the parking lot, with Tom holding the door open for him.

Ahmed was able to get into the car without help. He adjusted the seat so his right foot could reach the pedals. "Okay. Here goes." He started the car and then tried to back it out of the parking space. After a few minutes of unsuccessfully moving the car, he said, "This thing is just too big. I can't move it from the accelerator to the brake. Something down there is in the way. I'm sorry, Tom, but it looks like you'll have to drive it for me."

"No problem. Can you walk around the car?"

"I think so." He got out and walked slowly to the other side of the car and got in. Tom got in the driver's seat, and they drove back to College Park. Tom unloaded the wheelchair and moved Ahmed into the house. He then moved the car two blocks away, parked it, and walked home.

"I'm glad we did that," Tom told Ahmed when he got to the house. "At least you can put some weight on your feet and walk a little. I need to get going to my two o'clock class. I'll be back in about an hour and a half."

His mother was watching. "Do you have time for lunch?"

Tom glanced at his watch. "No. I'll eat when I get back." He picked up his backpack and left.

"How about you, Ahmed. Would you like some lunch?"

"Thanks, but I'll wait until Tom comes back." He collapsed on the couch and fell asleep.

In late afternoon Lauren thought, *I'd really like to talk to Tom. I guess I could call to ask about Ahmed. And I need to know if we're*

going to Greenbelt tomorrow night. Yeah, sure. She tapped his name on her contacts list.

Tom answered, "Hi Lauren. How're you doing?"

Encouraged by Tom's enthusiastic tone, she said, "I just needed to hear your voice."

He laughed. "I'm glad to hear yours too."

"Hey, how's Ahmed doing?"

"I don't know. He doesn't seem to be improving much. We were able to get him some padded shoes today, which make it more comfortable for him to stand. He tried to drive his car, but that didn't work. It's going to be a while."

"Oh, I'm so sorry. So I guess he'll continue to be your houseguest for some time, huh?"

"Yeah. That's not a problem, though. He's not a very demanding guest."

"That's good. Are we going to Greenbelt tomorrow?"

"Are you learning anything from George?"

"I think I'm getting to know Nadira a lot more since she's been living at home than when we were both in the dorm. And I'm beginning to see how George's lessons make sense. So yes, I think I'm learning a lot."

"Good. Then we should go."

"All three of us?"

"Uh," he spoke slowly, "I think for now we should all go. It's part of CCA's standard operating procedure. I think Martha should go too. I mean, it would look sort of, you know, disrespectful of the rules if she didn't."

"I suppose you're right."

"I do think that we should evaluate after tomorrow's meeting to see if we should keep it up, or if we've learned enough. Maybe we should involve George in that conversation."

"Yeah. That sounds like a good idea. Okay. Will you pick me up at the regular time?"

"Yes. About six thirty."

"Okay, Tom. Thanks. I'm glad I got to hear your voice. I'll see you tomorrow."

"I'm looking forward to it. Bye."

CHAPTER 39

The temperature had increased to typical mid-October weather by Wednesday morning, and Tom was enjoying the walk across campus to his nine o'clock class. When his phone rang, he resented the intrusion until he saw that Martha was calling. "Sister Martha, to what may I attribute this early morning call?"

"Early morning? I don't think you understand the meaning of the word. It was early when I went out for my run this morning at six thirty."

"I think of that as night. It was dark then, wasn't it?"

"Only because of daylight saving time. By the correct time of day, it was light."

"And it was cold then."

"Nippy. Are we going to see George tonight?"

"Of course. Why do you ask?"

"After what happened to Ahmed, I thought perhaps we should regroup or something. The world seems to be falling down around us. First Nadira, then Ahmed."

"Maybe we just don't know enough to understand what's happening."

"Oh. So more schooling is required. So be it. Listen, I'd like to drive myself tonight and take Lauren with me."

"That's fine with me, but Lauren needs to agree. She may be reluctant."

"I understand that. But as her discipler, I need some time alone with her."

"Well, that makes sense, as long as you don't tell her bad things about me."

"I suppose I could make some up. But really, I just want her to get to know me a little better. She might find out that I'm a nice person after all."

"Okay. You'll have to call her. She's expecting me to be at her curb at six thirty."

"Of course, of course, of course."

"All right. I'll see you at the church at seven. I'm here at my class, so I must turn off my cell phone or face the wrath of my professor."

"Ha. I'd like to watch that. Does he use a whip?"

"Just the common paddle. But seriously, I must go. Bye."

Lauren had been surprised when Martha called to say she'd be picking her up, rather than Tom. *I know I shouldn't be anxious, but I am, and for good reason. There's no question that she's trying to win Tom over. So, why does she want to talk to me? To warn me? Or to tell me she's better for Tom than I am? On Sunday she was very complimentary to me. Maybe she was trying to set me up for tonight.* On and on her thoughts dwelled on the coming drive with Martha. Anxiety was an unkind stimulant for her mind.

At six thirty she was at the door of Cecil Hall waiting. *I feel like a little girl about to be lectured to by an unloved aunt. Not that I don't love Martha. I just don't know her very well. I will try to be a quiet, submissive niece.* Martha arrived.

Lauren got into the car. "Hi." she sang. Martha was her old self, wearing a ball cap with her ponytail growing out of its back and no makeup. Lauren was glad to see that.

Martha didn't move the car but rather just sat and looked at Lauren. She said, "Lauren, I owe you an apology. I did you a terrible disservice last Wednesday, and I want to ask for your forgiveness." Lauren said nothing, not knowing what to say. Martha took her hand. "I had no business interfering between you and Tom, acting like a siren or something. I know you were offended. But when I heard about how you and Tom worked together to rescue Ahmed last Saturday, I knew I was wrong. So I wanted to ask for your forgiveness."

Lauren was shaken. *I never imagined this,* she thought. *What should I say?* Her silence would be misinterpreted, she knew. "I don't know what to say. Yes I forgive you, but I didn't think you'd done anything that needed my forgiveness."

"Well, nothing shocking. Just something a girl shouldn't do to a sister in the Lord." She smiled.

Lauren paused again and then said, "Thank you." They hugged and with that all the tension that had built up inside her over the past few hours disappeared. She laughed.

Martha laughed too and started the car. As they drove, she said, "I'll be leaving Maryland in December, after this semester is over. My employer notified me yesterday that they have received a grant and need to staff up quickly for it."

"Oh, do you have a job already?"

"Yes, at Lawrence-Livermore Laboratory."

"Where's that?"

"About an hour from San Francisco."

"That's a long way from Chicago."

"Yeah. But I've been a long way from Chicago for three years. I'm used to it."

"But what about your degree?"

"I'll do my last semester on line."

After a moment of thought Lauren said, "I wonder if Tom will ever leave Maryland."

"I doubt it."

"Why?"

"For the same reason he went to school here. It's convenient. There are plenty of opportunities for engineers and managers around here. And he seems to have a good home life."

"I suppose you're right."

After another brief pause, Martha said, "Tom and I are like brother and sister. He knew what I was doing, but he never fell for it. We're good friends. He sees into my mind, and we have good conversations. Great conversations. But there's no romance between us."

Lauren, wondering if Martha was crying, looked but could see no tears in the gathering dark. She could think of nothing else to say. The rest of the drive to Greenbelt was quiet.

Tom recognized Martha's car, beside George's Cadillac in the parking lot at the church. *They're all here. I wonder what kind of shape Lauren's in after her ride with Martha.* He went inside and to the room where they always met. "Hello, everyone. I hope I'm not late." He looked at his watch, and he saw that he was not late. He sat at the nearest seat, beside Lauren, and glanced at her to see how she looked. He was pleased to see her smiling at him.

"Hi." she said, softly.

"Hi to you." Tom smiled back at her. He turned toward George. "What's our agenda tonight?"

George said, "I thought we should talk about dos and don'ts when relating to Muslims."

Tom said, "I think Lauren and I have been having some real hands on experience with Muslims."

"Oh? How so?"

"Did you see the picture of the botched crucifixion in Sunday's *Post*?"

"Tom, you're not going to tell me you were there." George's eyes were wide open.

"Yes. And so was Lauren. And Nadira." He was nodding his head.

George rose halfway out of his seat. "Oh my—this is incredible. Oh my. Oh my." He sat back down. "You must tell me all about it."

Tom told him the entire episode, from planning the dinner, to the abduction, to the crucifixion, to the hospital, and then to bringing Ahmed to his house.

Midway through the story George turned to Martha. "Did you know about this?"

"He told me about it Saturday night, after the police had called me."

"Why did they call you?" George looked puzzled.

"They were trying to find out how the abductors knew where to find Ahmed. Tom had told me earlier in the day that he'd be meeting with Ahmed that night. So I was probably the only person outside of the four of them that knew they'd be together. They, the police, asked if I'd told anyone. I hadn't. So that was the end of that."

George waved his hand at Tom. "Is that the end of the story?"

"Lauren has also had quite a bit of contact with Nadira since her attack. So that's what I meant when I said what I did about hands-on experience."

George said to Lauren, "What have you learned about Muslims?"

She replied, "Nothing really. Nadira and I have become very good friends. We talk a lot. And sometimes we talk about religion, but I'm not learning much from her, and I'm not teaching her much about Christianity."

349

"Hmm." George looked at his notes and then at his watch. "I think I need to revise my plan for this session. Would you all object if we adjourned early tonight? I have something I really need to do, and with what you've told me I need to make some changes to my lesson plan."

"Yeah, I think we've taken most of our time with the story of Ahmed's crucifixion anyway. I don't mind." Tom looked at Lauren, who shook her head.

Martha said, "I've learned quite a bit just listening to that story again. Not all of it is uplifting."

"All right, then," George said. "Let's adjourn until next Wednesday."

Martha said, "Mind if we stay here and talk for a while?"

"No, not at all. This is Tom's church too, you know. Take as long as you please. Good-night." With that, George hustled out.

When they heard the door close Martha said, "Will you check to make sure he actually left?"

Tom frowned, but got up, went out of the room, down the hall to the door, and looked out into the parking lot to see if George had actually gone. The car was no longer there, so he went back and said, "He's gone."

Martha said, "There's more to George's need to go than revising the lesson plan. Tom, remember when we talked about who knew about your conversations with Ahmed?"

"Yes. Pete, George, and you. And Lauren, of course."

"Did either of you watch George's face when you told the story?"

"No." Tom said.

"Me neither," Lauren said.

"When I told him the police were searching for anyone who knew where Ahmed would be Saturday night his expression changed. It was a look of alarm. Then when you told him that Lauren had taken pictures of the abductors' car, his face turned absolutely white. And the color didn't come back before he left.

Something's going on with him. I think there's more to it than just being a blabbermouth."

Tom turned and looked out a window into the night, seeing nothing; but thinking. He turned back to Martha. "I don't know. I've only gotten to know him since we began these meetings. I can't imagine how he could be involved. He may have realized he'd said something to one of his customers that helped them find Ahmed. But who knows?"

Lauren said, "I thought it was odd a few weeks ago when he brought the pastor in to teach us about Christianity, didn't you? Do you know how long he's been a Christian?"

"That's interesting. I didn't think about it at the time. I have no idea how long he's been a Christian. I should ask my dad how long he's come here."

Martha said, "The first issue with me is Ahmed's crucifixion. Somehow those people must have known that Ahmed had been talking to you about Christianity. Otherwise they wouldn't have tried to crucify him. The second issue is knowing how to find him Saturday night."

"Did you know that the police found a GPS tracking device in his car?"

Martha's head jerked toward Tom. "We talked about that Saturday night, didn't we?"

"Ahmed thinks it was placed by his ex-business partners while he was taking a midterm. But did you know that Ahmed took his car to Glimus Motors for a recall repair on Saturday morning?"

"Are you kidding me? This is getting serious, Tom. We've got to do something."

"I'll talk to my dad about it tonight and see what he thinks. This could all be just speculation, or we might be on to something."

Lauren said, "I've got some studying to do tonight for a quiz in the morning. I really should be getting back to the dorm."

"Yeah, I do too. I'll let you know what Dad thinks tomorrow."

They filed out, turning off the lights, and locking the door behind them. At the parking lot exit, Tom let Martha go first. *What a mind that woman has,* he thought. *Who would have ever suspected George? I don't know if I suspect him or not.* Driving toward home, his mind swirling with questions, he passed Glimus Motors and slowed down, more by instinct than by purpose. It was now about eight thirty, and Glimus was closed, although well lighted. As he drove slowly by, he saw a Cadillac with a GLIMUS license plate parked by the side of the showroom. *That's George's car!* A sudden pang of anxiety filled him.

He stopped and parked on the side of the road across from the showroom and watched to see if anyone could be seen inside. He saw no one. *Why would George be here?* he thought. *I've got to take a look.* Tom crossed the road and walked to the showroom door and tried it, but it was locked. The showroom with all the service bays behind it made the building huge. He walked alongside the garage doors of the darkened bays with his heart pounding. *Why am I doing this? I must be crazy.* But he continued on to the back of the building. He could see two structures separated from the main building, and lights were on in the larger of the two. *Body shop, I bet. And the small one's probably the paint shop.*

Sitting in front of the paint shop was a car that Tom instantly recognized. It was the car he'd followed for a half an hour Saturday night. *Keep in the shadows,* he mentally instructed himself as he quietly and slowly walked toward the side of the paint shop. He pulled out his phone and pointed it at the car. *There's plenty of light here. I'll turn off the flash. Two shots will be enough to match it with those Lauren took during the chase.* He took six anyway.

He walked behind the paint shop to the adjacent building. He stood far enough away from the windows that anyone inside couldn't see him. He moved from window to window until he could see someone. First he saw George, then another man, apparently addressing George. A third man was off to the side, watching. Tom couldn't hear their conversation. No one was smiling. Again he took pictures.

I have enough, he thought. Quietly he slipped away, back to his car, and drove on home. He sat in front of the house to review all the photos on his camera. There were dozens. And clearly the car he'd seen at Glimus was the car used by Ahmed's abductors. *How in the world is George involved in this? And why? Maybe he's just assigned to take care of the car but doesn't know what's happening. No, he knows. He's the only person other than Lauren and Martha, and to some extent, Pete, who knows about Ahmed. But does the Glimus management know what's going on?*

When Tom went in he saw Ahmed asleep on the couch. Martin was in the family room, sitting in his recliner watching TV. "Dad, can I talk to you?"

"Sure, come on in. Do you mind if we wait for a commercial?"

"This is very important, Dad."

Martin turned toward Tom. "In that case, I'll turn this off." He pointed the remote at the television, clicked, and then said, "Here, sit down," gesturing toward the couch that faced the television. He looked at Tom with eyebrows raised.

Tom took a deep breath. "Dad, I believe George Lyon is involved with the terrorists. We've been trying to figure out how the terrorists knew about Ahmed's conversations with me, and how they knew where to find him Saturday night."

"Who's we?"

"Martha, Lauren, and me. Martha and me, mostly."

"Go on."

"We thought that Ahmed's crucifixion was a sign that they knew Ahmed had been talking to a Christian about religion. The only people that knew that were Martha, Lauren, George, and Pete. You know Pete, don't you?"

"Yes, of course." Martin was sitting absolutely still.

"On Saturday night, other than Ahmed, only Lauren, Nadira, and I knew where we were going. But somehow the terrorists knew and caught him at the restaurant. Martha and I suspected a GPS tracking device, and sure enough, that's what the police found in his car. Ahmed thought Rashid and Masoud put it there while Ahmed was taking a midterm last week. But Ahmed had also taken his car to Glimus on Saturday, at George's request, to install a recall fix."

"Really. Had Ahmed received a recall notice?"

"No. In fact, George had called me last Thursday to see if I could find Ahmed and tell him to take the car in. George said he hadn't been able to contact him. I knew that Ahmed had gotten a new cell phone, and George didn't know the number. In fact, Ahmed had begged me to not tell the number to anyone. So when Ahmed called me later that day I gave him the message. And that's why he took his car in Saturday."

"And it was Saturday night that the terrorists caught him. Hmm."

"But that's just the background."

"Oh?"

"Tonight at our meeting we told George about Saturday night and about having photos of the car. George cut the meeting short and left, saying he had another appointment."

"So?"

"After he left, Martha said that he looked pretty shaken up."

"How did she mean that?"

"She said that his face turned absolutely white, and that his expression was one of alarm."

"I see."

"Well, Martha and Lauren left—they'd come together in Martha's car—and I started home. But when I passed Glimus, I saw George's car there. They were closed, so I went over to see if I could talk to George, but the door was locked. Just on a hunch I walked on back behind the main building. There's a body shop, and I think a paint shop back there. Sitting in front of the paint shop was the car that had abducted Ahmed."

Martin stood, like he'd been prodded with a nail. "Are you sure?"

Tom pulled out his phone. "Here, look."

Martin sat beside him. Tom narrated, "Here are the pictures of the car we followed on Saturday night." He flicked slowly from one shot to the next so Martin could get a good look. "Now here are the pictures I took tonight."

"You took them at Glimus?"

"Yeah. See, it's the exact same car."

"Well, it sure looks the same, but—"

"It doesn't even have a license plate, just like on Saturday."

"But, Tom, this doesn't implicate George Lyon."

"But wait." He flicked to the next shot. "Here are George and two guys in the body shop. These other guys look like Middle Easterners, don't they?"

Martin studied the photographs. "Yes, but still—"

"Dad, it's after hours. The place is closed. I bet if we go over there in the morning, we'll find that car in a different color."

Tom and Martin were both startled by a voice from behind them, "May I see the photographs?" It was Ahmed in his wheelchair. "I've seen the face of one of the terrorists."

Martin said, "Come over here and take a look."

Tom held the cell phone in front of Ahmed. He took only a brief look. "That's the man who grabbed me Saturday night. The police also have pictures of him. They showed them to me yesterday."

"Are you sure?" Martin prodded.

"I'm very sure, Mr. Parker. But we should let the police see these pictures, so they can decide."

Silence permeated the room. Tom looked at Martin, who was staring ahead. *This is troubling him. I can see that. George is one of us, or so we thought. How can Dad turn in a fellow church member? But how can he not?* Tom looked at Ahmed, who started to say something, but Tom shook his head and put his forefinger to his lips. Ahmed understood and stopped.

Martin spoke slowly, "Many things can cause a person to do what we think George has done." Martin was not looking at either Tom or Ahmed. "An evil heart is only one of them. We can't judge George Lyon's motives. On the other hand, we think we can see sin. Sin falls into three categories—disrespecting or even ignoring God, disrespecting parents, or harming or disrespecting other people. We think we can see that George has committed sin by harming others, namely, Ahmed."

Ahmed added, "and Nadira."

"Yes. And Nadira." Martin glanced at Ahmed but then returned his gaze toward the blank television. "Fortunately, George is able to call on Jesus to atone for his apparent sin, if he repents. But unless he has reason to repent, it is unlikely that he will, depending on what motivates him. For that reason, we will be doing him a favor by taking this information to the police. Am I making sense, Ahmed?"

"Oh, yes, very much. I have been through this myself."

"Then you know that forces of evil live within all of us, in one form or another. We, on our own, can't eliminate them. We have to rely on Jesus to do that for us, either in this life or the next."

Tom looked at Ahmed, who was nodding his assent.

Martin continued. "I'll be going with you tomorrow but with a very heavy heart. We can show the police the evidence, but we should not pass judgment on George Lyon. Ultimately, only God will do that. Do you understand that?"

"Yes," Ahmed said.

"Sure, Dad. Thanks for putting this in perspective for us."

"Okay, let's plan to leave here at seven thirty."

CHAPTER 40

A hmed was up and waiting when Martin descended the stairway. "Well, good morning, Ahmed. Looks like you're ready to go. How about a bite to eat before we go?"

"Good-morning, sir. A bite would be good, thanks."

"Seen anything of Tom yet?"

"No, sir. Mrs. Parker is here."

"I knew that. I'd better check on Tom." Back up the stairs he went.

Mrs. Parker peeked around the doorway. "Would you like some eggs and toast?"

"I certainly would, thanks." He wheeled into the kitchen.

"How are your feet feeling today?"

"With the pads in the shoes I can at least stand and take a few steps. In fact, I was thinking about leaving the wheelchair here this morning."

"That's progress, isn't it?"

Martin reappeared. "Tom was in the bathroom. He'll be down shortly. We need to leave in ten minutes."

Ahmed and Martin began eating, and soon Tom joined them. As soon as they finished, Martin said, "Okay, men, let's get going. Do you have your cell phone, Tom?"

"Yeah, sure." Tom patted his pants pocket.

Ahmed said, "I'm going to try to go without the wheelchair this morning." He stood and gingerly walked toward the door.

"That's fine, but I think we should take the wheelchair along with us, just in case." Martin had already started pushing it toward the door.

They reached the police station in ten minutes and told the desk clerk they wanted to see Captain Parsons.

"He's not here yet," the night-shift desk clerk said. "I expect him right at eight. Have a seat."

Ahmed was already seated. *This may not have been a good idea. My feet still hurt too much to walk very far.* They sat and talked of weather and football. Martin said to Ahmed, "Do you miss Morocco? What's it like there this time of year?"

"Very nice, a little cool, and rainy. About twenty-two in the day. That's about seventy, maybe seventy-two Fahrenheit?"

"Isn't it desert there?" Tom asked.

"Oh, no." Ahmed laughed. "I live near the sea. It's much the same as Portugal."

Captain Parsons appeared. "I'm surprised to see you here this morning. What can I do for you?"

Martin said, "Tom has some new information that you need to hear."

He glanced at Tom. "All right," he said with enthusiasm. "Come right this way. Oh, I see you're walking." He was looking at Ahmed. "You must be better."

Ahmed replied, "Just a little, Captain. I may be a little optimistic." He walked slowly behind them.

They sat down again in Parsons' office, along with another officer. "What do you have, son," Parsons said to Tom.

Tom told him the same thing he'd told Martin the night before. He showed him the pictures, both those he'd taken last night and those Lauren had taken Saturday night. After studying them carefully, Parsons said to the officer, "Take these and compare the shots of the men with those we looked at on Tuesday. And have Judy see if we have any information on George Lyon." The officer took Tom's camera and left.

Parsons said, "Tell me all you can about George Lyon." He waved his open palm over the three of them.

Martin began. "I've known George for probably fifteen years. He attends my church."

"What church is that?"

"Greenbelt Christian Church."

"Is he active?"

"I don't think he attends every Sunday. Off and on. But he seems to be consistent. He claims to be the top salesman at Glimus Motors and says he sells a lot of cars to students. He must do well. He wears flashy clothes and a large diamond ring, and he talks loud."

"What about you, Tom? What's your connection with him?"

"He's been leading a small study group on how Christians can relate to Muslims. There are just three of us, two other students and me."

"How did that come about?"

"Lauren Stevenson, a friend of mine who rooms with Nadira Shalash, asked me if we, the Collegiate Christian Association, could teach her how to relate her Christian faith to her Muslim roommate. Our church has a committee that recommended George since he's thought to be well versed in Islam. That's why we were meeting at Greenbelt Christian Church. We meet every Wednesday night."

"So he knew about Nadira?"

"Of course."

Ahmed thought, *This is interesting. Pretty funny. I wish I'd had something like that before coming to America.* His thoughts were interrupted by a knock on the door. A woman walked in and handed Parsons a file folder. He took it and held his hand up, his palm facing Tom, and looked at the material in the file.

He examined it for a few minutes without speaking. Finally he said, "Mr. Parker, are you aware that Mr. Lyon is a naturalized citizen?"

"No." he sounded surprised.

"He came here from Italy, and his name was Giorgio Leone. He came here at age thirteen. His city of origin was Alcamo, Sicily." He raised eyebrows without raising his head and looked at Martin. Then he looked down at the file again. "Other than that, there doesn't seem to be anything of interest here. I only told you that much because it's public information."

While he was speaking, the other officer returned. Parsons said to him, "What did you find out?"

"They're the same two men that were in the post office." He laid some still shots from the post office video beside Tom's photographs on the desk.

Parsons studied them for several minutes. Without looking up he said, "It looks like this guy is wearing the same jacket in both, doesn't it? These are the same people. No question about it. I wonder what they're cooking up."

Ahmed thought, *Cooking up? These people have such strange ways of saying things.*

Parsons looked up and said, "Gentlemen, you've brought us some very valuable information. Again, I must commend you, Tom, for your investigative work. You might have a future in law enforcement."

"Thank you, sir."

Martin smiled.

Parsons stood. "We have work to do. We'll be in touch when we have this figured out."

They left, with Ahmed hobbling slowly. In the lobby Martin said, "Tom, why don't you go get Ahmed's wheelchair. I'll wait here with him."

Ahmed sat down, with gratitude.

Within twenty minutes they were back at the Parker home. Ahmed saw that the sheets and blanket on his makeshift bed had been straightened carefully. Soon Martin left for work and Tom went to class. Mrs. Parker was in and out, asking if he needed anything. He said, "No."

What I need is to talk to Hashim. When he was confident that he wouldn't be overheard, he called.

Hashim was quick to answer. "Hello Ahmed. I was expecting you to call."

"Why?"

"Captain Parsons just called and said he'd just met with you and that you brought some valuable matter to him. I'm on my way there right now."

"Good. I couldn't bring your name up there because Tom Parker and his father were with me."

"That's good. I'd like to talk to you later today but not by telephone. Can you walk yet?"

"A little. If you come by for me, I can walk to the curb."

"Where are you?"

Ahmed gave him the address.

"That's close. I'll call before I come."

"Okay. Thanks."

At lunchtime Lauren called Nadira. "Hey, Roomy, how are things going?"

"Same as usual. Pacing my cell."

"Did you hear anything about your picture in the paper?"

"No," She said in a loud whisper. "He hasn't said a word about it. I would have heard a lot about it if he'd seen it."

"Yeah, I'm sure."

"The police were here on Tuesday. They showed me some pictures, and I identified the man who attacked me."

"You did?" Lauren almost shouted. "Who is he?"

"They don't know his name yet. But they know where he lives."

"That's the best news I've ever heard. How did your dad react?"

"He asked me a lot of questions, like had I ever seen him before, did I know his name, was he involved with the Servants of Mercy, and that kind of stuff. Of course I had no idea who he is or anything like that. He wants him arrested, that was clear."

"Are they going to do that?"

"They've got to build a case against him before they arrest him."

"Well, do they think he's one of the guys that abducted Ahmed?"

"They didn't say. But surely they showed the pictures to him."

"I should ask Tom. I wonder if Ahmed is still at the Parkers' house."

"Let me know if you find out anything."

"I will. Wow. That's great, Nadira. You might be out of protective custody before long."

"I hope you haven't gotten used to living alone."

"Nope. Not at all. I'll be so happy when you can move in with me."

"I'm looking forward to it too. How are things with you and Tom?"

"Okay, I guess. I was with him at a meeting last night, but there were other people there, so we couldn't talk or anything. Martha's still in the picture, but I think she's becoming a nonfactor. I'll tell you about it sometime. It's a long story."

"Sounds interesting."

"Not."

"Oh. Sorry."

"Yeah, I'm a little confused about things at the moment. I'm waiting for the fog to clear. Well, I've got to go right now. I've got to eat and get to class. Anyway, I hope things are more settled soon."

"Me too. For both of us."

Lauren laughed. "My situation's nothing like yours. But you're bearing up well."

"I hope you are too."

"Yeah, I am. I'll be okay."

"I'm sure you will. Keep me posted."

"Maybe I'll ride over to see you this weekend."

"Oh, please do. That would make my day."

"All right. I'll let you know."

"Okay, bye."

Ahmed was sitting at his laptop with his cell phone beside it when Hashim called. It was midafternoon on Thursday. "This is Ahmed."

"I can pick you up in ten minutes. Will that work for you?"

"That would be great. Tom is at class, and Mr. Parker is at work. Mrs. Parker's the only other person here."

"Good. I'll be there soon."

Ten minutes later Ahmed started toward the door. He saw Mrs. Parker standing in the kitchen, looking at him. He said, "A friend of mine is coming by to talk to me. I'm going out to meet his car when he arrives." She smiled and nodded.

Hashim was already there when he went out. He hobbled to the curb as fast as the discomfort would permit and got into the car. Hashim said, speaking in Arabic as he drove away, "It looks like you're still in a lot of pain."

"Mostly in my feet." He wiggled his fingers. "My hands don't hurt very much and my shoulders just hurt a little."

"They've made an arrest. A car salesman named George Lyon. I hear he's someone you know."

"Yes, I do. I didn't expect his arrest this soon."

"Apparently they knew he's a big talker, so they expected to get some information from him."

"Have they learned anything from him yet?"

"He brought in his lawyer. Parsons promised him reduced charges if he'd cooperate. Lyon didn't need much convincing. It appears that he is the link between foreign terrorists and the local community, and possibly with an organized crime family in Sicily. He not only supplies the terrorists with cars, but he also gathers information for them. For a price. As soon as he saw the pictures Tom took, he began to talk. The police initially charged him as an accessory in your attack."

"What about Nadira?"

"He admitted that he'd informed the terrorists about Nadira's relationship with you. Had you told him about her?"

"No. He must have known about Nadira and me from his meetings with Tom and Lauren."

"I would assume so."

"What's to assume? They were meeting to discuss Lauren's ability to communicate with Nadira, who is her roommate. Lauren is a Christian and Nadira is a Muslim, you know. Tom or Lauren must have told him something about me."

"So your friends unwittingly gave the terrorists, through George Lyon, the information they needed to injure Nadira. What good friends." He shook his head.

"But surely they didn't tell him with any evil purpose."

"I know. I know. But how ironic."

"George Lyon is a Christian. It makes sense that they trusted him. I find Tom and his father to be very trustworthy."

"I hope they are."

"I see them as men of principle."

"You know George. What did you think of him?"

"I know him only as a car salesman. He talks a lot." He stopped for a second as another thought struck him. *He could have placed the GPS device in my car. That was through Tom too.* "George asked Tom to tell me to take my car in for a warranty fix, which I did last Saturday. That could easily have been when the GPS device was put in my car."

Hashim was silent for a moment. He glanced at Ahmed. "Instead of Rashid and Masoud."

"Possibly. Probably."

"Were Rashid and Masoud involved Saturday night?"

"I don't know."

"So George, through Tom, arranged for the GPS device."

"Yes."

"But you trust Tom."

"Yes, and I expect he trusted George. Tom was just passing on a message."

"Ahmed, I'm trying to determine if there is any probability that Tom is involved with the terrorists."

"Hashim, it was Tom who saved me. Lauren, at Tom's direction, took pictures of the car. And Tom took the pictures of George with the terrorists. No, I don't suspect Tom in the least. If it hadn't been for Tom, we wouldn't know anything, and I would be dead."

"Yes. You're right."

"So, will you arrest them?"

"Ahmed, with as much evidence we have, we still don't have a case. We need enough evidence to put these guys away for a long time."

"What about George?"

"He's a talker. We think he will give us the evidence we need. He will probably be charged as an accessory in Nadira's attack."

"So I'm still vulnerable."

"I'm afraid so. But as long as you stay with the Parkers' you should be safe, don't you think?"

Ahmed closed his eyes. "I hope so." He sighed.

When Mr. Shalash arrived home from work on Thursday, he burst into the house and announced, "They've made an arrest!"

His wife stood up from her chair where she had been reading a magazine. She clasped her hands together in front of her. "Oh, that's wonderful. Is it that boy, Ahmed?"

"No. And apparently it's not the perpetrator but an accessory. But it's progress."

Nadira listened to this conversation from her room. She ran down the stairs. "Who was it?"

"A car salesman from Greenbelt."

"A car salesman?" she exclaimed, stopping on the last step. "Not the man whose picture they showed me?"

"No. They said this man was involved in supporting the terrorists."

"Terrorists?" Nadira stepped to the floor and walked slowly toward her father.

"That's what they said. They apparently think a terrorist group did this to you."

"Why on earth—"

"Nadira, that's all I know. They expect more arrests soon."

"Terrorists." She felt the scars on her neck. "Why me?"

He shook his head. Her mother stood and embraced her. She said, "Just calm down. Soon this will all be over, and we'll know the whole story. We need to be patient. All of us." She glanced at her husband.

"Yes, you're right," he said. "I'm very encouraged by today's news, though. I think they're about to end this search."

Her mother stepped away. Nadira closed her eyes. "I hope so," she whispered.

CHAPTER 41

Friday dawned with a clear sky and unseasonable warmth. Martin appeared at breakfast, still wearing the pain that had shown on his face last night when the Parkers had learned from Ahmed about the arrest of George Lyon. Tom too seemed unusually somber. Ahmed, on the other hand, was happier than he had been since Nadira was attacked. He thought, *Perhaps I can understand their gloom. But Tom was the one who discovered George's association with the terrorists. He ought to be happy, especially on a day like this.*

"Why so solemn this morning?" Mrs. Parker said to Martin. "You and Tom look like you've lost your best friends."

Martin said, "I guess I'm just disappointed. Terribly disappointed."

Tom added, "Yeah. Here's a guy you thought you could trust and now look."

Mrs. Parker said, "I never have trusted George. To me he's a big mouth braggart. I know I shouldn't say that, but that's how I've always felt about him."

"Still," Martin said, "He's a fellow Christian and for that reason one should expect better."

"Everyone has secrets," she said. "Some are just more serious than others."

"I know you're right. And we don't know what lies behind George's activities. We shouldn't judge him until we hear all the facts—if we ever do."

Tom said, "Please excuse me. I have to go to class. We're leaving at two?"

"Right. Maybe that'll brighten up our day."

Ahmed thought, *My day's very bright already. A parade will make it even better.* "Will you be going with us, Mrs. Parker?"

"It's such a beautiful day, I think I will."

"I'm glad that you'll be with us," Ahmed said. Tom gave a thumbs-up as he walked out the front door.

Soon Martin left for work, and Ahmed returned to the living room and began his studies.

Lauren was walking to class when her cell phone rang. She saw it was Nadira. *I wonder if she knows about George.* "Hi, Nadira."

"Hi. Have you heard the news?"

"About George?"

"The car salesman? Is that his name?"

"Yeah. Tom told me last night. It was late, so I didn't want to wake you."

"We already knew. The police notified my father. What's his last name?"

"Lyon. George Lyon."

"How did Tom find out?"

"From Ahmed. George was also involved in Ahmed's abduction."

"What did a car salesman have to do with us?"

"Apparently he was helping the terrorists find ways to get money. So he provided information about Ahmed, his partners, and their friends, so they could find a way to threaten the Servants to go along with their demands."

"And I was just an available target."

"Yeah."

"How did he know about Ahmed and me?"

"You know the times I went to church on Wednesday nights?"

"Yes."

"I was attending a class to learn about your religion, so I wouldn't offend you if I said the wrong thing. He was teaching the class."

"Oh, Lauren. Why—"

"It just seemed like something I should do. I also wanted to learn how to talk to you about my religion. It was early in the year, and I didn't know you very well yet. I'm sure I said something to George about you and Ahmed. I'm so sorry. I was just trying to do the right thing."

The line was silent for a while. "Nadira, are you there?"

"Yes, I'm still here. Lauren, I know you didn't mean any harm. It's just, you know, hard to take in."

"I just found this out today."

"When you found out about the car salesman?"

"Yes."

"He must have known all along that he had misused your trust. I hope they lock that man up and throw away the key."

"I hope so too."

"Lauren, I don't blame you for this. You saved my life. And you helped save Ahmed's life. You were deceived. And that makes me mad."

"Thank you, Nadira."

"They said there would be more arrests soon."

"I hope so. They need to put someone in jail, so you can get out."

"That's a good way to look at it."

"Hey, my class is starting. I need to shut up."

"Okay, bye."

"Hi, Martha. This is Tom."

"Oh. Hi Tom," she answered with a lilt in her voice.

Tom laughed. "I have some interesting news."

"Go on."

"Are you free for lunch?"

"Any time, Tom."

"Where are you now?"

"Walking toward my car. Where are you?"

"Walking toward my car."

"Close to the Stamp?"

"Fairly."

"Let's meet there."

"Okay."

Tom and Martha arrived at the same time. Martha was her old self: ball cap with ponytail and no makeup. She said, "How about Adele's. It's quiet there. Lunch is on me."

"If you're buying, that's fine."

They found an empty table and quickly ordered.

Tom began. "After you told us what you thought about George Wednesday night, I drove by Glimus Motors, which I have to do when I go straight home. I saw George's car there, even though they were closed. Out of curiosity I thought I'd go poke around." He related how he found the car and saw George talking to the terrorists. "So I took some pictures of them and left without being seen."

"Tom, you're crazy."

"I know, in retrospect. But I had no idea what I'd find."

"Is that the end of the story?"

"No. Yesterday my dad, Ahmed and I took the pictures to the police. That was in the morning. Yesterday afternoon I learned that they had arrested George."

"Are you kidding? George Lyon? A criminal?"

"The police compared my pictures with the pictures Lauren took of the car on Saturday night. And they identified my pictures of the men with George as known terrorists."

"So they must have been the people that abducted Ahmed."

"Apparently."

"Wow. Wow. Who would have ever guessed that George—"

"You did."

Martha stared at him, her eyes wide open.

Tom nodded once. "You put it all together."

A long silence followed. Finally, she said, "I guess I did, didn't I. But you did the hard stuff."

"The crazy stuff. Yeah."

"Tom, Tom, Tom. What a team we would have made."

"Would have?"

She reached out and put her hand on his arm. "Earlier this week I was notified by Lawrence-Livermore that they had just received a federal grant and had to staff it up very quickly. They wanted me to come in January, instead of after graduation. They had already talked to the university about my finishing my course work online. So when I leave here at the end of this semester, it will be for good, except that I'll be able to come back for commencement in May."

Tom opened his mouth but couldn't speak. *I don't know what to think. This lovely girl is about to exit my life before I really had a chance to get to know her.* He took her hand in his.

"Tom, say something."

He looked into her eyes and shook his head slightly. "I don't know what to say. I am completely shocked."

"Well, here comes our lunch."

He released her hand. "I missed my chance, didn't I?"

"No," she said. "I missed my chance."

He stared at his sandwich. "I'm just completely bummed."

"I'm flattered."

He grinned. "I'll miss you, Martha Jenkins."

"I'll miss you too. Yes, we would have made a great team."

"I think we already have. At least I hope so."

"I think you're right." She smiled and picked up her sandwich.

Later that day, Ahmed sat in the backseat with Tom for the drive to Annapolis. *These people make me feel so well accepted, as if it were my own family. I'm excited for this diversion. Something very different from my usual life.*

They found a parking place on Maryland Avenue and walked several blocks to gate 3, with Tom pushing Ahmed in his wheelchair. As they approached Worden Field, Tom said, "There're a lot of people here already. It's a good thing we got here early."

Martin said, "I want to get as close to the reviewing stand as possible, so we can see more of what goes on there. Let's walk on past the reviewing stand. It looks like there are more seats available on that end." They found front row seats about forty yards from the reviewing stand.

They sat and chatted while the seats around them filled up. Eventually, officers and enlisted sailors arrived at the reviewing stand, and soon Ahmed heard drums in the distance. He said, "Tom, do you hear the drums?"

Tom cocked his head. "Yes, they should be here soon."

Martin pointed to the opposite corner of the field. "They'll be coming from there."

Ahmed glanced around to see if the other people were looking for the marching midshipmen. Suddenly his heart froze. He pulled on Tom's sleeve. "Tom, don't look now, but the terrorist is here. Just over to our left."

372

"Are you sure?"

"I have no question." He immediately pulled out his cell phone and called Hashim. As it rang he saw Tom tell Martin.

Hashim answered. "Ahmed?"

"Yes. Hashim, I am in Annapolis with Tom Parker and his parents. We're here for a parade. But standing very close to me, perhaps no more than thirty meters away, is the terrorist."

"Are you certain?"

"Absolutely."

"What is he doing?"

"Just watching."

"Ask Tom to move closer to him and follow him no matter where he goes. I'm calling for help. It should be there in minutes. Tell me exactly where you are."

"Looking out at the field, I am to the left of the official's position, perhaps forty meters."

"Hold on a minute."

While he was on hold, Ahmed relayed Hashim's message to Tom, who told Martin and then slowly moved closer to the terrorist. Martin eased over beside Ahmed.

In a few minutes Hashim came back on the line. "Ahmed, this morning our agents searched the house of the terrorists in D.C. They found no one there. They discovered many bomb making materials but no actual bombs. Security people from the Navy are already on the way to the parade ground. They will find you, and you must point out the terrorist to them. If he suspects anything, he will probably try to slip away. If he does, Tom must follow him. Understand?"

"Yes. Let me tell Mr. Parker." Martin was looking at Ahmed. "Mr. Parker, we are to do nothing that will alert the terrorist that he has been seen. If he tries to flee, Tom is to follow him. Security people are on the way now."

Martin nodded. He stepped slowly toward Tom and repeated Ahmed's instructions.

The band had already entered the field and was marching toward the north end. Close behind the band were companies of midshipmen marching onto the field. In less than five minutes a man in civilian clothes walked casually toward Ahmed. "Are you Ahmed Suliman?"

"Yes, sir."

"Without pointing or looking at him, describe the man you say is the terrorist."

"He is obviously Middle Eastern, and he is wearing a brown shirt, a shirt like mine, with long sleeves. He is about thirty meters from me. He has short black hair. Tom Parker is watching him to make sure he doesn't get away."

"Who's he?"

"A friend of mine who brought me here. The FBI agent told me to have him follow the terrorist." He held up his cell phone. "FBI, on the line," he explained.

The agent pulled out a folded paper, unfolded it, and showed it to Ahmed. "Is this the man?"

Ahmed looked at the picture, obviously a faxed copy, long enough to be certain. "Yes." He glanced at the terrorist, who was looking at him. At that moment the terrorist began walking away. Ahmed said, "He's starting to leave. Tom is following him. See?" He looked at the official, who said something he couldn't hear, seemingly speaking into his shoulder, and then started walking toward Tom.

Ahmed, sitting in his wheelchair in front of the bleachers, had a full view of the terrorist, who now was walking fast with Tom following. Another man appeared in front of the terrorist, coming toward him. The terrorist veered onto the parade ground toward the band and began to run. Tom ran after him. By now four agents were following Tom.

Mrs. Parker said loudly, "What's Tom doing? What's going on?"

Martin said, "That guy's a terrorist. Tom doesn't know that agents are behind him." He yelled, "Tom!"

The crowd was now making so much noise that Martin couldn't be heard. Ahmed watched the terrorist make a broad sweeping turn toward the corner of the field. Tom was getting closer. Suddenly Tom lunged, making a flying tackle, and the terrorist went down, rolling head over heels. The four agents immediately converged on the terrorist. "Place your hands on your head and come with us," they demanded.

Ahmed watched the terrorist begin to reach into his pocket. One of the officers grabbed his arm and pulled it behind him in a half nelson. Another officer pulled the terrorist's cell phone from his pocket and checked his other pockets. Then they marched the terrorist away, and out of Ahmed's sight.

The crowd broke into excited conversation. Tom picked himself up and started back to the bleachers. One of the agents stopped him and said something to him. Ahmed could see Tom smile and then walk back. The crowd began to clap, and the midshipmen cheered. Tom smiled again. He waved casually as he rejoined Ahmed and his parents. Martin patted him on the back, and his mother chided him and then hugged him. Others nearby shook his hand and smiled. Ahmed couldn't hear what they were saying.

As soon as the crowd noise abated, Ahmed spoke again to Hashim. "They've captured the terrorist. Tom chased him and tackled him on the parade field. Officers were there to arrest him."

"Well, good for Tom."

"Tom is a fearless hero. He saved my life, you know."

Ahmed recognized that the band had stopped playing, and the midshipmen had been halted. Naval officers were running to give instructions to the leaders of each of the companies. An announcement then came over the loud speaker, "As a precaution the parade will be delayed while a search for an explosive device is conducted. All spectators are directed to vacate the field and move to Upshur Road."

"Hashim, we have to leave the bleachers, now. They have directed all of us to leave."

"Okay. I'll hang up now. But call me if they find anything."

The bleachers were quickly emptied and the spectators gathered on the road behind them. When Ahmed and the Parkers were on the road, Ahmed turned to watch the midshipmen. Each company had turned around and marched onto the road on the other side of the field. He saw several vehicles pull onto the edge of the field, and men with dogs began their search for explosives. Ahmed turned to Tom, "This is amazingly efficient. Where did all these security men come from?"

Martin overheard his question. "Ahmed, many of them are stationed here. If you look across the river, you can see other navy facilities. They are always ready. Some of those in navy uniforms are probably SEALs who are trained in explosive ordinance disposal. They were here as part of the ceremony to honor them. You can see how they search under the bleachers and any area that a bomb could have been placed. See the dogs at work? They are trained to smell explosives."

Ahmed was watching the dogs. *This is fascinating. It looks like some of the dogs are leading their handlers.* He watched as one of the dogs sat down and stared at the earth in front of the reviewing stand. *His handler is pulling him away. Why? He might have found something.*

"Hey, Tom. Look at the dog in front of the tent." He hesitated. "Oh, they know he's found something."

"Yeah, that officer is backing all the others away. They're probably waiting for a disposal expert."

Ahmed heard a cheer coming from across the field. Soon a man appeared wearing what to Ahmed looked like a space suit. He walked up to the spot where the dog had stopped and then kneeled and placed a packet of tools beside him. Ahmed called Hashim again.

"Ahmed. What's happening?"

"Now they've removed everyone from the parade ground and are searching for a bomb. I think they've found it, buried in the ground in front of where the officials stand."

"That's very good news. Keep me on the line and tell me what happens."

"Okay. A man in a space suit, or something like it, is kneeling at the spot found by a search dog...bomb dog? What are they called?"

"Bomb sniffing dogs."

"One of them smelled the bomb. The man in the special suit is trying to disable it. Everyone is very quiet now. The students cheered when he came out. But now they are watching in silence."

"Was only one terrorist there?"

"I think so. I could only identify one."

"We'll have to pick up the other one, or other ones, when they return to the house. You'll be pleased to know that Rashid and Masoud were arrested today. For tax evasion and money laundering."

"I'm sorry for them. Not for Masoud so much. But Rashid is a man with many admirable traits."

"He'll have his opportunity in the US court."

"Ha. Some opportunity."

"You never know. If they have good lawyers, they might have a chance at a reasonable sentence."

"This bomb removal is going very slowly."

"They're trained to be careful."

"Hold on a minute. I want to ask Mr. Parker something." He turned to Martin. "Mr. Parker, how could they get that bomb in here?"

"This place really isn't very secure. There are places where someone could get in without too much trouble. Or you could just come in by boat. That would be easier, especially if you're carrying a bomb and tools."

Ahmed looked around. "I don't see any lights around here, at least on the field."

"Right. Basically this is a college. But they have to be careful to prevent this sort of thing."

"Hashim, the bomb man has apparently disabled the bomb, and now he's picking it up. A little truck is driving out to meet him."

"Good."

"Listen to the cheer from the students. Can you hear it?"

"No, not really."

"The other men and the dogs have been searching all the time he's been removing the bomb. Now they're coming back onto the field to finish searching it."

Tom said, "Hey, look. I think that dog has found another bomb."

Martin said, "He's sitting right under the path of the midshipmen where they'd march by the reviewing stand."

"Hashim, it looks like they've found another bomb."

Just then Ahmed heard another announcement, "Ladies and gentlemen, the parade for today has been cancelled. We will not permit either the midshipmen or spectators to be endangered by explosive devices. We regret very much the inconvenience, but I think you understand and will support our decision."

"Hashim, they've cancelled the parade."

"Good idea. They may have planted a lot of bombs there. I'm going to hang up again but call me as soon as you have any more news."

Ahmed heard the drums begin again, and the midshipmen marched away. *All very disciplined and well organized. I wonder if international students can come here.*

As the spectators began to leave, Martin said, "Maybe we should be going. But maybe not. Here come some official looking people toward us."

A man in a business suit and a high-ranking naval officer, judging by the gold stripes on his sleeve, accompanied by several lower ranking officers, were approaching. The man in civilian clothes said, "Folks, Admiral Hepperson, the superintendent of the Academy, would like a word with you."

The admiral turned to Tom, "Son, you made a magnificent open field tackle out there today. I want to thank you for stopping the bomber from escaping. Well done." He extended his hand.

"Thank you, sir. But the real credit goes to Ahmed Suliman here." The admiral turned toward him. "It was he that recognized him. He was the terrorist that attempted to kill Ahmed last Saturday by crucifixion."

"Oh my Lord," the admiral said. "I read about that in the Post."

"You can see the bandages on his hands, and he still can't walk very far."

The admiral turned to Martin and said, "I'd like to invite you all to my quarters and join with some other officers and faculty for a little relaxation. Would you join us?"

Martin turned to his wife, who nodded her consent. "Thank you, Admiral. We'd be delighted."

"Good. I'll leave Commander Phillips with you to show you the way. I'll see you in just a bit." He smiled and strode off with the others.

As they made their way from Worden Field, Ahmed looked back to see that the field was now ringed with uniformed policemen, and many other men and dogs were still searching for bombs as the second bomb was being disabled. *What frightening work that would be,* he thought.

As they walked to the superintendent's quarters, Commander Phillips collected their names, home towns, college, occupations, and some of the history of the past few weeks, which he would provide to the admiral and to the public information office. Ahmed overheard Mrs. Parker telling Martin that she needed someplace to comb her hair. Commander Phillips suggested that they stop at the Officers' Club, which is nearby, to freshen up.

After a brief stop, they moved on to the superintendent's residence, adjacent to the chapel. Looking around at the others there, Ahmed felt inappropriately dressed, surrounded by uniformed officers and tastefully clothed ladies. *I expect Mrs. Parker will be embarrassed. She looks nice but is dressed far more casually than all the other women here.* She was quiet but didn't appear to him to be intimidated. *I'm sure she realizes that most of the attention will be on Tom and me. Especially Tom.*

Shortly after they arrived, Admiral Hepperson asked the Parkers and Ahmed to stand by him. "Ladies and gentlemen, I am honored to introduce to you Mr. Tom Parker, his parents, Mr. and Mrs. Martin Parker, and Mr. Ahmed Suliman. Tom is the young man who ran down the terrorist and tackled him, preventing his escape before the security personnel could get to him. Tom, tell us a little about yourself and how you did what you did today."

Tom smiled and gathered his thoughts. "Thanks for inviting us to be here this afternoon. We didn't plan on all this." The people laughed. "I'm a junior at Maryland. We live right there in College Park. My dad is an old Navy man, so we come here every now and then."

"Oh," they seemed to say, approvingly.

Tom continued, "While we were waiting for the parade to start, Ahmed, here"—he gestured to him— "recognized a man in the crowd as a suspected terrorist, who had led an attack on him last Saturday night. That's why he's in a wheelchair." Ahmed held up his bandaged hands. "Ahmed called someone who had been working on the case, and that guy alerted the police here. He also told Ahmed to have me watch the terrorist and go wherever he went until the police arrive. So when he started running I ran after him. I was afraid he was going to get away, so when I had the chance I just tackled him."

Everyone clapped and congratulated him.

The admiral said, "I wish we'd have known about Tom a couple of years ago. We could use him on the football team." They all laughed. "Do you play football, Tom?"

"I did in high school. I'm not big enough to play at Maryland."

The admiral turned to Ahmed. "So you're the man who identified the bomber. Tell us about yourself."

Ahmed stood. "I am Ahmed Suliman, from Morocco."

"Ohh," they said, apparently expressing their understanding of his accent.

"I am an exchange student at Maryland. It is a long story leading up to last Saturday. It ended with terrorists kidnapping me and nailing my hands to a wall, like Jesus was nailed to the cross." He held both his arms out, with his bandaged palms facing the crowd, which reacted in horror. "I am still unable to walk very far, but I am improving quickly. The man I saw at the parade was the one who had taken me, with help from some others. They were known to be preparing a bomb attack someplace. When I saw him here, I called the police contact, and they told me they had searched the terrorists' house today, and found bomb-making equipment, but no bomb. So they thought, because of the nature of the parade I suppose, that there might be a bomb hidden nearby. So they notified the police here, and they immediately came with a picture of the man. When they showed it to me, the terrorist saw them and began to escape. So Tom, a hero not just because of today, but also because he saved my life last Saturday, caught him so he could be arrested."

The people applauded loudly. When they became quiet, Admiral Hepperson said, "We are deeply grateful to both of you for your bravery and quick thinking." He looked at the attendees. "Please continue to enjoy yourselves. I'll be having a photograph made of these heroes and asking the public information officer to prepare a news release, so I'll be gone for a few minutes." With that he led Ahmed and the Parkers into another room. After a group photograph, he left them there with the photographer and another officer, who took more pictures and conducted interviews of Tom and Ahmed.

Afterward, they returned to the reception room, where they were inundated with questions. The other guests were especially interested in Ahmed's abduction and crucifixion. He thought, *I don't think I should tell them about the Servants or about Nadira. Someday, perhaps, they will learn of them and understand.* They were there about forty-five minutes longer, and when the other guests began to leave, they also left and returned to College Park.

At the Parker house Ahmed waited until the family members dispersed into different rooms, and then he called Hashim. "They arrested the terrorist."

"I heard that they had. Tell me about it."

Ahmed told him the complete story.

Hashim did not interrupt. At the end he said, "Well done, Ahmed. Your friend, Tom, did very well. Unfortunately, I must forever remain unidentified to him. To everyone. Otherwise I become useless here. Now I have other news. We have captured and arrested the other terrorists who lived at the house in D.C."

"What great news! How many were there?"

"Three others. Our agents simply waited for them to come home. They all came together. We suspect they had all been in Annapolis but maybe not inside the Naval Academy, waiting for the explosions. We think that when the bombs didn't go off and their partner did not return, they rushed back to collect their belongings and then leave Washington, in fear their colleague would give them away."

"Does Captain Parsons know?"

"Of course."

"Hashim, all my enemies have been captured. This is a wonderful day for me."

"It is for the United States too."

"You are the one who made it happen," Ahmed said.

"I had help. You were as instrumental as the FBI."

"Before this I was afraid of the FBI. Now I see it in a different light."

"Good. Well, please enjoy the evening and tell your friend, Tom, that his work today was very helpful to his country."

"Who should I say told me that?"

"A federal agent. Just don't mention my name."

"Okay. Thank you."

"And thank you."

The Parkers had snacked at the superintendent's reception, and so waited until eight to have a light dinner. Martin said, "Ahmed, you look very pleased tonight. You must be very happy about today's events."

"I am very happy. I have been informed that three other terrorists were also captured today, partners of the man Tom caught. Not only that, Rashid and Masoud were arrested. All the men who wanted to hurt me are in jail."

"What spectacular news," Martin said.

"Yes, that's wonderful news," Mrs. Parker said.

Tom reached over the table to shake Ahmed's hand. "And I guess Nadira's attacker was one of them?"

"I don't know. I hope so."

"I do too. We'll know soon if he was."

CHAPTER 42

Nadira dreamed she heard someone calling her name. It woke her. She lay still, wanting to go back to sleep.

"Nadira!" It was not a dream. It was her father.

She rolled out of bed and groggily found her robe and slippers and opened the bedroom door. "Are you calling me, Father?"

"Yes. Please come down here."

"Why?"

"I need to show you something in the paper. It's about your friend, Ahmed."

What now, she thought. Dread suddenly filled her, as she quickly descended the stairs. Her father handed her the front section of the *Washington Post.* He pointed to an article on the lower right of the front page. The heading read, "Students Foil Bomb Plot at Naval Academy."

She began reading. It identified Ahmed Suliman and Tom Parker as having identified and caught a terrorist, and who notified security authorities about possible explosive devices. It said that two bombs were discovered buried beneath the parade route at a formal parade to honor Navy SEALs. It directed her to turn to page 3. There was a picture. It was Ahmed, Tom, and two adults, standing with a naval officer. She read the caption. "Ahmed Suliman, Tom Parker, Martin Parker, Mary Parker and Vice Admiral Hepperson at Annapolis." She looked at her father, who was watching her intently. She read the remainder of the article. It identified them as students at Maryland and told of Ahmed's crucifixion a week ago.

She looked at Mr. Shalash and handed him the paper. He said, "That's your friend, isn't it?"

"Yes."

Her mother had come in. "What's this about?" she asked.

He handed her the paper and pointed to the article. "What do you know about this, Nadira?"

"Just that he had been abducted and crucified. But some friends of his followed them and saved him."

"Crucified?" her mother exclaimed.

She nodded.

He said, "Why didn't you tell us?"

"I didn't think you'd want to hear anything about him."

"And now he's a national hero. Can you imagine the national outcry if those bombs had gone off under the feet of marching midshipmen? It would have been a catastrophe of immense proportion."

"I told you he was a good man."

"I think you were right."

Mrs. Shalash said, "Isn't this Tom Parker the same young man who came here with Lauren?"

"Yes, Mother."

"He endangered his own life to capture a terrorist. Won't Lauren be proud?"

"I'm sure she will."

The telephone rang. Mrs. Shalash answered. "Oh, yes, of course. Yes, she's here. All right, we'll see you in thirty minutes. Good-bye."

"It was the president of the university," she said breathlessly. "He wants to meet with us in thirty minutes."

"I'd better get dressed," Nadira said, and she turned and went back upstairs. She closed the door behind her and leaned on it, a smile spreading across her face, until she wanted to shout. Instead she simply said, "Yes," and pumped her fist.

The president was smiling when Mr. Shalash opened the door. The president was wearing a sport shirt, open at the collar. Helen McGovern was with him, dressed in her normal working outfit. "Please come in. We're very happy to see you this morning."

Both Nadira and her mother were standing in the entry hall, covered with headscarves. Mrs. Shalash said, "Welcome to our house, sir. We hope you're bringing good news."

"Thank you. Yes, we have some good news. Good-morning, Miss Shalash."

"Good-morning, sir."

Mrs. Shalash ushered them into the living room and offered them seats. "Would either of you care for a cup tea or coffee?"

"None for me," the president said. Helen McGovern also declined. She was carrying a newspaper.

The president said, "I was contacted this morning by the county police. They have arrested the man whom they believe attacked your daughter."

Nadira smiled. Her father said, "What is his name?"

"They would not release his name until they have a positive identification of him."

"Is there some uncertainty that he's the one?"

"I am told that he must be identified by Nadira and that will probably take place this morning. I asked that I could bring the news to you before the police contact you."

"Is he, by any chance, the same man that was arrested in Annapolis yesterday?"

"Yes, it is."

Helen held up the newspaper, "Have you seen this morning's paper?"

"Yes. The two students that caught him are friends of Nadira."

Helen added, "And I understand that Nadira helped save the one who'd been crucified last week."

Mr. Shalash sat up straight and his head snapped toward Nadira. "She did? Were you—"

Nadira's face instantly turned red. She hunched her shoulders.

"Nadira!" her mother stared at her.

Mr. Shalash turned toward the president. "We knew nothing of that. There might be some mistake."

"I suppose it's possible that we were misinformed. What about that, Miss Shalash?"

In a small voice she said, "Yes, I was there." She was looking down at her lap.

"How modest," the president said. "I commend you for helping to save him. It might have caused an international incident if he hadn't been rescued."

"We didn't know," Mr. Shalash said.

Mrs. Shalash's eyes were wide open.

The president continued, "I was told that Ahmed Suliman had been working with the FBI to find the man who attacked Nadira. Over the past few weeks—ever since she was attacked—Ahmed has been in hiding. An attempt was made on his life by a bomb placed under his car, and at another time several men chased him across the campus but he eluded them, and then the crucifixion. Still, he stayed on here until Nadira's attacker was found."

"Well, we just—" Mrs. Shalash was without words.

"We are very proud of her, sir." Mr. Shalash said.

"And so are we," the president said. "Well, I wanted to come here and personally give you the good news. The police will be calling very soon. I assume you'll have to go to the station for the identification." He stood, and Helen McGovern also stood. As they moved into the entry hall, he said to Nadira, "I suppose you'll be coming back to class soon. Monday, perhaps?"

"I hope so."

The Shalashes thanked him and watched as he and his assistant walked to the car, then they both turned to Nadira. "Well, Miss Shalash, I think you owe us an explanation," her father said.

"May I have some breakfast first," Nadira asked.

"Let's talk first."

She said, "All right. I was very tired of being confined to the house, so while you were gone last weekend I organized a short trip with Lauren, Tom, and Ahmed to Josie's for dinner. I'd just be gone for two hours, and I'd be with people that you know are honorable." She looked at both of them. "Let me sit down to finish the story." She returned to the living room and sat in one of the overstuffed chairs. "I didn't tell you because I knew you'd disapprove." Neither of them responded, so she continued with the entire story but omitted having spent the night in Ahmed's hospital room. "Please forgive me for not following your wishes, but I was desperate to see my friends and talk to them face to face. I didn't think it would create a problem. Obviously, it did though. I don't know how they knew where to find Ahmed. But it was clear that they didn't know Tom, Lauren, and I were there. Otherwise we wouldn't have been able to follow them."

Mr. Shalash stood. "Do you think your planned outing led to Ahmed's abduction?"

"I don't know, Father."

He stood at the window, staring out at nothing. He rubbed his face. The silence was long and filled with tension. Finally he said, "In America I cannot punish my eighteen-year-old daughter. You disobeyed our instructions, which we gave you for your own good. You could have been injured or even killed. Do you understand the reasons why a father's instructions should be carried out?"

"Of course, Father."

"I hope this is a lesson that you will never forget."

She felt a tear trickle down her cheek. She looked at her mother, whose face showed deep agony. "Oh, Mother." She went to her and hugged her.

After a long hug her mother said, "Let's have some breakfast."

The police called while they were eating. Mr. Shalash told them that Nadira could be there in an hour. Nadira had taken a few bites, but her hands began to shake. She put down her fork, looked up from her plate, and said, "I can't eat any more, not until this is over. Excuse me." In her room she squeezed into her rocking chair and rocked gently with her eyes closed, her thoughts incoherent. *I do not want to see him. I will know him, but I don't want him to see me. I have to do this. But I don't want to see him.* She rocked until her father called for her to leave.

He drove her to the police station, and they were met at the entrance by Captain Parsons. He introduced himself and led them into a room with part of one wall covered by a curtain. *I can hardly breathe,* she thought. *Please, make this quick.* Her eyes were closed.

"Are you okay, Miss Shalash?" Parsons asked.

She nodded.

"They won't be able to see you. The glass is one way. Are you ready?"

She breathed deeply. "Yes." The curtain opened.

Four men were standing in a line facing the glass. Nadira saw him immediately. She stared at him. *He looks like an everyday man. But his eyes are staring, like he can see me. His eyes are dark. I can see evil there.* "It's the one second from the left."

"Number two?"

She realized they were numbered. "Yes."

"Are you sure?"

"Absolutely."

The curtain closed. "Thank you," Parsons said. "Before you go, will you take a few minutes to speak to me in my office? There is one other question that you might help us to answer."

Nadira looked at her father, who answered for them both, "Certainly, Captain. We want to see this whole affair brought to a close."

When they were seated in his office he said, "It is obvious that this man had to have help from a student to get into your dormitory. Somehow he had to know when you would be alone and what room you live in. It seems logical that the only person who would know all that information is your roommate. Do you have any indication that she could have assisted this man's entry into the dorm and to your room?"

"Lauren? Oh, no. She couldn't have done that. She's the one who found me, and she has been the only one, other than my parents, who have helped me since the attack. She is so loving and kind. No. It's not possible that she could have done that."

"Do you know of anyone else who would have assisted him?"

Nadira looked with questioning eyes at her father.

He said, "Did Ahmed know your class schedule? Could he have given it to his business partners?"

"Father, I barely knew him before I was attacked. I wouldn't have given him my class schedule. I know of no way his partners could have known it."

Parsons asked, "Is there anyone else your roommate could have given it to? Or that you might have given it to?"

Nadira stared at the floor, searching her mind. The room was silent for over a minute. Then she said, "Yes. Yes there is. A week or two before I was attacked another girl, a Muslim, invited me to pray with her in her room. I had told her that sometimes I couldn't pray in my room because Lauren was there. So she suggested I pray in her room if she was there. We gave each other our class schedules. She asked me to use yellow highlight to show when I couldn't pray in my room because Lauren would be there, and she did the same thing. So she knew from that when I'd be alone."

"She would, of course, know your room number, right?"

"Of course. She came to my room once. I think just once."

"Is she a first-year student?" her father asked.

"Second year. She's an international student from Saudi Arabia, I think."

Parsons handed her a note pad and a pen. "Will you write her name and room number here for me?"

As she wrote, she said, "I can't imagine that she would have knowingly let him in and helped him to find me, she's so devout."

"Is there anyone else who could have possibly known your schedule and who could have gotten him into the building?"

"No. Not that I can think of."

"We will follow up with this lead, but if you can think of anyone else, please let me know."

Her father said, "Yes, of course."

"Thank you for your time. We will inform you of any further developments. You're free to go now."

Once in the car, her breathing became normal. Her father asked, "Are you all right, Nadira?"

"I'm very, very glad that is over with. I'm very shocked to think that my prayer partner could have assisted my attacker. I need some time to recover."

"I understand," he said.

Just before they arrived at home Nadira said abruptly, "I want to know why he did that to me."

"So do I. I suspect your friend, Ahmed, can tell us."

That was a curious thing to say. Why does he still think Ahmed had something to do with it? Back in the house Nadira returned to her room. She lay on her back and stared at the ceiling. Eventually she drifted off to sleep. When she awoke, she did not know how long she'd been sleeping, but she knew the lump inside her was gone, and her fear had left her. She got up, feeling better than she had felt in a week.

She went downstairs and said to her mother, "Can I speak to you and Father for a minute?"

"I'll see if he can come up. He's in the basement."

She returned in a few minutes with her husband behind her. Nadira was sitting at the kitchen table, and they both joined her.

"Am I free to go out now?"

Her parents looked at each other and nodded. "Yes, of course," her father said.

"I would like to go out to dinner with my friends and have the dinner we missed last Saturday night."

"Do you mean Ahmed, Lauren, and Tom?"

"Yes."

He said, "Yes, but I would like for them to come here first. I want to meet your friend, Ahmed, and the others. I wish to express my admiration for what they've done for you."

Nadira was speechless. As she looked at him, she began to smile. It spread from her lips to her entire face. Her parents began to smile too. "Thank you, thank you," she finally said. She stood and hugged her father and then her mother. "Shall I have them come at five?"

"Five will be fine," He said.

"Well, I have some calls to make. Excuse me." She stood.

"Just a minute," her father said. "While you were sleeping, we had a call from Captain Parsons. They brought your prayer partner in for questioning, and she confessed to giving access and information to your attacker. It seems she had been severely threatened if she did not help him. She was very remorseful, but she was charged as an accessory to the crime and released on her own recognizance."

"Oh, that poor thing." Nadira said. "She must have felt awful. Those cruel people! I'm so glad they've been arrested."

"And so are we, Nadira," her father said. Her mother nodded.

Lauren was still in her pajamas and robe when her cell phone rang. "Nadira. I'm glad that's you."

"I'm happy that I didn't have to wake you up."

"Yeah. Well, if you'd called thirty minutes ago, you would have. It's Saturday, you know."

"Listen. I have some amazing news."

"I'm listening."

"They've caught my attacker."

"What? Yay," she shouted. "Who was it?"

"I don't know his name, but I saw him at the police station. I identified him."

"Was that hard?"

"Yes, very. And they've also found the person that let him into the dorm and gave him my class schedule and information about when I'd be alone. It was the girl I prayed with sometimes."

"Oh, really? Why was she—"

"They threatened her. She did it because they would have hurt her if she hadn't."

"How awful."

"She easily confessed, probably because the terrorists had been arrested."

"So, can you come back to the dorm?"

"I hope so. The president of the university was here this morning to tell us the news. He mentioned that I'd be going back to class on Monday. I haven't discussed it with my parents. But they did say I could go out. So I want to have the dinner that we missed last Saturday."

"Oh, Nadira. This is such good news. Really. I'm so happy for you. I need to call Tom and see if he can go."

"Are things okay with you and Tom?"

"I think so. I have hope, anyway."

"Good. Tell him to call Ahmed. And let me know if everyone can come."

"I think Ahmed's still staying at Tom's."

"Good. Tell them my father wants you all to come to the house first, at five, so he can talk to you."

"Oh. That's kind of—heavy?"

"Oh, no. Tom and Ahmed are heroes now. Wait till you see this morning's *Post*."

"Just tell me. I don't get the paper."

"Tom and Ahmed were at Annapolis yesterday, and they saw this guy. He's the one who crucified Ahmed too."

"Really." *This is incredible.*

"Tom chased him down and tackled him, and the police arrested him. They found two bombs buried on the parade ground, but because of Ahmed and Tom they caught this guy before he could set them off."

"Tom tackled him? Wow."

"It's on the front page of the *Post*. So my father wants to congratulate them."

"Save your paper so I can read it. This is huge."

"Yeah, so don't worry about my father."

"Well, I have to call Tom. This is great!"

"Okay, bye."

Lauren immediately called Tom.

"Good-morning," he said, cheerily.

"Good-morning, Mr. Hero."

"So you've seen the paper."

"No, Nadira told me. Did you know that the guy you caught is the man who attacked Nadira too?"

"Are you serious? Ahmed's attacker was also Nadira's attacker?"

"Yes, and now she's free. And she wants to have the dinner tonight that we tried to have last week."

"Hold on a minute. I'll ask Ahmed."

After a moment Tom came back on the line. "Ahmed said yes. So what time? Seven again?"

"Actually, Nadira's dad wants us to come to their house first, at five. He wants to talk to you and Ahmed."

"Hmmm. So I'll pick you up at about a quarter till five. Will that be okay?"

"Are you going to the football game?"

"It's away this week."

"Actually, I'm thinking about riding Nadira's bike over to her house this afternoon and just meet you there. But you could bring me back to the dorm after dinner."

"Lauren, I'd be very happy to take you anywhere."

A sudden warmth exploded inside her. "I'm smiling, Tom."

"Was that funny?"

"No. I'm smiling at you. It's the nicest thing you've said to me in a week."

"Maybe you should ride her bike to my house."

"I'd love to, but I need to return it to her. I won't need it anymore, now that she's free."

"That's fine. Then we'll see you at five at the Shalash house."

"Good. I'll see you then."

"Bye, Lauren."

As soon as she disconnected, she wanted to call him back and talk some more. *Tom, my love, please don't ever leave me.* Basking in the glow that had unexpectedly engulfed her, Lauren waltzed about the room for a few turns, her robe flowing like an elegant gown around her.

Eventually she returned to normalcy and called Nadira. "Hello again, my free friend. The boys both said yes."

"Oh, good. At five?"

"Yes, but I'd like to ride your bike over to your house earlier and be there when the guys arrive. Would that work for you?"

"That would be wonderful. But come earlier. At two or three. Anytime really. I'm starving for someone to talk to."

"Okay. I'll be there at two-ish."

"Good. I'll see you soon."

This is odd, Ahmed thought, sitting in Tom's car on the way to the Shalash residence. *I'm on my way to meet Nadira's father but at his invitation, not my request. He will have questions. I'll answer honestly.*

Tom said, "You're awfully quiet."

"I'm just thinking about meeting Nadira's father."

"I've met her mother. She is a very beautiful and dignified lady."

"I would expect that, because Nadira is beautiful."

"Yes, she is. Well here we are."

Ahmed looked at the house from the car. *A nice house. A nice neighborhood. He must be very successful.* Ahmed had left the wheelchair at the Parkers' house, so he made his way somewhat slower than Tom, walking up the walk and the steps to the porch, but not feeling much pain, although still wearing the post-op shoes and silicone pads. The door opened before them, and Nadira stood waiting, her head covered, as usual. *Yes, she is a beautiful girl,* he thought.

"Come in," she smiled.

Behind her was Lauren. *She's very attractive too, but not with the natural beauty of Nadira.*

Tom said, "Hello, Nadira."

"Hello, Tom. Hello, Ahmed. Come in and meet my parents."

Ahmed said, "I'm happy to see you again, Nadira."

They said hello to Lauren as Mr. and Mrs. Shalash appeared.

Nadira introduced them. Mr. Shalash said, "It's an honor to have you great heroes in my house. We are eager to hear all that has happened, rather than to read it in the *Washington Post*. Please come in and sit."

Mrs. Shalash offered them candy, tea, and soft drinks. Mr. Shalash said, "Ahmed, I am so sorry to hear of your abuse. I can see that your hands are still bandaged. How are you doing?"

Ahmed said, "Thank you very much for inviting us into your home. I am very pleased to have met your daughter, Nadira. She is a very kind and upright woman. Thank you for asking about my wounds. My hands are healing well and my feet have progressed so that I no longer need a wheelchair, but I still have some pain in them. The pain that was in my shoulders is now gone."

"They say that crucifixion is very painful."

"I can assure you, sir, that it is. If it had not been for my friends here," he gestured to them, "I would not have survived long, especially because it was very cold and they had taken away my clothes."

"Why did they do this to you?"

"It is a long story."

"That's okay. I'm prepared to listen to whatever you have to say."

"I'll go back to the beginning." Ahmed explained that he had become part of a nonprofit company that raised money for an orphanage in Iraq, and that they had been targeted by terrorists as a source of revenue. "We decided to tell them no. Shortly after that, Nadira was attacked. I could see that her attack was by the hand of terrorists."

Mr. Shalash said, "So Nadira was attacked to force *your* organization to share the contributions with them. That's preposterous. What was Nadira's connection with your organization?"

"Nadira had no connection, except that I had once told her about the Servants. We have only learned this week that the terrorists found out about us and about Nadira from a car salesman, George Lyon, who had learned of our organization and about Nadira from Tom and Lauren."

Tom interjected, "George Lyon is a member of my church, and he was teaching a small class to familiarize us with Islam, especially since Lauren's roommate is a Muslim. I think it came up at one of the classes that Nadira had a friend that was operating the nonprofit company, a very commendable thing to do. We didn't know that George was gathering information for the terrorists. He was arrested this week."

"Oh," Mrs. Shalash said. "We learned this week from the police that this car salesman had been arrested. But we didn't know his connection."

Ahmed said, "Obviously, the terrorists must have thought that Nadira and I knew each other better than we did. As it was, we were just acquaintances that enjoyed talking to each other." He paused and looked at Mr. Shalash.

"Go on," Mr. Shalash said, a slight frown on his face.

"We were very frightened when Nadira was attacked. When my partners decided to share the proceeds with the terrorists, I immediately resigned from the Servants of Mercy. I went to the police and began helping them to find Nadira's attacker. The FBI became involved a little later on. It was through my contact with the FBI that the arrest of the terrorist was carried out. As soon as they arrested the man that Tom tackled on the parade ground, they also arrested three other members of the terrorist organization that they had been watching at their house in D.C. Yesterday morning the FBI searched the terrorists' house and found the bomb-making materials but found no bombs. So they knew something was about to happen but didn't know where. When I called them from the parade ground, they knew that was the place, probably because of the SEALs."

"What about the SEALs?"

"The parade was to honor them."

"Ah, I understand." Mr. Shalash said, with eyebrows raised. "But why did they attack you?"

"My partners knew I had gone to the police because the police questioned them. I believe they told the terrorists that I was a threat to them. Even before last Saturday they tried to blow up my car. I found the device before setting it off."

"So it was you! We saw it in the newspaper. But they didn't give your name."

Nadira said, "I saw it too. You must have been terrified."

I'd like to say something about being chased across the campus, Ahmed thought. *But that would open up a whole new subject, a subject I'm reluctant to discuss today.*

Tom said, "I'd like to say this about Ahmed. I asked him why he didn't return to Morocco. He said he could not go until Nadira's attacker was found."

A momentary silence filled the room.

Then Mr. Shalash said. "Are you saying that in spite of the attacks, you remained here just to find Nadira's attacker?"

Ahmed hesitated and then said, "Mr. Shalash, if I had never met Nadira, she would not have been wounded. It was, as you can see, because of me that she was attacked. I could not leave that crime unpunished."

Mr. Shalash turned toward Nadira and nodded. She looked at her father with eyes wide open.

Mrs. Shalash said, "But you had no evil intent. You and Nadira were becoming friends, isn't that all?"

Ahmed answered quickly, "Yes, of course. But that made it even more sinister. To harm an innocent girl, one so...one so vulnerable, was a cowardly thing to do and could not be ignored."

"Ahmed, I think you are a man of honor." Mr. Shalash stood up. He extended his hand to Ahmed. "Let me have your hand. I will hold it gently." He grasped Ahmed's wrist to avoid the bandage. "Thank you, Ahmed, for what you have done for my daughter. I will always be grateful."

Nadira looked at her watch. "Father, it's time for us to go now."

He removed his wallet from his hip pocket, took out a credit card, and handed it to Nadira. "Use this to pay for tonight's dinner."

She smiled. "Thank you." She tiptoed up and kissed him on his cheek. She looked at Lauren, Tom, and Ahmed. "It's time to go."

As they began to file out Ahmed said, "Go on, I'll be there in a moment. He turned to Mr. Shalash. "Sir, I would like to ask for your permission to begin seeing Nadira."

Mr. Shalash said, "I couldn't ask for a more honorable man to be seeing my daughter. Yes, with my blessing."

Mrs. Shalash added, "And mine." She smiled broadly.

Ahmed said, "Thank you." He turned and walked out. Nadira was waiting on the porch, smiling at him. He smiled at her and at Tom and Lauren, who were walking slowly, hand in hand, toward the car.

Also by Jon K. Elliott
the hands of Christ

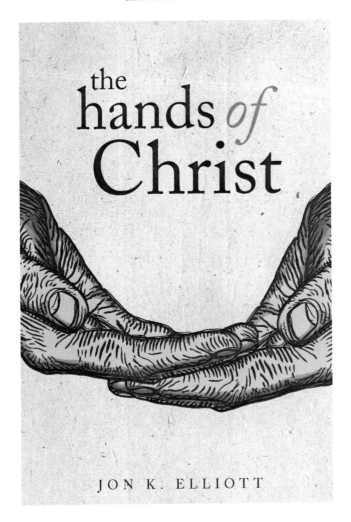

What happens when the perfect marriage comes to a crashing halt? *The Hands of Christ* is the story of two people who found themselves unequipped for the chaos they faced, and of friends who cared enough to attempt to intervene.

TATE PUBLISHING